The Green Mirror

HUGH WALPOLE

The Green Mirror

A QUIET STORY

by HUGH WALPOLE

GROSSET & DUNLAP ～ *Publishers*
by arrangement *with* Doubleday-Doran & Company, Inc.

TO

DOROTHY

WHO FIRST INTRODUCED ME

TO

KATHERINE

"There's the feather bed element here brother, ach! and not only that! There's an attraction here—here you have the end of the world, an anchorage, a quiet haven, the navel of the earth, the three fishes that are the foundation of the world, the essence of pancakes, of savoury fish-pies, of the evening samovar, of soft sighs and warm shawls, and hot stoves to sleep on—as snug as though you were dead, and yet you're alive—the advantages of both at once."

DOSTOEFFSKY.

My dear Dorothy,

As I think you know, this book was finished in the month of August, 1914. I did not look at it again until I revised it during my convalescence after an illness in the autumn of 1915.

We are now in a world very different from that with which this story deals, and it must, I am afraid, appear slow in development and uneventful in movement, belonging, in style and method and subject, to a day that seems to us already old-fashioned.

But I will frankly confess that I have too warm a personal affection for Katherine, Philip, Henry and Millicent to be able to destroy utterly the signs and traditions of their existence, nor can I feel my book to be quite old-fashioned when the love of England, which I have tried to make the text of it, has in many of us survived so triumphantly changes and catastrophes and victories that have shaken into ruin almost every other faith we held.

Let this be my excuse for giving you, with my constant affection, this uneventful story.

Yours always,

HUGH WALPOLE.

Petrograd,
    May 11th, 1917.

CONTENTS

BOOK I: THE RAID

BOOK II: THE FEATHER BED

BOOK III: KATHERINE AND ANNA

BOOK I
THE RAID

CHAPTER I

THE CEREMONY

I

THE fog had swallowed up the house, and the house had submitted. So thick was this fog that the towers of Westminster Abbey, the river, and the fat complacency of the church in the middle of the Square, even the three Plane Trees in front of the old gate and the heavy old-fashioned porch had all vanished together, leaving in their place, the rattle of a cab, the barking of a dog, isolated sounds that ascended, plaintively, from a lost, a submerged world.

The House had, indeed, in its time seen many fogs for it had known its first one in the days of Queen Anne and even then it had yielded, without surprise and without curiosity, to its tyranny. On the brighest of days this was a solemn, unenterprising unimaginative building, standing four-square to all the winds, its windows planted stolidly, securely, its vigorous propriety well suited to its safe, unagitated surroundings. Its faded red brick had weathered many London storms and would weather many more: that old, quiet Square, with its uneven stones, its church, and its plane-trees, had the Abbey, the Houses of Parliament, the river for its guardians . . . the skies might fall, the Thames burst into a flaming fire, Rundle Square would not stir from its tranquillity.

The old house—No. 5, Rundle Square—had for its most charming feature its entrance. First came an old iron gate guarded, on either side, by weatherbeaten stone pillars. Then a cobbled path, with little green lawns to right and left of it, ran to the door whose stolidity was crowned with an old porch of dim red brick. This was unusual enough for London, but there the gate, the little garden, the Porch had stood for some hundreds of years, and that Progress that had already its throttling fingers about London's neck, had, as yet, left Rundle Square to its staid propriety.

Westminster abides, like a little Cathedral town, at the heart of London. One is led to it, through Whitehall, through Victoria Street, through Belgravia, over Westminster Bridge with preparatory caution. The thunder of London sinks, as the traveller approaches, dying gradually as though the spirit of the town warned you, with his finger at his lip. To the roar of the traffic there succeeds the solemn striking of Big Ben, the chiming of the Abbey Bells; so narrow and winding are many of the little streets that such traffic as penetrates them proceeds slowly, cautiously, almost sleepily; there are old buildings and grass squares, many clergymen, schoolboys in black gowns and battered top hats, and at the corners one may see policemen, motionless, somnolent, stationed one supposes, to threaten disturbance or agitation.

There is, it seems, no impulse here to pile many more events upon the lap of the day than the poor thing can decently hold. Behind the windows of Westminster life is passing, surely, with easy tranquillity; the very door-bells are, many of them, old and comfortable, unsuited to any frantic ringing; there does not sound, through every hour, the whirring clang of workmen flinging, with eager haste, into the reluctant air, hideous and contemptuous buildings; dust does not rise in blinding clouds from the tortured corpses of old and happy houses. . . . Those who live here live long.

No. 5, Rundle Square then, had its destiny in pleasant places. Upon a fine summer evening the old red brick with its windows staring complacently upon a comfortable world showed a fine colour. Its very chimneys were square and solid, its eaves and water pipes regular and mathematical. Whatever horrid catastrophe might convulse the rest of London, No. 5 would suffer no hurt; the god of propriety—the strongest of all the gods—had it beneath His care.

Now behind the Fog it waited, as it had waited so often before, with certain assurance, for its release.

II

Inside the house at about half-past four, upon this afternoon November 8th, in the year 1902, young Henry Trenchard was sitting alone; he was straining his eyes over a book that interested him so deeply that he could not leave it in order to switch on the electric light; his long nose stuck into the book's very heart and his eyelashes almost brushed the paper. The drawing-room where he was had caught some of the fog and kept it, and Henry Trenchard's only light was the fading glow of a red cavernous fire. Henry Trenchard, now nineteen years of age, had known, in all those nineteen years, no change in that old drawing-room. As an ugly and tiresome baby he had wailed before the sombre indifference of that same old stiff green wall-paper—a little brighter then perhaps,—had sprawled upon the same old green carpet, had begged to be allowed to play with the same collection of little scent bottles and stones and rings and miniatures that lay now, in the same decent symmetry, in the same narrow glass-topped table over by the window. It was by shape and design a heavy room, slipping into its true spirit with the London dusk, the London fog, the London lamp-lit winter afternoon, seeming awkward, stiff, almost affronted before the sunshine and summer weather. One or two Trenchards—two soldiers and a Bishop—were there in heavy old gold frames, two ponderous glass-fronted bookcases guarded from any frivolous touch high stiff-backed volumes of Gibbons and Richardson and Hooker.

There were some old water-colours of faded green lawns, dim rocks and seas with neglected boats upon the sand—

all these painted in the stiff precision of the 'thirties and the 'forties, smoked and fogged a little in their thin black frames.

Upon one round-table indeed there was a concession to the modern spirit in the latest numbers of the "Cornhill" and "Blackwood" magazines, the "Quarterly Review" and the "Hibbert Journal."

The chairs in the room were for the most part stiff with gilt backs and wore a "Don't you dare to sit down upon me" eye, but two armchairs, near the fire, of old green leather were comfortable enough and upon one of these Henry was now sitting. Above the wide stone fireplace was a large old gold mirror, a mirror that took into its expanse the whole of the room, so that, standing before it, with your back to the door, you could see everything that happened behind you. The Mirror was old and gave to the view that it embraced some old comfortable touch so that everything within it was soft and still and at rest. Now, in the gloom and shadow, the reflection was green and dark with the only point of colour the fading fire. Before it a massive gold clock with the figures of the Three Graces stiff and angular at its summit ticked away as though it were the voice of a very old gentleman telling an interminable story. It served indeed for the voice of the mirror itself. . . .

Henry was reading a novel that showed upon its back Mudie's bright yellow label. He was reading, as the clock struck half-past four, these words:—

"I sat on the stump of a tree at his feet, and below us stretched the land, the great expanse of the forests, sombre under the sunshine, rolling like a sea, with glints of winding rivers, the grey spots of villages, and here and there a clearing, like an islet of light amongst the dark waves of continuous tree-tops. A brooding gloom lay over this vast and monotonous landscape; the light fell on it as if into an abyss. The land devoured the sunshine; only far off, along the coast, the empty ocean, smooth and polished within the faint bays, seemed to rise up to the sky in a wall of steel.

And there I was with him, high on the sunshine on the top of that historic hill. . . ."

The striking of the clock brought him away from the book with a jerk, so deep had he been sunk in it that he looked now about the dusky room with a startled uncertain gaze. The familiar place settled once more about him and, with a little sigh, he sank back into the chair. His thin bony legs stuck out in front of him; one trouser-leg was hitched up and his sock, falling down over his boot, left bare part of his calf; his boots had not been laced tightly and the tongues had slipped aside, showing his sock. He was a long thin youth, his hair untidy, his black tie up at the back of his collar; one white and rather ragged cuff had slipped down over his wrist, the other was invisible. His eyes were grey and weak, he had a long pointed nose with two freckles on the very end of it, but his mouth was kindly although too large and indeterminate. His cheeks were thin and showed high cheekbones; his chin was pronounced enough to be strong but nevertheless helped him very little.

He was untidy and ungainly but not entirely unattractive; his growth was at the stage when nature has not made up its mind as to the next, the final move. That may, after all, be something very pleasant. . . .

His eyes now were dreamy and soft because he was thinking of the book. No book, perhaps, in all his life before had moved him so deeply and he was very often moved—but, as a rule, by cheap and sentimental emotions.

He knew that he was cheap; he knew that he was sentimental; he, very often, hated and despised himself.

He could see the Forests "rolling like a sea". It was as though he, himself, had been perched upon that high, bright hill, and he was exalted, he felt, with that same exultation; the space, the freedom, the liberty, the picture of a world wherein anything might happen, where heroes, fugitives, scoundrels, cowards, conquerors all alike might win their salvation. "Room for everyone . . . no one to pull one up—

No one to make one ashamed of what one says and does. No crowd watching one's every movement. Adventures for the wishing and courage to meet them."

He looked about the room and hated it,—the old, shabby, hemmed-in thing! He hated this life to which he was condemned; he hated himself, his world, his uninspiring future.

"My God, I must do something! . . . I *will* do something! . . . But suppose I can't!" His head fell again— suppose he were out in that other world, there in the heart of those dark forests, suppose that he found that he did no better there than here! . . . That would be, indeed, the most terrible thing of all!

He gazed up into the Mirror, saw in it the reflection of the room, the green walls, the green carpet, the old faded green place like moss covering dead ground. Soft, damp, dark, —and beyond outside the Mirror, the world of the Forests —"the great expanse of Forests" and "beyond, the Ocean —smooth and polished . . . rising up to the sky in a wall of steel."

His people, his family, his many, many relations, his world, he thought, were all inside the Mirror—all embedded in that green, soft, silent enclosure. He saw, stretching from one end of England to the other, in all Provincial towns, in neat little houses with neat little gardens, in Cathedral Cities with their sequestered Closes, in villages with the deep green lanes leading up to the rectory gardens, in old Country houses hemmed in by wide stretching fields, in little lost places by the sea, all these persons happily, peacefully sunk up to their very necks in the green moss. Within the Mirror this . . . Outside the Mirror the rolling forests guarded by the shining wall of sea. His own family passed before him. His grandfather, his great-aunt Sarah, his mother and his father, Aunt Aggie and Aunt Betty, Uncle Tim, Millicent, Katherine. . . . He paused then. The book slipped away and fell on to the floor.

Katherine . . . dear Katherine! He did not care what

she was! And then, swept by a fresh wave of feeling springing up, stretching his arms, facing the room, he did not care what *any* of them were! *He* was the Idiot, the discontented, ungrateful Idiot! He loved them all—he wouldn't change one of them, he wouldn't be in any other family in all the world!

The door opened; in came old Rocket, the staff and prop of the family, to turn up the lights, to poke up the fire. In a minute tea would come in. . . .

"Why, Mr. Henry, no fire nor lights!" He shuffled to the windows, pulling the great heavy curtains across them, his knees cracking, very slowly he bent down, picked up the book, and laid it carefully on the table next to the "Hibbert Journal."

"I hope you've not been reading, Mr. Henry, in this bad light," he said.

III

Later, between nine and half-past, Henry was sitting with his father and his uncle, smoking and drinking after dinner. To-night was an evening of Ceremony—*the* Family Ceremony of the year—therefore, although the meal had been an extremely festive one with many flowers, a perfect mountain of fruit in the huge silver bowl in the centre of the table, and the Most Sacred Of All Ports (produced on this occasion and Christmas Day) nevertheless only the Family had been present. No distant relations even, certainly no friends. . . . This was Grandfather Trenchard's birthday.

The ladies vanished, there remained only Henry, his father and Uncle Tim. Henry was sitting there, very self-conscious over his glass of Port. He was always self-conscious when Uncle Tim was present.

Uncle Tim was a Faunder and was large-limbed and absent-minded like Henry's father. Uncle Tim had a wild head of grey hair, a badly-kept grey beard and clothed his long, loose figure in long, loose garments. He was here to-

day and gone to-morrow, preferred the country to the town
and had a little house down in Glebeshire, where he led an
untidy bachelor existence whose motive impulses were birds
and flowers.

Henry was very fond of Uncle Tim; he liked his untidiness, his careless geniality, his freedom and his happiness.

Henry's father—George Trenchard—was "splendid"—
that, thought Henry, was the only possible word—and the
boy, surveying other persons' fathers, wondered why Katherine, Millicent, and himself should have been chosen out
of all the world to be so favoured.

George Trenchard, at this time about sixty years of age,
was over six feet in height and broad in proportion. He
was growing too stout; his hair was grey and the top of his
head bald; his eyes were brown and absent-minded, his mouth
large with a lurking humour in its curves; his cheeks were
fat and round and there was the beginning of a double chin.
He walked, always, in a rambling, rolling kind of way, like
a sea-captain on shore, still balancing himself to the swing
of his vessel, his hands deep sunk in his trouser-pockets.
Henry had been privileged, sometimes, to see him, when, absorbed in the evolution of an essay or the Chapter of some
book (he is, of course, one of our foremost authorities on
the early Nineteenth Century period of English Literature,
especially Hazlitt and De Quincey) he rolled up and down
his study, with his head back, his hand sunk in his pockets,
whistling a little tune . . . very wonderful he seemed to
Henry then.

He was the most completely careless of optimists, refused
to be brought down to any stern fact whatever, hated any
strong emotion or stringent relations with anyone, treated his
wife and children as the most delightful accidents against
whom he had, most happily tumbled; his kindness of heart
was equalled only by the lightning speed with which he forgot the benefits that he had conferred and the persons upon
whom he had conferred them . . . like a happy bird, he

went carolling through life. Alone, of all living beings, his daughter Katherine had bound him to her with cords; for the rest, he loved and forgot them all.

Now, on this family occasion of his father's birthday—his father was eighty-seven to-day—he was absolutely happy. He was proud of his family when any definite occasion, such as this, compelled him to think of it; he considered that it had all been a very jolly, pleasant dinner, that there would certainly follow a very jolly, pleasant evening. He liked, especially, to have his brother, Timothy, with him—he loved them all, bless their hearts—he felt, as he assured them, "Not a day more than twenty."

"How do you really think Father is, George?" asked Timothy.

"Sound as a bell," said Henry's father, "getting deaf of course—must expect that—but it's my belief that the harder his hearing the brighter his eyes—never knew anyone so sharp. Nothing escapes him, 'pon my soul."

"Well," said George Trenchard, "I think it a most satisfactory thing that here we should all be again—healthy, happy, sound as so many bells—lively as crickets—not a happier family in England."

"Don't say that, George," said Uncle Tim, "most unlucky."

"Nonsense," said George Trenchard, brushing Uncle Tim aside like a fly, "Nonsense. We're a happy family, a healthy family and a united family."

"I drink my gratitude to the God of Family Life, whoever He is. . . ." He finished his glass of Port. "Here, Timothy, have another glass. It's a Port in a million, so it is."

But Uncle Tim shook his head. "It's all very well, George, but you'll have to break up soon. The girls will be marrying—Katherine and Millicent—"

"Rot," said George, "Millie's still at school."

"She's coming home very soon—very shortly I believe. And besides you can't keep a family together as you used to.

You can't. No one cares about the home at all now-a-days. These youngsters will find that out soon enough. You'll be deserting the nest immediately, Henry, my friend, won't you?"

This sudden appeal, of course, confused Henry terribly. He choked over his wine, coloured crimson, stammered out:

"No, Uncle Tim—Of course—Of course—not."

George Trenchard looked at his son with approval.

"That's right. Stick to your old father while you can. The matter with you, Tim, is that you live outside the world and don't know what's going on."

"The matter with you, George, is," his brother, speaking slowly and carefully, replied, "That you haven't the ghost of an idea of what the modern world's like—not the ghost. Up in the clouds you are, and so's your whole family, my sister and all—But the young ones won't be up in the clouds always, not a bit of it. They'll come down one day and then you'll see what you *will* see."

"And what'll that be?" said George Trenchard, laughing a little scornfully.

"Why you and Harriet doing Darby and Joan over the dying fire and no one else within a hundred miles of you —except a servant who's waiting for your clothes and sleeve-links."

"There, Henry—Listen to that!" said his father, still laughing—"See what an ungrateful fellow you're going to be in a year or two!"

Henry blushed, swallowed in his throat, smiled idioti-cally. They were all, he thought, laughing at him, but the effect was very pleasant and genial. . . .

Moreover he was interested. He was, of course, one of the young ones and it was his future that was under dis-cussion. His mind hovered over the book that he had been reading that afternoon. Uncle Tim's words had very much the same effect upon Henry's mind that that book's words had had, although from a different angle so to speak. . . .

Henry's eyes lingered about a little silver dish that contained sugared cherries. . . . He liked immensely sugared cherries. Encouraged by the genial atmosphere he stretched out his hand, took two cherries, and swallowed them, but, in his agitation, so swiftly that he did not taste them at all.

Then he drank two glasses of Port—he had never before drunk so much wine. He was conscious now that he must not, under any circumstances, drink any more. He was aware that he must control, very closely, his tongue; he told himself that the room was not in reality so golden and glowing a place as it now seemed to him, that it was only the same old dining-room with which he had all his life, been familiar. He convinced himself by a steady gaze that the great silver dish with the red and purple and golden fruit piled upon it *was* only a silver dish, was not a deep bowl whose sides, like silver walls stretched up right into the dim electric clusters of electric light hanging from the ceiling. He might convince himself of these facts, he might with a great effort steady the room that very, very slightly swayed about him . . . what he could not deny was that Life was gorgeous, that this was an Evening of all the Evenings, that he adored his father, his uncle and all the family to such a height and depth of devotion that, were he not exceedingly careful, he would burst into tears—burst into tears he must not because then would the stud in his shirt most assuredly abandon its restraints and shame him, for ever, before Uncle Tim.

At this moment his father gave the command to move. Henry rose, very carefully, from his seat, steadied himself at the table for an instant, then, very, very gravely, with his eye upon his shirt-stud, followed his uncle from the room.

IV

He retained, throughout the rest of that eventful evening, the slightly exaggerated vision of the world. It was not that, as he followed his father and uncle into the drawing-room, he did not know what he would see. He would find them sitting there—Grandfather in his chair, his feet on a stool, his bony hands pressed upon his thin knees with that fierce, protesting pressure that represented so much in his grandfather. There would be, also, his Great-Aunt Sarah with her high pyramid of white hair, her long black ear-trumpet and her hard sharp little eyes like faded blue pebbles, there would be his mother, square and broad and placid with her hands folded on her lap, there would be Aunt Aggie, with her pouting, fat little face, her cheeks quivering a little as she moved her head, her eyes searching about the room, nervously, uneasily, and there would be Aunt Betty, neat and tiny, with her little trembling smile and her quiet air of having something very important to do of which no one else in the family had the ghost of an idea! Oh! he knew them all so well that they appeared to him, now, to be part of himself and to exist only as his ideas of the world and life and his own destiny. They could not now do anything that would ever surprise or disconcert him, he knew their ideas, their schemes, their partialities, their disgusts, and he would not—so he thought now with the fire of life burning so brightly within him—have them changed, no, not in any tiniest atom of an alteration.

He knew that they would sit there, all of them, and talk quietly about nothing, and then when the gold clock was approaching half-past nine they would slip away,—save only grandfather and Aunt Sarah—and would slip up to their rooms and then they would slip down again with their parcels in their hands and at half-past nine the Ceremony would take place. So it had been for years and years and so it would continue to be until Grandfather's death, and, after that, Henry's father would take his place, and then, one day, perhaps, it would be the turn of Henry himself.

He paused for a moment and looked at the room—Katherine was not there. She was always until the very last moment, doing something to Grandfather's present, tying it up in some especial ribbon, writing something on the paper wrapping, making it, in some way, more perfect. He knew that, as he came in, his mother would look up and smile and say "Well, Henry," and then would resume her placidity, that Uncle Tim would sit down beside Aunt Betty and begin, very gently, to chaff her, which would please her immensely, and that Aunt Sarah would cry "What did you say, Timothy?" and that then he would shout down her ear-trumpet, with a good-humoured smile peeping down from his beard as though he were thinking "One must humour the old lady you know."

All these things occurred. Henry himself sat in a low chair by the fire and looked at his father, who was walking up and down the other end of the room, his hands deep in his pockets, his head back. Then he looked at his two aunts and wondered, as he had wondered so many times before, that they were not the sisters of his mother instead of his father. They were so small and fragile to be the sisters of such large-limbed, rough-and-tumble men as his father and Uncle Timothy. They would have, so naturally, taken their position in the world as the sisters of his mother.

Aunt Aggie, who thought that no one was paying her very much attention, said:

"I can't think why Katherine wouldn't let me get that silk for her at Liberty's this afternoon. I could have gone up Regent Street so easily—it wouldn't have been very much trouble—not very much, but Katherine always must do everything for herself."

Mrs. Trenchard said: "It was very kind of you, Aggie dear, to think of it—I'm sure it was very kind," and Aunt Betty said: "Katherine would appreciate your thinking of her."

"I wonder, with the fog, that any of you went out at all," said Uncle Tim, "I'm sure I was as nearly killed as nothing just coming back from the Strand."

Aunt Aggie moved her hands on her lap, looked at them, suspiciously, to see whether they meant what they said, and then sighed—and, to Henry, this all seemed to-night wonderful, magical, possessed of some thrilling, passionate quality; his heart was beating with furious, leaping bounds, his eyes were misty with sentimental happiness. He thought that this was life that he was realising now for the first time. . . . It was not—it was two glasses of Port.

He looked at his grandfather and thought of the wonderful old man that he was. His grandfather was very small and very thin and so delicate was the colour of his white hair, his face, and his hands that the light seemed to shine through him, as though he had been made of glass. He was a silent old man and everything about him was of a fine precious quality—his black shoes with the silver buckles, the gold signet ring on his finger, the black cord with the gold eye-glasses that lay across his shirt-front; when he spoke it was with a thin, silvery voice like a bell.

He did not seem, as he sat there, to be thinking about any of them or to be caring for anything that they might do.

His thoughts, perhaps, were shining and silver and precious like the rest of him, but no one knew because he said so little. Aunt Betty, with a glance at the clock, rose and slipped from the room. The moment had arrived. . . .

V

Very soon, and, indeed, just as the clock, as though it were summoning them all back, struck the half-hour, there they all were again. They stood, in a group by the door and each one had, in his or her hand, his or her present. Grandfather, as silent as an ivory figure, sat in his chair, with Aunt Sarah in her chair beside him, and in front of him was a table, cleared of anything that was upon it, its mahogany shining in the fire-light. All the Trenchard soldiers and the Trenchard Bishop looked down, with solemn approval, upon the scene.

"Come on, Henry, my boy, time to begin," said his father.

Henry, because he was the youngest, stepped forward, his present in his hand. His parcel was very ill-tied and the paper was creased and badly folded. He was greatly ashamed as he laid it upon the table. Blushing, he made his little speech, his lips together, speaking like an awkward schoolboy. "We're all very glad, Grandfather, that we're all—most of us—here to—to congratulate you on your birthday. We hope that you're enjoying your birthday and that—that there'll be lots more for you to enjoy."

"Bravo, Henry," came from the back of the room. Henry stepped back still blushing. Then Grandfather Trenchard, with trembling hands, slowly undid the parcel and revealed a purple leather blotting-book with silver edges.

"Thank you, my boy—very good of you. Thank you."

Then came Katherine. Katherine was neither very tall nor very short, neither fat nor thin. She had some of the grave placidity of her mother and, in her eyes and mouth, some of the humour of her father. She moved quietly and easily, very self-possessed; she bore herself as though she had many more important things to think about than anything that concerned herself. Her hair and her eyes were dark brown, and now as she went with her present, her smile was as quiet and unself-conscious as everything else about her.

"Dear Grandfather," she said, "I wish you many, many happy returns—" and then *she* stepped back. Her present was an old gold snuff-box.

"Thank you, my dear," he said. "Very charming. Thank you, my dear."

Then came Aunt Aggie, her eyes nervous and a little resentful as though she had been treated rather hardly but was making the best of difficult circumstances. "I'm afraid you won't like this, Father," she said. "I felt that you wouldn't

when I got it. But I did my best. It's a silly thing to give
you, I'm afraid."

She watched as the old man, very slowly, undid the parcel.
She had given him a china ink-stand. It had been as though
she had said: "Anything more foolish than to give an old
man who ought to be thinking about the grave a china ink-
stand I can't imagine."

Perhaps her father had felt something of this in her voice
—he answered her a little sharply—

"Thank 'ye—my dear Aggie—Thank 'ye."

Very different Aunt Betty. She came forward like a cheerful and happy sparrow, her head just on one side as though
she wished to perceive the complete effect of everything that
was going on.

"My present is handkerchiefs, Father. I worked the ini-
tials myself. I hope you will like them," and then she bent
forward and took his hand in hers and held it for a moment. As he looked across at her, a little wave of colour
crept up behind the white mask of his cheek. "Dear Betty
—my dear. Thank 'ye—Thank 'ye."

Then followed Mrs. Trenchard, moving like some fragment of the old house that contained her, a fragment anxious
to testify its allegiance to the head of the family—but anxious—as one must always remember with Mrs. Trenchard—
with no very agitated anxiety. Her slow smile, her solid
square figure that should have been fat but was only broad,
her calm soft eyes—cow's eyes—from these characteristics
many years of child-bearing and the company of a dreamy
husband had not torn her.

Would something ever tear her? . . . Yes, there was something.

In her slow soft voice she said: "Father dear, many
happy returns of the day—*many* happy returns. This is
a silk muffler. I hope you'll like it, Father dear. It's a
muffler."

They surveyed one another calmly across the shining table.

Mrs. Trenchard was a Faunder, but the Faunders were kin by breeding and tradition to the Trenchards—the same green pastures, the same rich, packed counties, the same mild skies and flowering Springs had seen the development of their convictions about the world and their place in it.

The Faunders. . . . The Trenchards . . . it is as though you said Tweedledum and Tweedledee. Mrs. Trenchard looked at her father-in-law and smiled, then moved away.

Then came the men. Uncle Tim had a case of silver brushes to present and he mumbled something in his beard about them. George Trenchard had some old glass, he flung back his head and laughed, gripped his father by the hand, shouted something down Aunt Sarah's trumpet. Aunt Sarah herself had given, at an earlier hour, her offering because she was so deaf and her brother's voice so feeble that on earlier occasions, her presentation, protracted and embarrassing, had affected the whole evening. She sat there now, like an ancient Boadicea, looking down grimly upon the presents, as though they were so many spoils won by a raid.

It was time for the old man to make a Speech: It was—"Thank 'ye, Thank 'ye—very good of you all—very. It's pleasant, all of us together—very pleasant. I never felt better in my life and I hope you're all the same. . . . Thank 'ye, my dears. Thank 'ye."

The Ceremony was thus concluded; instantly they were all standing about, laughing, talking, soon they would be all in the hall and then they would separate, George and Timothy and Bob to talk, perhaps, until early hours in the morning. . . . Here is old Rocket to wheel grandfather's chair along to his bedroom.

"Well, Father, here's Rocket come for you."

"All right, my dear, I'm ready. . . ."

But Rocket had not come for his master. Rocket, perplexity, dismay, upon his countenance, was plainly at a loss, and for Rocket to be at a loss!

"Hullo, Rocket, what is it?"

"There's a gentleman, sir—apologises profoundly for the lateness of the hour—wouldn't disturb you but the fog—his card. . . ."

VI

Until he passes away to join the glorious company of Trenchards who await him, will young Henry Trenchard remember everything that then occurred—exactly he will remember it and to its tiniest detail. It was past ten o'clock and never in the memory of anyone present had the Ceremony before been invaded. . . . Astonishing impertinence on the part of someone! Astonishing bravery also did he only realise it!

"It's the fog, you know," said Henry's mother.

"What's the matter!" screamed Aunt Sarah.

"Somebody lost in the fog."

"Somebody what?"

"Lost in the Fog."

"In the what?"

"IN THE FOG!"

"Oh! . . . *How* did you say?"

"FOG!"

George Trenchard then returned, bringing with him a man. The man stood in the doorway, confused (as, indeed, it was only right for him to be), blushing, holding his bowler hat nervously in his hand, smiling that smile with which one seeks to propitiate strangers.

"I say, of all things," cried George Trenchard. "What *do* you think, all of you? Of all the coincidences! This is Mr. Mark. You know, mother dear (this to Mrs. Trenchard, who was waiting calmly for orders), son of Rodney Mark I've so often told you of. . . . Here's his son, arrived in London yesterday after years' abroad, out to-night, lost his way in the fog, stopped at first here to enquire, found it of all remarkable things ours where he was coming to call to-morrow! . . . Did you ever!"

"I really must apologise—" began Mr. Mark, smiling at everyone.

"Oh no! you mustn't," broke in George Trenchard—"Must he, mother? He's got to stop the night. Of course he has. We've got as much room as you like. Here, let me introduce you."

Mr. Mark was led round. He was, most certainly, (as Aunt Betty remarked afterwards upstairs) very quiet and pleasant and easy about it all. He apologised again to Mrs. Trenchard, hadn't meant to stop more than a moment, so struck by the coincidence, his father had always said first thing he must do in London. . . .

Rocket was summoned—"Mr. Mark will stop here to-night." "Certainly—of course—anything in the world—"

Grandfather was wheeled away, the ladies in the hall hoped that they would see Mr. Mark in the morning and Mr. Mark hoped that *he* would see *them*. Good-night—good-night. . . .

"Come along now," cried George Trenchard, taking his guest's arm. "Come along and have a smoke and a drink and tell us what you've been doing all these years! . . . Why the last time I saw you! . . ."

Mrs. Trenchard, unmoved by this ripple upon the Trenchard waters, stopped for a moment before leaving the drawing-room and called Henry—

"Henry dear. Is this your book?" She held up the volume with the yellow Mudie's label.

"Yes, Mother."

"I hope it's a nice book for you, dear."

"A very nice book, Mother."

"Well I'm sure you're old enough to know for yourself now."

"Good-night, Mother."

"Good-night, dear."

Henry, with the book under his arm, went up to bed.

CHAPTER II

EXTRACTS from a letter written by Philip Mark to Mr. Paul Alexis in Moscow:—

". . . because, beyond question, it was the oddest chance that I should come—straight out of the fog, into the very house that I wanted. That, mind you, was a week ago, and I'm still here. You've never seen a London fog. I defy you to imagine either the choking, stifling nastiness of it or the comfortable happy indifference of English people under it. I couldn't have struck, if I'd tried for a year, anything more eloquent of the whole position—my position, I mean, and theirs and the probable result of our being up against one another. . . .

This will be a long letter because, here I am quite unaccountably excited, unaccountably, I say, because it's all as quiet as the grave—after midnight, an old clock ticking out there on the stairs. Landseer's 'Dignity and Impudence' on the wall over my bed and that old faded wall-paper that you only see in the bedrooms of the upper middles in England, who have lived for centuries and centuries in the same old house. Much too excited to sleep, simply I suppose because all kinds of things are beginning to reassert themselves on me—things that haven't stirred since I was eighteen, things that Anna and Moscow had so effectually laid to rest. All those years as a boy I had just this wall-paper, just this ticking-clock, just these faded volumes of 'Ivanhoe,' 'Kenilworth', 'The Scarlet Letter' and Lytton's 'Night and Morning' that I see huddled together in the window. Ah, Paul,

32

you've never known what all that means—the comfort, the
safety, the muffled cosiness, the gradual decline of old familiar things from shabbiness to shabbiness, the candles, and
pony-traps and apple-lofts and going to country dances in old,
jolting cabs with the buttons hopping off your new white
gloves as you go . . . it's all back on me to-night, it's been
crowding in upon me all the week—The Trenchards are
bathed, soaked, saturated with it all—they ARE IT ! . . . Now,
I'll tell you about them, as I've seen them so far.

Trenchard, himself, is fat, jolly, self-centred, writes about
the Lake Poets and lives all the morning with Lamb, Hazlitt
and De Quincey, all the afternoon with the world as seen by
himself, and all the evening with himself as seen by the world.
He's selfish and happy, absent-minded and as far from all
reality as any man could possibly be. He likes me, I think, because I understand his sense of humour, the surest key to
the heart of a selfish man. About Mrs. Trenchard I'm not
nearly so sure. I've been too long out of England to understand her all in a minute. You'd say right off that she's
stupider than any one you'd ever met, and then afterwards
you'd be less and less certain. . . . Tremendously full of
family (she was a Faunder), muddled, with no power over
words at all so that she can never say what she means, outwardly of an extremely amiable simplicity, inwardly, I am
sure, as obstinate as a limpet . . . not a shadow of humour.
Heaven only knows what she's thinking about really. She
never lets you see. I don't think she likes me.

There are only two children at home, Henry and Katherine. Henry's at 'the awkward age'. Gauche, shy, sentimental, rude, frightfully excitable from the public school conviction that he must never show excitement about anything,
full of theories, enthusiasms, judgments which he casts aside,
one after the other, as fast as he can get rid of them—at the
very crisis of his development—might be splendid or no
good at all, according as things happen to him. He's interested in me but isn't sure of me.

Then there's Katherine. Katherine is the clue to the house—know Katherine and you know the family. But then Katherine is not easy to know. She is more friendly than any of them—and she is farther away. Very quiet with all the calm security of someone who knows that there are many important things to be done and that you will never be allowed, however insistent you may be, to interfere with those things. The family depends entirely upon her and she lives for the family. Nor is she so limited as that might seem to make her. She keeps, I am sure, a great many things down lest they should interfere, but they are all there—those things. Meanwhile she is cheerful, friendly, busy, very, very quiet—and distant—miles. Does she like me? I don't know. She listens to all that I have to say. She has imagination and humour. And sometimes when I think that I have impressed her by what I have said I look up and catch a glimpse of her smiling eyes, as though she thought me, in spite of all my wisdom, the most awful fool. The family do more than depend upon her—they adore her. There is no kind of doubt—they adore her. She alone in all the world awakes her father's selfish heart, stirs her mother's sluggish imagination, reassures her brother's terrified soul. They love her for the things that she does for them. They are all—save perhaps Henry—selfish in their affection. But then so are the rest of us, are we not? You, Paul, and I, at any rate. . . .

And, all this time, I have said nothing to you about the guardians of the House's honour. Already, they view me with intense suspicion. There are two of them, both very old. An aged, aged man, bitter and sharp and shining like a glass figure, and his sister, as aged as he. They are, both of them, deaf and the only things truly alive about them are their eyes. But with these they watch everything, and above all, they watch me. They distrust me, profoundly, their eyes never leave me. They allow me to make no advances to them. They cannot imagine why I have been admitted—they will, I am sure, take steps to turn me out very soon. It is as though I were a spy in a hostile country. And yet they all press me to stay—all of them. They seem to like to have me. What I have to tell them interests them and they are pleased, too, to be hospitable in a large and comfortable manner. Trenchard was deeply attached to my father and speaks of him to me with an emotion surprising in so selfish a man. They like me to stay and yet, Paul, with it all I tell you that I am strangely frightened. Of what? Of whom? . . . I have no idea. Isn't it simply that the change from Russia and, perhaps, also Anna is so abrupt that it is startling? Anna and Miss Trenchard—there's a contrast for you! And I'm at the mercy—you know, of anyone—you have always said it and it *is* so—most unhappily. Tell Anna from me that I am writing.

Because I couldn't, of course, explain to her as I do to you the way that these old, dead, long-forgotten things are springing up again in me. She would never understand. But we were both agreed—she as strongly as I—that this was the right thing, the only thing. . . . You know that I would not hurt a fly if I could help it. No, tell her that I won't write. I'll keep to my word. Not a line from either of us until Time has made it safe, easy. And Stepan will be good to her. He's the best fellow in the world, although so often I hated him. For his sake, as well as for all the other reasons, I will not write. . . . Meanwhile it is really true enough that I'm frightened for, perhaps, the first time in my life. . . .''

Suspicion was the key-note of young Henry Trenchard at this time. He was so unsure of himself that he must needs be unsure of everyone else. He was, of course, suspicious of Philip Mark. He was suspicious and he also admired him. On the day after Mark had sat up writing his letter 'half the night because he was excited', on the afternoon of that day they were sitting in the green dim drawing-room waiting for tea. Mark was opposite Henry, and Henry, back in the shadow, as he liked to sit, huddled up but with his long legs shooting out in front of him as though they belonged to another body, watched him attentively, critically, inquisitively. Mark sat with a little pool of electric light about him and talked politely to Mrs. Trenchard, who, knitting a long red woollen affair that trailed like a serpent on to the green carpet, said now and then such things as:

"It must be very different from England" or "I must say I should find that very unpleasant," breaking in also to say: "Forgive me a moment. Henry, that bell did ring, didn't it?" or "Just a little more on the fire, Henry, please. That big lump, please." Then, turning patiently to Mark and saying: "I beg your pardon, Mr. Mark—you said?"

Henry, having at this time a passion for neatness and orderly arrangements, admired Mark's appearance. Mark was short, thick-set and very dark. A closely-clipped black moustache and black hair cut short made him look like an officer, Henry thought. His thick muscular legs proved him a rider, his mouth and ears were small, and over him from head to foot was the air of one who might have to be 'off' on a dangerous expedition at any moment and would moreover know exactly what to do, having been on many other dangerous expeditions before. Only his eyes disproved the man of action. They were dreamy, introspective, wavering eyes—eyes that were much younger than the rest of him and eyes too that might be emotional, sentimental, impetuous, foolish and careless.

Henry, being very young, did not notice his eyes. Mark was thirty and looked it. His eyes were the eyes of a boy of twenty. . . . From Henry his dark neat clothes, his compact and resourceful air compelled envy and admiration—yes, and alarm. For Henry was, now, entirely and utterly concerned with himself, and every fresh incident, every new arrival was instantly set up before him so that he might see how he himself looked in the light of it. Never before, within Henry's memory, had anyone not a relation, not even the friend of a relation, been admitted so intimately into the heart of the house, and it seemed to Henry that now already a new standard was being set up and that, perhaps, the family by the light of this dashing figure, who knew Russia like an open book and could be relied upon at the most dangerous crisis, might regard himself, Henry, as something more crudely shabby and incompetent than ever. Moreover he was not sure that Mark himself did not laugh at him. . . .

Beyond all this there was the sense that Mark had, in a way, invaded the place. It was true that the family had, after that first eventful evening, pressed him to stay, but it had pressed him as though it had, upon itself, felt pressure— as though its breath had been caught by the impact of some new force and, before it could recover from its surprise, behold the force was there, inside the room with the doors closed behind it.

"It's hardly decent for him to stay on like this," thought Henry, "and yet after all we asked him. And . . . he *is* jolly!"

Jolly was something that only Henry's father and Uncle Tim of the Trenchard family could be said to be, and its quality was therefore both enlivening and alarming.

"Mother won't like it, if he's too jolly," thought Henry, "I'm not sure if she likes it now."

Henry had, upon this afternoon, an extra cause for anxiety; a friend of his, a friend of whom he was especially proud, was coming to tea. This friend's name was Seymour and he was a cheerful young man who had written several novels and was considered 'promising'—

The Trenchards had a very slight knowledge of that world known as 'the Arts' and they had (with the exception of Henry) a very healthy distrust of artists as a race.

But young Seymour was another affair. He was a gentleman, with many relations who knew Trenchards and Faunders; his novels were proper in sentiment and based always upon certain agreeable moral axioms, as for instance "It is better to be good than to be bad" and "Courage is the Great

Thing" and "Let us not despise others. They may have more to say for themselves than we know."

It was wonderful, Mrs. Trenchard thought, that anyone so young should have discovered these things. Moreover he was cheerful, would talk at any length about anything, and was full of self-assurance. He was fat, and would soon be fatter; he was nice to everyone on principle because "one doesn't know how much a careless word may harm others." Above all, he was 'jolly'. He proclaimed life splendid, wished he could live to a thousand, thought that to be a novelist was the luckiest thing in the world. Some people said that what he really meant was "To be Seymour was the luckiest thing in the world" . . . but everyone has their enemies.

Henry was nervous about this afternoon because he felt— and he could not have given his reasons—that Mark and Seymour would not get on. He knew that if Mark disliked Seymour he, Henry, would dislike Mark. Mark would be criticising the Trenchard taste—a dangerous thing to do. And, perhaps, after all—he was not sure—he looked across the dark intervening shadow into the light where Mark was sitting— the fellow *did* look conceited, supercilious. No one in the world had the right to be so definitely at his ease.

There came in then Rocket and a maid with the tea, Katherine, and finally Aunt Aggie with Harvey Seymour.

"I found Mr. Seymour in the Hall," she said, looking discontentedly about her and shivering a little. "Standing in the Hall."

Seymour was greeted and soon his cheerful laugh filled the room. He was introduced to Mark. He was busy over tea. "Sugar? Milk?"

"Nice sharp twang in the air, there *is*. Jolly weather. I walked all the way from Knightsbridge. Delightful. Cake? Bread and butter? Hello, Henry! You ought to have walked with me—never enjoyed anything so much in my life."

Mrs. Trenchard's broad, impassive face was lighted with

approval as a lantern is lit. She liked afternoon-tea and her drawing-room and young cheerful Seymour and the books behind the book-case and the ticking of the clock. A cosy winter's afternoon in London! What could be pleasanter? She sighed a comfortable, contented sigh. . . .

Mark was seized, as he sat there, with a drowsy torpor. The fire seemed to draw from the room all scents that, like memories, waited there for some compelling friendly warmth. The room was close with more than the Trenchard protection against the winter's day—it was packed with a conscious pressure of all the things that the Trenchards had ever done in that room, and Mrs. Trenchard sat motionless, placid, receiving these old things, encouraging them and distributing them. Mark was aware that if he encouraged his drowsiness he would very shortly acquiesce in and submit to—he knew not what—and the necessity for battling against this acquiescence irritated him so that it was almost as though everyone in the room were subtly taking him captive and he would be lost before he was aware. Katherine, alone, quiet, full of repose, saying very little, did not disturb him. It was exactly as though all the other persons present were wishing him to break into argument and contradiction because then they could spring upon him.

His attention was, of course, directed to Seymour's opinions, and he knew, before he heard them, that he would disagree violently with them all.

They came, like the distant firing of guns, across the muffled drowsiness of the room.

"I assure you, Mrs. Trenchard. . . . I assure you . . . assure you. You wouldn't believe. . . . Well, of course, I've heard people say so but I can't help disagreeing with them. One may know very little about writing oneself—I don't pretend I've got far—and yet have very distinct ideas as to how the thing should be done. There's good work and bad, you know—there's no getting over it. . . .

"But, my dear Henry . . . dear old chap . . . I assure

you. But it's a question of Form. You take my word a
man's nothing without a sense of Form . . . Form . . .
Form. . . . Yes, of course, the French are the people. Now
the Russians. . . . Tolstoi, Dostoevsky . . . Dostoevsky,
Mrs. Trenchard. Well, people spell him different ways.
You should read 'War and Peace'. Never read 'War and
Peace'? Ah, you should and 'Crime and Punishment'. But
compare 'Crime and Punishment' with 'La maison Tel-
lier' . . . Maupassant—The Russians aren't in it. But what
can you expect from a country like that? I assure you. . . ."

Quite irresistibly, as though everyone in the room had said:
"There now. You've simply got to come in now", Mark was
drawn forward. He heard through the sleepy, clogged and
scented air his own voice.

"But there are all sorts of novels, aren't there, just as
there are all sorts of people? I don't see why everything
should be after the same pattern."

He was violently conscious then of Seymour's chin that
turned, slowly, irresistibly as the prow of a ship is turned,
towards him—a very remarkable chin for its size and
strength, jutting up and out, surprising, too, after the chubby
amiability of the rest of his face. At the same moment it
seemed to Mark that all the other chins in the room turned
towards him with stern emphasis.

A sharp litle dialogue followed then: Seymour was eager,
cheerful and good-humoured—patronising, too, perhaps, if
one is sensitive to such things.

"Quite so. Of course—of course. But you will admit,
won't you, that style matters, that the way a thing's done, the
way things are arranged, you know, count?"

"I don't know anything about writing novels—I only know
about reading them. The literary, polished novel is one
sort of thing, I suppose. But there is also the novel with
plenty of real people and real things in it. If a novel's too
literary a plain man like myself doesn't find it real at all. I
prefer something careless and casual like life itself, with

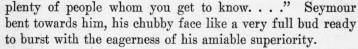

plenty of people whom you get to know. . . ." Seymour
bent towards him, his chubby face like a very full bud ready
to burst with the eagerness of his amiable superiority.

"But you can't say that your Russians are real people—
come now. Take Dostoevsky—take him for a minute. Look
at them. Look at 'Les Frères Karamazoff'. All as mad as
hatters—all of 'em—and no method at all—just chucked on
anyhow. After all, Literature is something."

"Yes, that's just what I complain of," said Mark, feeling
as though he were inside a ring of eager onlookers who were
cheering his opponent. "You fellows all think literature's
the only thing. It's entirely unimportant beside real life.
If your book is like real life, why then it's interesting. If
it's like literature it's no good at all except to a critic or
—"

"And I suppose," cried Seymour, scornfully, his chin rising higher and higher, "that you'd say Dostoevsky's like real
life?"

"It is," said Mark, quietly, "if you know Russia."

"Well, I've never been there," Seymour admitted. "But
I've got a friend who has. He says that Russian fiction's
nothing like the real thing at all. That Russia's just like
anywhere else."

"Nonsense"—and Mark's voice was shaking—"Your
friend . . . rot—" He recovered himself. "That's utterly
untrue," he said.

"I assure you—" Seymour began.

Then Mark forgot himself, his surroundings, his audience.

"Oh—go to Blazes!" he cried. "What do you know about
it? You say yourself you've never been there. I've lived in
Moscow for years!"

There was then a tremendous silence, Mrs. Trenchard,
Aunt Aggie, Henry, all looked at Seymour as though they
said "Please, please, don't mind. It shall *never* happen
again."

Katherine looked at Mark. During that moment's silence

the winter afternoon with its frost and clear skies, its fresh
colour and happy intimacies, seemed to beat about the house.
In Mark, the irritation that he had felt ever since Seymour's
sentence, seemed now to explode within him, like the bursting
of some thunder cloud. He was for a moment deluged
most drowned by his impotent desire to make some so
short, to fight, anything that would break the hot stuff
ness of the air and let in the sharp crispness of th
world.

But the episode was at an end. Katherine closed it
"Tell Mr. Seymour some of those things that you
telling us last night—about Moscow and Russian life."

Mrs. Trenchard's eyes, having concluded their wo
consoling Seymour, fastened themselves upon Mark,—v
ing like eyes behind closed windows; strangely in add
to their conviction that some outrage had been comm
there was also a suspicion of fear—but they were the i
glazed eyes of a stupid although kindly woman. . . .

Mark that evening, going up to dress for dinner, thou
to himself, "I really can't stay here any longer. It isn't
cent, besides, they don't like me." He found, half in th
dusk, half in the moonlight of the landing-window Katherine
looking for an instant before she went to her room, at the dark
Abbey-towers, the sky with the stars frosted over, it seemed,
by the coldness of the night, at the moon, faintly orange and
crisp against the night blue.

He stopped. "I'm sorry," he said abruptly, looking into
her eyes, very soft and mild but always with that lingering
humour behind their mildness. "I'm afraid I was rude to
that fellow this afternoon."

"Yes," she said, turning to him but with her eyes still on
the black towers. "You were—but it would have no effect on
Mr. Seymour."

He felt, as he stood there, that he wished to explain that
he was not naturally so unpolished a barbarian.

"Russia," he began, hesitating and looking at her almost appealingly, "is a sore point with me. You can't tell—unless you've lived there how it grows upon you, holds you, and, at last, begs you to stand up for it whenever it may be attacked. And he didn't know—really he didn't—"

"You're taking it much too seriously," she said, laughing at him, he felt. "No one thought that he *did* know. But Mother likes him and he's Henry's friend. And we all stick together as a family."

"I'm afraid your mother thought me abominable," he said, looking up at her and looking away again.

"Mother's old-fashioned," Katherine answered. "So am I —so are we all. We're an old-fashioned family. We've never had anyone like you to stay with us before."

"It's abominable that I should stay on like this. I'll go to-morrow."

"No, don't do that. Father loves having you. We all like you—only we're a little afraid of your ways"—she moved down the passage. "We're very good for you, I expect, and I'm sure you're very good for us." She suddenly turned back towards him, and dropping her voice, quite solemnly said to him, "The great thing about us is that we're fond of one another. That makes it all the harder for anyone from outside. . . ."

"I'll tell you one thing," he said, carrying on her note of confidence, "I like people to like me. I'm very foolish about it. It's the chief thing I want."

"I like people to like me, too," Katherine answered, raising her voice and moving now definitely away from him. "Why shouldn't one?" she ended. "Don't you be afraid, Mr. Mark. It's all right."

He dressed hurriedly and came down to the drawing-room, with some thought in the back of his mind that he would, throughout the evening, be the most charming person possible. He found, however, at once a check. . . .

Under a full blaze of light Grandfather Trenchard and Great Aunt Sarah were sitting, waiting for the others. The old man, his silver buckles and white hair gleaming, sat, perched high in his chair, one hand raised before the fire, behind it the firelight shining as behind a faint screen.

Aunt Sarah, very stiff, upright and slim, was the priestess before the Trenchard temple. They, both of them, gazed into the fire. They did not turn their heads as Mark entered; they had watched his entry in the Mirror.

He shouted Good-evening, but they did not hear him. He sat down, began a sentence.

"Really a sharp touch in the air—" then abandoned it, seizing 'Blackwood' as a weapon of defence. Behind his paper, he knew that their eyes were upon him. He felt them peering into 'Blackwood's' cover; they pierced the pages, they struck him in the face.

There was complete silence in the room. The place was thick with burning eyes. They were reflected, he felt, in the Mirror, again and again.

"How they hate me!" he thought.

CHAPTER III

KATHERINE TRENCHARD'S very earliest sense of
morality had been that there were God, the Trenchard's
and the Devil—that the Devil wished very much to win the
Trenchards over to His side, but that God assured the Trenchards that if only they behaved well He would not let them
go—and, for this, Troy had burnt, Carthage been razed to
the ground, proud kings driven from their thrones and hum-
bled to the dust, plague, pestilence, and famine had wrought
their worst. . . .

The Trenchards were, indeed, a tremendous family, and
it was little wonder that the Heavenly Powers should fight
for their alliance. In the county of Glebeshire, where Katherine had spent all her early years, Trenchards ran like spid-
ers' webs, up and down the lanes and villages.

In Polchester, the Cathedral city, there were Canon
Trenchard and his family, old Colonel Trenchard, late of the
Indian army, the Trenchards of Polhaze and the Trenchards
of Rothin Place—all these in one small town. There were
Trenchards at Rasselas and Trenchards (poor and rather unworthy Trenchards) at Clinton St. Mary. There was one
Trenchard (a truculent and gout-ridden bachelor) at Polwint—all of these in the immediate neighbourhood of Katherine's home. Of course they were important to God. . . .

In that old house in the village of Garth in Roselands,
where Katherine had been born, an old house up to its very
chin in deep green fields, an old house wedded, hundreds of
years ago to the Trenchard Spirit, nor likely now ever to be
divorced from it, Katherine had learnt to adore with her

body, her soul and her spirit Glebeshire and everything that belonged to that fair county, but to adore it, also, because it was so completely, so devoutly, the Trenchard heritage. So full were her early prayers of petitions for successive Trenchards. "God bless Father, Mother, Henry, Millie, Vincent, Uncle Tim, Uncle Wobert, Auntie Agnes, Auntie Betty, Cousin Woger, Cousin Wilfrid, Cousin Alice, etc., etc.," that, did it ever come to a petition for someone unhappily not a Trenchard the prayer was offered with a little hesitating apology. For a long while Katherine thought that when Missionaries were sent to gather in the heathen they were going out on the divine mission of driving all strangers into the Trenchard fold.

Not to be a Trenchard was to be a nigger or a Chinaman.

And here I would remark with all possible emphasis that Katherine was never taught that it was a fine and a mighty thing to be a Trenchard. No Trenchard had ever, since time began, considered his position any more than the stars, the moon and the sun consider theirs. If you were a Trenchard you did not think about it at all. The whole Trenchard world with all its ramifications, its great men and its small men, its dignitaries, its houses, its Castles, its pleasure-resorts, its Foreign Baths, its Theatres, its Shooting, its Churches, its Politics, its Foods and Drinks, its Patriotisms and Charities, its Seas, its lakes and rivers, its Morality, its angers, its pleasures, its regrets, its God and its Devil, the whole Trenchard world was a thing intact, preserved, ancient, immovable. It took its stand on its History, its family affection, its country Places, its loyal Conservatism, its obstinacy and its stupidity. Utterly unlike such a family as the Beaminsters with their preposterous old Duchess (now so happily dead) it had no need whatever for any self-assertion, any struggle with anything, any fear of invasion. From Without nothing could attack its impregnability. From Within? Well, perhaps, presently . . . but no Trenchard was aware of that.

A young Beaminster learnt from the instant of its breaking the Egg that it must at once set about showing the world that it was a Beaminster.

A young Trenchard never considered for a single second that he was supposed to show anyone anything. HE WAS . . . that was enough.

The Trenchards had never been conceited people—conceit implied too definite a recognition of other people's position and abilities. To be conceited you must think yourself abler, more interesting, richer, handsomer than someone else—and no Trenchard ever realised anyone else.

From the security of their Mirror they looked out upon the world. Only from inside the House could the Mirror be broken—surely then they were secure. . . .

Katherine was always a very modest little girl, but her modesty had never led to any awkward shyness or embarrass-ment; she simply did not consider herself at all. She had been, in the early days, a funny little figure, 'dumpy', with serious brown eyes and a quiet voice. She was never in the way, better at home than at parties, she never 'struck' strang-ers, as did her younger sister Millicent, 'who would be bril-liant when she grew up'; Katherine would never be brilliant.

She had, from the first, a capacity for doing things for the family without atracting attention—and what more can selfish people desire? She was soon busy and occupied—nec-essary to the whole house. She very seldom laughed, but her eyes twinkled and she was excellent company did anyone care for her opinion. Only Uncle Tim of them all realised her intelligence—for the rest of the family she was slow 'but a dear.'

It was in her capacity of 'a dear' that she finally stood to all of them. They adored because they knew that they never disappointed her. Although they had, none of them (save Henry) any concern as to their especial failings or weaknesses, it was nevertheless comforting to know that they might put anything upon Katherine, behave to her always in the way that was easiest to them, and that she would always think them splendid. They would not in public places put Katherine forward as a Fine Trenchard. Millicent would be a Fine Trenchard one day—but at home, in their cosy fortified security, there was no one like Katherine.

Katherine was perfect to them all. . . . Not that she did not sometimes have her tempers, her impatiences, her 'moods'. They were puzzled when she was short with them, when she would not respond to their invitations for compliments, when she seemed to have some horrible doubt as to whether the Trenchard world was, after all, the only one—but they waited for the 'mood' to pass, and it passed very swiftly . . . it is noteworthy however that never, in spite of their devotion to her, did they during these crises, attempt to help or console her. She stood alone, and at the back of their love there was always some shadow of fear.

Very happy had her early years been. The house at Garth, rambling, untidy, intimate, with the croquet-lawn in front of it, the little wild wood at the right of it, the high sheltering green fields at the left of it, the old church Tower above the little wood, the primroses and cuckoos, the owls and moon-light nights, the hot summer days with the hum of the reaping machine, the taste of crushed strawberries, the dim-sleepy voices from the village street. *This* was a world! The Old House had never changed—as she had grown it had dwindled perhaps, but ever, as the years passed, had enclosed more securely the passion of her heart. She saw herself standing in the dim passage that led to her bedroom, a tiny, stumpy figure. She could hear the voice of Miss Mayer, the governess, "Now, Katherine—come along, please—Millie's in bed."

She could smell the tallow of the candle, could hear the owls' hoot from the dark window, could smell apples and roses somewhere, could remember how intensely she had caught that moment and held it, and carried it, for ever and ever, away with her. Yes, that *was* a World!

And, beyond the House, there was the Country. Every

lane and wood and hill did she know. Those thick, deep,
scented lanes that only Glebeshire in all the world can pro-
vide—the road to Rafiel, running, at first, with only a moment's peep now and again of the sea, then plunging with dramatic fling, suddenly down into the heart of the Valley.
There was Rafiel—Rafiel, the only Cove in all the world!
How as the dog-cart bumped down that precipice had her
heart been in her mouth, how magical the square harbour,
the black Peak, the little wall of white-washed cottages, after
that defeated danger!

There were all the other places—St. Lowe and Polwint,
Polchester with the Cathedral and the Orchards and the cobbled streets, Grane Woods and Grane Castle, Rothin Woods,
Roche St. Mary, Moore with the seadunes and the mists and
rabbits, the Loroe river and the fishing-boats at Pelynt—
world of perfect beauty and simplicity, days stained with the
high glory of romance. And this was Trenchard Country!

London, coming to her afterwards, had, at first, been hated,
only gradually accepted. She grew slowly fond of the old
Westminster house, but the crowds about her confused and
perplexed her. She was aware now that, perhaps, there were
those in the world who cared nothing for the Trenchards.
She flew from such confusion the more intensely into her devotion to her own people. It was as though, at the very
first peep of the world, she had said to herself—"No. That
is not my place. They have no need of me nor I of them.
They would change me. I do not wish to be changed."

She was aware of her own duty the more strongly because
her younger sister, Millicent, had taken always the opposite
outlook. Millicent, pretty, slender, witty, attractive, had always found home (even Garth and its glories) 'a little slow'.

The family had always understood that it was natural
for Millicent to find them slow—no pains had been spared
over Millicent's development. She had just finished her education in Paris and was coming back to London. Always

future plans now were discussed with a view to finding amusement for Millicent. "Millie will be here then". "I wonder whether Millie will like him." "You'd better accept it. Millie will like to go."

Beyond all the family Katherine loved Millicent. It had begun when Millie had been very small and Katherine had mothered her,—it had continued when Millie, growing older, had plunged into scrapes and demanded succour out of them again—it had continued when Katherine and Millie had developed under a cloud of governesses, Millie brilliant and idle, Katherine plodding and unenterprising, it had continued when Millie, two years ago, had gone to Paris, had written amusing, affectionate letters, had told "Darling Katie that there was no one, *no one,* no ONE, anywhere in all the world, to touch her—Mme. Roget was a pig, Mlle. Lefresne, who taught music, an angel, etc. etc."

Now Millicent was coming home. . . . Katherine was aware that from none of the family did she receive more genuine affection than from Henry, and yet, strangely, she was often irritated with Henry. She wished that he were more tidy, less rude to strangers, less impulsive, more of a comfort and less of an anxiety to his father and mother. She was severe sometimes to Henry and then was sorry afterwards. She could 'do anything with him,' and wished therefore that he had more backbone. Of them all she understood her mother the best. She was very like her mother in many ways; she understood that inability to put things into words, that mild conviction that 'everything was all right', a conviction to be obtained only by shutting your eyes very tight. She understood, too, as no other member of the family understood, that Mrs. Trenchard's devotion to her children was a passion as fierce, as unresting, as profound, and, possibly, as devastating as any religion, any superstition, any obsession. It *was* an obsession. It had in it all the glories, the dangers, the relentless ruthlessness of an overwhelming 'idée fixe'—that 'idée fixe' which is at every human being's heart, and that, often undiscovered, unsuspected, transforms the world. . . . Katherine knew this.

For her father she had the comradeship of a play-fellow. She could not take her father very seriously—he did not wish that she should. She loved him always and he loved her in his 'off' moments, when he was not thinking of himself and his early Nineteenth Century—if he had any time that he could spare from himself it was given to her. She thought it quite natural that his spare time should be slender.

And, of them all, no one enquired as to her own heart, her thoughts, her wonders, her alarms and suspicions, her happiness, her desires. She would not if she could help it, enquire herself about these things—but sometimes she was aware that life would not for ever, leave her alone. She had one friend who was not a Trenchard, and only one. This was Lady Seddon, who had been before her marriage a Beaminster and grand-daughter of the old Duchess of Wrexe. Rachel Beaminster had married Roddy Seddon. Shortly after their marriage he had been flung from his horse, and from that time had been always upon his back—it would always be so with him. They had one child—a boy of two—and they lived in a little house in Regent's Park.

That friendship had been of Rachel Seddon's making. She had driven herself in upon Katherine and, offering her baby as a reward, had lured Katherine into her company—but even to her, Katherine had not surrendered herself. Rachel Seddon was a Beaminster, and although the Beaminster power was now broken, about that family there lingered traditions of greatness and autocratic splendour. Neither Rachel nor Roddy Seddon was autocratic, but Katherine would not trust herself entirely to them. It was as though she was afraid that by doing so she would be disloyal to her own people.

This, then, was Katherine's world.

Upon the morning of the November day when Millicent was to make, upon London, her triumphal descent from Paris, Katherine found herself, suddenly, in the middle of Wigmore Street, uneasy—Wigmore Street was mild, pleasantly lit with a low and dim November sun, humming with a little stir and scatter of voices and traffic, opening and shutting its doors, watching a drove of clouds, like shredded paper, sail through the faint blue sky above it. Katherine stopped for an instant to consider this strange uneasiness. She looked about her, thought, and decided that she would go and see Rachel Seddon.

Crossing a little finger of the Park, she stopped again. The shredded clouds were dancing now amongst the bare stiff branches of the trees and a grey mist, climbing over the expanse of green, spread like thin gauze from end to end of the rising ground. A little soughing wind seemed to creep about her feet. She stopped again and stood there, a solitary figure. For, perhaps, the first time in her life she considered herself. She knew, as she stood there, that she had for several days been aware of this uneasiness. It was as though someone had been knocking at a door for admittance. She had heard the knocking, but had refused to move, saying to herself that soon the sound would cease. But it had not ceased, it was more clamorous than before. She was frightened—why? Was it Millie's return? She knew that it was not that. . . .

Standing there, in the still Park, she seemed to hear something say to her "You are to be caught up. . . . Life is coming to you. . . . You cannot avoid it. . . . You are caught."

She might have cried to the sky, the trees, the little pools of dead and sodden leaves "What is it? What is it? Do you hear anything?" A scent of rotting leaves and damp mist, brought by the little wind, invaded her. The pale sun struck through the moist air and smiled down, a globe of gold, upon her. There came to her that moment of revelation that tells human beings that, fine as they may think them-

selves, full of courage and independent of all men, Life, if it
exert but the softest pressure, may be too strong for them—
the armies of God, with their certain purpose, are revealed
for a brief instant entrenched amongst the clouds. "If we
crush you what matters it to Us?"

She hurried on her way, longing for the sound of friendly
voices, and, when she found Rachel Seddon with her son in
the nursery, the fire, the warm colours, the absurd rocking-
horse, armies of glittering soldiers encamped upon the red
carpet, the buzz of a sewing-machine in the next room, above
all, Michael Seddon's golden head and Rachel's dark one,
she could have cried aloud her relief.

Rachel, tall and slender, dark eyes and hair from a Russian mother, restless, impetuous, flinging her hands out in
some gesture, catching her boy, suddenly, and kissing him,
breaking off in the heart of one sentence to begin another, was
a strange contrast to Katherine's repose. Soon Katherine
was on the floor and Michael, who loved her, had his arms
about her neck.

"That's how she ought always to be," thought Rachel,
looking down at her. "How could anyone ever say that she
was plain! Roddy thinks her so. . . . He should see her
now."

Katherine looked up. "Rachel," she said, "I was frightened just now in the Park. I don't know why—I almost
ran here. I'm desperately ashamed of myself."

"You—frightened?"

"Yes, I thought someone was coming out from behind a
tree to slip a bag over my head, I—Oh! I don't know what
I thought. . . ."

Then she would say no more. She played with Michael
and tried to tell him a story. Here she was, as she had
often been before, unsuccessful. She was too serious over
the business, would not risk improbabilities and wanted to
emphasise the moral. She was not sufficiently absurd . . .
gravely her eyes sought for a decent ending. She looked up

and found that Michael had left her and was moving his soldiers.

The sun, slanting in, struck lines of silver and gold from their armour across the floor.

As she got up and stood there, patting herself to see whether she were tidy, her laughing eyes caught Rachel.

"There! You see! I'm no good at *that!*—no imagination —father's always said so."

"Katie," Rachel said, catching her soft, warm, almost chubby hand, "there's nothing the matter, is there?"

"The matter! No! what should there be?"

"It's so odd for you to say what you did just now. And I think—I don't know—you're different to-day."

"No, I'm not." Katherine looked at her. "It was the damp Park, all the bare trees and nobody about."

"But it's so unlike you to think of damp Parks and bare trees."

"Well—perhaps it's because Millie's coming back from Paris this afternoon. I shall be terrified of her—so smart she'll be!"

"Give her my love and bring her here as soon as she'll come. She'll amuse Roddy." She paused, searching in Katherine's brown eyes—"Katie—if there's ever—anything—*anything*— I can help you in or advise you—or do for you. You know, don't you? . . . You always *will* be so independent. You don't *tell* me things. Remember I've had my times—worse times than you guess."

Katherine kissed her. "It's all right, Rachel, there's noth- ing the matter—except that . . . no, nothing at all. Good- bye, dear. Don't come down. I'll bring Millie over."

She was gone—Rachel watched her demure, careful prog- ress until she was caught and hidden by the trees.

There had been a little truth in her words when she told Rachel that she dreaded Millie's arrival. If she had ever, in the regular routine of her happy and busy life, looked forward to any event as dramatic or a crisis, that moment had always been Millie's return from Paris. Millie had been happy and affectionate at home, but nevertheless a critic. She had never quite seen Life from inside the Trenchard Mirror nor had she quite seen it from the vision of family affection. She loved them all—but she found them slow, un-adventurous, behind the times. That was the awful thing—'behind the times'—a terrible accusation. If Millie had felt that (two years ago) how vehemently would she feel it now! . . . and Katherine knew that as she considered this criticism of Millie's she was angry and indignant and warm with an urgent, passionate desire to protect her mother from any criticism whatever. "Behind the times", indeed—Millie had better not. . . . And then she remembered the depth of her love for Millie . . . nothing should interfere with that.

She was in her bedroom, after luncheon, considering these things when there was a tap on the door and Aunt Betty entered. In her peep round the door to see whether she might come in, in the friendly, hopeful, reassuring butterfly of a smile that hovered about her lips, in the little stir of her clothes as she moved as though every article of attire was assuring her that it was still there, and was very happy to be there too, there was the whole of her history written.

It might be said that she had no history, but to such an assertion, did she hear it, she would offer an indignant denial, could she be indignant about anything. She had been per-fectly, admirably happy for fifty-six years, and that, after all, is to have a history to some purpose. She had nothing whatever to be happy about. She had no money at all, and had never had any. She had, for a great number of years, been compelled to live upon her brother's charity, and she was the most independent soul alive. In strict truth she had, of her own, thirty pounds a year, and the things that she did with those thirty pounds are outside and beyond any cal-culation. "There's always *my* money, George," she would say when her brother had gloomy forebodings about investments. She lived, in fact, a minute, engrossing, adventurous, flaming life of her own, and the flame, the colour, the fire were drawn from her own unconquerable soul. In her bedroom—faded wall-paper, faded carpet, faded chairs because no one ever thought of her needs—she had certain possessions, a cedar-wood box, a row of books, a water-colour sketch, photographs of the family (Katherine 3½, Vincent 8 years old, Millicent 10 years, etc., etc.), a model of the Albert Memorial done in pink wax, a brass tray from India, some mother-of-pearl shells, two china cats given to her, one Christmas day, by a very young Katherine—those possessions were her world. She felt that within that bedroom everything was her own. She would allow no other pictures on the wall, no books not hers in the bookcase. One day when she had some of the thirty pounds 'to play with' she would cover the chairs with beautiful cretonne and she would buy a rug—so she had said for the last twenty years. She withdrew, when life was tiresome, when her sister Aggie was difficult, when there were quarrels in the family (she hated quarrels) into this world of her own, and would suddenly break out in the midst of a conversation with "I might have the bed *there*" or "There isn't really room for another chair if I had one," and then would make a little noise like a top, 'hum, hum, hum'. In defiance of her serenity she could assume a terrible rage and indignation were any member of the family attacked. Her brother George and Katherine she loved best—she did not, although she would never acknowledge it, care greatly for Henry—Millie she admired and feared. She had only to think of Katherine and her eyes would fill with tears . . . she was a very fount of sentiment. She had suffered much from her sister Agnes, but she had learnt now the art of withdrawal so perfectly that she could escape at any time without her sister being aware of it. "You aren't listening, Elizabeth," Agnes would cry suspiciously.

"Yes, dear Aggie, I am. I don't think things as bad as you say. For instance," and a wonderful recovery would re-

assure suspicion. The real core of her life was Katherine
and Katherine's future. There was to be, one day, for Katherine a most splendid suitor—a Lord, perhaps, a great poli-
tician, a great Churchman, she did not know—but someone
who would realise first Katherine's perfection, secondly the
honour of being made a Trenchard, thirdly the necessity of
spending all his life in the noble work of making Katherine
happy. "I shall miss her—we shall all miss her—but we
mustn't be selfish—hum, hum—she'll have one to stay, perhaps."

Very often she came peeping into Katherine's room as she
came to-day. She would take Katherine into her confidence;
she would offer her opinion about the events of the hour.
She took her stand in the middle of the room, giving little
excited pecks at one of her fingers, the one that suffered most
from her needle when she sewed, a finger scarred now by a
million little stabs. So she stood now, and Katherine, sitting
on the edge of her bed, looked up at her.

"I came in, my dear, because you hardly ate any luncheon.
I watched you—hardly any at all."

"Oh, that's all right, Aunt Betty. I wasn't hungry."

"I don't like your not eating—hum, hum. No, I don't.
Mother always used to say 'Don't Eat, can't Beat'—of mili-
tary forces, you know, dear, or anything that had a hard
task to perform."

She looked about her with an aimless and rather nervous
smile, which meant that she had something to say but was
afraid of it.

"Katie, dear, do you know?" (This with an air of intense
importance.) "I don't think I'll show Millie my room—not
just at first at any rate."

"Oh, but you must. She'll be longing to see it."

"Well, but—will she, do you think? Oh, no, she won't,
not after Paris. . . . Paris is so grand. Perhaps, later I
will—show it her. I mean when she's more accustomed to the
old life."

But even now it was plain that she had not delivered her purpose. It was imprisoned, like a mouse in a very woolly moth-eaten trap. Soon there will be a click and out it will come!

Her wandering, soft, kindly eyes looked gravely upon Katherine.

"My dear, I wish you'd eaten something. Only a little mince and two of those cheese biscuits. . . . Katie dear, did you hear what Mr. Mark said at luncheon about leaving us?"

"Yes, Aunt Betty."

"He said he'd got somewhere from next Monday. Poor young man—not *so* young now either—but he seems lonely. I'm glad we were able to be kind to him at first. Katie, I have an 'Idea'." Impossible to give any picture of the eagerness with which now her eyes were lit and her small body strung on a tiptoe of excitement, "I have an idea. . . . I think he and Millie—I think he might be just the man for Millie—adventurous, exciting, knowing so much about Russia—and, after Paris, she'll want someone like that."

Katherine turned slowly away from her aunt, gazing vaguely, absent-mindedly, as though she had not been thinking of the old lady's words.

"Oh, no, Aunt Betty. I don't think so—What an old matchmaker you are!"

"I love to see people happy. And I like him. I think it's a pity he's going on Monday. He's been here a fortnight now. I like him. He's polite to me, and when a young man is polite to an old woman like me that says a lot—hum, hum —yes, it does. But your mother doesn't like him—I wonder why not—but she doesn't. I always know when your mother doesn't like anybody. Millie will. . . . I know she will. But I don't think I'll show her my things—not at first, not right after Paris."

"Perhaps it would be better to wait a little." Katherine went and sat in front of her mirror. She touched the things on her dressing-table.

"I'll go now, dear—I can't bear to think of you only having had that mince. My eye will be on you at dinner, mind."

She peeped out of the door, looked about her with her bright little eyes, then whisked away.

Katherine sat before her glass, gazing. But not at herself. She did not know whose face it was that stared back at her.

Millie's entrance that afternoon was very fine. There were there to receive her, her grandfather, her great-aunt (in white boa), her father, her mother, Henry, Katherine, Aunt Betty and Aggie, Philip Mark, Esq. She stood in the doorway of the drawing-room radiant with health, good spirits and happiness at being home again—all Trenchards always are. Like Katherine in the humour of her eyes, otherwise not at all—tall, dark, slim in black and white, a little black hat with a blue feather, a hat that was over one ear. She had her grandfather's air of clear, finely cut distinction, but so alive, so vibrating with health was she that her entrance extinguished the family awaiting her as you blow out a candle. Her cheeks were flushed, her black eyes sparkled, her arms were outstretched to all of them.

"Here I am!" she seemed to say, "I'm sure you've forgotten in all this time how delightful I am!—and indeed I'm ever so much more delightful than I was before I went away. In any case here I am, ready to love you all. And there's no family in the world I'd be gladder to be a member of than this!"

Her sharp, merry, inquisitive eyes sought them all out—sought out the old room with all the things in it exactly as she had always known them, and then the people—one after the other—all of them exactly as she had always known them. . . .

She was introduced to Philip Mark. Her eyes lingered up him, for an instant, mischievously, almost interrogatively.

To him she seemed to say: "What on earth are you doing inside here? How did you ever get in? And what are you here for?" She seemed to say to him: "You and I—we know more than these others here—but just because of that we're not half so nice."

"Well, Henry," she said, and he felt that she was laughing at him and blushed. He knew that his socks were hanging loosely. He had lost one of his suspenders.

"Well, Millie," he answered, and thought how beautiful she was.

It was one of the Trenchard axioms that anyone who crossed the English Channel conferred a favour—it was nice of them to go, as though one visited a hospital or asked a poor relation to stay. Paris must have been glad to have had Millie—it must have been very gay for Paris—and that not because Millie was very wonderful, but simply because Paris wasn't English.

"It must be nice to be home again, Millie dear," said Mrs. Trenchard comfortably.

Millie laughed and for a moment her eyes flashed across at Philip Mark, but he was looking at Katherine. She looked round upon them all, then, as though she were wondering how, after all, things were going to be now that she had come home 'for good'—now that it would be always and always—well, perhaps not always. She looked again at Philip Mark and liked him. She surrendered herself then to the dip and splash and sparkle of the family waters of affection. They deluged and overwhelmed her. Her old grandfather and the great-aunt sat silently there, watching, with their bird-like eyes, everything, but even upon their grim features there were furrowed smiles.

"And the crossing was really all right?" "The trees in the Park were blowing rather. . . ." "And so, Milly dear, I said you'd go. I promised for you. But you can get out of it as easily as anything. . . ."

"You must have been sorry, as it was the last time, but

you'll be able to go back later on and see them. . . ."

And her father. "Well, *they've* had her long enough, and now it's our turn for a bit. She's been spoiled there. . . . She won't get any spoiling here. . . ."

He roared with laughter, flinging his head back, coming over and catching Millie's head between his hands, laughing above her own laughing eyes. Henry watched them, his father cynically, his sister devotedly. He was always embarrassed by the family demonstrations, and he felt it the more embarrassing now because there was a stranger in their midst. Philip was just the man to think this all odd. . . . But Henry was anxious about the family behaviour simply because he was devoted to the family, not at all because he thought himself superior to it.

Then Milly tore herself away from them all. She looked at Katherine.

"I'm going up to my room. Katy, come up and help me—"

"I'd better come and help you, dear," said Mrs. Trenchard. "There's sure to be a mess. . . ."

But Milly shook her head with a slight gesture of impatience. "No, no, Mother . . . Katy and I will manage."

"Hilda will do everything if—"

"No, I want to show Katy things. . . ."

They went.

When the two girls were alone in the bedroom and the door was closed Milly flung her arms round Katherine and kissed her again and again. They stood there, in the silence, wrapped in one another's arms.

"Katy—darling—if you only knew, all this time, how I've longed for you. Sometimes I thought 'I *must*—I *must* —see her'—that's you. I'd run away—I'd do anything. I don't think anything matters now that I've got you again— *and* I've so much to tell you!"

They sat down on the bed, Millie vibrating with the excitement of her wonderful experiences, Katherine quiet, but with one hand pressing Millie's and her eyes staring into distance.

Suddenly Millie stopped.

"Katie, dear, who's this man?"

"What man?"

"The nice-looking man I saw downstairs."

"Oh, he's a Mr. Mark. Son of a great friend of father's. He's lived in Russia—Moscow—for years. He came in by mistake one night in a fog and found that ours was the house he was coming to next day—then Father asked him to stay—"

"Do you like him?"

"Yes. He's very nice."

"He looks nice."

Milly went on again with her reminiscences. Katherine, saying only a word now and then, listened.

Then, exactly as though she had caught some unexpected sound, Milly broke off again.

"Katy—Katy."

"Yes."

"You're different, something's happened to you."

"My dear!—nothing, of course."

"Yes, something has.—Something . . . Katy!" And here Milly flung her arms again about her sister and stared into her eyes. "You're in love with someone."

But Katherine laughed. "That's Paris, Milly dear—Paris—Paris."

"It isn't. It isn't. It's *you*. There is someone. Katy, darling, tell me—you've always told me everything: who is he? tell me."

Katherine drew herself away from Milly's embrace, then turned round, looking at her sister. Then she caught her and kissed her with a sudden urgent passion. "There's no one, of course there's no one. I'm the old maid of the family. You know we, long ago, decided that. I'm not . . ." she broke off, laughed, got up from the bed. She looked at Milly as though she were setting, subduing some thoughts in her mind. "I'm just the same, Milly. *You're* different, of course."

At a sudden sound both the girls looked up. Their mother stood in the doorway, with her placidity, her mild affection; she looked about the room.

"I had to come, my dears, to see how you were getting on." She moved forward slowly towards them.

CHAPTER IV

THE FOREST

PART of a letter that Philip Mark wrote to his friend:—
"... I couldn't stay any longer. They'd had me there a fortnight and then one of the daughters came home from being 'finished' in Paris, so that they've really no room for strangers. I've moved here—not very far away—three furnished rooms in an upper part in a small street off Victoria Street. It's quiet with an amazing quietness considering its closeness to all the rattle. The Roman Catholic Cathedral is just round the corner—hideous to look at, but it's nice inside. There's a low little pub. opposite that reminds me comfortably of one of our beloved 'Trakteer'—you see I'm sentimental about Moscow already—more so every day.

"I've so much to tell you, and yet it comes down to one very simple thing. I've found, I believe, already the very soul I set out to find, set out with yours and Anna's blessing, remember. You mayn't tell her yet. It's too soon and it may so easily come to nothing, but I do believe that if I'd searched England through and through for many years I could never have found anyone so—so—exactly what I need. You must have guessed in that very first letter that it had, even then, begun. It began from the instant that I saw her—it seems to me now to be as deeply seated in me as my own soul itself. But you know that at the root of everything is my own distrust in myself. Perhaps if I had never gone to Russia I should have had more confidence, but that country, as I see it now, stirs always through the hearts of its lovers, questions about everything in heaven or earth and then tells one at the end that nothing matters. And the Englishman that

is in me has always fought that distrust, has called it sentimental, feeble, and then again I've caught back the superstition and the wonder. In Russia one's so close to God and the
Devil—in England there is business and common-sense. Between the two I'm pretty useless. If you had once seen Katherine you'd know why she seems to me a refuge from all that
I've been fighting with Anna for so long. She's clear and
true as steel—so quiet, so sure, so much better and finer than
myself that I feel that I'm the most selfish hound in the
world to dream of attaching her to me. Mind you, I don't
know at present that she's interested; she's so young and
ignorant in so many ways, with all her calm common-sense,
that I'm terrified of alarming her, and if she doesn't care for
me I'll never disturb her—never. But if she should—well,
then, I believe that I can make her happy—I know myself
by now. I've left my Moscow self behind me just as Anna
said that I must. There's nothing stranger than the way
that Anna foretold it all. That night when she shewed me
that I must go she drew a picture of the kind of woman whom
I must find. She had never been to England, she had only,
in all her life, seen one or two Englishwomen, but she knew,
she knew absolutely. It's as though she had seen Katherine
in her dreams. . . .

"But I'm talking with absurd assurance. Putting Katherine entirely aside there is all the family to deal with. Trenchard himself likes me—Mrs. Trenchard hates me. That's
not a bit too strong, and the strange thing is that there's
no reason at all for it that I can see, nor have we been, either
of us, from the beginning anything but friendly to one
another. If she suspected that I was in love with Katherine
I might understand it, but that is impossible. There has been
nothing, I swear, to give anyone the slightest suspicion. She
detects, I think, something foreign and strange in me. Russia of course she views with the deepest suspicion, and it
would amuse you to hear her ideas of that country. Nothing,
although she has never been near it nor read anything but

silly romances about it, could shake her convictions. Because I don't support them she knows me for a liar. She is always calm and friendly to me, but her intense dislike comes through it all. And yet I really like her. She is so firm and placid and determined. She adores her family—she will fight for them to the last feather and claw. She is so sure and so certain about everything, and yet I believe that in her heart she is always afraid of something—it's out of that fear, I am sure, that her hatred of me comes. For the others, the only one who troubled about me was the boy, and he is the strangest creature. He'd like me to give him all my experiences: he hasn't the slightest notion of them, but he's morbidly impatient of his own inexperience and the way his family are shutting him out of everything, and yet he's Trenchard enough to disapprove violently of that wider experience if it came to him. He'd like me, for instance, to take him out and show him purple restaurants, ladies in big hats, and so on. If he did so he'd feel terribly out of it and then hate me. He's a jumble of the crudest, most impossible and yet rather touching ideas, enthusiasms, indignations, virtues, would-be vices. He adores his sister. About that at least he is firm—and if I were to harm her or make her unhappy! . . .

"I suppose it's foolish of me to go on like this. I'm indulging myself, I can talk to no one. So you . . . just as I used to in those first days such years ago when I didn't know a word of Russian, came and sat by the hour in your flat, talked bad French to your wife, and found all the sympathy I wanted in your kind fat face, even though we could only exchange a word or two in the worst German. How good you were to me then! How I must have bored you! . . . There's no one here willing to be bored like that. To an Englishman time is money—none of that blissful ignoring of the rising and setting of sun, moon, and stars that for so many years I have enjoyed. 'The morning and the evening were the first day. . . .' It was no Russian God who said that. I've found some old friends—Millet, Thackeray, you'll remember—they were in Moscow two years ago. But with them it is 'Dinner eight o'clock sharp, old man—got an engagement nine-thirty.' So I'm lonely. I'd give the world to see your fat body in the doorway and hear your voice rise into that shrill Russian scream of pleasure at seeing me. You should sit down—You should have some tea although I've no Samovar to boil the water in, and I'd talk about Katherine, Katherine, Katherine—until all was blue. And you'd say 'Harosho' 'Harosho'—and it would be six in the morning before we knew. . . . God help us all, I mustn't talk about it. It all comes to this, in the end, as to whether a man can, by determination and resolve, of his own will, wipe out utterly the old life and become a new man. All those Russian years—Anna, Paul, Paul's death, all the thought, the view, the vision of life, the philosophy that Russia gave me—those things have got to disappear. . . . They never existed. I've got again what, all those years, you all said that I wanted—the right to be once again an English citizen with everything, morals and all, cut and dried. I can say, like old Vladimir after his year in Canada, 'I'd never seen so many clean people in my life.' I've . : what I wanted, and I mustn't—I musn't—look back.

"I believe I can carry it all through i   can get Katherine—get her and keep her and separate her om the family. She's got to belong to me and not to the Tr hards. Moscow—The Trenchards! Oh, Paul, there's a Co dy there—and a tragedy too perhaps. I'm an ass, but I'm ghtened. I think I'm doing the finest things and, when the done, they turn out the rottenest. Supposing I become   ren-chard myself? Think of that night when Paul died.   er-wards we went up to the Kremlin, you remember. how quiet it was and how entirely I seemed to have died with Paul, and then how quickly life was the same again. But at any rate Moscow cared for me and told me that it cared—London cares nothing . . . not even for the Trenchards. . . .

"Think of me, Paul, as often as you can. Think of that afternoon in the restaurant when you first showed me how to drink Vodka and I told you in appalling German that Byron and Wilde weren't as good as you thought them. . . . Think of me, old man. I believe I'm in for a terrible business. If Katherine loves me the family will fight me. If she doesn't love me nothing else now seems to matter . . . and, with it all, I'm as lonely as though I were a foreigner who didn't know a word of English and hadn't a friend. . . . I've got my Ikon up on the right corner—Near it is a print of 'Queen Victoria receiving news of her accession to the throne of England' . . ."

Philip Mark sat, day after day, in his ugly sitting-room and thought of Katherine Trenchard. It was nearly a fortnight now since he had come to these rooms—he had not, during that time, seen Katherine; he had called once at the Trenchard's house; he had spent then half an hour alone with Mrs. Trenchard and Aunt Aggie.

In these fourteen days she had grown from an attractive thought into a compelling, driving impulse. Because his rooms were unattractive and because he was sick for Moscow (although he would not admit that) therefore he had turned to the thought of her to comfort him; now he was a slave to the commination of it. . . . He must see her, he must speak to her, he must have something to remember. . . . He must not speak to her, he must not see her lest he should be foolish and ruin all his friendship with her by frightening her; and, meanwhile, in these long, long evenings the lamp from the street below trembled and trembled on his wall as though London, like some hostile policeman, were keeping its eye upon him, and warned him not to go too far.

The history of Philip Mark, its past, its present, and its future, is to be found clearly written in the character of his mother. His mother had been a woman of great force, resolve and determination. She had in complete subjection those who composed her world. She was kind as the skilful executioner is kind who severs a head with one neat blow; her good-humoured husband, her friendly, sentimental, idealistic son submitted, utterly, without question, to her kindness. She had died when Philip was twenty-one, and instantly Philip and his father had discovered, to their immense surprise, their immense relief. Philip's father had married at once a young clergyman's daughter of no character at all, and was compelled to divorce her four years later. Philip, to show his new and splendid independence, had discovered an opening in a cloth business in Moscow. He went there and so remained until, in his thirtieth year, the death of his father had presented him with fifteen hundred pounds a year.

Always, through all the Russian time, it had been his dream that he would one day be an English landowner with a house and a wood, fields and children, white gates and a curving drive. He had come home now to realise this ambition.

The central motive of Philip's existence was that he always desired, very seriously, sometimes desperately, to be all these things that the elements in his character would always prevent him from being. For instance, awaking, at his mother's death, from her relentless domination, he resolved that he would never be influenced by anyone again; five minutes after this determination he was influenced by the doctor who had attended his mother, the lawyer who read her will, and the clergyman who buried her.

It had seemed to him, as he grew up in England, that the finest thing in the world was to be (when he was sixteen) like St. Francis of Assisi, (when he was nineteen) like Shelley, (when he was twenty-one) like Tolstoi, and the worst thing in the world was to be a commonplace English Squire. He went to Russia and, at once, concluded that there was nothing like the solid, sensible beef-eating English Squire for helping on the World, and that, as I have said, as soon as he was rich enough he would settle down in England, with his estate, his hunters and his weekly 'Spectator'.

Meanwhile he was influenced more and more by Russia and the Russians. He did not really desire to be strong, sober, moral, industrious, strong-minded, but only kindly, affectionate, tolerant, with every one man for his friend. . . . He found in Russia that the only thing demanded of him was that he should love his brother. He made an immense number of friends, lived with a Russian girl, Anna Petrovna Semyonov, (she danced in the Moscow Imperial Ballet) for three years, and had, by her, a son who died. At the end of that time his father's death gave him the opportunity of doing what he had always declared to every Russian was the ambition of his life—to settle in England as an English land-owner. Anna was fond of him now, but not at all in love with him—they were the best friends in the world. She believed, very seriously, that the greatest thing for him would be to find a nice English girl whom he could love, marry, and make the mother of his children.

Philip had, during these Russian years, grown stronger in character, and still was determined that the worst thing in the world was to be under anyone's domination. He was however under the power of anyone who showed him affection; his outlook was now vehemently idealistic, romantic and sentimental, although, in the cloth business, he was hard-headed, cynical, and methodical. Did a human being care for him, and he would do anything for him; under the influence of anyone's affection the world became so rosy to him that he lost all count of time, common-sense and digestion.

Anna was really fond of him, although often enough she was desperately bored with him. She had always mothered him, but thought now that an English girl would mother him better. She sent him home. He was very young for his thirty years, but then from the age of anyone who has lived in Russia for long, you may take away, always, twenty years.

He was resolved now to be the most English of all English—to be strong, hard-headed, a little cynical, unsentimental. . . . He had, of course, fallen in love with the first English girl whom he met. Meanwhile he did not entirely assist his cynical hardheadedness by writing long, introspective letters to his Russian friend. However, to support his resolute independence, he had always in front of him on his writing-table a photograph of his mother.

"It shall never be like that again", he would say to himself, looking fixedly at the rather faded picture of a lady of iron-grey hair and a strong bosom clad in shining black silk. "Won't it, my son?" said his mother, looking back at him with a steely twinkle somewhere in her eye. "Won't it?"

Meanwhile there was no place in London where, at three in the morning, he might drink with his friends and discover that all the world loved him. He was very lonely in London, and wanted Katherine more desperately with every tick of the Ormolu clock on the marble mantelpiece; but he would not go to see her. . . . One glance at his mother's photograph was enough to settle that. *No, he would not.* . . .

Then he met her. Upon a lonely November afternoon he walked along the Embankment, past Lambeth Bridge, into the melancholy, deserted silences of Pimlico. He turned back, out of the little grey streets on to the river again, and stood, for a while, looking back over the broad still sheet of the river, almost white in colour but streaked with black lines of shadow that trembled and wavered as though they were rods about to whip the water into storm. The sky was grey, and all the buildings clustered against it were grey, but slowly, as though some unseen hand were tearing the sky like tissue paper, a faint red background was stealing into the picture and even a little faint gold that came from God knows where flitted, in and out, upon the face of the river.

Heavy black barges lay, like ancient prehistoric beasts, in the slime left now by the retreating tide. One little tug pushed desperately up stream as though it would force some energy into this dreaming, dying world—a revolutionary striving to stir the dim silences that watched, from either bank, into protest.

The air was sharply cold and there was a smell of smoke somewhere—also of tar and cabbage and mud. . . . The red light pushed and pushed its way upwards.

The silence emphasised, with rather a pleasing melancholy, Philip's loneliness. It seemed, down here, as though London were a dead city and he, only, alive in it. Katherine, too, was alive somewhere. . . . He looked and, as in one's dreams absurdity tumbles upon the heels of absurdity, he saw her walking alone, coming, as yet without any recognition in her eyes, towards him.

The world was dead and he was dead and Katherine—let it stay so then. . . . No, the world was alive. She had recognised him; she had smiled—the air was suddenly warm and pulsating with stir and sound. As she came up to him he could think of nothing but the strange difference that his fortnight's absorption in her had made for him. His being with her now was as though he had arrived at some long-desired Mecca after a desperate journey of dust and strain and peril. As he greeted her he felt "A fortnight ago we had only just met, but now we have known each other for years and years and years—but perhaps she does not know that yet."

But he knew, as she gave him her hand, that she felt a little awkwardness simply because she was so glad to see him—and she had never been awkward with him before.

"You've been hiding from us," she said. Her cheeks were flaming because she had walked fast, because the air was frosty—because she was glad to see him. Her coat and muff were a little old-fashioned and not very becoming to her—all the more did he praise the beautiful kindliness of her eyes. "I'm in love with you," he wanted to say to her. "Do you care that I am?" . . . He turned at her side and they faced together the reddening sky. The whole city lay in absolute silence about them as though they were caught together into a ball of grey evening cloud.

"I haven't hidden," he said, smiling, "I came and called, but you were not there."

"I heard," she answered, "Aunt Aggie said you were very agreeable and amusing—I hope you're happy in your rooms."

"They're all right."

"We miss you. Father's always beginning to tell you something and then finding that you're gone. Henry—"

"Your Mother?"

"Ah, you were quite wrong about Mother. You thought that she disliked you. You care much too much, by the way, whether people like you or no. But Mother's hard, perhaps, to get to know. You shocked and disturbed her a little, but she didn't dislike you."

Although he had asserted so definitely that Mrs. Trenchard hated him, he had reassured himself, in his own heart, that she rather liked him—now when he saw in spite of Katherine's words that she really had disliked him, he felt a little shock of dismay.

"You may say what you like," he said, "I know—"

"No, you don't understand. Mother is so absorbed by all of us. There are a great many of us, you know—that it takes a long time for her to realise anyone from outside. You were so much from outside. She was just beginning to realise you when you went away. We are all so much to her. In a family as big as ours there are always so many things. . . ."

"Of course," he said, "I know. As to myself, it's natural enough. At present I miss Moscow—but that will be all right soon."

She came a little closer to him, and her eyes were so kindly that he looked down upon the ground lest his own eyes should betray him.

"Look here—come to us whenever you like. Why, all this time, have you kept away? Wasn't it what you were always telling us about your friends in Moscow that their houses were open to everyone always? You must miss that. Don't be lonely whatever you do. There are ever so many of us, and some of us are sure to be in."

"I will," he said, stammering, "I will."

"Henry's always asking questions about Russia now. You've had a great effect upon him, and he wants you to tell him ever so much more. Then there's Millie. She hasn't seen you at all yet. You'll like her so much. There's Vincent coming back from Eton. Don't be lonely or homesick. I know how miserable it is."

They were in the Square by the Church outside her house; above the grey solid building the sky had been torn into streaming clouds of red and gold.

He took her hand and held it, and suddenly as she felt his pressure the colour flooded her face; she strove to beat it down—she could not. She tried to draw her hand away—but her own body, as though it knew better than she, defied her. She tried to speak—no words would come.

She tried to tell him with her eyes that she was indifferent, but her glance at him showed such triumph in his gaze that she began to tremble.

Then he released her hand. She said nothing—only with quick steps hurried into the house. He stood there until she had disappeared, then he turned round towards his rooms.

He strode down Victoria Street in such a flame of exultation as can flare this World into splendour only once or twice in a lifetime. It was the hour when the lights come out, and it seemed to him that he himself flung fire here, there, for all the world to catch, now high into a lamp-post, now low beneath some basement window, now like a cracker upon some distant trees, now, high, high into the very evening blue itself. The pavement, the broad street, the high, mysterious buildings caught and passed the flame from one to another.

An ancient newspaper man, ragged in a faded tail coat, was shouting "Finals! Finals! All the Finals!" but to Philip's ear he was saying—"She cares for you! she cares for you! Praise God! What a world it is."

He stumbled up the dark stairs of his house past the door from whose crevices there stole always the scent of patchouli, past the door, higher up, whence came, creeping up his stairs the suggestion of beef and cabbage, into his own dark lodging. His sitting-room had its windows still open and its blinds still up. The lamp in the street below flung its squares of white light upon his walls; papers on his table were blowing in the evening breeze, and the noise of the town climbed up, looked in through the open windows, fell away again, climbed up again in an eternal indifferent urgency. He was aware that a man stood by the window, a wavering shadow was spread against the lighted wall.

Philip stopped in the doorway.

"Hullo!" he said, "who's there?"

A figure came forward. Philip, to whom all the world was, to-night, a fantasy, stared, for a moment, at the large bearded form without recognising it—wild and unreal as it seemed in the dim room. The man chuckled.

"Well, young man. I've come to call, I got here two minutes before you."

It was Uncle Tim, Mrs. Trenchard's brother, Timothy Faunder, Esq.

"I beg your pardon," said Philip, "the room was dark and—and—as a matter of fact I was thinking of something rather hard as I came in. Wait a minute. You shall have some light, tea and a cigarette in a moment."

"No, thanks." Uncle Tim went back to the window again. "No tea—no cigarette. I hate the first. The second's poisonous. I've got a pipe here—and don't light up—the room's rather pleasant like this. I expect it's hideous when one can see it."

Philip was astonished. He had liked Tim Faunder, but had decided that Tim Faunder was indifferent to *him*—quite indifferent. For what had he come here? Sent by the family? . . . Yes, he liked Uncle Tim, but he did not want him or anyone else in the world there just then. He desired to sit by the open window, alone, to think about Katherine, to worship Katherine!

They both sat down; Faunder on the window-seat, Philip near by. The noise of the town was distant enough to make a pleasant rumbling accompaniment to their voices. The little dark public-house opposite with its beery eye, a dim hanging lamp in the doorway, watched them.

"Well, how are you?" said Faunder, "lonely?"

"It was at first," said Philip, who found it immensely difficult to tie his thoughts to his visitor. "And I hadn't been lonely for so long—not since my first days in Moscow."

"*They* were lonely then?"

"Oh, horribly. My first two months there were the worst hours in all my life. I wanted to learn Russian, so I kept away from English people—and Russian's difficult to pick up at first."

Faunder made one of the rumbling noises in his throat that always testified to his interest.

"I like what you said—over there, at my sister's," he waved his hand, "about Russia—and about everything. I listened, although perhaps you didn't think it. I hope you're going to stick to it, young man."

"Stick to what?"

"Your ideas about things—everything being for the best. There's a great time coming—and the Trenchards are damned fools."

"But I never—"

"Oh, yes, you did. You implied it. Nobody minded, of course, because the Trenchards know so well that they're not. *They* don't bother what people think, bless them. Besides, you don't understand them in the least—nor won't ever, I expect."

"But," said Philip, "I really never thought for a moment."

"Don't be so afraid of hurting people's feelings. I liked your confidence. I liked your optimism. I just came this afternoon to see whether a fortnight alone had damped it a little."

Philip hesitated. It would be very pleasant to say that no amount of personal trouble could alter his point of view; it would be very pleasant to say that the drearier his personal life was the surer he was of his Creed. He hesitated—then spoke the truth.

"As a matter of fact, I'm afraid it *was* dimmed for a bit. Russia seemed so far away and so did England, and I was hanging in mid-air, between. But now—everything's all right again."

"Why now? . . . Because I've paid you a call?"

Uncle Timothy laughed.

Philip looked down at the little public-house. "I'm very glad you have. But this afternoon—it's been the kind of day I've expected London to give me, it seemed to settle me suddenly with a jerk, as though it were pushing me into my place and saying, 'There! now I've found a seat for you'."

He was talking, he knew, at random, but he was very conscious of Uncle Timothy, the more conscious, perhaps, because he could not see his face.

Then he bent forward in his chair. "It was very jolly of you," he said, "to come and see me—but tell me, frankly, why you did. We scarcely spoke to one another whilst I was at your sister's house."

"I listened to you, though. Years ago I must have been rather like you. How old are you?"

"Thirty."

"Well, when I was thirty I was an idealist. I was impatient of my family although I loved them. I thought the world was going to do great things in a year or two. I believed most devoutly in the Millennium. I grew older—I was hurt badly. I believed no longer, or thought I didn't. I determined that the only thing in life was to hold oneself absolutely aloof. I have done that ever since. . . . I had forgotten all these years that I had ever been like you. And then when I heard once again the same things, the same beliefs . . ." He broke off, lit his pipe, puffed furiously at it and watched the white clouds sail into the night air.

"Whatever I have felt," said Philip, slowly, "however I have changed, to-night I know that I am right. To-night I know that all I believed in my most confident hour is true."

The older man bent forward and put his hand on Philip's arm.

"Stick to that. Remember at least that you said it to me. If before I died. . . . There have been times. . . . After the Boer War here in England it seemed that things were moving. There was new life, new blood, new curiosity. But then I don't know—it takes so long to wake people up. *You* woke me up a little with your talk. You woke them all up—a little. And if people like my sister and my brother-in-law—whom I love, mind you—wake up, why then it will be painful for them but glorious for everyone else."

Philip was more alarmed than ever. He had not, at all, wished to wake the Trenchards up—he had only wanted them to like him. He was a little irritated and a little bored with Uncle Timothy. If only Mr. and Mrs. Trenchard allowed him to love Katherine, he did not care if they never woke up in all their lives. He felt too that he did not really fill the picture of the young ardent enthusiast. He was bound, he knew, to disappoint Uncle Timothy. He would have liked to have taken him by the hand and said to him: "Now if only you will help me to marry Katherine I will be as optimistic as you like for ever and ever."

But Uncle Tim was cleverer than Philip supposed. "You're thinking—how tiresome! Here's this old man forcing me into a stained-glass window. Don't think that. I know you're an ordinary nice young fellow just like anyone else. It's your age that's pleasant. I've lived very much alone all these years at a little house I've got down in Glebeshire. You must come and see it. You're sure to stay with my sister there; she's only five minutes away. But I've been so much alone there that I've got into the habit of talking to myself."

Philip at once loved Uncle Tim.

"I'm delighted that you came. If you'll let me be a friend of yours I shall be most awfully proud. It was only that I didn't want you to expect too much of me. One gets into the way in Russia of saying that things are going to be splendid because they're so bad—and really there they do *want* things to be better. And often I do think that there's going to be, one day, a new world. And many people now think about it and hope for it—perhaps they always did."

Uncle Timothy got up. "That's all right, my son. We'll be friends. Come and see me. London's a bit of a forest— one can't make out always quite what's going on. You'll get to know all of us and like us, I hope. Come and see me. Yes?"

"Of course I will."

"I've got a dirty little room in Westminster, 14 Barton Street. I go down to Glebeshire for Christmas, thank God. Good-night."

He clumped away down the stairs. He had stayed a very short time, and Philip felt vaguely that, in some way or another, Uncle Tim had been disappointed in him. For what had he come? What had he wanted? Had the family sent him? Was the family watching him?

That sense that Philip had had during the early days in London suddenly returned. He felt, in the dark room, in the dark street, that the Trenchards were watching him. From the old man down to Henry they were watching him, waiting to see what he would do.

Did Uncle Tim think that he loved Katherine? Had he come to discover that?

Although it was early, the room was very cold and very dark. Philip knew that for an instant he was so afraid that he dared not look behind him.

"London's a forest. . . ."

And Katherine! At the thought of her he rose, defied all the Trenchards in the world, lit his lamp and pulled down the blinds. The smell of Uncle Tim's tobacco was very strong in the room.

CHAPTER V

THE FINEST THING

WHEN a stranger surveys the life of a family it is very certain that the really determining factor in the development of that group of persons will escape his notice. For instance, in surveying the Trenchards, Philip had disregarded Aunt Aggie.

As this is a record of the history of a family and not only of individuals, Aunt Aggie must be seriously considered; it was the first ominous mistake that Philip made that he did not seriously consider her. Agnes Trenchard, when quite a young girl, had been pretty in a soft and rounded manner. Two offers of marriage had been made to her, but she had refused these because she had a great sense of her destiny. From her first thinking moment she had considered herself very seriously. She had very high ideals; the finest thing in this world was a life of utter unselfishness, a life of noble devotion and martyred self-interest. She looked about her and could see no signs of such lives; all the more then was it clear that she was set apart to give the world such an example. Unfortunately, allied to this appreciation of a fine self-sacrificing character was a nature self-indulgent, indolent and suspicious. Could she be unselfish without trouble or loss then how unselfish she would be! She liked the idea of it immensely. . . .

For some years she was pretty, sang a little and obviously 'thought more' than either of her sisters. People listened then to her creed and believed in her intentions. She talked often of unselfishness, was always ready to do anything for

anybody, and was always prevented or forestalled by less altruistic people. When, after her two offers of marriage, she
stepped very quickly into the shapes and colours of an old
maid, went to live with her sister-in-law and brother, and
formed 'habits', people listened to her less readily. She herself however, quite unaware that at thirty-five, life for a
woman is, sexually, either over or only just commencing,
hoped to continue the illusions of her girlhood. The nobility
of unselfishness appealed to her more than ever, but she found
that the people around her were always standing in her way.
She became, therefore, quite naturally, rather bitter. Her
round figue expressed, in defiance of its rotundity, peevish-
ness.

She had to account for her failures in self-sacrificing al-
truism, and found it not in her own love of ease and dislike
of effort, but, completely, in other people's selfishness. Had
she been permitted she would have been the finest Trenchard
alive, and how fine that was only a Trenchard could know!
But the world was in a conspiracy against her—the world,
and especially her sister Elizabeth, whom she despised and
bullied, but, somewhere in her strange suspicious crust of a
heart, loved. That was, perhaps, the strangest thing about
her—that, in spite of her ill-humour, discontents and irri-
tations, she really loved the family, and would like to have
told it so were she not continually prevented by its extraordinary habit of being irritating just when she felt most affectionate! She really did love them, and she would go down
sometimes in the morning with every intention of saying so,
but in five minutes they had destroyed that picture of herself which, during her absence from them, she had painted—
for that, of course, she could not forgive them.

In the mansion of the human soul there are many cham-
bers; Aunt Aggie's contradictions were numberless; but, on
broad lines it may be said that her assurance of the injustice
of her own fate was balanced only by her conviction of the
good luck of everyone else. She hoped, perpetually, that

they would all recognise this—namely, that their Life had treated them with the most wonderful good fortune. Her brother George Trenchard, for instance, with his careless habits, his indifference to the facts of life, his obvious selfishness. What disasters he would, had he not been incredibly favoured, most surely have encountered! Aunt Aggie was afraid that he did not sufficiently realise this, and so, in order that he might offer up thanks to God, she reminded him, as often as was possible, of his failings. Thus, too, with the others. Even Katherine, for whom she cared deeply, betrayed, at times, a haughty and uplifted spirit, and frequently forestalled her aunt's intended unselfishness, thus, in a way, rebuking her aunt, a thing that a niece should never do. With this consciousness of her relations' failings went an insatiable curiosity. Aunt Aggie, because she was the finest character in the family, should be rewarded by the trust and confidence of the family; she must, at any rate, maintain the illusion that she received it. Did they keep her quiet with little facts and stories that were of no importance, she must make them important in order to support her dignity. She made them very important indeed. . . .

A great factor was her religion. She was, like her sister, a most sincere and devout member of the Church of England. She believed in God as revealed to her by relations and clergymen in the day of her baptism; time and a changing world had done nothing to shake her confidence. But, unlike her sisters, she believed that this God existed chiefly as a friend and supporter of Miss Agnes Trenchard. He had other duties and purposes, of course, but did not hide from her His especial interest in herself. The knowledge of this gave her great confidence. She was now fifty years of age, and believed that she was still twenty-five; that is not to say that she dressed as a young woman or encouraged, any longer, the possibility of romantic affairs. It was simply that the interest and attraction that she offered to the world as a fine and noble character were the same as they had ever been—and if the world did not recognize this that was because fine and noble characters were few and difficult to discover. One knew this because the Trenchard family offered so seldom an example of one, and the Trenchards were, of course, the finest people in England.

She had great power with her relations because she knew, so intimately, their weaknesses. People, on the whole, may be said to triumph over those who believe in them and submit to those who don't. The Trenchards, because life was full and time was short, submitted to Aunt Aggie and granted anything in order that they might not be made uncomfortable. They could not, however, allow her to abuse them, one to another, and would submit to much personal criticism before they permitted treachery. Their mutual affection was a very real factor in their lives. Aunt Aggie herself had her share in it. She possessed, nevertheless, a genius for creating discomfort or for promoting an already unsteady atmosphere. She was at her best when the family was at its worst, because then she could perceive, quite clearly, her own fine nobility.

Philip Mark had made a grave mistake when he disregarded her.

She had disliked Philip from the first. She had disapproved of the way that he had burst in upon the family just when she had been at her best in the presentation to her father. He had not known that she had been at her best, but then that was his fault. She had been ready to forgive this, however, if, in the days that followed, he had shown that he appreciated her. He had not shown this, at all—he had, in fact, quite obviously preferred her sister Elizabeth. He had not listened to her with close attention when she had talked to him about the nobility of unselfishness, and he had displayed both irritation and immorality in his views of life. She had been shocked by the abruptness with which he had rebuked Mr. Seymour, and she thought his influence on

Henry was, already, as bad as it could be. It was of course only too characteristic of George that he should encourage the young man. She could see what her father and Aunt Sarah thought of him, and she could only say that she entirely shared their opinion.

Philip's visit had upset her, and Millie's return from Paris upset her still more. She had never cared greatly about Millie, who had never showed her any deference or attention, but Millie had until now always been a Trenchard. She had come back from Paris only half a Trenchard. Aunt Aggie was grievously afraid that troublesome times were in store for them all.

It was just at this point that her attention was directed towards Katherine. She always considered that Katherine knew her better than any other member of the family did, which simply meant that Katherine considered her feelings. Lately, however, Katherine had not considered her feelings. She had, on at least two occasions, been deliberately uncivil! Once Aunt Aggie had suffered from neuralgia, and Katherine had promised to come and read her to sleep and had forgotten to do so. Next morning, her neuralgia being better, Aunt Aggie said—"I can't, dear Katherine, imagine myself, under similar conditions, acting as you have done. . . . I had a sleepless night. . . . But of course you had more important duties"—and Katherine had scarcely apologised. On the second occasion Aunt Aggie at breakfast, (she was always bitter at breakfast, mildly unhappy over her porridge and violently sarcastic by marmalade time) had remarked with regret that Millie, who was late, had "picked up these sad habits abroad. She had never known anyone the finer, whether in character or manners, for living abroad;" here was a little dust flung at the inoffensive person of Philip, now soundly asleep in Jermyn Street. At once Katherine was "in a flurry." "What right had Aunt Aggie to say so? How could she tell? It might be better if one went abroad more, lost some of one's prejudices . . ." quite a little scene! Very unlike Katherine!

Aunt Aggie did not forget. Like some scientist or mathematician, happily let loose into some new theory or problem, so now did she consider Katherine. Katherine was different, Katherine was restless and out of temper. She had been so ever since Philip Mark's visit. . . . With her sewing or her book Aunt Aggie sat in a corner by the drawing-room fire and watched and waited.

Upon that afternoon that had seen Katherine's meeting with Philip by the river Aunt Aggie had been compelled to have tea alone. That had been annoying, because it looked as though the gay world was inviting everyone except Aunt Aggie to share in its excitements and pleasures. At last there arrived Mrs. Trenchard and Millie, and finally Katherine. Aunt Aggie had sat in her warm corner, pursuing with her needle the green tail of an unnatural parrot which she was working into a slowly-developing cushion cover and had considered her grievances. It had been a horrible day, cold and gloomy. Aunt Aggie had a chilblain that, like the Waits, always appeared about Christmas and, unlike them, stayed on well into the spring. It had made its appearance, for the first time this season, during the past night. Millie talked a great deal about very little, and Mrs. Trenchard received her remarks with the nonchalant indifference of a croupier raking in the money at Monte Carlo. Katherine sat staring into the fire and saying nothing.

Aunt Aggie, watching her, felt quite suddenly as though the firelight had leapt from some crashing coal into a flaring splendour, that something strange and unusual was with them in the room. She was not at all, like her sister Elizabeth, given to romantic and sentimental impressions. She seldom read novels, and cared nothing for the theatre. What she felt now was really unpleasant and uncomfortable, as though she had soap in her eyes or dropped her collection under the seat during the Litany. The room positively glowed, the dim shadows were richly coloured, and in Aunt Aggie's heart was alarm and agitation.

She stared about her; she looked about the room and pierced the shadows; she sewed a wrong stitch into the parrots' tail, and then decided that it was Katherine's eyes. . . . She looked at the girl—she looked again and again—saw her bending forward a little, her hands pressed together on her lap, her breast rising and falling with the softest suspicion of some agitation, and, in her eyes, such a light as could come from no fire, no flame from without, but only from the very soul itself. Katherine's good-tempered, humorous eyes, so charged with common-sense, affectionate but always mild, unagitated, calm, like her mother's—now what was one to say?

Aunt Aggie said nothing. Her own heart felt for an instant some response. She would have liked to have taken the girl into her arms and kissed her and petted her. In a moment the impulse passed. What was the matter with Katherine? *Who* was the matter with Katherine? It was almost improper that anyone should look like that in a drawing-room that had witnessed so much good manners. Moreover it was selfish, this terrible absorption. If Katherine began to think of herself, whatever would happen to them all! And there were Millie and her mother, poor things, chattering blindly together. Aunt Aggie felt that the business of watching over this helpless family did indeed devolve upon her. From that moment Katherine and the things that were possibly happening to Katherine never left her thoughts. She was happier than she had been for many months.

But Katherine, in the days that followed, gave her curiosity no satisfaction. Aunt Aggie dated, in future years, all the agitation that was so shortly to sweep down upon the Trenchard waters from that afternoon when 'Katherine's eyes had seemed so strange', but her insistence on that date did not at all mean that it was then that Katherine invited her aunt's confidence, Aunt Aggie was compelled to drive on her mysterious way alone. She was now assured that 'something was the matter', but the time had not yet arrived when all the family was concerned in it.

In any case, to begin with, what was her sister-in-law Harriet Trenchard thinking? No one ever knew what Harriet Trenchard thought; and foolish and hasty observers said that that was because Harriet Trenchard never thought at all. Aggie Trenchard was neither foolish nor hasty; she was afraid of Harriet because, after all these years, she knew nothing about her. She had never penetrated that indifferent stolidity. Harriet had never spoken to her intimately about anything, nor had Harriet once displayed any emotions, whether of surprise or anger, happiness or grief, but Aggie was penetrating enough to fear that brooding quiet.

At least Aggie knew her sister-in-law well enough to realise that her children were an ever-present, ever-passionate element in her life. On certain occasions, concerning Millie, Katherine, Henry or Vincent, Aggie had seen that silence, for a moment, quiver as a still lake trembles with a sudden shake or roll when the storm is raging across the hills—especially was Katherine linked to her mother's most intimate hold upon life, even though the words that they exchanged were of the most commonplace; Aunt Aggie knew that, and strangely, obscurely, she was moved, at times, to sudden impulses of bitter jealousy. Why was it that no one cared for her as Katherine cared for her mother? What was there in Harriet to care for? . . . and yet—nevertheless, Aggie Trenchard loved her sister-in-law. With regard to this present business Aggie knew, with sufficient assurance, that Harriet disliked Philip Mark, had disliked him from the first. Had Harriet noticed this change in her daughter, and had she drawn her conclusions? What would Harriet say if . . .? Aunt Aggie added stitches to the green parrot's tail with every comfortable assurance that 'in a time or two', there would be plenty of trouble.

Ultimately, through it all, it was her jealousy that moved

her and her jealousy that provoked the first outburst . . .
instantly, without warning, new impulses, new relationships,
new motives were working amongst them all, and their world
was changed.

Upon an afternoon, Aunt Aggie hearing that Henry
wished to change a novel at Mudie's Library (that very
novel that he had been reading on the day of Philip's arrival) offered to take it for him. This was at luncheon, and
she felt, because she liked her food and barley-water, a sudden impulse towards the Ideal Unselfishness. She made
her offer, and then reflected that it would be very troublesome to go so far as Oxford Street; she therefore allowed
Katherine to accept the mission, retaining at the same time
her own nobility. She became quite angry: "Of course,"
she said, "you consider me too old to do anything—to sit
in a corner and sew is all I'm good for—well, well—you'll
be old yourself one day, Katherine, my dear. I should
have liked to have helped Henry. . . . However . . ."

She was conscious, during the afternoon, of some injustice; she had been treated badly. At dinner that night
Rocket forgot the footstool that was essential to her comfort; she was compelled at last to ask him for it. He had
never forgotten it before; they all thought her an old woman
who didn't matter; no one troubled now about her—well, they
should see. . . .

Great Aunt Sarah was, as often happened to her, rheu-
matic but Spartan in bed. The ladies, when they left the
dining-room and closed around the drawing-room fire, were
Mrs. Trenchard, Aunt Aggie, Aunt Betty, Katherine and
Millie. Happy and comfortable enough they looked, with
the shadowed dusky room behind them and the blaze in
front of them. In the world outside it was a night of intense frost: here they were reflected in the Mirror, Mrs.
Trenchard's large gold locket (Henry as a baby inside it),
Aggie's plump neck and black silk dress, Aunt Betty's dart-
ing, sparkling eyes, Millie's lovely shoulders, Katherine's

rather dumpy ones—there they all were, right inside the Mirror, with a reflected fire to make them cosy and the walls ever so thick and old. The freezing night could not touch them.

"Rocket's getting very old and careless," said Aggie.

Everyone had known that Aunt Aggie was out of temper this evening, and everyone, therefore, was prepared for a tiresome hour or two. Rocket was a great favourite; Mrs. Trenchard, her arms folded across her bosom, her face the picture of placid content, said:

"Oh, Aggie, do you think so? . . . I don't."

"No, of couse, you don't, Harriet," answered her sister sharply. "He takes care with you. Of course he does. But if you considered your sister sometimes—"

"My dear Aggie!" Mrs. Trenchard, as she spoke, bent forward and very quietly picked up a bright green silk thread from the carpet.

"Oh, I'm not complaining! That's a thing I don't believe in! After all, if you think Rocket's perfection I've no more to say. I want others to be comfortable—for myself I care nothing. It is for the rest of the family."

"We're *quite* comfortable, Aunt Aggie, thank you," said Millie laughing.

"I hope you don't think, Harriet," said Aggie, disregarding her niece, "that I'm complaining—I—"

Mrs. Trenchard leant towards her, holding out the thread of green silk!

"That must be from your silks, Aggie dear," she said. "It's just the colour of your parrot's tail. I couldn't think what it was, lying there on the carpet."

It was then that Katherine, who had paid no attention to this little conversation but had followed her own thoughts, said:

"Oh! how careless of me! I never took Henry's book, after all—and I went right up Oxford Street too!"

This was unfortunate, because it reminded Aunt Aggie of

something that she had very nearly forgotten. Of course Katherine had never intended to take the book—she had simply offered to do so because she thought her Aunt old, feeble, and incapable.

"Really, Katherine," said Aunt Aggie, "you might have let me take it after all. I may be useless in most ways and not worth anyone's consideration, but at least I'm still able to walk up Oxford Street in safety!"

Her aunt's tones were so bitter that Katherine looked across at her in some dismay.

Aunt Betty did not assist the affair by saying:

"Why, Aggie dear, who ever supposed you couldn't; I'm sure you can do anything you want to!"

"Well, perhaps, next time," Aunt Aggie said sharply. "When I offer some help someone will listen to me. *I* should not have forgotten the book."

"I *can't* think why *I* did," said Katherine, "I remembered it just before I started, and then something happened—"

Aunt Aggie looked about her, and thought that this would be a very good opportunity for discovering the real state of Katherine's mind.

"You must take care, Katherine dear," she said, "you don't seem to me to have been quite yourself lately. I've noticed a number of little things. You're tired, I think."

Katherine laughed. "Why should I be? I've had nothing to make me."

It was then that Aunt Aggie caught a look of strange, almost furtive anxiety in Harriet's eyes. Following this, for the swiftest moment, Katherine and her mother exchanged a gleam of affection, of reassurance, of confidence.

"Ah!" thought Aunt Aggie, "they're laughing at me. *Everyone's* laughing at me."

"My dear Katherine," she snapped, "I'm sure *I* don't know what's tired you, but I think you must realise what I mean. You are not your normal self; and, if your old aunt may say so, that's a pity."

Millie, looking across at her sister, was astonished to see the colour rising in her cheeks. Katherine was annoyed! Katherine minded Aunt Aggie! Katherine, who was never out of temper—never perturbed! and at Aunt Aggie!

"Really, Aunt Aggie," Katherine said, "it's very tiresome if all the family are going to watch one day and night as though one were something from the Zoo. Tiresome is not nearly strong enough."

Her aunt smiled bitterly.

"It's only my affection for you," she said. "But of course you don't want that. Why should you? One day, however, you may remember that someone once cared whether you were tired or not."

Aunt Aggie's hands trembled on her lap.

Katherine shook her head impatiently.

"I'm very grateful for your kindness—but I'd much rather be left alone. I'm not tired, nor odd, nor anything —so, please, don't tell me that I am."

Aggie rose from her chair, and very slowly with trembling fingers drew her work together. "I think," she said, her voice quivering a little, "that I'll go to bed. Next time you wish to insult me, Katherine, I'd rather you did it when we were alone."

A very slow and stately figure, she walked down the drawing-room and disappeared.

There was a moment's silence.

"Oh, dear!" cried Katherine, "I'm so sorry!" She looked round upon them all, and saw quite clearly that they were surprised at her. Again behind Mrs. Trenchard's eyes there hovered that suspicion of anxiety.

"What did I do? What did I say? Aunt Aggie's so funny." Then, as still they did not answer, she turned round upon them: "*Have* I been cross and tiresome lately? *Have* you all noticed it? Tell me."

Aunt Betty said, "No, dear, of course not."

Millie said, "What *does* it matter what Aunt Aggie says?"

Mrs. Trenchard said, "There's another of Aggie's green threads. Under your chair, Millie dear. I'd better go up and see whether she wants anything."

But Katherine rose and, standing for an instant with a little half-smile, half-frown, surveying them, moved then slowly away from them down the room.

"No. I'll go, Mother, and apologise. I suppose I was horrid." She left them.

She went up through the dark passages slowly, meditatively. She waited for a moment outside her aunt's door and then knocked, heard then her aunt's voice, "Come in!" —in tones that showed that she had been expecting some ambassador.

Katherine stood by the door, then moved forward, put her arms about Aunt Aggie and kissed her.

"I'm so sorry. I'm afraid that I hurt you. You know that I didn't mean to."

Upon Aunt Aggie's dried cheeks there hovered a tiny cold and glassy tear. She drew back from Katherine's embrace, then with a strange, almost feverish movement caught Katherine's hand.

"It wasn't, my dear, that you hurt me. I expect I'm too sensitive—that has always been my misfortune. But I felt" (another glassy tear now upon the other cheek) "that you and Millie are finding me tiresome now."

"Aunt Aggie! Of *course* not!"

"I wish to be of some use—it is my continual prayer— some use to someone—and you make me feel—but of course you are young and impatient—that I'd be better perhaps out of the way."

Katherine answered her very gravely: "If I've ever made you feel that for a moment, Aunt Aggie, there's nothing too bad for me. But how can you say such a thing? Aren't you a little unjust?"

The two tears had disappeared.

"I daresay I am, my dear, I daresay I am—or seem so

to you. Old people often do to young ones. But I'm not unjust, I think, in fancying that you yourself have changed lately. I made you angry when I said that just now, but I felt it my duty—"

Katherine was silent. Aunt Aggie watched her with bright, inquisitive eyes, from which tears were now very far away.

"Well, we won't say any more, dear. My fault is, perhaps, that I am too anxious to do things for others, and so may seem to you young ones interfering. I don't know, I'm sure. It has always been my way. I'm glad indeed when you tell me that nothing is the matter. To my old eyes it seems that ever since Mr. Mark stayed here the house has not been the same. You have not been the same."

"Mr. Mark?" Katherine's voice was sharp, then suddenly dropped and, after an instant's silence, was soft, "You've got Mr. Mark on the brain, Aunt Aggie."

"Well, my dear, I didn't like him. I'm sure he was very bad for Henry. But then I'm old-fashioned, I suppose. Mr. Mark shocked me, I confess. Russia must be a very wild country."

Then, for a space, they looked at one another. Katherine said nothing, only, her cheeks flushed, her breath coming sharply, stared into the mirror on the dressing-table. Aunt Aggie faced in this silence something alarming and uneasy; it was as though they were, both of them, listening for some sound, but the house was very still.

"I think I'll go to bed, my dear. Kiss me, Katherine. Don't forget that I'm older than you, dear. I know something of the world—yes . . . good-night, my dear."

They embraced; Katherine left the room. Her cheeks were flaming; her body seemed wrapt in dry, scorching heat. She hurried, her heart beating so loudly that it seemed to her to fill the passage with sound, into her own room.

She did not switch on the electric-light, but stood there in the darkness, the room very cool and half-shadowed; some reflected outside light made a pool of grey twilight upon the floor, and just above this pool Katherine stood, quite motionless, her head raised, her hands tightly clasped together. She knew. That moment in her aunt's room had told her!

She was lifted, by one instant of glorious revelation, out of herself, her body, her life, and caught up into her divine heaven, could look down upon that other arid, mordant world with eyes of incredulous happiness.

She loved Philip Mark. She had always loved him. She had never loved anyone before. She had thought that life was enough with its duties, its friendships, its little pleasures and little sorrows. She had never lived; she was born now here in the still security of her room. . . . The clocks were striking ten, the light on the carpet quivered, dimly she could see her books, her bed, her furniture. Some voice, very far away, called her name, waited and then called again —called the old Katherine, who was dead now . . . dead and gone . . . buried in Aunt Aggie's room. The new Katherine had powers, demands, values, insistences, of which the old Katherine had never dreamed.

Katherine, at this instant, asked herself no questions— whether he loved her, what the family would say, how she herself would face a new world, why it was that, through all these weeks, she had not known that she loved him? She asked herself nothing. . . . Only waited, motionless, staring in front of her.

Then suddenly her heart was so weighed down with happiness that she was utterly weary; her knees trembled, her hands wavered as though seeking some support. She turned, fell down on her knees beside the bed, her face sank deep in her hands and so remained, thinking of nothing, conscious of nothing, her spirit bathed in an intensity of overwhelming joy.

She recovered, instantly in the days that followed, her natural sweetness; she was, as all the household, with relief, discovered, the real Katherine again. She did not to herself seem to have any existence at all. The days in this early December were days of frost, red skies, smoking leaves, and hovering silver mists that clouded the chimneys, made the sun a remotely yellow ball, shot sunset and sunrise with all rainbow colours.

Beautiful days—she passed through them with no consciousness of herself, her friends, not even of Philip. No thought of anything was possible, only that breathless, burning, heart-beat, the thickness of the throat, the strange heat and then sudden cold about her face, the vision of everyone near her as ghosts who moved many, many worlds away. Her daily duties were performed by someone else—some kindly, considerate, sensible person, who saw that she was disturbed and preoccupied. She watched this kind person, and wondered how it was that the people about her did not notice this. At night for many hours she lay there, thinking of nothing, feeling the beating of her heart, wrapped in a glorious ecstasy of content, then suddenly soothed as though by some anaesthetic she would sleep, dumbly, dreamlessly, heavily.

For a week this continued—then Philip came to dinner, scarcely a dinner-party, although it had solemnity. The only invited guests were Philip, Rachel Seddon, her fat uncle, Lord John Beaminster, and an ancient Trenchard cousin. Lord John was fat, shining, and happy. Having survived with much complacency the death of his mother, the Duchess of Wrexe, and the end of the Beaminster grandeur, he led a happy bachelor existence in a little house behind Shepherds Market. He was the perfect symbol of good temper, good food, and a good conscience. Deeply attached to his niece, Rachel, he had, otherwise, many friends, many interests, many happinesses, all of a small bird-like amiable character. He bubbled with relief because he was not compelled, any longer, to sustain the Beaminster character. He had beautiful white hair, rosy cheeks, and perfect clothes. He often dined at the Trenchard's house with Rachel—he called him-

self 'Roddy's Apology.' The Trenchards liked him because he thought very highly of the Trenchards.

He sat beside Katherine at dinner and chattered to her.
Philip sat on her side of the table, and she could not see
him, but when he had entered the drawing-room earlier in
the evening the sudden sight of him had torn aside, as though
with a fierce, almost revengeful gesture, all the mists, the
unrealities, the glories that had, during the last weeks, surrounded her. She saw him and instantly, as though with
a fall into icy water, was plunged into her old world again.
He looked at her, she thought, as he would look at a stranger.
He did not care for her—he had not even thought about her.
Why had she been so confident during all these strange days?
Her one longing now was to avoid him. With a great effort
she drove her common-sense to her service, talked to him for
a moment or two with her customary quiet, half-humorous
placidity, and went into dinner. She heard his voice now
and then. He was getting on well with Rachel. They would
become great friends. Katherine was glad. Dinner was
interminable; Lord John babbled and babbled and babbled.
Dinner was over. The ladies went into the drawing-room.

"I like your friend, Katie," said Rachel. "He's interesting."

"I'm glad you do," said Katherine.

The men joined them. Philip was conveyed by Mrs.
Trenchard to the ancient Trenchard cousin, who had a bony
face and an eager, unsatisfied eye. Philip devoted himself
to these.

Katherine sat and talked to anyone. She was so miserable
that she felt that she had never known before what to be
miserable was. Then, when she was wondering whether the
evening would ever end, she looked up, across the room.
Philip, from his corner, also looked up. Their eyes met
and, at that moment, the fire, hitherto decorously confined
behind its decent bounds, ran golden, brilliant about the
room, up to the ceiling, crackling, flaming. The people in

the room faded, disappeared; there was no furniture there, the bookcases, the chairs, the tables were gone, the mirror, blazing with light, burning with some strange heat, shone down upon chaos. Only, through it all, Katherine and Philip were standing, their eyes shining, for all to see, and Heaven, let loose upon a dead, dusty world, poured recklessly its glories upon them.

"I was saying," said Lord John, "that it's these young fellows who think they can shoot and can't who are doin' all the harm."

Slowly, very slowly Katherine's soul retreated within its fortresses again. Slowly the fires faded, Heaven was withdrawn. For a moment she closed her eyes, then, once more, she regarded Lord John. "Oh, God! I'm so happy!" something within her was saying, "I shall be absurd and impossible in a moment if I can't do something with my happiness!"

She was saved by the ancient cousin's deciding that it was late. She always ended an evening party by declaring that it was later than she could ever have supposed. She was followed by Rachel, Lord John and Philip.

When Philip and Katherine said good-bye their hands scarcely touched, but they were burning.

"I will come to-morrow afternoon," he whispered.

"Yes," she whispered back to him.

Through the history of that old Westminster house there ran the thread of many of such moments, now it could not be surprised nor even so greatly stirred, whispering through its passages and corridors. "Here it is again. . . . Pleasant enough for the time. I wish them luck, poor dears, but I've never known it answer. This new breath, out through my rafters, up through my floors, down my chimneys, in at my windows—just the same as it used to be. Very pleasant while it lasts—poor young things."

It was only natural that the House, long practised in the

affairs of men, should perceive these movements in advance
of the Trenchard family. As to warning the Trenchards,
that was not the House's business. It was certainly owing
to no especial virtue of perception that Aunt Aggie decided
that she would spend the afternoon of the day following the
dinner-party in the drawing-room.

This decision was owing to the physical fact that she
fancied that she had a slight cold, and the spiritual one
that her sister Harriet had said: would she mind being most
unselfish: would she stay in and receive callers as she, Harriet, was compelled to attend an unfortunate Committee?
There was nothing that Aunt Aggie could have preferred
to sitting close to the drawing-room fire, eating muffin if
alone, and being gracious were there company. However,
Harriet had said that it would be unselfish—therefore unselfish it was.

Katherine, it appeared, also intended to stay at home.

"You needn't, my dear," said Aunt Aggie, "I promised
your mother. I had rather looked forward to going to the
Misset-Faunders', but never mind—I promised your
mother."

"I'm sure it's better for your cold that you shouldn't go
out," said Katherine. "*I* think you ought to be upstairs—
in bed with a hot bottle."

"My cold's nothing"—Aunt Aggie's voice was sharp.
"Certainly the Misset-Faunders wouldn't have hurt it. I
could have gone in a cab. But I promised your mother.
. . . It's a pity. They always have music on their second
Fridays. Alice plays the violin very well . . . and I dare
say, after all, no one will come this afternoon. You really
needn't bother to stay in, Katherine."

"I think I will to-day," said Katherine quietly.

So aunt and niece sat, one on each side of the fire, waiting. Katherine was very quiet, and Aunt Aggie, who, like
all self-centred people, was alarmed by silence, spun a little
web of chatter round and round the room.

"It was all quite pleasant last night I thought; I must say Lord John can make himself very agreeable if he pleases. How did you think Rachel was looking? I wanted to ask her about Michael, who had a nasty little cold last week, but Mr. Mark quite absorbed her—talking about his Russia, I suppose. I don't suppose anyone will come this afternoon. The very last thing Clare Faunder said on Sunday was 'Mind you come on Friday. We've some special music on Friday, and I know how you love it.' But of course one must help your mother when one can. Your Aunt Betty would take one of her walks. Walking in London seems to me such an odd thing to do. If everyone walked what would the poor cabmen and busses do? One must think of others, especially with the cold weather coming on."

Her voice paused and then dropped; she looked sharply across at Katherine, and realized that the girl had not been listening. She was staring up into the Mirror; in her eyes was the look of burning, dreaming expectation that had on that other afternoon been so alarming.

At that moment Rocket opened the door and announced Philip Mark.

Katherine's eyes met Philip's for an instant, then they travelled to Aunt Aggie. That lady rose with the little tremor of half-nervous, half-gratified greeting that she always bestowed on a guest. She disliked Mr. Mark cordially, but that was no reason why the memory of an hour or two filled with close attention from a young man should not brighten to-morrow's reminiscences. She was conscious also that she was keeping guard over Katherine. Not for an instant would she leave that room until Mr. Mark had also left it. She looked at the two young people, Katherine flushed with the fire, Philip flushed with the frosty day, and regarded with satisfaction their distance one from the other. Tea was brought; life was very civilised; the doors were all tightly closed.

Philip had come with the determined resolve of asking

Katherine to marry him. Last night he had not slept. With a glorious Katherine at his side he had paced his room, his soul in the stars, his body somewhere underground. All day he had waited for a decent hour to arrive. He had almost run to the house. Now he was faced by Aunt Aggie. As he smiled at her he could have taken her little body, her bundle of clothes, her dried little soul, crunched it to nothing in his hands and flung it into the fire.

Although he gave no sign of outward dismay, he was raging with impatience. He would not look at Katherine lest, borne upon some wave of passion stronger than he, he should have rushed across the room, caught her to his side, and so defied all the Trenchard decencies; he knew that it was wiser, at present, to preserve them.

They talked about Rachel Seddon, Dinner-parties, Cold Weather, Dancing, Exercise, growing Stout, Biscuits, the best Church in London, Choirs, Committees, Aunt Aggie's duties, growing Thin, Sleeplessness, Aunt Aggie's trials, Chilblains, Cold Weather. . . . At this renewed appearance of the weather Philip noticed an old calf-bound book lying upon a little table at his side. Behind his eyes there flashed the discovery of an idea.

"Pride and Prejudice," he said.

"Oh!" cried Katherine. "That's one of Father's precious Jane Austen's—a first edition. He keeps them all locked up in his study. Henry must have borrowed that one. They're never allowed to lie about."

Philip picked it up. From between the old leaves, brown a little now, with the black print sunk deep into their very heart, there stole a scent of old age, old leather, old tobacco, old fun and wisdom.

Philip had opened it where Mr. Collins, proposing to Elizabeth Bennet, declines to accept her refusal.

"I am not now to learn," replied Mr. Collins, with a formal wave of the hand, "that it is usual with young ladies to reject the addresses of the man whom they secretly mean to accept, when he first applies for their favour; and that sometimes the refusal is repeated a second, or even a third time. I am, therefore, by no means discouraged by what you have just said, and shall hope to lead you to the altar ere long."

"Upon my word, sir," cried Elizabeth, "your hope is rather an extraordinary one after my declaration. I do assure you that I am not one of those young ladies (if such young ladies there are) who are so daring as to risk their happiness on the chance of being asked a second time. I am perfectly serious in my refusal. You could not make me happy, and I am convinced that I am the last woman in the world who would make you so. Nay, were your friend Lady Catherine to know me, I am persuaded she would find me in every respect ill-qualified for the situation."

"Were it certain that Lady Catherine would think so," said Mr. Collins very gravely—"but I cannot imagine that her ladyship would at all disapprove of you. And you may be certain that when I have the honour of seeing her again, I shall speak in the highest terms of your modesty, economy, and other amiable qualifications."

" 'Pride and Prejudice,' I always thought," said Aunt Aggie with amiable approval, "a very pretty little tale. It's many years since I read it. Father read it aloud to us, I remember, when we were girls."

Philip turned a little from her, as though he would have the light more directly over his shoulder. He had taken a piece of paper from his pocket, and in an instant he had written in pencil:

"I love you. Will you marry me? Philip."

This he slipped between the pages.

He knew that Katherine had watched him; very gravely he passed the book across to her, then he turned to Aunt Aggie, and with a composure that surprised himself, paid her a little of the deference that she needed.

Katherine, with hands that trembled, had opened the

book. She found the piece of paper, saw the words, and then, in a sort of dreaming bewilderment, read to the bottom of the old printed page.

"Mr. Collins thus addressed her:

"When I do myself the honour of speaking to you next on this subject, I shall hope to receive a more favourable answer than you have now given me; though I am far from accusing you of cruelty at present, because I know it to be the established custom of your sex to reject a man on the first—"

She did not turn the page; for a moment she waited, her mind quite empty of any concentrated thought, her eyes seeing nothing but the shining, glittering expanse of the Mirror.

Very quickly, using a gold pencil that hung on to her watch chain, she wrote below his name: "Yes. Katherine."

"Let me see the book, my dear," said Aunt Aggie. "You must know, Mr. Mark, that I care very little for novels. There is so much to do in this world, so many people that need care, so many things that want attention, that I think one is scarcely justified in spending the precious time over stories. But I own Miss Austen is a memory—a really precious memory to me. Those little simple stories have their charm still, Mr. Mark. . . . Yes. . . . Thank you, my dear."

She took the book from Katherine, and began very slowly to turn over the pages, bending upon Miss Austen's labours exactly the look of kindly patronage that she would have bent upon that lady herself had she been present.

Katherine glanced at Philip, half rose in her chair, and then sat down again. She felt, as she waited for the dreadful moment to pass, a sudden perception of the family—until this moment they had not occurred to her. She saw her mother, her father, her grandfather, her aunts, Henry, Millie. Let this affair be suddenly flung upon them as a result of Aunt Aggie's horrified discovery and the tumult would be, indeed, terrible. The silence in the room, during those moments, almost forced her to cry out.

Had Philip not been there she would have rushed to her aunt, torn the book from her hands, and surrendered to the avalanche.

Aunt Aggie paused—she peered forward over the page. With a little cry Katherine stood up, her knees trembling, her eyes dimmed, as though the room were filled with fog.

"I doubt very much," said Aunt Aggie, "whether I could read it now. It would seem strangely old-fashioned, I daresay, I'm sure to a modern young man like yourself, Mr. Mark."

Philip took the book from her; he opened it, read Katherine's answer, laid the volume very carefully upon the table.

"I can assure, Miss Trenchard," he said, "a glance is enough to assure me that 'Pride and Prejudice' is and always will be my favourite novel."

Katherine moved to the table, picked up the book, and slipped the paper from the leaves into her belt. For an instant her hand touched Philip's.

Aunt Aggie looked at them, and satisfied with hot tea, a fire, a perfect conscience and a sense of her real importance in the business of the world, thought to herself—"Well, this afternoon at any rate those two have had no chance."

She was drowsy and anxious for a little rest before dinner, but her guard, she assured herself with a pleasant little bit of conscious self-sacrifice, should not be relaxed. . . .

Eleven had boomed that night, from the Abbey clock, when Philip Mark took his stand opposite the old house, looking up, as all the lovers in fiction and most of the lovers in real life have done, at his mistress' window. A little red glow of light was there. The frosty night had showered its sky with stars, frozen into the blue itself in this clear air, a frozen sea; an orange moon scooped into a dazzling curve, lay like a sail that had floated from its vessel, idly above the town; the plane trees rustled softly once and again, as though, now that the noise of men had died away, they might whisper in comfort together. Sometimes a horn blew from the river, or a bell rang.

Philip waited there, and worshipped with all the humility and reverence of a human soul at the threshold of Love.

The lights in the house went out. Now all the Trenchards were lying upon their backs, their noses towards the ceilings, the ceilings that shut off that starry sky. They were very secure, fenced round by Westminster. No danger could threaten their strong fortress. . . . Their very dreams were winged about with security, their happy safety was penetrated by no consciousness of that watching, motionless figure.

CHAPTER VI

GEORGE TRENCHARD'S study expressed, very pleasantly, his personality. The room's walls were of a deep warm red, and covering three sides ran high bookcases with glass fronts; within these bookcases were beautiful new editions, ugly old ones, books, for the greater part, relating to his favourite period, all ranged and ordered with the most delicate care. The windows of the room were tall and bright even on dull and foggy days, the carpet soft and thick, the leather chairs large and yielding, the fireplace wide and shining. Most significant of all was his writing-table; upon this lay everything that any writer could possibly desire, from the handsomest of gold inkstands to the minutest of elastic bands. There was also here a little bust of Sir Walter Scott. Within this room George Trenchard knew, always, perfect happiness—a very exceptional man, indeed, that he could know it so easily. He knew it by the simple expedient of shutting off entirely from his consciousness the rest of mankind; his study door once closed, he forgot his family absolutely. No one was allowed to disturb or interrupt him; it was understood that he was at work upon a volume that would ultimately make another of that series that contained already such well-known books as "William Wordsworth and his Circle," "Hazlitt—The Man in his Letters" and "The Life of Thomas de Quincey." These had appeared a number of years ago; he had been indeed a young man when he had written them. It was supposed that a work entitled

"The Lake Poets, a Critical Survey" would appear 'Next Autumn'.

For some time now the literary schemes of the weekly journals had announced this. George Trenchard only laughed at enquiries: "It takes a damned long time, you know," he said, " 'tisn't any use rushing the thing." He enjoyed, however, immensely, making notes. From half-past nine in the morning until half-past one, behind his closed doors, he considered the early Nineteenth Century, found it admirable (Scott seemed to him the perfect type) took first one book, then another from his book-shelves, wrote a few lines, and before his fire imagined the Trenchards of that period, considered their food and their drink, their morals, their humour and their literature. Hazlitt's essays seemed to him the perfection, not of English prose, but of a temporal and spiritual attitude. "Hang it all," he would conclude, "we're a rotten lot now-a-days." He did not worry over this conclusion, but it gave him the opportunity of a superior attitude during the rest of the day when he joined the world. "If you knew as much about the early Nineteenth Century as I do," he seemed to say, "you wouldn't be so pleased with yourselves." He did not, however, express his superiority in any unpleasant manner. There was never anyone more amiable. All that he wanted was that everyone should be happy, and to be that, he had long ago discovered, one must not go too deep. "Keep out of close relationships and you're safe" might be considered his advice to young people. He had certainly avoided them all his life, and avoided them by laughing at them. He couldn't abide "gloomy fellows" and on no account would he allow a 'scene'. He had never lost his temper.

During the months that he spent at his place in Glebeshire he pursued a plan identically similar. He possessed an invaluable 'factotum', a certain James Ritchie, who took everything in a way of management off his hands. Ritchie in Glebeshire, Mrs. Trenchard and Rocket in London. Life was made very simple for him.

As has been said elsewhere, Katherine, alone of his family, had in some degree penetrated his indifferent jollity; that was because she really did seem to him to have some of the Early Nineteenth Century characteristics. She seemed to him (he did not know her very well) tranquil, humorous, unadventurous, but determined. She reminded him of Elizabeth Bennet, and he always fancied (he regarded her, of course, from a distance,) that she would make a very jolly companion. She seemed to him wiser than the others, with a little strain of satirical humour in her comment on things that pleased him greatly. "She should have been the boy, and Henry the girl," he would say. He thought Henry a terrible ass. He was really anxious that Katherine should be happy. She deserved it, he thought, because she was a little wiser than the others. He considered sometimes her future, and thought that it would be agreeable to have her always about the place, but she must not be an old maid. She was too good for that. "She'd breed a good stock," he would say. "She must marry a decent fellow—one day." He delighted in the gentle postponement of possibly charming climaxes. His size, geniality and good appetite may be attributed very largely to his happy gifts of procrastination. "Always leave until to-morrow what ought to be done to-day" had made him the best-tempered of men.

After luncheon on the day that followed Philip's tea with Aunt Aggie, George Trenchard retired to his study "to finish a chapter". He intended to finish it in his head rather than upon paper, and it was even possible that a nap would postpone the conclusion; he lit his pipe and preferred to be comfortable—it was then that Rocket informed him that Mr. Mark had called, wished to see him alone, would not keep him long, apologised, but it was important.

"Why the devil couldn't he come to lunch? What a time

to appear!" But Trenchard liked Philip, Philip amused him—he was so alive and talked such ridiculous nonsense. "Of course he would see him!"

Then when Trenchard saw Philip Mark standing inside the room, waiting, with a smile half-nervous, half-friendly, the sight of that square, sturdy young man gave him to his own uneasy surprise a moment of vague and unreasonable alarm. George Trenchard was not accustomed to feelings of alarm; it was his principle in life that he should deny himself such things.

He connected now, however, this very momentary sensation with other little sensations that he had felt before in Philip's company. The young man was so damnably full of his experiences, so eager to compare one thing with another, so insistent upon foreign places and changes in England and what we'd all got to do about it. Trenchard did not altogether dislike this activity. That was the devil of it. It would never do to change his life at this time of day. . . .

He stood, large, genial, and rosy, in front of his fire. "Well, young man, what are you descending upon us at this hour for? Why couldn't you come to lunch?"

"I wanted to speak to you seriously about something. I wanted to see you alone."

"Well, here I am. Sit down. Have a cigar." Trenchard saw that Philip was nervous, and he liked him the better for that. "He's a nice young fellow, nice and clean and healthy—not too cocksure either, although he's clever."

Philip, on his part, felt, at this moment, a desperate determination to make all the Trenchard family love him. They *must*. . . . They MUST.

His heart was bursting with charity, with fine illusions, with self-deprecation, with Trenchard exultation. He carried the flaming banner of one who loves and knows that he is loved in return.

He looked round upon George Trenchard's bookcases and

thought that there could, surely, be nothing finer than writing critical books about early Nineteenth Century Literature.

"I love Katherine," he said, sitting on the very edge of his arm-chair. "And she loves me. We want to be married."

George Trenchard stared at him.

"Well, I'm damned!" he said at last, "you've got some cheek!" His first impression was one of a strange illumination around and about Katherine, as though his daughter had been standing before him in the dark and then had suddenly been surrounded with blazing candles. Although he had, as has been said, already considered the possibility of Katherine's marriage, he had never considered the possibility of her caring for someone outside the family. That struck him, really, as amazing. That made him regard his daughter, for a moment, as someone quite new and strange.

He burst into laughter.

"It's ridiculous!" he said. "Why! you two have scarcely seen one another!"

Philip blushed, but looked up into Trenchard's face with eyes that were strangely pleading for a man who could, at other times, be so firmly authoritative.

"I know that it must seem so to you," he said. "But really we *have* met a good deal. I knew from the very beginning. . . . I'll make her happy," he ended, almost defiantly, as though he were challenging some unseen enemy.

"Well, state your case," said Trenchard.

"I love her," he stammered a little, then his voice cleared and he stared straight before him at Trenchard's velvet waistcoat. "Of course there've been people in my life before, but I've never felt anything like this. I should like to tell you that my life is absolutely free from any entanglements—of any kind. I'm thirty and as fit as a fiddle. My share in the business and some other things come to about fifteen hundred a year. It's all very decently invested, but, of course, I'd show you all that. I'm not bad about manag-

ing those things, although you mightn't think so. I want
to buy a little place somewhere in England and settle down
—a little place with a bit of land. I do think I could make
Katherine happy—I'd devote myself to that."

"She cares for you?" asked Trenchard.

"Yes," said Philip quite simply.

"Well, I'm damned," said Trenchard.

This was not so rude as it appeared to be. He was not
thinking about Philip at all—only about Katherine. She
had fallen in love, she, Katherine, the staid, humorous,
comfortable companion. He had not realised, until now,
that he had always extracted much complacent comfort from
the belief that she cared for him more than for any other
member of the family. He did not know that every individual member extracted from Katherine the same comfort.
He looked at Philip. What did she see in the man to lead
her to such wild courses? He was nice enough to look at,
to listen to—but to love? It seemed to him that his quiet
daughter must have been indulging in melodrama.

"Why, you know," he cried at last, "it never entered my
head—Katherine's marrying anybody. She's very young—
you're very young too."

"I don't know," said Philip, "I'm thirty—lots of men
have families by then."

"No, but you're young though—both of you," persisted
Trenchard. "I don't think I want Katherine to marry anybody."

"Isn't that rather selfish?" said Philip.

"Yes. I suppose it is," said Trenchard, laughing, "but
it's natural."

"It isn't, you see," said Philip eagerly, "as though I
wanted to take her away to Russia or in any way deprive
you of her. I know how much she is to all of you. She's
sure to marry some day, isn't she? and it's much better that
she should marry someone who's going to settle down here

and live as you all do than someone who'd go right off with her."

"It's all right, I shouldn't let him," said Trenchard. He bent his eyes upon the eager lover, and again said to himself that he liked the young man. It would certainly be much pleasanter that Katherine should care about a fine healthy young fellow, a good companion after dinner, a good listener with a pleasant sense of humour, than that she should force into the heart of the family some impossibility—not that Katherine was likely to care about impossibilities, but you never knew; the world to-day was so full of impossibilities. . . .

"I think we'll send for Katherine," he said.

He rang the bell, Rocket came, Katherine was summoned. As they waited Trenchard delivered himself of a random, half-humorous, half-conscious, half-unconscious discourse:

"You know, I like you—and I don't often like modern young men. I wouldn't mind you at all as a son-in-law, and you'd suit me as a son much better than Henry does. At least I think so, but then I know you very slightly, and I may dislike you intensely later on. We none of us know you, you see. We never had anybody drop in upon us as you did. . . . It doesn't seem to me a bit like Katherine —and I don't suppose she knows you any better than the rest of us do. *She* mayn't like you later on. I can't say that marriage is going to be what you think it is. You're very unsettling. You won't keep quiet and take things easily, and Katherine is sure not to like that. She's as quiet as anything. . . . If it were Millie now. I suppose you wouldn't care to have Millie instead? she'd suit you much better. Then, you know, the family won't like your doing it. My wife won't like it." He paused, then, standing, his legs wide apart, his hands deep in his pockets, roared with laughter: "It *will* disturb them all—not that it won't be good for them perhaps. You're not to think though that I've given my consent—at any rate you're not to marry her for a long time until we see what you're like. I'm not to give her just to anyone who comes along, you know. I rather wish you'd stayed in Russia. It's very unsettling."

The door opened—Katherine entered. She looked at Philip, smiled, then came across to her father and put her arm through his. She said nothing, but was radiant; her father felt her hand tremble as it touched his, and that suddenly moved him as, perhaps, nothing had ever moved him before.

"Do you want to marry him?" he asked.

"Yes," she answered.

"But you hardly know him."

"I know him very well indeed," she said, looking at Philip's eyes.

"But I don't want you to marry anyone," her father went on. "We were all very nice as we were. . . . What'll you do if I say you're not to marry him?"

"You won't say that," she answered, smiling at him.

"What do you want to marry him for?" he asked. "He's just an ordinary young man. You don't know him," he repeated, "you can't yet, you've seen so little of him. Then you'll upset us all here very much—it will be very unpleasant for everybody. Do you really think it's worth it?"

Katherine laughed. "I don't think I can help it, father," she answered.

Deep in Trenchard's consciousness was the conviction, very common to men of good digestion over fifty, that had he been God he would have managed the affairs of the world very agreeably for everybody. He had not, often, been in the position of absolute power, but that was because he had not often taken the trouble to come out of his comfortable shelter and see what people were doing. He felt now that he could be Jove for a quarter of an hour without any discomfort to himself—a very agreeable feeling.

He was also the most kind-hearted of men. "Seriously, Katherine," he said, separating himself from her, drawing his legs together and frowning, "you're over age. You can do what you like. In these days children aren't supposed to consider their parents, and I don't really see why they should . . . it's not much I've done for you. But you're fond of us. We've rather hung together as a family. . . . I like your young man, but I've only known him a week or two, and I can't answer for him. You know *us,* but you don't know *him.* Are you sure you're making a wise exchange?"

Here Philip broke in eagerly but humbly. "It isn't that there need be any change," he said. "Katherine shall belong to you all just as much as ever she did."

"Thank you," said Trenchard laughing.

"I'll be proud," Philip cried, impulsively, jumping up from his chair, "if you'll let me marry Katherine, but I'll never forget that she was yours first. Of course I can't come into the family as though I'd always been one of you, but I'll do my best. . . . I'll do my best. . . ."

"My dear boy," said Trenchard, touched by the happy atmosphere that he seemed, with a nod of his head, to fling about him, "don't think *I'm* preventing you. I want everyone to be pleased, I always have. If you and Katherine have made up your minds about this, there isn't very much for me to say. If I thought you'd make her miserable I'd show you the door, but I don't think you will. All I say is —we don't know you well enough yet. Nor does she. After all, does she?" He paused, and then, enjoying the sense of their listening attention, thought that he would make a little speech. "You're like children in a dark wood, you know. You think you've found one another—caught hold of one another—but when there's a bit of a moon or something to see one another by you may find out you've each of you caught hold of someone quite different. Then, there you are, you see. That's all I can tell you about marriage; all your lives you'll be in the forest, thinking you've made a clutch at somebody, just for comfort's sake. But you never know whom you're catching—it's someone different every five minutes, even when it's the same person. Well, well —all I mean is that you mustn't marry for a year at least."

"Oh! a year!" cried Philip.

"Yes, a year. Won't hear of it otherwise. What do you say, Katherine?"

"I think Philip and I can wait as long as that quite safely," she answered, looking at her lover.

Trenchard held out his hand to Philip. "I congratulate you," he said. "If you've made Katherine love you you're a lucky fellow. Dear me—yes, you are." He put his hand on Philip's shoulder. "You'd better be good to her," he said, "or there'll be some who'll make you pay for it."

"Be good to her! My God!" answered Philip.

"Now you'd better clear. Reveal yourselves to the family. . . . There, Katherine, my dear, give me a kiss. Don't neglect me or I shall poison the villain. . . . There, there —God bless you."

He watched them depart with real affection both for them and for himself.

"I'm not such a bad father after all," he thought as he settled down into his chair.

Outside the study door, in the dark corner of the little passage, Philip kissed Katherine. Her lips met his with a passion that had in it complete and utter self-surrender.

They did not speak.

At last, drawing herself gently away from him, she said: "*I'll* tell Mother—I think it would be better not for both of us. . . ."

"Yes," he whispered back, as though they were conspirators. "I don't think I'll face them all now—unless you'd like me to help you. I'll come in to-night."

With a strange, fierce, almost desperate action she caught his arm and held him for a moment with his cheek against hers.

"Oh! Philip . . . my *dear!*" Her voice caught and broke. They kissed once again, and then, very quietly, went back into the world.

Meanwhile they had been watched; Henry had watched them. He had been crossing at the farther end of the little passage, and stopping, holding himself back against the wall, had seen, with staring eyes, the two figures. He knew instantly. They were Philip and Katherine. He saw Katherine's hand as it pressed into Philip's shoulder; he saw Philip's back set with so fierce a strength that Henry's knees trembled before the energy of it. He was disgusted—he was wildly excited. "This is real life. . . . I've seen something at last. I didn't know people kissed like that, but they oughtn't to do it in the passage. Anyone might see them. . . . Katherine!"

Staggered by the contemplation of an utterly new Katherine with whom, for the rest of his life, he would be compelled to deal, he slipped into a room as he heard their steps. When they had gone he came out; he knocked on his father's door:

"I'm sorry to bother you, Father," he began. "I wanted to know whether I might borrow—" he stopped; his heart was beating so wildly that his tongue did not belong to him.

"Well, get it and cut." His father looked at him. "You've heard the news, I see."

"What news?" said Henry.

"Philip and Katherine. They're engaged, they tell me. Not to marry for a year though. . . . I thought you'd heard it by the look of you. What a mess you're in! Why can't you brush your hair? Look at your tie up the back of your collar! Get your book and go! I'm busy!"

But Henry went without his book.

Katherine went up to her mother's room. She would catch her alone now for half an hour before tea-time, when many of the family would be assembled, ready for the news.

With such wild happiness was she surrounded that she saw them all in the light of that happiness; she had always shared so readily in any piece of good fortune that had ever befallen any one of them that she did not doubt that now they too would share in this fortune—this wonderful fortune!—of hers. She stopped at the little window in the passage where she had had the first of her little personal scraps of talk with Philip. Little scraps of talks were all that they had been, and yet now, looking back upon them, how weighted they seemed with heavy golden significance. The sky was amber-coloured, the Abbey tower sharply black, and the low archway of Dean's Yard, that she could just catch with her eye, was hooped against the sky, pushing upwards to have its share in the evening light. There was perfect quiet in the house and beyond it, as she went to her mother's room. This room was the very earliest thing that she could remember, this, or her mother's bedroom in the Glebeshire house. It was a bedroom that exactly expressed Mrs. Trenchard, large, clumsy, lit with five windows, mild and full of unarranged trifles that nevertheless arranged themselves. At the foot of the large bed, defended with dark sateen faded curtains, was a comfortable old-fashioned sofa. Further away in the middle of a clear space was a table with a muddle of things upon it—a doll half-clothed, a writing-case, a silver inkstand, photographs of Millie, Henry and Katherine, a little younger than they were now, a square silver clock, a pile of socks with a needle sticking sharply out of them, a little oak book-case with 'Keble's Christian Year', Charlotte Yonge's 'Pillars of the House', two volumes of Bishop Westcott's 'Sermons' and Mrs. Gaskell's 'Wives and Daughters'. There was also a little brass tray with a silver thimble, tortoiseshell paper-knife, a little mat made of bright-coloured beads, a reel of red silk and a tiny pocket calendar. Beside the bed there was a small square oaken table with a fine silver Crucifix and a Bible and a prayer book and copy of 'Before the

Throne' in dark blue leather. The pictures on the walls—
they hung against a wall-paper of pink roses, faded like the
bedroom curtains and the dark red carpet, but comfortably,
happily faded—were prints of 'Ulysses Deriding Poly-
phemus', 'Crossing the Brook', and 'Christ leaving the
Temple'. These three pictures were the very earliest things
of Katherine's remembrance. There were also several photographs of old-fashioned but sturdy ladies and gentlemen—an
officer in uniform, a lady with high shoulders against a background of a grey rolling sea. There were photographs of
the children at different ages. There were many cupboards,
and these, although they were closed, seemed to bulge, as
though they contained more clothes than was comfortable
for them.

There was a faint scent in the room of eau-de-cologne and
burning candles. The little clock on the table gave an
irritating, self-important whirr and clatter now and then,
and it had been doing that for a great many years.

Mrs. Trenchard was lying upon her sofa making a little
crimson jacket for the half-clothed doll. She did not move
when Katherine came in, but went on with her work, her
fat, rather clumsy-looking fingers moving very comfortably
up and down the little piece of red cloth.

"Who is that?" she said.

"It's I, Mother," said Katherine, remaining by the door.

"Ah, it's you, dear," her mother answered. "Just give
me that doll on the table. It's for Miss Sawyer's Bazaar
in the Hampstead Rooms. I said I'd dress three dolls, and
I only remembered this morning that they've got to go off to-
morrow. I thought I'd snatch this quiet time before tea.
Yes, it's for Miss Sawyer, poor thing. I'm sure I shall
run out of red silk, and I don't suppose there's any in the
house. Did you want anything, Katherine?"

Katherine came forward, picked up the doll from the
table and gave it to her mother. Then she went to one of
the broad high windows and stood looking out. She could

see the river, over whose face the evening, studded with golden lamps, was dropping its veil. She could see, very dimly, Westminster Bridge, with dots and little splashes of black passing and repassing with the mechanical indifference of some moving toy. The sight of her mother's room had suddenly told her that her task would be a supremely difficult one; she did not know why she had not realised that before. Her personal happiness was overwhelmed by her consciousness of her mother; nothing at this moment seemed to be of importance save their relations, the one to the other. "I'm going to hurt her," she thought, as she turned round from the window. All her life it had been her urgent passion to save her mother from pain.

"Mother dear," she said, "I've got something very important to tell you. Mr. Mark has asked me to marry him, and I've accepted him. Father says we're to wait for a year."

She moved forward and then stopped. Mrs. Trenchard looked at her, suddenly, as a house of cards crumples up at a single touch, her face puckered as though she were going to cry. For an instant it was like the face of a baby. It was so swift that in a flash it was gone, and only in the eyes there was still the effect of it. Her hands trembled so that she forced them down upon her lap. Then her face, except for her eyes, which were terrified, wore again exactly her look of placid, rather stupid composure. The force that she had driven into her hands had done its work, for now she could raise them again; in one hand she held the doll and in another the little red jacket.

"My *dear* Katherine!" she said. Then—"Just give me that reel of silk, dear, on the table." Then—"But it's absurd—you don't—" she seemed to struggle with her words as though she were beating back some other personality that threatened to rise and overwhelm her. "You don't—" She found her words. "You don't know him."

Katherine broke in eagerly. "I loved him at the very

beginning I think. I felt I knew him at once. I don't know; it's so hard to see how it began, but I can't help it, Mother. I've known it myself for weeks now; Mother—" She knelt down beside the sofa and looked up, and then, at something in her mother's eyes, looked down again. "Please —please—I know it seems strange to you now, but soon you'll get to know him—then you'll be glad—" She broke off, and there followed a long silence.

Mrs. Trenchard put down the doll very carefully, and then, with her hands folded on her lap, lay back on her sofa. She watched the dark evening as it gathered in beyond the windows; she heard her maid's knock on the door, watched her draw the curtains and switch on the light.

It was only four o'clock, but it was very cold.

"I think I'll have my shawl, dear," said Mrs. Trenchard. "The Indian one that your Uncle Timothy gave me—it's in the third drawer—there—to the right. . . . Thank you. I must go down. Grandfather's coming down to tea this afternoon."

Katherine drew closer to the sofa, after she had brought the shawl; she laid her hand upon her mother's, which were very cold.

"But, Mother, you've said nothing! I know that now it must seem as though I'd done it without asking you, without telling you, but I didn't know myself until yesterday afternoon. It came so suddenly."

"Yesterday afternoon?" Mrs. Trenchard drew her shawl closely about her. "But how could he—Mr. Mark—yesterday afternoon? You weren't alone with him—Aggie was there. Surely she—"

"No. He wrote on a piece of paper and slipped it across to me, and I said 'yes.' We both felt we couldn't wait."

"I don't like him," Mrs. Trenchard said slowly. "You knew that I didn't like him."

The colour rose in Katherine's cheeks.

"No," she said, "I knew that you thought some of his ideas odd. But you didn't know him."

"I don't like him," said Mrs. Trenchard again. "I could never like him. He isn't a religious man. He has a bad effect upon Henry. You, Katherine, to accept him when you know that he doesn't go to church and was so rude to poor Mr. Seymour and thinks Russia such a fine country! I can't think," said Mrs. Trenchard, her hands trembling again, "what's come over you."

Katherine got up from her knees. "You won't think that when you know him better. It's only that he's seen more of the world than we have. He'll change and we'll change, and perhaps it will be better for all of us. Down in Glebeshire we always have done so much the same things and seen the same people, and even here in London——"

Her mother gave a little cry, not sharp for anyone else in the world, but very sharp indeed for Mrs. Trenchard.

"You! Katherine—you! If it had been Millie!"

They looked at one another then in silence. They were both of them conscious of an intensity of love that they had borne towards one another through the space of a great many years—a love that nothing else had ever approached. But it was an emotion that had always been expressed in the quietest terms. Both to Katherine and her mother demonstrations were unknown. Katherine felt now, at what promised to be, perhaps, the sharpest crisis that her life had yet experienced, an urgent desire to break through, to fling her arms round her mother, to beat down all barriers, to assure her that whatever emotion might come to her, nothing could touch their own perfect relationship. But the habits of years muffled everything in thick, thick wrappings—it was impossible to break through.

"Your father is pleased?" said Mrs. Trenchard.

"Yes," answered Katherine. "He likes Philip. But we must wait a year."

"Your father has never told me anything. Never." She got up slowly from the sofa.

"He couldn't have told you," Katherine said eagerly. "He has only just known. I came straight to you from him."

Mrs. Trenchard now stood, looking rather lost, in the middle of her room; the shawl had slipped half from her shoulders, and she seemed, suddenly, an old woman.

The vision of something helpless in her, as she stood there, stirred Katherine passionately.

She took her mother into her arms, stroking her hair, kissing her cheeks and whispering to her: "Darling—darling—it doesn't make any difference to us—it can't—it can't. Nothing can. Nothing. . . . Nothing!"

Mrs. Trenchard kissed her daughter very quietly, remained in her embrace for a little, then drew herself away and went to her mirror. She tidied her hair, patted her dress, put some eau-de-Cologne on her handkerchief, laid the shawl carefully away in the drawer.

"I must go down now. Father will want his tea. I'll take the doll—I shan't have another chance of finishing it." She walked to the door, then, turning, said with an intensity that was amazing in its sudden vehemence and fire: "No one shall take you from me, Katherine. No one. Let him do what he likes. No one shall take you."

She did not appear an old woman, then, as she faced her daughter.

Meanwhile, in the drawing-room, the family had already gathered together as though it were aware that something had occurred. Mr. Trenchard, Senior, surrounded by his rugs, his especial table, his silver snuff-box (he never took snuff in the drawing-room, but liked his box to be there), a case of spectacles, and the last number of 'Blackwood's Magazine'. Great Aunt Sarah, Aunt Aggie, Aunt Betty, and Millie. Millie, watching them, was, to her own immense surprise, sorry for them.

Millie, watching them, wondered at herself. What had happened to her? She had returned from Paris, eager to find herself as securely inside the family as she had always been—longing after the wide, vague horizons of the outside world to feel that security. She had laughed at them a little, perhaps, but she had always understood and approved of their motives.

Now she found herself at every turn criticising, wondering, defending against her own intelligence, as though she had been the merest stranger. She loved them—all of them —but—how strong they were! And how terrible of her that she should find them strange! They were utterly unaware of any alteration in her; she seemed to herself to be a spy in their midst. . . .

Happily, however, they were all, this afternoon, most comfortably unaware of any criticism from anyone in the world. They sat about the room, waiting for their tea and saying very little. They knew one another so well that conversation was a mere emphasis of platitudes. Aunt Aggie talked, but nobody listened, unless one of the above-mentioned assurances were demanded.

Her dry, sharp little voice, like the fire and the ticking of the clock, made an agreeable background.

Upon this innocent gathering, so happy and tranquil, Henry burst with his news. He came with all the excited vehemence sprung from his own vision of the lovers. He could see only that; he did not realise that the others had not shared his experience. It was almost as though he had tumbled into the middle of them, so abrupt, so agitated, so incoherent was he!

"They're engaged!" he burst out.

"My dear Henry!" said Millie. "What's the matter?"

"I tell you! Katherine and Mark. They've been into father, and he says they're to wait a year, but it's all right. He says that he didn't know till they told him. Katherine's with Mother now,—Mark's coming in to-night; Katherine!"

He broke off, words failed him, and he was suddenly conscious of his Uncle's eye.

"What?" said Aunt Aggie.

"They're engaged," repeated Henry.

"Whom?" cried Aunt Aggie, ungrammatically, with a shrill horror that showed that she had already heard.

"Katie and Philip," Henry almost screamed in reply.

What Aunt Aggie, whose eyes were staring as though she saw ghosts or a man under her bed, would have said to this no one could say, but Aunt Sarah drove, like a four-wheeled coach, right across her protruding body.

Aunt Sarah said: "What are you all talking about? What's the matter with Henry? Is he ill? I can't hear."

Millie went up to her. "Katherine's engaged, Aunt Sarah, to Mr. Mark."

"What do you say about Katherine?"

"She's engaged."

"She's what?"

"ENGAGED!"

"Who to?"

"Mr. Mark."

"Eh? What?"

"Mark!"

At the shouting of that name it did indeed seem that the very walls and ceiling of that old room would collapse. To Aunt Aggie, to Millie, to Henry, to Aunt Betty, this raid upon Katherine struck more deeply than any cynical student of human nature could have credited. For the moment Philip Mark was forgotten—only was it apparent to them all from Grandfather Trenchard and Great Aunt Sarah to Henry that Katherine, their own absolute property, the assurance given to them that life would be always secure, solid, unalterable, had declared publicly, before the world, that she preferred a stranger, a complete, blown-from-anywhere stranger, to the family. What would happen to them all, to their comforts, their secret preferences and habits (known as they all, individually, believed, only to Katherine), to their pride, to their self-esteem? They loved one another, yes, they loved the Trenchard family, the Trenchard position, but through all these things, as a skewer through beef, ran their reliance upon Katherine. It was as though someone had cried to them: "The whole of Glebeshire is blown away—fields and houses, roads and rivers. You must go and live in Yorkshire. Glebeshire cares for you no longer!"

"THEY'RE TO WAIT A YEAR, FATHER SAYS!" shouted Millie.

Aunt Sarah shook her white-plumed head and snorted: "Katherine! Engaged! To a Stranger! Impossible!"

Aunt Aggie was conscious, at the moment, of nothing except that she herself had been defeated. They had tricked her, those two. They had eluded her vigilance. . . . They were now, in all probability, laughing at her.

"The last thing I want to do," she said, "is to blame anybody, but if I'd been listened to at the beginning, Mr. Mark would never have been asked to stay. . . . It was thoughtless of George. Now we can all see—"

But Millie, standing before them all, her face flushed, said:

"The chief thing is to consider Katherine's happiness. Mr. Mark is probably delightful. She was sure to marry somebody. How can people help falling in love with Katherine? We all love her. She loves us. I don't see what Mr. Mark can do to prevent that—and he won't want to. He *must* be nice if Katherine loves him!"

But the final word was spoken by Grandfather Trenchard, who had been hitherto utterly silent. In his clear, silvery voice he said:

"A great deal can happen in a year!"

At that moment Katherine and her mother came in.

BOOK II

THE FEATHER BED

CHAPTER I

KATHERINE IN LOVE

KATHERINE TRENCHARD, although she had, for a number of years now, gone about the world with open eyes and an understanding heart, was, in very many ways, absurdly old-fashioned. I say "absurd" because many people, from amongst her own Trenchard relations, thought her prejudices, simplicities, and confidences absurd, and hoped that she would grow out of them. The two people who really knew her, her Uncle Timothy and Rachel Seddon, hoped that she never would. Her "old-fashioned" habits of mind led her to believe in "people" in "things" and in "causes", and it was her misfortune that up to this year of which I am speaking she had never been disappointed. That may be because she had grown up amongst the rocks, the fields, the lanes of Glebeshire, true ground where sincerity and truth flourish yet in abundance—moreover it is assured that man lives up to the qualities with which he is by his friends credited, and all the Trenchard family lived up to Katherine's belief in their word of honour.

She was not so simple a character that she found the world perfect, but she was in no way subtle, and, because she herself acted in her faults and virtues, her impetuosities and repentances, her dislikes and affections with clear-hearted simplicity, she believed that other persons did the same. Her love for her mother was of this quite unquestioning sort; her religion too was perfectly direct and unquestioning: so, then, her love for Philip. . . .

She had never before been in love, nor had she ever con-

129

sidered men very closely as anything but visitors or relations. The force and power of the passion that now held her was utterly removed from anything that had ever encountered her before, but she was a strong character, and her simplicity of outlook helped her. Philip seemed to her to be possessed of all the qualities of the perfect hero. His cleverness, his knowledge of the world, his humour were only balanced by his kindness to everyone and everything, his unselfishness, his honesty of speech and eye. She had thought him, once, a little weak in his anxiety to be liked by all the world, but now that was forgotten. He was, during these days, a perfect character.

She had not, however, lost her clear-sighted sense of humour; that humour was almost cynical sometimes in its sharp perception of people and things, and did not seem to belong to the rest of Katherine at all. It was driven more often upon herself than upon anyone else, but it was, for a character of Katherine's simplicity, strangely sharp. A fair field for the employment of it was offered to her just now in the various attitudes and dispositions of her own immediate family, but, as yet, she was unable to see the family at all, so blinding was Philip's radiance.

That year England enjoyed one of the old romantic Christmases. There were sparkling dazzling frosts. The snow lay hard and shining under skies of unchanging blue, and on Christmas Eve, when the traffic and smoke of the town had stolen the purity away, more snow fell and restored it again.

It had always been the rule that the Trenchards should spend Christmas in Glebeshire, but, this year, typhoid fever had visited Garth only a month or two before, and London was held to be safer. Katherine had not had, in her life, so many entertainments that she could afford to be blasé about them, and she still thought a Pantomime splendid "The Only Way" certainly the most magnificent play in the world, and a dance a thing of perfect rapture, if only

she could be more secure about the right shapes and colours
of her clothes. She had no vanity whatever—indeed a little
more would have helped her judgment: she never knew
whether a dress would suit her, nor why it was that one
thing "looked right" and another thing "looked wrong".
Millie could have helped her, because Millie knew all about
clothes, but it was always a case with Katherine of something else coming first, of having to dress at the last minute,
of "putting on any old thing because there was no time."

Now, however, there was Philip to dress for, and she did
really try. She went to Millie's dressmaker with Millie as
her guide, but unfortunately Mrs. Trenchard, who had as
little idea about dress as Katherine, insisted on coming too,
and confused everyone by her introduction of personal motives and religious dogmas into something that should have
been simply a matter of ribbons and bows. Katherine, indeed, was too happy to care. Philip loved her in any old
thing, the truth being that when he went about with her,
he saw very little except his own happiness. . . .

It is certainly a fact that during these weeks neither of
them saw the family at all.

Rachel Seddon was the first person of the outside world
to whom Katherine told the news.

"So that was the matter with you that day when you
came to see me!" she cried.

"What day?" said Katherine.

"You'd been frightened in the Park, thought someone
was going to drop a bag over your head, and ran in
here for safety."

"I shall always run in here for safety," said Katherine
gravely. Rachel came, in Katherine's heart, in the place
next to Mrs. Trenchard and Philip. Katherine had always
told Rachel everything until that day of which Rachel had
just spoken. There had been reticence then, there would be
reticences always now.

"You will bring him very quickly to see me?" said Rachel.

"I will bring him at once," answered Katherine.

Rachel had liked Philip when she met him at the Trenchards; now, when he came to call, she found that she did not get on with him. He seemed to be suspicious of her: he was awkward and restrained. His very youthful desire to make the person he was with like him, seemed now to give way to an almost truculent surliness. "I don't care whether you like me or not," he seemed to say. "Katherine's mine and not yours any longer."

Neither Philip nor Rachel told Katherine that they did not like one another. Roddy Seddon, Rachel's husband, on the other hand, liked Philip very much. Lying for many years on his back had given him a preference for visitors who talked readily and gaily, who could tell him about foreign countries, who did not too obviously pity him for being "out of the running, poor beggar."

"You don't like the feller?" Roddy said to his wife.

"He doesn't like me," said Rachel.

"Rot," said Roddy. "You're both jealous. You both want Katherine."

"I shan't be jealous," answered Rachel, "if he's good enough for her—if he makes her happy."

"He seems to me a very decent sort of feller," said Roddy.

Meanwhile Rachel adored Katherine's happiness. She had chafed for many years now at what she considered was the Trenchards' ruthless sacrifice of Katherine to their own selfish needs.

"They're never going to let her have any life of her own," she said. Now Katherine *had* a life of her own, and if only that might continue Rachel would ask no more. Rachel had had her own agonies and disciplines in the past, and they had left their mark upon her. She loved her husband and her child, and her life was sufficiently filled with their demands upon her, but she was apprehensive of happiness—

she saw the Gods taking away with one hand whilst they gave with the other.

"I knew more about the world at ten," she thought, "than Katherine will ever know. If she's hurt, it will be far worse for her than it ever was for me."

Although she delighted in Katherine's happiness, she trembled at the utter absorption of it. "We aren't meant to trust anything so much," she thought, "as Katherine trusts his love for her."

Katherine, perhaps because she trusted so absolutely, did not at present ask Philip any questions. They talked very little. They walked, they rode on the tops of omnibuses, they went to the Zoo and Madame Tussaud's and the Tower, they had tea at the Carlton Restaurant and lunch in Soho, they went to the Winter Exhibition at Burlington House, and heard a famous novelist give a portentous lecture on the novel at the "Times" Book Club. They were taken to a solemn evening at the Poets' Club, where ladies in evening dress read their own poetry, they went to a performance given by the Stage Society, and a tea-party given by four lady novelists at the Lyceum Club: old Lady Carloes, who liked Katherine, chaperoned her to certain smart dances, whither Philip also was invited, and, upon two glorious occasions, they shared a box with her at a winter season of German Opera at Covent Garden. They saw the Drury Lane pantomime and Mr. Martin Harvey and one of Mr. Hall Caine's melodramas and a very interesting play by Sir Arthur (then Mr.) Pinero. They saw the King driving out in his carriage and the Queen driving out in hers.

It was a wild and delirious time. Katherine had always had too many duties at home to consider London very thoroughly, and Philip had been away for so long that everything in London was exciting to him. They spoke very little; they went, with their eyes wide open, their hearts beating very loudly, side by side, up and down the town, and the town smiled upon them because they were so young, so happy, and so absurdly confident.

Katherine was confident because she could see no reason for being otherwise. She knew that it sometimes happened that married people did not get on well together, but it was ridiculous to suppose that that could be the case with herself and Philip. She knew that, just at present, some members of her family did not care very greatly for Philip, but that was because they did not know him. She knew that a year seemed a long time to wait, but it was a very short period compared with a whole married lifetime. How anyone so clever, so fine of soul, so wise in his knowledge of men and things could come to love anyone so ordinary as herself she did not know—but that had been in God's hands, and she left it there.

There was a thing that began now to happen to Katherine of which she herself was only very dimly perceptive. She began to be aware of the living, actual participation in her life of the outside, abstract world. It was simply this—that, because so wonderful an event had transformed her own history, so also to everyone whom she saw, she felt that something wonderful must have happened. It came to more than this; she began now to be aware of London as something alive and perceptive in the very heart of its bricks and mortar, something that knew exactly her history and was watching to see what would come of it. She had always been concerned in the fortunes of those immediately about her—in the villages of Garth, in all her Trenchard relations —but they had filled her world. Now she could not go out of the Westminster house without wondering—about the two old maids in black bonnets who walked up and down Barton Street, about a tall gentleman with mutton-chop whiskers and a white bow, whom she often saw in Dean's Yard, about a large woman with a tiny dog and painted eyebrows, about the young man with the bread, the young man with the milk, the very trim young man with the post, the very fat young man with the butcher's cart, the two smart nursemaids with the babies of the idle rich, who were always together and deep in whispered conversation; the policeman at the right corner of the Square, who was friendly and human, and the policeman at the left corner who was not; the two young men in perfect attire and attaché cases who always lounged down Barton Street about six o'clock in the evening with scorn for all the world at the corners of their mouths, the old man with a brown muffler who sold boot laces at the corner of Barton Street, and the family with the barrel-organ who came on Friday mornings (man once been a soldier, woman pink shawl, baby in a basket), a thick-set, grave gentleman who must be somebody's butler, because his white shirt was so stiff and his cheeks blue-black from shaving so often, a young man always in a hurry and so untidy that, until he came close to her, Katherine thought he must be Henry . . . all those figures she had known for years and years, but they had been only figures, they had helped to make the pattern in the carpet, shapes and splashes of colour against the grey.

Now they were suddenly alive! They had, they must have, histories, secrets, triumphs, defeats of a most thrilling order! She would like to have told them of her own amazing, stupendous circumstances, and then to have invited their confidences. The world that had held before some fifty or sixty lives pulsated now with millions. But there was more than that before her. Whereas she had always, because she loved it, given to Garth and the country around it a conscious, individual existence, London had been to her simply four walls with a fire and a window. From the fire there came heat, from the window a view, but the heat and the view were made by man for man's convenience. Had man not been, London was not. . . . Garth had breathed and stormed, threatened and loved before Man's spirit had been created.

Now, although as yet she did not recognise it, she began

to be aware of London's presence—as though from some hidden corner, from long ago some stranger had watched her; now, because the room was lit, he was revealed to her. She was not, as yet, at all frightened by her knowledge, but even in quiet Westminster there were doorways, street corners, trees, windows, chimneys, houses, set and square and silent, that perceived her coming and going—"Tum— te tum—Tat—Tat—Tat . . . Tat—Tat—Tat—Tum—te —tum. . . .

"We know all about it, Katherine Trenchard—We know what's going to happen to you, but we can't tell you—We're older and wiser, much older and much, much wiser than you are—Tat—Tat—Tat. . . ."

She was so happy that London could not at present disturb her, but when the sun was suddenly caught behind black clouds, when a whirr of rain came slashing down from nowhere at all, when a fog caught with its yellow hand London's throat and squeezed it, when gusts of dust rose from the streets in little clouds as though the horses were kicking their feet, when a wind, colder than snow came, blowing from nowhere, on a warm day, Katherine needed Philip, clung to him, begged him not to leave her . . . she had never, in all her life, clung to anyone before.

But this remains that, during these weeks, she found him perfect. She liked nothing better than his half-serious, half-humorous sallies at himself. "You've got to buck me up, Katherine—keep me from flopping about, you know. Until I met you no one had any real influence on me—never in all my days. Now you can do anything with me. Tell me when I do anything hateful, and scold me as often as you can. Look at me with the eyes of Aunt Aggie if you can—she sees me without any false colouring. I'm not a hero—far from it—but I can be anything if you love me enough."

"Love him enough!" Had anyone ever loved anyone before as she loved him? She was not, to any ordinary observer, very greatly changed. Quietly and with all the matter-of-fact half-serious, half-humorous common-sense she went about her ordinary daily affairs. Young Seymour came to tea, and she laughed at him, gave him teacake, and asked him about the latest novel just as she had always done. Mr. Seymour had come expecting to see love's candle lit for the benefit of his own especial genius. He was greatly disappointed, but also, because he hated Mark, gratified. "I don't believe she loves him a bit," he said afterwards. "He came in while I was there, and she didn't colour up or anything. Didn't show anything, and I'm pretty observant. She doesn't love him, and I'm jolly glad—I can't stand the man."

But those who were near her knew. They felt the heat, they watched the colour, of the pure, unfaltering flame. Old Trenchard, the Aunts, Millie, Henry, her mother, even George Trenchard felt it. "I always knew," said Millie, "that when love came to Katherine it would be terrible". She wrote that in a diary that she kept.

Mrs. Trenchard said nothing at all. During those weeks Katherine was, for the first time in her life, unaware of her mother.

The afternoon of the Christmas Eve of that year was never afterwards forgotten by Katherine. She had been buying last desperate additions to Christmas presents, had fought in the shops and been victorious; then, seeing through the early dusk the lights of the Abbey, she slipped in at the great door, found a seat near the back of the nave, and remembered that always, at this hour, on Christmas Eve, a Carol Service was held. The service had not yet begun, and a hush, with strange rhythms and pulsations in it, as though some phantom conductor were leading a phantom orchestra, filled the huge space. A flood of people, dim and very silent, spread from wall to wall. Far away, candles fluttered, trembled and flung strange lights into the web of shadow that seemed to swing and stir as though driven by

some wind. Katherine sank into a happy, dreamy bewilderment. The heat of the building after the cold, frosty air,
some old scent of candles and tombstones and ancient walls,
the consciousness of utter, perfect happiness carried her into
a state that was half dream, half reality. She closed her
eyes, and soon the voices from very far away rose and fell
with that same phantom, remotely inhuman urgency.

A boy's voice that struck, like a dart shot by some heavenly
archer, at her heart, awoke her. This was "Good King
Wenceslaus". A delicious pleasure filled her: her eyes
flooded with tears and her heart beat triumphantly. "Oh!
how happy I am! And I realise it—I *know* that I can never
be happier again than I am now!"

The carol ceased. After a time, too happy for speech,
she went out.

In Dean's Yard the snow, with blue evening shadows upon
it, caught light from the sheets of stars that tossed and
twinkled, stirred and were suddenly immovable. The Christmas bells were ringing: all the lights of the houses in the
Yard gathered about her and protected her. What stars
there were! What beauty! What silence!

She stood, for a moment, taking it in, then, with a little
shiver of delight, turned homewards.

CHAPTER II

MRS. TRENCHARD

MILLIE, like many of the Trenchard ladies before her, kept a diary. She had kept it now for three years, and it had not during that time, like the diaries of other young ladies, died many deaths and suffered many resurrections, but had continued with the utmost regularity and discipline. This regularity finds its explanation in the fact that Millie really was interested in other people as well as in herself, was sometimes surprised at her cleverness and in turn suspicious of it—in fact, she knew as much about the world as most girls of eighteen who have been "finished" in Paris: she thought that she knew more than she did, and was perfectly determined to know a great deal more than she thought she knew.

These were some entries:

"*Dec. 6th.* Tried on the new white silk, but it won't do even now—too tight and makes me skimpy—Refused to let mother come with me this time. Took Aunt Betty instead, and we saw a *peach* of a hat at Renée's which I'd give my eyes for, only of course I haven't got the money now with Christmas coming and everything. Aunt Betty said it was much better wanting things you can't have, because then you go on being excited, but that's of course *absurd* and just like Aunt Betty.

Bought Aunt Aggie a calendar-blotter thing for Christmas which she won't like (blue leather with silver corners) but I *can't* help it. I'm sick of thinking what to get her, and she won't be contented whatever it is. Meanwhile, in the afternoon: the sensation of a lifetime—All sitting in the drawing-room, waiting for tea. When in bursts Henry with the wild news that Katie's engaged herself to Philip Mark. We all turned blue—I'd like to have been someone outside and seen us. No one had really suspected it. *I* hadn't myself—although one might have, I suppose, if one had watched more closely. It's very exciting, and if Katie's happy I don't care about anything else. At least I do. It was so lovely coming back from Paris and having her all to oneself. We understand one another so *much better* than any of the others do. I'm the only one in the family who really knows her. I never thought of her as being married, which was silly, I suppose. It's funny to think of her liking a man, whom she's only just seen, better than all of us. It wouldn't be funny with most people, but Katherine's so *quiet* and so *steady*. It all depends on what *he's* like. Finished 'La Faute de l'abbé Mouret'. *Loved* it. Downstairs I'm reading 'Sesame and Lilies'—well-written but awfully silly.

Dec. 9th. Dreary day buying presents with mother at the Stores. *Why* she will go there I can't think, and she takes it like a week on the Riviera or a box at the opera. She says nothing about Philip—not a word. He dined last night, and was most tactful. I never saw anyone so determined to make us all devoted to him, but he's got a difficult business with Aunt Aggie and mother. I *like* him, and have a kind of idea that I understand him better than any of the others do. He's certainly not the God that Katherine thinks him—and he knows he isn't. He's a little uncomfortable about it, I think. He's certainly very much in love with her. Letter from Louise Pougé—She's engaged —to no one very particular. She's younger than I am—*and* prettier—lots.

Spoke to Henry about clean handkerchiefs. He's really incredible at his age. Philip seems to influence him though. That may do something.

Dec. 13th. Dismal day. Out of sorts and cross. Dreadfully restless. I don't know why. It's all wrong this Christmas, not being down at Garth and Katherine so occupied. On days like these I have terrible scruples about myself. I suppose I *am* terribly conceited really—and yet I don't know. There are plenty of people I admire ever so much more than myself. I suppose it's seeing Katherine so happy that makes me restless. It must be nice to have anyone as devoted as that to you. . . . I've always been very cynical about being in love, but when one watches it, quite close, with anyone as good as Katherine . . . anyway it's been a beastly day, and Aunt Aggie went on like an old crow at dinner. I wish I knew what mother was feeling about it all—she's so quiet.

Dec. 17th. Had a long talk with Philip this evening. I must say I liked him—he was so modest about himself. He said that he wished he were a little more as Katherine thinks he is, and that he's going to try to be. I said that's all right so long as he made Katherine happy and didn't take her right away from us all. He said that he would do anything to make mother like him, and did I think that she liked him better now? I said that I was sure that she did—but I'm not sure really. It's impossible to know what mother thinks. Katherine came in whilst we were talking. Afterwards, I don't know why, I felt afraid somehow. Katie's so *sure*. I know I'd never be sure of anybody, least of all anyone in love with me. But then I know so much more about men than Katie does. And I'm sure Philip knows lots more about women than Katie thinks. Katie and mother are *so* alike in some ways. They're both as obstinate as anything. Such a lovely afternoon out with the Swintons—Snow in the Green Park, sparkling all over and the air like after you've eaten peppermints. Lady Perrot asked me to go with them to New Year's supper at the Savoy. Hope I'll be allowed.

Dec. 23rd. Had a walk with Katie—first walk had alone since her engagement. She was so happy that she was almost

—a beastly word—*frisky*. Katie frisky! We're miles away from one another just now, and that's the truth. I suppose one must simply wait until this period's passed away. But supposing it never passes away? Supposing she disappears altogether—from all of us. At any rate, what can one say? I like Philip, and can honestly say so, but I don't think him the angel Gabriel. Not that Katie at present cares, in the least, what one thinks—she doesn't wait to hear. She is making no plans, thinking of no possible future, imagining nothing. She never had any imagination, or at any rate never used it. Perhaps she'll get some now from Philip, who has *plenty*—far too much. It's *his* trouble, I believe that he's always imagining something a little better than he's got. . . . We Trenchards have none. I haven't any really—it's only curiosity. Henry and I might have some if we were all very uncomfortable. But of course the whole family only keeps together because it can't imagine things being different. *Are* things going to be different now? . . . Rachel Seddon came to tea. Don't like her. Thinks she owns Katie—and Katie's let her. Went with the Aunts to the Messiah. Very long, with nice bits. Aunt Aggie had a crick in the neck, and wriggled all the time. Hope I get some money on Christmas Day or I shall be in an *awful* hole.

Dec. 26th. Two pounds from father, one from grandfather, ten shillings Cousin Alice, five Aunt Grace, kettleholder Aunt Aggie, two dozen handkerchiefs Uncle Bob, fountain-pen father, new hat mother (quite hopeless), photogravure 'Happy Warrior' Aunt Betty, two books 'Reuben Hallard' by Westcott (Mudie second-hand) 'Rossetti's Poems' from Henry—lovely amethyst brooch Katie (darling!) two novels by Turgenieff from Philip—lots of other things.

Nice day on the whole, but not *quite right* somehow. Wish mother didn't always look so anxious when there's a dinner party. You always *expect* things to happen wrong, and really

Rocket knows his business by this time. All of us a little forced, I think. It seemed funny not being at Garth and Philip the first person we've ever had not of the family. Aunt Sarah keeps forgetting who he is, or pretends to. I wish he didn't make up to mother quite so much. That isn't the way to make her like him. I really *do* understand him much better than anyone else does—*much* better than Katie.

Dec. 31st. Going to the Savoy party to-night. Hope it will be fun. Never expected mother to let me, but she's awfully sweet to me lately. She's a darling, but we're really always just a little afraid of one another. Of course I'm not out yet, so I'll have to be quiet to-night. Mother never would have dreamt of letting me go six months back. End of the year—made several resolutions. Not to be snappy, nor superior, nor cynical, nor selfish. That's enough for any-one to look after! Wonder what things will be like this year, and how Katie and Philip will turn out. Feel as though things will all go wrong, and yet I don't know why. Bought the hat I saw a fortnight ago. Finished 'House of Gentlefolks'. *Adored* it. Discussed it with Philip. Going to get all the other Turgenieffs. Think Russia must be a wonderful country. Time to dress. I know I'll just *love* the party. . . ."

Only Mrs. Trenchard herself could say whether or no she had enjoyed this Christmas. She displayed the same busy placidity as on other occasions; of her fears, disappoint-ments, surprises, she said nothing. The turkey was a suc-cess, the plum-pudding burnt with a proper glow, no one was ill, she had forgotten, in sending out her parcels, no single Trenchard relation—surely all was well.

Her brother, Timothy, who knew her better than anyone else did, had long abandoned the penetration of her motives, aims, regrets. There had been a time when she had been almost intimate with him, then something (he never knew what) had driven her in more obstinately than ever upon herself. Something he had said. . . . He could point almost exactly to the day and hour. She had been a stranger to him from that moment.

Her history was, however, very simple.

When she had been a very, very small child she had decided for herself that the way to give life a real value was to fix one's affection upon someone: perhaps there had been also the fear of life as a motive, the discovery that the best way to be protected from all kinds of perils was to be so fond of someone that nothing else mattered. With a quiet, undemonstrative but absolutely tenacious hold she attached herself to her nurse, who deserted her on the appearance of a younger sister, to her mother, who died, to her father, who was always so busy that loving him was like being devoted to a blotting pad. When she was ten years of age she went to school, and clung to a succession of older girls, who, however, found, in her lack of all demonstrations, her almost cynical remarks, her inability to give any expression whatever to her emotions, something, at first, terrifying, and afterwards merely tiresome.

When she was about eighteen she discovered that the person to whom a woman should be properly attached was her husband. She waited then very calmly until she was twenty, when George Trenchard appeared, proposed to her, and was accepted. She took it so utterly for granted that her devotion to him would fill sufficiently the energy of her remaining days that it wasn't until the end of a year of married life that she discovered that, although he liked her very much, he could do quite beautifully without her, and did, indeed, for three-quarters of every day forget her altogether. No one, except herself, knew whether that discovery hurt her. She, of course, said nothing to anyone about it. She waited for the arrival of her children. Katherine, Henry and Mildred came, and at last it seemed that Mrs. Trenchard's ship had come into port. During their early years, at any rate, they clung to her tenaciously, did not in the least mind that she had nothing to say to them: they found her sure and safe and, best of all possible things in a parent, always the same. It was when Katherine was six years old that Timothy said to her one day:

"Look here, Harriet, don't get so wrapt in the children that you'll never be able to unwrap yourself again. I've seen it happen dozens of times, and it always gives endless trouble later on. It's all very well now, but the time will come when they'll break away—it *must* come, and you'll suffer horribly unless you're ready for it. I'm not married myself, it's true, but I see all the more for that very reason."

This was the speech that severed Mrs. Trenchard from her brother. She never forgot nor forgave it. She never forgave it because she could not forget it: his words were to haunt her from the moment of their utterance until the last conscious instant of her life. She had been born entirely without imagination, but she had not been born without the wish for romance. Moreover, the Faunder tradition (which is the same as the Trenchard tradition) taught her to believe that there was something enfeebling and dangerous about imagination, and that the more one thought about things not immediately within sight the less likely one was to do one's daily task with efficiency. Her longing for a romantic life therefore (that is for the justification of her own personal existence) was assisted by no private dreams nor castle-building. No Faunder or Trenchard had ever built a castle in the air when there were good square manors and vicarages waiting to be constructed on good solid ground. She directed the whole of her passionate life towards her relations with her children, but never even to herself would she admit that she had any passionate life at all. Take away the children and there was nothing left for her except her religion; because the loss of them would be the one tragedy that would drive her to question the justice of her God was justification of itself for her passionate determination.

Now Timothy had said that she would lose them—well, Timothy should see. With other children, with other mothers, it might be so. God Himself should not take them from her.

Nevertheless, as the children grew, the shadows of his words ever pursued her and hemmed her in. She watched, with close attention, other families, and saw that Timothy's warning was justified often enough, but always she was able to find for herself some reason. The weakness of selfishness or carelessness of the parent. Not weak, nor selfish, nor careless could any watching Powers, waiting to pounce, accuse her of being!

When the children grew older she discovered certain things about them. Henry often annoyed her with his untidiness and strangely unjustified egotism. He always thought about himself, and yet never did anything. She liked Henry least of her children.

Mildred was delightful, clever, the "show child", but for that very reason would in all probability be, afterwards, the most restless of them. As the two girls grew Mrs. Trenchard told herself that, perhaps, Millie would have to be sacrificed, and in telling herself this she implied that if she would only, when the time came, allow Millie without a murmur to depart, the Gods would be satisfied with that and Katherine would remain.

It came to this, that by the time that Katherine was twelve she was the centre of her mother's existence. Mildred and Henry would be held as long as it was possible to hold them, but, if the worst came, they should go. Katherine would always remain. . . .

It seemed indeed that she would. She loved her home, her parents, her relations, Glebeshire, the whole of the Trenchard inheritance. She placed her mother first in her life, and she was able to satisfy the love in her mother's heart without saying anything about it or drawing anyone's attention towards it. She had all the qualities that her

mother admired—sincerity, trust, common-sense, practical
punctuality, moral as well as physical: above all, she took
things for granted without asking endless questions, as was
Henry's unfortunate habit. There grew then in the lives
both of Mrs. Trenchard and Katherine a passionate affection, which was never allowed by either of them to find outward expression. This became, behind the commonplace
matter-of-fact of all their days, a kind of romantic conspiracy.
Even when Katherine was still a child Mrs. Trenchard knew
that the hours that they spent alone together had some strange
almost incoherent quality, something that was mixed, inex-
tricably, with the high lanes, the grassy lawns, the distant
strip of sea beyond the fields, the rooks in the high trees, the
smell of the village shop, boot-laces, liquorice, tallow, cheese
and cotton, the dark attic bedroom of Katherine's, the cries
of village children beyond the garden wall, afternoon Sunday
school upon hard benches under glazed lamps to the accompaniment of the harmonium; all the things that belonged to
Garth belonged also to the love between Mrs. Trenchard and
Katherine. Katherine had been first taken to the sea when
she had been a very little girl; she had been shown Rafiel and
the Pirates' Cove with its cave (too small for any but very
thin pirates), and the village with the cottages cut out of
the rock and the sea advancing and retreating as a lazy cat
stretches and withdraws its paws upon the pebbled beach.
Driving home through the twilight in the high dog-cart behind the fat and beloved family pony, Katherine had been besieged with questions. What had she thought of it all? What
had she liked best? Had it been wonderful? She had said
nothing. She was obstinately silent. At last, persecuted
beyond bearing, she looked, imploringly, at her mother. Her
eyes had met her mother's, and, as complete understanding
passed between them, it seemed that they made, there and
then, a compact of mutual help and protection that was never
afterwards to be broken. Mrs. Trenchard had never, never
been known to mention scenery, sunsets or buildings, except

for strictly practical reasons. She would say: "Come in, children, you'll catch cold, the sun's setting", or "I *don't* think we'll have rain to-day. There's not a cloud", or "It's so hot, there's quite a mist. I hope there'll be enough strawberries and cream for everyone." That was her attitude, and yet she loved Glebeshire, every stone and tree, with an unfaltering and unarguing devotion. She never said "Glebeshire is the loveliest spot in the world". But only: "Oh! you've never been to Glebeshire? You don't know the Clarence Faunders then? They're only five miles from us", or "Yes. We live in Glebeshire—a little village not far from Polchester. We're very lucky in our clergyman, a Mr. Smart, one of the Smarts, etc." Moreover, she never when she was quite alone said to herself: "Oh! what a heavenly day!" or "How lovely the new leaves are", or "Look at the primroses!" She only said to herself: "Lucy Cartwright's Annie has got to have that ointment", or "I must tell Rebekah about the poor Curtises. She could take them the things."

Nevertheless, when she discovered that Katherine cared for Glebeshire with a love as deep as her own, how happy she was! How firmly that discovery bound them together! For them both that journey twice a year from London to Garth was as exciting as though they had never taken it before. The stations, whose names were like the successive wrappers that enclose a splendid present, Rasselas, the little windy station where they changed from the London Express into the halting, stumbling little train that carried them towards the sea; then Stoep in Roselands, tiniest station of all, with the sea smell blowing across the dark fields, the carriage with its lights and Jacob, the coachman, the drive through the twilight lanes, the gleaming white gates, the house itself and old Rebekah on the doorstep . . . yes, of all these things was the love between Mrs. Trenchard and her daughter made.

Most wonderful of all was it that, with Katherine, Mrs. Trenchard never knew a moment's awkwardness or embarrassment. With everyone else in the world and, perhaps especially with her own family, Mrs. Trenchard was often awkward and embarrassed, although no one but herself was aware of it. Of this embarrassment Mrs. Trenchard had a horrible dread: it was to her as though she were suddenly lifted off her feet by a giant hand and held dangling: she felt that all the world must see how her skirts blew in the wind. With Katherine she was always safe: she grew, most urgently, to depend upon this safety. Then, as the years passed she felt that she might, with justice, consider Katherine secure. Katherine seemed to have no interest in young men: already she adopted a rather motherly attitude towards them and, perhaps because Henry was the young man immediately before her, considered them rather helpless, rather clumsy, rather unwieldy and ungainly. She was always kind but a little satirical in her relations to the other sex: young men were, perhaps, afraid of her.

Mrs. Trenchard did, of course, consider the possibility of Katherine's marriage, but, if that ever occurred, it would be, she knew, with someone in the family, someone like themselves, who would live near by, who would worship Katherine but never interfere with her, who would give her children, to whom Mrs. Trenchard could be a delightful grandmother. This surrender the Gods might demand—it would need more than such a marriage to separate, now, Katherine from her mother. Mrs. Trenchard, like all unimaginative people, relied very strongly upon little facts and well-accustomed places and familiar family relations. She did not believe that Victoria Street would walk away or that the old woman (Mrs. Pengello, an ancient widow with a pension, two granddaughters and a cast in her eye) at the Garth post office would appear one morning as a radiant young beauty, or that her brother Timothy would go on to the music halls. Her world was thus a place of security, and Katherine was one of the most secure things in it. "Ah! Timothy, you're wrong after all," she would sometimes, in the watches of the night, think to herself. "Nothing can take

Katherine from me now. You may be as right as you like about Millie and Henry. Katherine is enough. . . ."

She had, during these last years, been wrapped in with a strange, placid content: Millie had been at school in Paris: there was nothing inside the Trenchard fortress that spoke of the outside world. No secret spirit ever whispered to Mrs. Trenchard: "Are you not being selfish in keeping your daughter? You will die some day, and then she will have a lonely old maid's life when she might have been so happy. The children's lives are their own. What right have you to Katherine's life and ambitions and love? Would you, in your youth, have given up your future for your parents? Why should she?"

There was nothing that Mrs. Trenchard desired more than Katherine's happiness. If Katherine had not loved her she would have let her go, but now . . . Katherine's life was bound up with hers so tightly that nothing, nothing could part them. . . .

Then there came a night of fog, a stranger bowing in the doorway, and all the old days were dead. Mrs. Trenchard was still stunned, the fog was yet about her eyes, and in her heart was a dread that had not yet found its voice nor driven her to determine what she would do. . . . Meanwhile there was no one in the world who knew her. She did not know herself. Until now there had been in her life no crisis strong enough to force open that realisation.

One morning early in January Mrs. Trenchard said to Katherine at breakfast: "Will you come to the Stores with me this afternoon, Katherine? I have to buy some hot-water bottles and one or two other things. Two of them leak badly . . . some hot-water bottles . . . and I'd like you to help me."

"I'm lunching with Rachel, mother," Katherine said. "But I'll be back by three if that's time enough."

"Three o'clock. Very well, dear. They oughtn't to leak

—we've had them quite a short time. Shall I meet you there?"

"No. I'll come back. We might miss there. I'll be back by three."

At ten minutes past three in a large rather confused hat with a black bird and white feathers Mrs. Trenchard was seated waiting in the drawing-room. The fire had had coal poured upon it by Rocket, and it was very black: the room was cold and dark, and Mrs. Trenchard, feeling like an un-welcome guest in her own house, shivered. At twenty min-utes past three Mrs. Trenchard began to be afraid that there had been an accident. Katherine was always so punctual. Millie came in.

"Dear mother, what on earth!"

"I'm waiting for Katherine. She was to be back at three from Rachel Seddon's. We are—were—going to the Stores. You don't think there can have been an accident?"

"Katherine! Why, I saw her twenty minutes ago. I've just come back from Lady Carloes. Katie was at Hyde Park Corner with Philip."

"Philip!"

Mrs. Trenchard got up, took off one black glove, then put it on again. She looked at the clock.

"Will you come to the Stores with me, Millie? I've got to get some hot-water bottles and some other things. . . . Two of ours leak. . . . I'd like you to help me."

Millie looked once at the clock, and her mother saw her. Then Millie said:

"Of course I will. We won't be very long, will we?"

"Why, no, dear," said Mrs. Trenchard, who would have been happy to spend a week at the Stores had she the op-portunity. "Quite a little time."

They set off together.

Millie was not yet of such an age that she could disguise her thoughts. She was wondering about Katherine, and Mrs. Trenchard knew that this was so. Mrs. Trenchard always walked through the streets of London as a trainer in the company of his lions. Anything might happen, and one's life was not safe for a moment, but a calm, resolute demeanour did a great deal, and, if trouble came, one could always use the whip: the whip was the Trenchard name. To-day, however, she gave no thought to London: she was very gentle and kind to Millie—almost submissive and humble. This made Millie very uncomfortable.

"I'm rather foolish about the Stores, I'm afraid. I know several places where you can get better hot-water bottles *and* cheaper. But they know me at the Stores now."

Once she said: "I hope, Millie dear, I'm not keeping you from anything. We shall be home by half-past four."

In exchange for these two little remarks Millie talked a great deal, and the more she talked the more awkward she seemed. She was very unhappy about her mother, and she wished that she could comfort her, but she knew her so little and had been always on such careless terms with her that now she had no intuition about her.

"What is she thinking? . . . I know Katherine has hurt her terribly. She oughtn't to wear a hat like that: it doesn't suit her a bit. Why isn't it *I* who have forgotten, and Katie here instead to console her? Only then she wouldn't want consolation. . . ."

As they walked up the steps of the Stores they were stared at by a number of little dogs on chains, who all seemed to assert their triumphant claims on somebody's especial affections. The little dogs stirred Mrs. Trenchard's unhappiness, without her knowing why. All down Victoria Street she had been thinking to herself: "Katherine never forgot before—never. It was only this morning—if it had even been yesterday—but this morning! Millie doesn't understand, and she didn't want to come—Katie. . . ."

She walked slowly into the building, and was at once received by that friendly, confused smell of hams and medicines which is the Stores' note of welcome. Lights shone, warmth eddied in little gusts of hot air from corner to corner: there was much conversation, but all of a very decent kind: ladies, not very grand ones and not very poor ones, but comfortable, motherly, housekeeping ladies were everywhere to be seen.

No wonder, surely, that Mrs. Trenchard loved the Stores! Here was everything gathered in from the ends of the earth that was solid and sound and real. Here were no extravagances, no decadencies, no flowing creations with fair outsides and no heart to them, nothing foreign nor degenerate. However foreign an article might be before it entered the Stores, once inside those walls it adopted itself at once to the claims of a Cathedral City—even the Eastern carpets, stained though their past lives might be with memories of the Harem, recognised that their future lay along the floor of a Bishop's study, a Major's drawing-room or the dining-room of a country rectory. If ever Mrs. Trenchard was alarmed by memories of foreign influences, of German invasions, or Armenian atrocities, she had only to come to the Stores to be entirely reassured. It would be better for our unbalanced and hysterical alarmists did they visit the Stores more frequently. . . .

But frequent visits had bred in Mrs. Trenchard a yet warmer intimacy. Although she had never put her feeling into words, she was determined now that the Stores was maintained solely in the Trenchard and Faunder interests. So pleasant and personally submissive had the young men and young women of the place been to her all these years, that she now regarded them with very nearly the personal benevolence that she bestowed upon her own Rebekah, Rocket, Jacob and so on. She felt that only Trenchards and Faunders could have produced an organisation whose spirit was so entirely sprung from their own views and observances. She did not defend or extol those views. There simply they were! and out of them the Stores were born. She paid her call here, therefore, rather as a Patroness visits a Hospital in which she is interested—with no conceit or false pride, but with a maternal anxiety that everything should be well and prosperous. Everything always was well and prosperous. . . . She was a happy Patroness!

"That's a splendid ham!" were invariably her first words, and "I do like the way they arrange things here," her second. She could have wandered, very happily, all day from compartment to compartment, stopping continually to observe, to touch, to smile, to blow her nose (being moved, very often, quite emotionally) to beam happily upon the customers and then to turn, with a little smile of intimacy, to the young men in frock coats and shiny hair, as though she would say: "We've got a good crowd to-day. Everyone seems comfortable . . . but how can they help it when everything is so beautifully done?"

Her chief pride and happiness found its ultimate crown in the furniture department. Here, hung as it was somewhere up aloft, with dark bewildering passages starting into infinity on every side of it, was the place that her soul truly loved. She could gaze all day upon those sofas and chairs. Those wonderful leather couches of dark red and dark blue, so solid, so stern in their unrelenting opposition to flighty half-and-half, so self-supporting and self-satisfying, so assured of propriety and comfort and solid value for your money. She would sink slowly into a huge leather armchair, and from her throne smile upon the kind gentleman who washed his hands in front of her.

"And how much is this one?"

"Nine pounds, eight and sixpence, ma'am."

"Really. Nine pounds, eight and sixpence. It's a splendid chair."

"It is indeed, ma'am. We've sold more than two dozen of this same article in this last fortnight. A great demand just now."

"And so there ought to be—more than two dozen! Well, I'm not surprised—an excellent chair."

"Perhaps we can send it for you? Or you prefer— ?"

"No, thank you. Not to-day. But I must say that it's wonderful for the money. That sofa over there—"

Up here, in this world of solid furniture, it seemed that England was indeed a country to be proud of! Mrs. Trenchard would have made no mean Britannia, seated in one of the Stores' arm-chairs with a Stores' curtain-rod for her trident!

Upon this January afternoon she found her way to the furniture department more swiftly than was usual with her. The Stores seemed remote from her to-day. As she passed the hams, the chickens, the medicines and powders, the petticoats and ribbons and gloves, the books and the stationery, the cut-glass and the ironware, the fancy pots, the brass, the Chinese lanterns, the toys, the pianos and the gramophones, the carpets and the silver, the clocks and the pictures, she could only be dimly aware that to-day these things were not for her, that all the treasures of the earth might be laid at her feet and she would not care for them, that all the young men and young women in England might bow and smile before her and she would have no interest nor pleasure in them. She reached the furniture department. She sank down in the red-leather arm-chair. She said, with a little sigh:

"She has never forgotten before!"

This was, considering her surroundings and the moment of its expression, the most poignant utterance of her life.

Millie's chief emotion, until this moment, had been one of intense boredom. The Stores seemed to her, after Paris, an impossible anachronism; she could not understand why it was not instantly burnt up and destroyed, and all its solemn absurdities cast, in dirt and ashes, to the winds.

She followed her mother with irritation, and glances of cynical contempt were flung by her upon the innocent ladies who were buying and chatting and laughing together. Then she remembered that her mother was in trouble, and she was bowed down with self-accusation for a hard heartless girl who thought of no one but herself. Her moods always thus followed swiftly one upon another.

When, in the furniture department, she heard that forlorn exclamation she wanted to take her mother's hand, but was shy and embarrassed.

"I expect Katie *had* to go with Philip. . . . Something she *had* to do, and perhaps it only kept her a moment or two and she got back just after we'd left. We didn't wait long enough for her. She's been waiting there, I expect, all this time for us."

Mrs. Trenchard's cheek flushed and her eyes brightened.

"Why, Millie, that's most likely! We'll go back at once . . . that's most likely. . . . We'll go back at once."

"This is a very cheap article," said the young man, "or if Madame would prefer a chair with—"

"No, no," said Mrs. Trenchard quite impatiently. "Not to-day. Not to-day, thank you."

"There are the hot-water bottles," said Millie.

"Oh, of course. . . . I want some hot-water bottles. Ours leak . . . three of them. . . ."

"In the rubber department, Madam, first to the right, second to the left. . . ."

But Mrs. Trenchard hurried through the hot-water bottles in a manner utterly foreign to her.

"Thank you. I'm sure they're very nice. They won't leak, you say? How much? . . . Thank you . . . no, I prefer these. . . . If you're sure they won't leak. . . . Yes, my number is 2157. . . . Thank you."

Outside in Victoria Street she said: "I might have given her until quarter to four. I daresay she's been waiting all this time."

But Millie for the first time in all their days together was angry with Katherine. She said to herself: "She's going to forget us all like this now. We aren't, any of us, going to count for anything. Six months ago she would have died rather than hurt mother. . . ."

And behind her anger with Katherine was anger with herself because she seemed so far away from her mother, because she was at a loss as to the right thing to do, because she had said that she had seen Philip with Katherine. "You silly idiot!" she thought to herself. "Why couldn't you have kept your mouth shut?"

Mrs. Trenchard spoke no word all the way home.

Katherine was not in the house when they returned. Millie went upstairs, Mrs. Trenchard stared at the desolate drawing-room. The fire was dead, and the room, in spite of its electric light, heavy and dark. Mrs. Trenchard looked at the reflection of her face in the mirror; with both hands she pushed her hat a little, then, with a sudden gesture, took it off, drawing out the pins slowly and staring at it again. Mrs. Trenchard glanced at the clock, and then slowly went out, holding her hat in her hand, advancing with that trailing, half-sleepy movement that was peculiarly hers.

She did then what she had not done for many years: she went to her husband's study. This hour before tea he always insisted was absolutely his own: no one, on any pretext, was ever to disturb him. To-day, cosily, with a luxurious sense that the whole world had been made for him, and made for him exactly as he liked it, he was, with a lazy pencil, half-writing, half-thinking, making little notes for an essay on William Hazlitt.

As his wife entered he was reading: "How fine it is to enter some old town, walled and turreted, just at the approach of nightfall, or to come to some straggling village, with the lights streaming through the surrounding gloom; and then, after enquiring for the best entertainment the place affords, to take one's ease at one's inn! These eventful moments in our lives' history are too precious, too full of solid, heartfelt happiness to be frittered and dribbled away in imperfect sympathy. I would have them all to myself, and drain them to the last drop."

How thoroughly George Trenchard agreed with that. How lucky for him that he was able to defend himself from so much of that same "imperfect sympathy". Not that he did not love his fellow-creatures, far from it, but it was pleasant to be able to protect oneself from their too constant, their too eager ravages. Had he been born in his beloved Period, then he fancied that he might, like magnificent Sir Walter, have built his Castle and entertained all the world, but in this age of telephones and motorcars one was absolutely compelled. . . . He turned Hazlitt's words over on his tongue with a little happy sigh of regret, and then was conscious that his wife was standing by the door.

"Hullo!" he cried, starting up. "Is anything the matter?"

It was so unusual for her to be there that he stared at her large, heavy figure as though she had been a stranger. Then he jumped up, laughing, and the dark blue Hazlitt fell on to the carpet.

"Well, my dear," he said, "tea-time?"

She came trailing across the room, and stood beside him near the fire.

"No . . ." she said, "not yet . . . George. . . . You look very cosy here," she suddenly added.

"I am," he answered. He looked down at the Hazlitt, and her eyes followed his glance. "What have you been doing?"

"I've been to the Stores."

"Why, of course," he said, chaffing her. "You live there. And what have you been buying this time?"

"Hot-water bottles."

"Well, *that's* exciting!"

"Ours leaked. . . . Two of them, and we'd had them a very short time. I took Millie with me!"

"Very good for her. Clear some of her Parisian fancies."

There was a pause then, and he bent forward as though he would pick up the book, but he pulled himself up again.

"Katherine's been out with Philip all the afternoon."

He smiled one of his radiant, boyish smiles.

"She's happy, isn't she? It does one good to see her. She deserves it too if anyone in this world does. I like him—more and more. He's seen the world, and has got a head on his shoulders. And he isn't conceited, not in the least. He's charming to her, and I think he'll make her a very good husband. That was a lucky thing for us his coming along, because Katherine was sure to marry someone, and she might have set her heart on an awful fellow. You never know in these days."

"Ah! I don't think so," said Mrs. Trenchard, nervously turning her hat over in her hands, "that wouldn't be like Katie at all."

"No, well, perhaps it wouldn't," said George cheerfully. There was another pause, and now he bent right down, picked up the book, grunting a little, then stood, turning over the pages.

"I'm getting fat," he said, "good for all of us when we get down to Garth."

"George . . ." she began and stopped.

"Well, my dear." He put his hand on her shoulder, and then as though embarrassed by the unexpected intimacy that his action produced, withdrew it.

"Don't you think we might go out to the theatre one evening—theatre or something?"

"What! With the children? Family party! Splendid idea!"

"No, I didn't mean with the children—exactly. Just you and I alone. Dine somewhere—have an evening together."

It was no use to pretend that he was not surprised. She saw his astonishment.

"Why, of course—if you'd really care about it. Mostly pantomimes just now—but I daresay we could find something. Good idea. Good idea."

"Now that—now that—the children are beginning to

marry and go off by themselves. Why, I thought . . . you understand. . . ."

"Of course. Of course," he said again. "Any night you like. You remind me. . . ."

He whistled a gay little tune, and turned over the pages of the Hazlitt, reading sentences here and there.

"Tea in a minute? . . ." he said gaily. "Just got a line or two more to finish. Then I'll be with you."

She looked at him as though she would say something more: she decided, however, that she would not, and trailed away.

Returning to the drawing-room, she found Katherine standing there. Katherine's cheeks were flushed and her eyes sparkled: she was wearing a little black hat with red berries, and the black velvet ribbon round her neck had a diamond brooch in it that Philip had given her. Rocket was bending over the fire: she was laughing at him. When she saw her mother she waved her hand.

"Mother, darling—what kind of an afternoon have you had? I've had the loveliest time. I lunched at Rachel's, and there, to my immense surprise, was Philip. I hadn't the *least* idea he was coming. Not the slightest. We weren't to have met to-day at all. Just Lord John, Philip, Rachel and I. Then we had *such* a walk. Philip and I. Hyde Park Corner, right through the Park, Marble Arch, then through Regent's Park all the way up Primrose Hill—took a 'bus home again. *Never* enjoyed anything so much. You've all been out too, because here's the fire dead. I've been telling Rocket what I think of him. Haven't I, Rocket? . . . Where are the others? Millie, Aunt Aggie. It's tea-time."

"Yes, dear, it is," said Mrs. Trenchard.

It was incredible, Katherine was utterly unconscious. She remembered nothing.

Mrs. Trenchard looked at Rocket.

"That'll do, Rocket. That's enough. We'll have tea at once."

Rocket went out. She turned to her daughter.

"I'm glad you've enjoyed your afternoon, dear. I couldn't think what had happened to you. I waited until half-past three."

"Waited?"

"Yes—to go to the Stores. You said at breakfast that you'd come with me—that you'd be back by three. I waited until half-past. . . . It was quite all right, dear. Millie went with me. She had seen you—you and Philip at Hyde Park Corner—so, of course, I didn't wait any longer."

Katherine stared at her mother: the colour slowly left her face and her hand went up to her cheeks with a gesture of dismay.

"Mother! . . . How *could* I!"

"It didn't matter, dear, in the slightest . . . dear me, no. We went, Millie and I, and got the hot-water bottles, very good and strong ones, I think, although they said they couldn't positively guarantee them. You never can tell, apparently, with a hot-water bottle."

Katherine's eyes, now, were wide and staring with distress.

"How *could* I possibly have forgotten? It was talking about it at breakfast when Aunt Aggie too was talking about something, and I got confused, I suppose. No, I haven't any excuse at all. It was seeing Philip unexpectedly. . . ."

She stopped abruptly, realising that she had said the worst thing possible.

"You mustn't let Philip, dear, drive everything out of your head," Mrs. Trenchard said, laughing. "We have some claim on you until you are married—then, of course. . . ."

The colour mounted again into Katherine's face.

"No, mother, you mustn't say that," she answered in a low voice, as though she was talking to herself. "Philip makes *no* difference—none at all. I'd have forgotten in any case, I'm afraid, because we talked about it at breakfast when I was thinking about Aunt Aggie. It was nothing to do with Philip—it was my fault absolutely. I'll never forgive myself."

All the joy had left her eyes. She was very grave: she knew that, slight as the whole incident was, it marked a real crisis in her relations, not only with her mother, but with the whole house. Perhaps during all these weeks, she had forgotten them all, and they had noticed it and been hurt by it. She accused herself so bitterly that it seemed that nothing could be bad enough for her. She felt that, in the future, she could not show her mother enough attention and affection. But now, at this moment, there was nothing to be done. Millie would have laughed, hugged her mother and forgotten in five minutes that there had been any crime. But, in this, Katherine's character resembled, exactly, her mother's.

"Really, Katie, it didn't matter. I'm glad you liked the walk. And now it's tea-time. It always seems to be tea-time. There's so much to do."

They were then, both of them, conscious that Aunt Aggie had come in and was smiling at them. They wished intensely to fling into the pause some conversation that would be trivial and unimportant. They could think of nothing to say. . . .

"Why, Katherine," said Aunt Aggie, "where *have* you been? Millie says she's been to the Stores. . . . You said at breakfast . . ."

"I was kept . . ." said Katherine sharply, and left the room.

"I'll be down in five minutes, Aggie," said Mrs. Trenchard. "Tea time—"

Her sister watched her as she went out, carrying her hat in her hand. Half-way upstairs she saw Henry, who was half-tumbling, half-sliding from step to step: he was evidently hurrying, in his confused way, to do something that he had forgotten to do or to finish some task that he should long ago have completed.

"Henry," she said, "I wonder whether—"

"Right, mother," he called back to her. "I must—" the rest of his sentence was swallowed by distance. She turned and looked after him, then walked through the long passages to her room. She entered it, closed the door, and stood by her dressing-room staring in front of her. There was complete, intense silence here, and all the things lay about the room, as though waiting for her to address them.

"George, Millie, Henry, Katherine . . . Millie didn't want to go . . . Katherine. . . ."

On her table was a list of articles, the week's washing—her own list.

Handkerchiefs—12.

Stockings—8 pairs.

She looked at it without seeing it, then with a sudden, vindictive, passionate movement tore it in half, and then those halves into smaller pieces, tore the smaller pieces into little shreds of paper that fluttered in the air and then fell on to the floor at her feet.

CHAPTER III

LIFE AND HENRY

PHILIP was entirely happy during the first days of his engagement—so happy that he assured himself that he had never before known what happiness was. When, however, this glorious state had continued for four or five weeks he was aware that that most sensitive and unreliable of his spiritual possessions, his conscience, was being attacked. He was aware that there was something that he ought to do, something that he did not want to do—he was aware that he must tell Katherine about Anna and his life with her. Now when he had said to Mr. Trenchard that his life was free of all complications and that there was nothing in it that need be hidden from the world, he was, quite honestly, convinced that that was so. His life with Anna was entirely at an end: he had done her no wrong, she owed him no grudge, he did not know that he had ever taken any especial pains in Moscow to hide his relations with her, and he did not believe that any-one there thought the worse of him for them. He had come to England with that chapter closed, eager to begin another. His only thought of Anna when he had proposed to Katherine was that this was exactly what she had intended him to do —that she would be pleased if she knew. His conscience was always at rest when he thought that everyone liked him. . . .

Now he knew, quite definitely, after a month of his engagement to Katherine, that some of the members of the Trenchard family did not like him—No amount of *his* determination to like *them* could blind him to the truth of this unpleasant fact—Mrs. Trenchard did not like him, Aunt

Aggie did not like him, probably Mr. Trenchard, senior, and Great-Aunt Sarah did not like him (he could not tell, because they were so silent), and he was not sure whether Henry liked him or not. Therefore, in front of this alarming array of critics his conscience awoke.

The other force that stirred his conscience was Katherine's belief in him. In Moscow no one had believed in anyone— anyone there, proved to be faultless, would have been, for that very reason, unpopular. Anna herself had held the most humorous opinion of him. (She liked Englishmen, respected their restraint and silence, but always laughed at their care for appearances.) Although he had known that his love for Katherine had sprung partly from his sense of her difference from Anna, he, nevertheless, had expected the qualities that had pleased him in the one to continue in the other. He discovered that Katherine trusted him utterly, that she believed, with absolute confidence, in every word that fell from his lips, and he knew that, if the old whole world came to her and told her that he had had for several years a mistress in Moscow and he denied it to her, that she would laugh at the world. This knowledge made him extremely uncomfortable. First, he tried to persuade himself that he had never had a mistress, that Anna had never existed, then, when that miserably failed, he told himself that he could always deny it if she asked him, then he knew that he loved her so much that he would not lie to her (this discovery pleased him). He must, he finally knew, tell her himself. . . . He told himself that he would wait a little until she believed in him less completely; he must prepare her mind. He did not even now, however, consider that she would feel his confession very deeply; Anna would simply have laughed at his scruples.

Meanwhile he loved her so deeply and so completely that Anna's figure was a ghost, dimly recalled from some other life. He had almost forgotten her appearance. She had a little black mole on her left cheek—or was it her right? . . .

Somewhere in the beginning of February he decided that he would cultivate Henry, not because he liked Henry, but because he thought that Katherine would like it—also, although this he did not confess to himself, because Henry was so strange and unexpected that he was half afraid of him.

Of course Henry ought to be sent to one of the Universities, it was absurd to keep a great, hulking boy of nineteen hanging about, wasting his own time and the time of his family, suffering no discipline and learning nothing of any value. George Trenchard had told Philip that Henry was too young for Oxford, and was to have a year of "seeing the world" before he "went up". A fine lot of seeing the world Henry was doing, slouching about the house, reading novels and sulking! Philip, in spite of his years in Russia, felt very strongly that every Englishman should be shaven clean and wear clothes from a good tailor. About men of other nationalities it did not matter, but smartness was expected from an Englishman. Henry, however, was in that unpleasant condition known as "sprouting." He had a little down on one cheek, apparently none on the other; in certain lights his chin boasted a few hairs of a forlorn and desolate appearance, in other lights you would swear that there were none. His forehead often broke into pimples (these were a terrible agony to him).

"Why can't he do something with his hair?" thought Philip, "brush it and have it cut regularly. Why is it that awful dusty colour? He might at least do something to his clothes. Mrs. Trenchard ought to see to it."

Mrs. Trenchard did try to "see to it". She was perpetually buying new clothes for Henry; she took him to her husband's tailor and dragged him, again and again, to have things "tried on". Henry, however, possessed the art of reducing any suit, within twenty-four hours of his first wearing it, to chaos. He was puzzled himself to know what he did.

"But, Henry, it was new last week!"

"*I* know. How can I help it? I haven't done anything to the beastly thing. It simply came like that."

He affected a lofty indifference to clothes, but Philip, who saw him look frequently into the looking-glass, suspected the sincerity of this. Katherine said to Philip:

"You have so much influence on Henry. Do talk to him about his clothes and other things. He won't mind it from you. He gets so angry if we say anything."

Philip was not at all sure that Henry would "not mind it from him". When they were alone Henry would listen with the greatest interest to the things that Philip told him; his eyes would soften, his mouth would smile, his voice would quiver with his excitement. Then, quite suddenly, his face would cloud, he would blush and frown, almost scowl, then, abruptly, with some half-muttered word, fall into a sulky silence. Once he had broken in to Philip's information with: "Oh! I suppose you think I don't know anything about it, that I'm a stupid idiot. . . . Well, if I am, what do you bother to talk to me for?"

This, of course, annoyed Philip, who always liked to feel, after a conversation with anyone, that "everything had gone off all right". Had it not been for Katherine, he would not have bothered with the fellow. Another thing puzzled and even alarmed Philip. Henry would often, when he thought that he was unwatched, stare at Philip in a perplexed brooding fashion with a look in his eye that said: "I'll find out one day all right. You think that no one's watching you, that I'm not worth anyone's trouble. . . . You wait and see."

Henry would look at Philip's buttons, studs, tie, handkerchief with this same puzzled stare. It was another side of that surveillance of which Philip had been conscious ever since Tim Flaunder's visit to his rooms. "Ah!" thought Philip, "once I'm married, they can watch as much as they like. . . . A year's a long time though."

He decided then to cultivate Henry and to know the boy better. "I'll show him that there's nothing in me to be suspicious about—that I'm worthy of marrying his sister. I'll make a friend of him."

He asked George Trenchard whether he might give Henry an evening. "Take him out to dinner and a music-hall. I'll look after him."

Trenchard said:

"My dear fellow, if you can make Henry look something like an ordinary civilised being we'll all be in your debt for ever. I don't envy you your job . . . but, of course, do what you like with him."

When Philip told Mrs. Trenchard she said:

"How nice for Henry! How kind of you to bother with the boy! He goes out so little. How nice for Henry!"

When Philip asked Henry himself, Henry coloured crimson, looked at his boots, muttered something about shirts, stammered "Thanks . . . very glad . . . awful bore for you", and finally stumbled from the room.

Philip thought Jules for dinner, The Empire, The Carlton for supper. Katherine's delight when he told her compensated him for all the effort of the undertaking.

To understand Henry's emotion at Philip's invitation would be to understand everything about Henry, and that no one has ever done. His chief sensation was one of delight and excitement—this he hid from all the world. He had waited, during more years than he could remember, for the arrival of that moment when he would be treated as a man. Lately he had said to himself, "If they're all going to laugh at me always, I'll show them one day soon." He had a ferocious disgust at their lack of penetration. He had, from the very first, admired Philip's appearance. Here was a man still young, with perfect clothes, perfect ability to get in and out of a room easily, perfect tranquillity in conversation. He had been offended at Philip's treatment of Seymour, but even that had been a bold, daring thing to do, and Henry was forced to admit that he had been, since that episode, himself sometimes doubtful of Seymour's ability. Then Philip in his conversation had shown such knowledge of the world; Henry could listen all day to his talk about Russia. To be able to travel so easily from one country to the other, without fear or hesitation, that was, indeed, wonderful!

Afterwards had occurred one of the critical moments in Henry's career; his passionate memory of that afternoon when he had seen the embrace of Katherine and Philip, changed those two into miraculous beings, apart from all the world. He heard Philip for the audacity of it, he also admired him, envied him, speculated endlessly about it. "Ah! if somebody would love me like that", he thought. "I'd be just as fine. They think me a baby, not fit even to go to college, I could—I could . . ." He did not know what it was that he could do. Perhaps Philip would help him.

And yet he did not really like Philip. He thought that Philip laughed at him, despised him. His one continual fear was lest Philip should teach Katherine, Henry's adored and worshipped Katherine, also to despise him. "If he were to do that I'd kill him", he thought. He believed utterly in Katherine's loyalty, "but she loves Philip so now. It's changed her. She'll never belong to us properly again." Always his first thought was: "So long as he's good to her and makes her happy nothing matters."

Now it seemed that Philip *was* making her happy. Katherine's happiness lit, with its glow, the house, the family, all the world. When, therefore, Philip asked Henry to dine with him, the great moment of Henry's life seemed to have come, and to have come from a source honourable enough for Henry to accept it.

"If only I dare," Henry thought, "there are so many things that I should like to ask him." The remembered passion of that kiss told Henry that there could be nothing that Philip did not know. He was in a ferment of excitement and expectation. To the family he said:

"I'm afraid I shan't be in, Tuesday evening. Sorry, but

Philip and I are dining together. Expect I'll be in, Wednesday, though."

It is a fact, strange but true, that Henry had never entered one of the bigger London restaurants. The Trenchards were not among those more modern parents who spend their lives in restaurants and take their infant sons in Eton jackets to supper at the Savoy after the Drury Lane pantomime. Moreover, no one ever thought of taking Henry anywhere. He had been at school until a few months ago, and when, in the holidays, he had gone to children's parties he had always behaved badly. George Trenchard went very seldom into restaurants, and often, for days together, forgot that he had a son at all. Down in Glebeshire Henry was allowed to roam as he pleased; even in London no restrictions were placed on his movements. So long as he went to the Abbey twice on Sunday he could do what he liked. A friend of Seymour's had put him up as a member of a club in a little street off St. James: the entrance was only a guinea, and "anyone could be a member". Henry had, three months ago, received a book of club rules, a list of members, and a printed letter informing him that he was now elected, must pay five guineas entrance and a guinea subscription. He had extorted the money from his father, and, for twenty-four hours, was the proudest and happiest human being in London. He had never, alas! dared to venture inside the building. Seymour's friend had forgotten him. The Club had remained strangely ignorant of his existence. On three occasions he had started out, and on three occasions his fears had been too strong for him. Once he had arrived at the very club door, but a stout gentleman, emerging and staring at him haughtily, had driven the blood from his heart. He had hurried home, feeling that he had been personally insulted. He found, on his return, that some vehicle had splashed mud on to his cheek. "There! you see what happens! . . ."

He was not far from tears.

He had, behind his unhappy experiences, the resolved certainty that he was marked apart by destiny for some extraordinary future: his very misfortunes seemed to prove this. He had bought for himself a second-hand copy of that romance to which I have made earlier allusion. It exercised, at this time, an extraordinary influence upon him, and in the hero's fight against an overwhelming fate he saw his own history, even when the circumstance was as trivial as his search for a stud under the washing-stand. So young was he, so crude, so sentimental, impulsive, suspicious, self-confident, and lacking in self-confidence, loyal, ambitious, modest and conceited that it was not strange that Philip did not understand him.

On the evening of his dinner with Philip he dressed with the utmost care. There were three dress-shirts in his drawer, and it was, of course, fate that decided that there should be something the matter with all of them—one of them had been worn once already, one was frayed at the cuffs, one had a cracked and gaping stud hole. He pared the frayed cuffs with his scissors, and hoped for the best. He then produced the only valuable article in his possession, a pearl stud given to him by his Uncle Bob on his last birthday. He was greatly afraid of this stud, because the head of it screwed into the body of it, and he was never sure whether he had screwed it sufficiently. Suppose it were to leap into the soup! Suppose it were to fall off and he not see it and lose it! Such catastrophes were only too probable where he was concerned. He screwed it in so vigorously to-night that he made a grey mark round the stud-hole. He dabbed this with a sponge, and the grey mark was greyer. His father had told him that he must never wear a "made-up" evening tie, but he had not told him how to tie one that was not made-up, and Henry had been too timid to enquire. To-night, by a sudden twist of genius, he produced something that really seemed satisfactory; one end was longer

than the other, but his father approved of a little disorder
—when the tie was too neat it was almost "made-up".
Henry's dress-clothes, lying there upon the bed, seemed a
little faded. The trousers glistered in the electric light, and
the tails of the coat were sadly crumpled. But when they
were on his body Henry gazed at them with pleasure. One
trouser leg seemed oddly longer than the other, and his shirt
cuff had disappeared altogether, but the grey mark round the
stud was scarcely visible, and his collar was beautifully clean.

His face was red and shining, his hair was plastered
down with water; it was a pity that there were three red
pimples on his forehead, but there had been four yesterday.
His ears, too, were dreadfully red, but that was from excitement.

He had an opera hat and a black greatcoat with a velvet
collar, so that he felt very smart indeed as he slipped out
of the house. He was glad that he had escaped the family,
although he fancied that Aunt Aggie watched him from the
top of the stairs. He would have liked to have seen Katherine for a moment, and had he spoken his heart out, he
would have assured her that, for her sake, he would do his
best to love Philip. It was for her sake, after all, that he
had dressed so carefully, for her sake that he wanted to be
a fine figure in the world. If he *had* seen her, all that he
would have said would have been: "So long, Katherine.
Dining with Philip, you know. See you in the morning. . . ."

He rode on an omnibus from Whitehall to Piccadilly Cir-
cus, and walked then to Jules'. The clocks were striking half-
past seven, the appointed hour, as he entered. A stout man
like an emperor insisted on disrobing him of his greatcoat,
and he felt suddenly naked. He peeped into the room, which
was very empty, and all the waiters, like figures in Mme.
Tussaud's, stared at him together. He was sure that his tie
had mounted above his collar; he put up his hand, found that
this was so, and thought that the emperor was laughing at

him. He bent down to tie his shoe, and then, just as a large
party entered the restaurant, there was a little pop, and the
head of his pearl stud was gone. He was on his knees in a
second.

"Beg pardon, sir," said the Emperor. "Allow me."

"No," said Henry, whose face was purple, whose heart
was beating like a hammer, and through whose chasm in his
shirt a little wind was blowing against his vest.

"It's my stud. I can—I beg your—Oh, there—No, it
isn't—"

He was conscious of towering forms above him, of a lady's
black silk stockings, of someone saying: "Why, dammit";
of a sudden vision of the pearl and a large masculine boot
thundering towards it.

From his position on the floor he cried in agony: "Oh,
do look out, you're stepping on it! . . . I say . . . Please!"

He heard a sharp little cry, then, just as he seized it,
Philip's voice:

"Why, Henry!"

He staggered up from his knees, which were white with
dust: his purple face, his disordered hair, a piece of pink
vest that protruded from his shirt made an unusual picture.
Someone began to laugh.

"I say," said Philip quickly, "come in here." He led the
way into the lavatory. "Now, what's the matter?"

Henry stared at him. Why couldn't the silly fool see?

"It's my stud . . . the head came off . . . might have
happened to anyone."

"That's all right," said Philip cheerfully. "Got it now?
That's good. Look here, I'll screw it in for you."

"The other piece . . ." said Henry, who was near tears
. . . "It's slipped down—inside."

"I'm afraid you'll have to take your trousers off," said
Philip gravely. "Just let 'em down. It's all right. There's
no one here who matters."

Henry undressed. A smart man with hair like a looking-glass came in, stared and went out again. Two attendants watched sympathetically. After some time the stud was arranged, and Henry was dressed again.

"You'd better just let me tie your tie," said Philip. "It's so difficult in here. One can't see to do it oneself."

Henry said nothing. He brushed his hair again, suffered himself to be dusted and patted by the attendant, and followed Philip into the restaurant. He was so miserable that suicide was the only alternative to a disgraced and dishonoured life. He was sure that everyone in the restaurant was laughing at him; the grave waiter who brought him his soup, the fat, round button of a waiter who brought the champagne in a bucket of ice, the party opposite, two men and two women (beasts!), all these were laughing at him! His forehead was burning, his heart deadly cold. He glared at Philip, gulped down his food without knowing at all what it was that he was eating, said "yes" and "no"; never looked at Philip, but stared, fiercely, round him as though he were looking for someone.

Philip persisted, very bravely, in a succession of bright and interesting anecdotes, but at last he flagged. He was afraid that he had a terrible evening before him . . . never again. . . .

"He's thinking," said Henry to himself, "that I'm impossible. He's wondering what on earth he asked me for. Why did he if he didn't want to? Conceited ass . . . that about the stud might have happened to anyone. He'll tell Katherine. . . ."

"Coffee?" said Philip.

"No, thank you," said Henry.

"All right. We'll have it later. We'd better be getting on to the show. Ready?"

They moved away; they were in a cab; they were caught into the heart of some kaleidoscope. Lights flashed, men shouted, someone cried in a high treble. Lights flashed again, and they were sitting in the stalls at the "Empire" music-hall. Henry hailed the darkness with relief; he felt as though his body were bruised all over, and when he looked up and saw a stout man upside down on a tight-rope he thought to himself: "Well, he can't see me anyhow. . . . He doesn't know that the top of my stud came off."

There followed then a number of incredible people. (It must be remembered that he had never been to a music-hall before.) There was a man with two black eyes and a red nose who sang a song about the wives he had had (seven verses—one wife to every verse), there was a stout lady who sang about porter, and there were two small children who danced the Tango—finally a gentleman in evening dress and a large white button-hole who recited poems whilst his friends in the background arranged themselves in illustrative groups. In this strange world Henry's soul gradually found peace. It was a world, after all, in which it was not absurd to grope on one's knees for the top of one's stud—it was the natural and clever thing to do. When the lady who sang about the porter kissed her hand to the audience, Henry, clapping enthusiastically, felt a throb of sympathy. "I'm so glad she's been a success to-night," he thought to himself, as though she had been his cousin or his aunt. "She'll feel pleased." He wanted, by this time, everyone to be happy. . . . When, at the last, the fat man in evening clothes recited his tale of "the good old British Flag," and was surrounded instantly by a fluttering cloud of Union Jacks, Henry was very near to tears. "I'll make them send me to Oxford," he said to himself. "At once . . . I'll work like anything."

The lights went up—ten minutes' interval—whilst the band played tunes out of "Riogletta", and behind the curtain they prepared for that immensely popular ballet "The Pirate".

"Let's walk about a bit, shall we?" said Philip.

Henry, humbly, with a timid smile agreed. He tumbled over a lady as he passed out of his row, but he did not mind now, his eyes were shining and his head was up. He followed Philip, admiring his broad shoulders, the back of his head, his sturdy carriage and defiant movement of his body. He glared haughtily at young men lolling over the bar, and the young men glared back haughtily at him. He followed Philip upstairs, and they turned into the Promenade (Henry did not know that it was the Promenade). With his head in the air he stepped forward and plunged instantly into something that flung powder down his throat, a strange and acrid scent up his nose: his fingers scraped against silk.

"There! clumsy!" said a voice.

A lady wearing a large hat and (as it appeared to Henry) tissue of gold, smiled at him.

"It doesn't matter," she said, putting some fat fingers on his hand for a moment. "It doesn't, dear, really. Hot, isn't it?"

He was utterly at a loss, scarlet in the face, his eyes staring wildly. Philip had come to his rescue.

"Hot, it is," said Philip.

"What about a drink, dear?" said the lady.

"Not just now," said Philip, smiling at her as though he'd known her all his life. "Jolly good scrum up here, isn't there?"

"Everyone bangin' about so," said the lady. "What about a drink *now?* Rot waitin'."

"Sorry," said Philip. "Got an engagement. Very important—" The lady, however, had suddenly recognised an old friend. "Why, Charlie!" Henry heard her say: "Who ever . . ."

They sat down on a sofa near the bar and watched the group. Henry was thinking: "He spoke to her as though he had known her all his life. . . ." He was suddenly aware that he and his father and mother and aunts, yes, and Katherine too were babies compared with Philip. "Why, they don't know anything about him. Katherine doesn't know anything really. . . ." He watched the women who passed him: he watched their confidential whispers with gentlemen who al-

seemed to have red faces and bulging necks. He watched two
old men with their hats cocked to one side; they had faces
like dusty strawberries, and they wore white gloves and carried silver-topped canes. They didn't speak, and nothing
moved in their faces except their eyes. He watched a woman
who was angry and a man who was apologetic. He watched a
girl in a simple black dress who stood with grave, waiting
eyes. She suddenly smiled a welcome to someone, but the
smile was hard, practised, artificial, as though she had fastened it on like a mask. Philip belonged to these people;
he knew their ways, their talk, their etiquette, their tragedies
and comedies. Henry stared at him, at his gaze, rather un-
interested and tired. (Philip, at that moment, was thinking
of Katherine, of the bore that her young brother was: he was
remembering the last time that she had kissed him, of her
warm cheek against his, of a little laugh that she had given,
a laugh of sheer happiness, of trusting, confident delight.)
Henry sat there, frightened, thrilled, shocked, proud, indignant and terribly inquisitive. "I'm beginning to know about
life. Already I know more than they do at home."

Two boys who must have been younger than he passed him;
they were smart, shining, scornful. They had the derisive,
incurious gaze of old men, and also the self-assertive swagger
of very young ones. Henry, as he looked at them, knew that
he was a babe in arms compared with them; but it seemed
to him to-night that all his family was still in the cradle.
"Why, even father," he thought, "if you brought him here I
don't believe he'd know what to say or do."

They went downstairs, then found their seats, and the curtain rose on the ballet. The ballet was concerned with pirates
and Venice in the good Old Days. The first scene was on an
island in the Adriatic: there were any number of pirates and
ladies who loved them, and the sun slowly set and the dancers
on the golden sand sank, exhausted, at the feet of their lovers,
and the moon rose and the stars came out in a purple sky.
Then the Pirate Chief, an enormous Byronic figure with hair

jet black and tremendous eyebrows, explained through his hands, that there was a lady in Venice whom he loved, whom he must seize and convey to his island. Would his brave fellows follow him in his raid? His brave fellows would! One last dance and one last drink, then death and glory! The curtain came down upon figures whirling madly beneath the moon.

There followed then the Doge's Palace, a feast with much gold plate, aged senators with white beards, who watched the dancing with critical gaze, finally a lovely lady who danced mysteriously beneath many veils. She was, it appeared, a Princess, sought in marriage by the Doge, her heart, however, lost utterly to a noble Stranger whom she had once seen but never forgotten. The Doge, mad with love for her, orders her to be seized. She is carried off, wildly protesting, and the golden scene is filled with white dancers, then with fantastic masked figures, at last with dancers in black, who float like shadows through the mazes of the music.

The third scene is the Piazza. The country people have a holiday—drinking and dancing. Then enters a magnificent procession, the Doge leading his reluctant bride. Suddenly shouts are heard. It is the Pirates! A furious fight follows, the Pirates, headed by their chief, who wears a black mask, are, of course, victorious. The Princess is carried, screaming, to the Pirates' ship, treasure is looted, pretty village maidens are captured. The Pirates sail away. Last scene is the Island again. The ladies are expecting their heroes, the vessel is sighted, the Pirates land. There are dances of triumph, the spoil, golden goblets, rich tapestries, gleaming jewels are piled high, finally the captive lady Princess, who weeps bitterly, is led by the Chieftain, still masked, into the middle of the stage. She, upon her knees, begs for pity. He is stern (a fine melancholy figure). At last he removes the mask. Behold, it is the noble Stranger! With what rapture does she fall into his arms, with what dances are the triumphant Pirates made happy, upon what feasting does the sun again set. The moon rises and the stars appear. Finally, when the night-sky is sheeted with dazzling lights and the moon is orange-red, the Pirates and their ladies creep away. Only the Chieftain and his Princess, locked in one another's arms, are left. Someone, in the distance, pipes a little tune . . . the curtain descends.

Impossible to describe the effect that this had upon Henry. The nearest approach to its splendour in all his life before had been the Procession of Nations at the end of the Drury Lane pantomime, and, although he had found that very beautiful, he had nevertheless been disturbed by a certain sense of incongruity, Aladdin and his Princess having little to do with Canada and Australia represented, as those fine countries were, by two stout ladies of the Lane chorus. I think that this "Pirate" ballet may be said to be the Third Crisis in this critical development of Henry, the first being the novel about the Forest, the second his vision of Katherine and Philip.

It will be, perhaps, remembered that at Jules' restaurant Henry had drunk champagne and, because of his misery and confusion there, had had no consciousness of flavour, quantity or consequences. It was certainly the champagne that lent "The Pirate" an added colour and splendour.

As the boy followed Philip into Leicester Square he felt that any achievement would be now possible to him, any summit was to be climbed by him. The lights of Leicester Square circled him with fire—at the flame's heart were dark trees soft and mysterious against the night sky—beneath these trees, guarded by the flame, the Pirate and the Princess slept.

It seemed to him that now he understood all the world, that he could be astonished and shocked by nothing, that every man, be he never so degraded, was his brother. . . . He was unaware that his tie was again above his collar and his shoe lace unfastened. He strode along, thinking to himself: "How glorious! . . . How splendid! . . . How glorious!"

Philip, too, although the Empire ballet had once been com-

monplace enough, although, moreover, he had come so little
a time ago from the country where the ballet was in all the
world supreme, had been plunged by the Pirate into a most
sentimental attitude of mind. He was to-night terribly in love
with Katherine, and, when the lights had been turned down
and the easy, trifling music had floated out to him, caught
him, soothed and whispered to him, he had held Katherine
in his arms, her cheek touching his, her heart beating with
his, his hand against her hair.

Her confidence in him that, at other times, frightened him,
to-night thrilled him with a delicious pleasure. His old distrust of himself yielded, to-night, to a fine, determined assurance. "I will be all that she thinks I am. She shall see how
I love her. They shall all see."

"I think we'll go down into the Grill Room," said Philip,
when they arrived at the Carlton. "We can talk better
there."

It was all the same to Henry, who was busy feasting with
the Pirate upon the Adriatic Island, with the Princess dancing for them on the golden sand. They found a quiet little
table in that corner which is one of the pleasantest places in
London, so retired from the world are you and yet so easy is
it to see all that goes on amongst your friends, enemies and
neighbours.

"Oysters? . . . Must have oysters, Henry. . . . Then
grilled bones . . . then we'll see. Whisky and soda—split
soda, waiter, please. . . ."

Henry had never eaten oysters before, and he would have
drunk his whisky with them had Philip not stopped him.
"Never drink whisky with oysters—you'd die—you would
really."

Henry did not like oysters very much, but he would have
suffered the worst kind of torture rather than say so. The
bones came, and the whisky with them. Henry drank his
first glass very quickly in order to show that he was quite used
to it. He thought, as he looked across the table, that Philip

was the finest fellow in the world; no one had ever been so
kind to him as Philip—How could he ever have disliked
Philip? Philip was going to marry Katherine, and was the
only man in all the world who was worthy of her. Henry felt
a burning desire to confide in Philip, to tell him all his most
secret thoughts, his ambitions, his troubles. . . .

He drank his second glass of whisky, and began a long,
rather stumbling narration.

"You know, I shall never be able to tell you how grateful
I am to you for giving me such a ripping evening. All this
time . . . I've been very rude sometimes, I expect . . . you
must have thought me a dreadful ass, and I've wanted so
much to show you that I'm not."

"That's all right," said Philip, who was thinking of Katherine.

"No, it isn't all right," said Henry, striking the table with
his fist. "I must tell you, now that you've been so kind to
me. You see I'm shy really, I wouldn't like most people to
know that, but I am. I'm shy because I'm so unfortunate
about little things. You must have noticed long ago how
unlucky I am. Nothing ever goes right with me at home.
I'm always untidy and my clothes go to pieces and I break
things. People seem to think I want to . . ." His voice
was fierce for a moment.

"That's all right," said Philip again. "Have some more
bone."

"Yes, thank you," said Henry, staring darkly in front of
him. "I don't know why I'm so unfortunate, because I know
I *could* do things if I were given a chance, but no one will
ever let me try. What do they keep me at home for when
I ought to be at Oxford? Why don't they settle what I'm
going to be? It's quite time for them to make up their mind.
. . . It's a shame, a shame. . . ."

"So it is. So it is," said Philip. "But it will be all right
if you wait a bit."

"I'm always told I've got to wait," said Henry fiercely.

"What about other fellows? No one tells them to wait. . . . I'm nineteen, and there are plenty of men of nineteen I know who are doing all kinds of things. I can't even dress properly —soot and fluff always come and settle on *my* clothes rather than on anyone else's. I've often noticed it. Then people laugh at me for nothing. They don't laugh at other men."

"You oughtn't to care," said Philip.

"I try not to, but you can't help it if it happens often."

"What do you want to be?" said Philip. "What would you like to do?"

"I don't mind; anything," said Henry, "if only I did it properly. I'd rather be a waiter who didn't make a fool of himself than what I am. I'd like to be of use. I'd like to make people proud of me. I'd like Katherine—"

At that name he suddenly stopped and was silent.

"Well?" said Philip. "What about Katherine? . . . Have some more whisky. . . . Waiter, coffee."

"I want to do something," said Henry, "to make Katherine proud of me. I know it must be horrible for her to have a brother whom everyone laughs at. It's partly because of her that I'm so shy. But she understands me as none of the others do. She knows I've got something in me. She believes in me. She's the only one. . . . I can talk to her. She understands when I say that I want to do something in the world. *She* doesn't laugh. And I'd die for her. . . . Here, now, if it was necessary. And I'll tell you one thing. I didn't like you at first. When you got engaged to Katherine I hated it until I saw that she'd probably have to be engaged to someone, and it might as well be you."

"Thank you," said Philip, laughing.

"I saw how happy you made her. It's hard on all of us who've known her so long, but we don't mind that . . . if you *do* make her happy."

"So," said Philip, "it's only by the family's permission that I can keep her?"

"Oh, you know what I mean," said Henry. "Of course

she's her own mistress. She can do what she likes. But she *is* fond of us. And I don't think—if it came to it—that she'd ever do anything to hurt us."

"If it came to what?" said Philip.

But Henry shook his head. "Oh! I'm only talking. I meant that we're fonder of one another as a family than people outside can realise. We don't seem to be if you watch us, but if it came to pulling us apart—to—to—taking Katherine away, for instance, it—it wouldn't be easy."

"Another soda, waiter," said Philip. "But I don't want to take Katherine away. I don't want there to be any difference to anyone."

"There *must* be a difference," said Henry, shaking his head and looking very solemn. "If it had been Millie it mightn't have mattered so much, because she's been away a lot as it is, but with Katherine—you see, we've always thought that whatever misfortune happened, Katherine would be there—and now we can't think that any longer."

"But that," said Philip, who'd drunk quite a number of whiskies by this time, "was very selfish of you. You couldn't expect her never to marry."

"We never thought about it," said Henry. He spoke now rather confusedly and at random. "We aren't the sort of people who look ahead. I suppose we haven't got much imagination as a family. None of the Trenchards have. That's why we're fond of one another and can't imagine ever not being."

Philip leant forward. "Look here, Henry, I want us to be friends—real friends. I love Katherine so much that I would do anything for her. If she's happy you won't grudge her to me, will you? . . . I've felt a little that you, some of you, don't trust me, that you don't understand me. But I'm just what I seem: I'm not worthy of Katherine. I can't think why she cares for me, but, as she does, it's better, isn't it, that she should be happy? If you'd all help me, if you'd all be friends with me—"

He had for some minutes been conscious that there was something odd about Henry. He had been intent on his own thoughts, but behind them something had claimed his attention. Henry was now waving a hand in the air vaguely, he was looking at his half-empty glass with an intent and puzzled eye. Philip broke off in the middle of his sentence, arrested suddenly by this strangeness of Henry's eye, which was now fixed and staring, now red and wandering. He gazed at Henry, a swift, terrible suspicion striking him. Henry, with a face desperately solemn, gazed back at him. The boy then tried to speak, failed, and very slowly a large fat tear trembled down his cheek.

"I'm trying—I'm trying," he began. "I'll be your friend —always—I'll get up—stand—explain. . . . I'll make a speech," he suddenly added.

"Good Lord!" Philip realised with a dismay pricked with astonishment, "the fellow's drunk." It had happened so swiftly that it was as though Henry were acting a part. Five minutes earlier Henry had apparently been perfectly sober. He had drunk three whiskies and sodas. Philip had never imagined this catastrophe, and now his emotions were a confused mixture of alarm, annoyance, impatience and disgust at his own imperception.

Whatever Henry had been five minutes ago, there was no sort of question about him now.

"Someone's taken off my—b-boots," he confided very confidentially to Philip. "Who—did?"

The one clear thought in Philip's brain was that he must get Henry home quietly—from the Carlton table to Henry's bed, and with as little noise as possible. Only a few people now remained in the Grill Room. He summoned the waiter, paid the bill. Henry watched him.

"You must—tell them—about my boots," he said. "It's absurd."

"It's all right," said Philip. "They've put them on again now. It's time for us to be moving." He was relieved to see that Henry rose at once and, holding for a moment on to the table, steadied himself. His face, very solemn and sad, with its large, mournful eyes and a lock of hair tumbling forward over his forehead, was both ridiculous and pathetic.

Philip took his arm.

"Come on," he said. "Time to go home."

Henry followed very meekly, allowed them to put on his coat, was led upstairs and into a "taxi."

Then he suddenly put his head between his hands and began to sob. He would say nothing, but only sobbed hopelessly.

"It's all right," said Philip, as though he were speaking to a child of five. "There's nothing to cry about. You'll be home in a moment." He was desperately annoyed at the misfortune. Why could he not have seen that Henry was drinking too much? But Henry had drunk so little. Then he had had champagne at dinner. He wasn't used to it. Philip cursed his own stupidity. Now if they made a noise on the way to Henry's room there might follow fatal consequences. If anyone should see them!

Henry's sobs had ceased: he seemed to be asleep. Philip shook his arm. "Look here! We must take care not to wake anyone. Here we are! Quietly now, and where's your key?"

"Wash key?" said Henry.

Philip had a horrible suspicion that Henry had forgotten his key. He searched. Ah! there it was in the waistcoat pocket.

Henry put his arms round Philip's neck.

"They've turned the roa' upside down," he whispered confidentially. "We mustn't lose each other."

They entered the dark hall. Philip with one arm round Henry's waist. Henry sat on the lowest step of the stairs.

"I'll shtay here to-night," he said. "It's shafer," and was instantly asleep. Philip lifted him, then with Henry's boots tapping the stairs at each step, they moved upwards. Henry was heavy, and at the top Philip had to pause for breath.

Suddenly the boy slipped from his arms and fell with a crash. The whole house re-echoed. Philip's heart stopped beating, and his only thought was, "Now I'm done. They'll all be here in a moment. They'll drive me away. Katherine will never speak to me again." A silence followed abysmally deep, only broken by some strange snore that came from the heart of the house (as though it were the house that was snoring) and the ticking of two clocks that, in their race against one another, whirred and chuckled.

Philip picked Henry up again and proceeded. He found the room, pushed open the door, closed it and switched on the light. He then undressed Henry, folding the clothes carefully, put upon him his pyjamas, laid him in bed and tucked him up. Henry, his eyes closed as though by death, snored heavily. . . .

Philip turned the light out, crept into the passage, listened, stole downstairs, let himself into the Square, where he stood for a moment, in the cold night air, the only living thing in a sleeping world, then hastened away.

"Thank Heaven," he thought, "we've escaped." He had *not* escaped. Aunt Aggie, a fantastic figure in a long blue dressing-gown, roused by Henry's fall, had watched, from her bedroom door, the whole affair. She waited until she had heard the hall-door close, then stole down and locked it, stole up again and disappeared silently into her room.

When Henry woke in the morning his headache was very different from any headache that he had ever endured before. His first thought was that he could never possibly get up, but would lie there all day. His second that, whatever he did, he must rouse suspicion in no one, his third that he really *had* been terribly drunk last night, and remembered nothing after his second whisky at the Carlton, his fourth that someone must have put him to bed last night, because his clothes were folded carefully, whereas it was his own custom always to fling them about the room. At this moment

Rocket (who always took upon himself the rousing of Henry) entered with hot water.

"Time to get up, sir," he said. "Breakfast-bell in twenty minutes. Bath quite ready."

Henry watched. "He'll suspect something when he sees those clothes," he thought. But Rocket, apparently, suspected nothing. Henry got up, had his bath and slowly dressed. His headache was quite horrible, being a cold headache with a heavy weight of pain on his skull and a taste in his mouth of mustard and bad eggs. He felt that he could not possibly disguise from the world that he was unwell. Looking in the glass he saw that his complexion was yellow and muddy, but then it was never, at any time, very splendid. He looked cross and sulky, but then that would not surprise anyone. He went downstairs and passed successfully through the ordeal: fortunately Aunt Aggie was in bed. Only Millie, laughing, said to him: "You don't look as though evenings with Philip suited you, Henry—"

(How he hated Millie when she teased him!)

"Well, I'm sure," said Mrs. Trenchard placidly, "there must be thunder about—thunder about. I always feel it in my back. George dear, do put that paper down, your tea's quite cold."

"Well," said George Trenchard, looking up from the 'Morning Post' and beaming upon everyone, "what did Philip do with you last night, Henry. Show you the town— eh?"

"We had a very pleasant evening, thank you, father," said Henry. "We went to the Empire."

"You came in very quietly. I didn't hear you. Did you hear him, Harriet?"

"No," said Mrs. Trenchard. "I do hope you locked the front door, Henry."

"Oh, yes, mother. That was all right," he said hurriedly.

"Well, dear, I'm very glad you had a pleasant evening. It was kind of Philip—very kind of Philip. Yes, that's

Aunt Aggie's tray, Katie dear. I should put a little more marmalade—and that bit of toast, the other's rather dry— yes, the other's rather dry. Poor Aggie says she had a disturbed night—slept very badly. I shouldn't wonder whether it's the thunder. I always know by my back. Thank you, Katie. Here's a letter from Rose Faunder, George, and she says, 'etc., etc.' "

After breakfast Henry escaped into the drawing-room; he sank into his favourite chair by the fire, which was burning with a cold and glassy splendour that showed that it had just been lit. The room was foggy, dim and chill, exactly suited to Henry, who, with his thin legs stretched out in front of him and his headache oppressing him with a reiterated emphasis as though it were some other person insisting on his attention, stared before him and tried to think.

He wanted to think everything out, but could consider nothing clearly. It was disgusting of him to have been drunk, but it was Philip's fault—that was his main conclusion. Looking back, everything seemed to be Philip's fault—even the disaster to himself. There was in Henry a strange puritanical, old-maidish strain, which, under the persuasion of the headache, was allowed full freedom. Philip's intimacy with those women, Philip's attitude to drink, to ballets, even to shirt studs, an attitude of indifference bred of long custom, seemed to Henry this morning sinister and most suspicious. Philip had probably been laughing at him all the evening, thought him a fool for getting drunk so easily (terrible idea this), would tell other people about his youth and inexperience. Thoughts like these floated through Henry's aching head, but he could not really catch them. Everything escaped him. He could only stare into the old mirror, with its reflection of green carpet and green wall-paper, and fancy that he was caught, held prisoner by it, condemned to remain inside it for ever, with an aching head and an irritated conscience.

He was ill, he was unhappy, and yet through it all ran the

thought: "You are a man now. You have received your freedom. You'll never be a boy again. . . ."

He was aroused from his thoughts by the sudden vision of Katherine, who was, he found, sitting on the elbow of his armchair with her hand on his shoulder.

"Hullo," he said, letting her take his hand. "I didn't hear you come in."

"I didn't know you were in here," she answered. "You were hidden by the chair. I was looking for you, though."

"Why?" said Henry, suspiciously.

"Oh, nothing—except that I wanted to hear about last night. Did you enjoy it?"

"Very much."

"Was Philip nice?"

"Very nice."

"What did you do?"

"Oh, we dined at Jules, went to the Empire, had supper at the Carlton, and came home." He looked at Katherine's eyes, felt that he was a surly brute and added: "The ballet was called 'The Pirate'. I thought it was fine, but it was the first one I'd seen—I don't think Philip cared much for it, but then he's seen so many in Moscow, where they go on all night and are perfectly splendid."

Katherine's hand pressed his shoulder a little, and he, in response, drew closer to her.

"I'm glad Philip was nice to you," she said, gazing into the fire. "I want you two to be great friends." There sprang then a new note into her voice, as though she were resolved to say something that had been in her mind a long time. "Henry—tell me—quite honestly, I want to know. Have I been a pig lately? A pig about everybody. Since I've been engaged have I neglected you all and been different to you all and hurt you all?"

"No," said Henry, slowly. "Of course you haven't . . . but it has been different a little—it couldn't help being."

"What has?"

"Well, of course, we don't mean so much to you now. How can we? I suppose what Philip said last night is true, that we've been all rather selfish about you, and now we're suffering for it."

"Did Philip say that?"

"Yes—or something like it."

"It isn't true. It simply shows that he doesn't understand what we all are to one another. I suppose we're different. I've been feeling, since I've been engaged, that we *must* be different. Philip is so continually surprised at the things we do."

Henry frowned. "He needn't be. There's nothing very wonderful in our all being fond of you."

She got up from the chair and began to walk up and down the room. Henry's eyes followed her.

"I don't know what it is," she said suddenly. "But during these last weeks it's as though you were all hiding something from me. Even you and Millie. Of course I know that Aunt Aggie hates Philip. She never *can* hide her feelings. But mother . . ." Katherine broke out. "Oh! it's all so silly! Why can't we all be natural? It's unfair to Philip. He's ready for anything, he wants to be one of us, and you, all of you—"

"It isn't quite fair," said Henry slowly, "to blame only us. We've all been very nice to Philip, I think. I know Aunt Betty and Millie and father like him very much."

"And you?" said Katherine.

"I don't think I'd like anyone who was going to take you away."

"But he isn't going to take me away. That's where you're all so wrong. He's just going to be one more of the family."

Henry said nothing.

Katherine then cried passionately: "Ah, you don't know him! you simply don't know him!" She stopped, her eyes shining, her whole body stirred by her happiness. She came over and stood close to him: "Henry, whatever happens, *whatever* happens, nothing can take me away from you and mother and the rest. Nor from Garth. . . . If you're *sure* of that then you needn't be afraid of Philip."

Henry looked up at her. "Suppose, Katherine—just suppose—that he insisted on your going, leaving us all, leaving Garth, going right away somewhere. What would you do?"

Katherine smiled with perfect confidence. "He wouldn't insist on anything that would make me so unhappy—or anyone unhappy. All he wants is that everyone should like everyone else, and that no one should be hurt."

"I'm not sure," said Henry, "whether it isn't that sort who hurt people most in the end." He took her hand in his. "He can do anything he likes, Katherine, anything, and I'll adore him madly, so long as he doesn't hurt you. If he does that—"

Aunt Aggie, standing in the doorway with the look of one who must live up to having had breakfast in bed, interrupted him:

"Ah, Katherine, there you are. The last thing I want is to give trouble to anyone, but I passed so poor a night that I feel quite unequal to marking those pillow-cases that I offered yesterday to do for your mother. I was so anxious yesterday afternoon to help her, as indeed I always am, but of course I couldn't foretell that my night would be so disturbed. I wonder whether you—"

"Why, of course, Aunt Aggie," said Katherine.

Henry's morning reflections resolved themselves finally into the decision that to continue his emancipation he would, definitely, before the day closed, penetrate into the heart of his Club. He found, when he arrived there, that he was so deeply occupied with thoughts of Katherine, Philip and himself that he knew no fear. He boldly passed the old man in the hall who exactly resembled a goat, climbed the stairs with the air of one who had been doing it all his life, and discovered a room with a fire, a table with papers, some bookcases with ancient books, and Seymour. That gentleman was standing before the fire, a smile of beaming self-satisfaction upon his red fat face; he greeted Henry with that altruistic welcome that was peculiarly his own. A manner that implied that God had sent him especially into the world to show other men how to be jolly, optimistic, kind-hearted and healthy.

"Why, who ever expected to see you here?" he cried. "You're yellow about the gills, my son. Have a whisky and soda."

"No, thank you," said Henry, with an internal shudder. "I thought I'd just look in."

"Why, of course," said Seymour. "How jolly to see you!"

They drew their chairs in front of the fire and talked— at least Seymour talked. He told Henry what a lucky fellow he, Seymour, was how jolly the world was, how splendid the weather was. He let slip by accident the facts that three publishers were fighting for his next book, that America had gone mad about his last one ("although I always said, you know, that to be popular in America was a sure sign that one was no good"), and that he'd overheard some woman at a party saying that he was the most interesting young man of the day. He told these tales with an air as though he would imply—"How absurd these people are! How ridiculous!"

Then, suddenly, he paused. It seemed that he had remembered something.

"By the way, Trenchard—I knew there was something. There's a fellow in this Club, just been lunching with him. I don't expect he's gone. I want you to meet him, I was thinking about you at luncheon. He's just come from Moscow, where he's been two years."

"Moscow?" said Henry.

"Yes. I'll go and find him. He may have left if I don't go now."

Seymour hurried away to return an instant later with a very-much dressed young man in a purple suit and a high, shrill voice. He gave Henry a languid finger, said that he wouldn't mind a drink, and sat down in front of the fire. Seymour began a fresh monologue, the young man (Morrison was his name) drank his whisky with a delicate foreign attitude which Henry greatly admired, said at last that he must be going. It was only then that Henry plucked up courage.

"I say—Seymour tells me you've just come from Moscow."

"Yes—damned rotten town," said Morrison, "two years of it—nearly killed me."

"Did you happen to know," said Henry, "a man there called Mark?"

"What! Phil Mark! Think I did! . . . Everyone knew Phil Mark! Hot stuff, my word!"

"I beg your pardon?" said Henry.

Mr. Morrison looked at Henry with curiosity, stared into his glass, found that it was empty, rose and brushed his trousers.

"Went the pace—had a mistress there for years—a girl out of the ballet. Everyone knew about it—had a kid, but the kid died . . . conceited sort o' feller—no one liked him. Know I didn't."

"It can't have been the same man," said Henry slowly.

"No? daresay not," said Morrison languidly, "name of Philip though. Short square feller, bit fat, black hair; he was in Maddox and Custom's—made a bit of money they said. He chucked the girl and came to England—here somewhere now I believe. . . ."

He looked at Henry and Seymour, found them silent, disliked the stare in Henry's eyes, saw a speck of dust on his waistcoat, was very serious about this, found the silence unpleasant and broke away—

"Well, so long, you fellows. . . . Must be toddling."

He wandered out, his bent shoulders expressing great contempt for his company.

Seymour had watched his young friend's face. He was, for once, at a loss. He had known what would occur; he had produced Morrison for no other purpose. He had hated Mark since that day at the Trenchard's house with all the unresting hatred of one whose whole peace of mind depends on the admiration of others. Morrison had told him stories about Mark: he did not, himself, wish to inform Henry, because his own acquaintance with the family and knowledge of Miss Trenchard's engagement made it difficult, but he had no objection at all to Morrison's agency. He was frightened now at Henry's white face and staring eyes.

"Did you know this?" Henry said.

"'Pon my word, Trenchard—no idea. Morrison *was* talking the other day about Englishmen in Moscow, and mentioned Mark, I think, but I never connected him. If I'd thought he was coming out with it like that of course I'd have stopped it, but *he* didn't know—"

"He's lying."

"Don't know why he should. He'd no idea your sister was engaged. It's a bit rotten, isn't it? I'm awfully sorry—"

Henry stared at him. "I believe you *did* know: I believe you meant him to tell me. That's what you brought him for —you hate Mark anyway." Henry laughed, then broke off, stared about him as though he did not know where he was, and rushed from the room. He did not know through what streets he passed; he saw no people, heard no noise; was conscious neither of light nor darkness. He knew that it was true. Mark was a blackguard. Katherine—Katherine. . . .

As he crossed the bridge in St. James' Park he tumbled against a man and knocked off his hat. He did not stop to apologise. What was he to do? What was he to do? Why had it been he who had heard this?

In the dark hall of the house he saw Katherine. She spoke to him; he tore past her, tumbling upstairs, running down the passage as though someone pursued him. His bedroom door banged behind him.

CHAPTER IV

GARTH IN ROSELANDS

PHILIP, on the day following his evening with Henry, left London to spend three weeks with some relations who lived near Manchester. This was the first parting from him that Katherine had suffered since the beginning of their engagement, and when she had said good-bye to him at the station, she seemed to return through empty streets, through a town without colour or movement, and the house, when she entered it, echoed, through its desolate rooms and passages, to her steps.

She resolved at once, however, that now was the time to show the family that she was the same Katherine as she had ever been. As she waited for a little in her bedroom, finally dismissing Philip's presence and summoning the others, she laughed to think how simply now she would brush away the little distrusts and suspicions that seemed, during those last weeks, to have grown about her.

"They *shall* know Phil," she thought to herself. "They can't help loving him when they see him as he really is. Anyway, no more keeping anything back." It seemed to her, at that moment, a very simple thing to impart her happiness to all of them. She had no fear that she would fail. Then, almost at once, the most delightful thing occurred.

Two or three days after Philip's departure Mrs. Trenchard, alone with Katherine in the dining-room before breakfast, said:

"I've written to Philip, my dear, to ask him to go down with us to Garth."

Katherine's eyes shone with pleasure.

"Mother! . . . How delightful of you! I was hoping that perhaps you might ask him later. But isn't it tiresome to have him so soon?"

"No—my dear—no. Not tiresome at all. I hope he'll be able to come."

"Of course he'll be able to come," laughed Katherine.

"Yes—well—I've written to ask him. We go down on the fifth of March. Your father thinks that's the best day. Griffiths writes that that business of the fences in Columb meadow should be looked into—Yes. No, Alice, not the ham —tell Grace to boil two more eggs—not enough—I'm glad you're pleased, Katherine."

Katherine looked up, and her eyes meeting her mother's, the confidence that had been clouded ever since that fatal affair with the hot-water bottles seemed to leap into life between them. Mrs. Trenchard put out her hand, Katherine moved forward, but at that moment Aunt Aggie and Aunt Betty entered; breakfast began.

"I believe," thought Katherine, "Aunt Aggie waits outside the door and chooses her moment. She's always interrupting. . . ." The fact that there was now some restraint between her mother and herself was only emphasised the more by the feeling of both of them that an opportunity had been missed.

And why, Katherine wondered afterwards, had her mother asked Philip? If he had been invited to come to them after Easter—but now, to go down with them, as one of the family! Was not this exactly what Katherine had been desiring? And yet she was uncomfortable. She felt sometimes now that her mother, who had once been her other self, in whose every thought, distress, anxiety she had shared, was almost a stranger.

"It's just as though there were ghosts in the house," she thought. As she went to bed she was, for the first time in her life, lonely. She longed for Philip . . . then suddenly, for no reason that she could name, began to cry and, so crying, fell asleep. She was much younger than everyone thought her. . . .

Throughout the three weeks that followed she felt as though she were beating the air. Rachel Seddon had taken her husband abroad. There was no one to whom she could speak. She wrote to Philip every day, and discovered how useless letters were. She tried to approach Millie, but found that she had not the courage to risk Millie's frankness. Her sister's attitude to her was: "Dear Katie, let's be happy and jolly together without talking about it—it's much better. . . ." There had been a time, not so very long ago, when they had told one another everything. Henry was the strangest of all. He removed himself from the whole family, and would speak to no one. He went apparently for long solitary walks. Even his father noticed his depression, and decided that something must really be done with the boy. "We might send him abroad for six months—learn some French or German . . ." but of course nothing was done.

Aunt Betty was the only entirely satisfactory member of the family. She frankly revelled in the romance of the whole affair. She was delighted that Katherine had fallen in love "with such a fine manly fellow" as Philip. Her attention was always centred upon Katherine to the exclusion of the others, therefore she noticed no restraint nor awkwardness. She was intensely happy, and went humming about the house in a way that annoyed desperately her sister Aggie. She even wrote a little letter to Philip, beginning "My dear Boy," saying that she thought that he'd like to know from one of the family that Katherine was in perfect health and looking beautiful. She received a letter from Philip that surprised and delighted her by its warmth of feeling. This letter was the cause of a little battle with Aggie.

They were alone together in Betty's room when she said, half to herself:

"*Such* a delightful letter from the 'dear boy'."

"*What* dear boy?" said Aunt Aggie sharply.

Aunt Betty started, as she always did when anyone spoke to her sharply, sucked her fingers, and then, the colour mounting into her cheeks, said:

"Philip. He's written to me from Manchester."

"I do think, Betty," Aggie answered, "that instead of writing letters to young men who don't want them you might try to take a little of the burden of this house off my shoulders. Now that Katherine has lost all her common-sense I'm supposed to do everything. I don't complain. They wish me to help as much as I can, but I'm far from strong, and a little help from you . . ."

Then Aunt Betty, with the effect of standing on her toes, her voice quite shrill with excitement, spoke to her sister as she had never, in all her life, spoken to anyone before.

"It's too bad, Aggie. I used to think that you were fond of Katherine, that you wished her happiness—Now, ever since her engagement, you've done nothing but complain about her. Sometimes I think you really want to see her unhappy. We ought to be glad, you and I, that she's found someone who will make her happy. It's all your selfishness, Aggie; just because you don't like Philip for some fancied reason . . . it's unfair and wicked. At anyrate to me you shan't speak against Katherine and Philip. . . . I love Katherine, even though you don't."

Now it happened that, as I have said elsewhere, Aggie Trenchard loved her niece very deeply. It was a love, however, that depended for its life on an adequate return. "That young man has turned Katherine against me. Ever since he first came into the house I knew it." Now at her sister's accusation her face grew grey and her hands trembled.

"Thank you, Betty. I don't think we'll discuss the matter. Because you're blind and know nothing of what goes on under your nose is no reason that other people's sight should be blinded too. Can't you see for yourself the change in Katherine? If you loved her a little more sensibly than you do, instead of romancing about the affair, you'd look into the future. I tell you that the moment Philip Mark entered this house was the most unfortunate moment in Katherine's life. Nothing but unhappiness will come of it. If you knew what I know—"

Aunt Betty was, in spite of herself, struck by the feeling and softness in her sister's voice.

"What do you mean?" she asked.

"I mean nothing. I'm right, that's all. *You're* a silly, soft fool, Elizabeth, and so you always were. But Harriet . . . asking him to go down to Garth with us, when she hates him as I know she does! *I* don't know what it means. Do you suppose that I don't love Katherine any longer? I love her so much that I'd like to strangle Mr. Philip Mark in his sleep!"

She flung from the room, banging the door behind her.

Philip arrived on the evening before the departure into the country. He came well pleased with all the world, because his Manchester relations had liked him and he had liked his Manchester relations. Viewed from that happy distance, the Trenchards had been bathed in golden light. He reviewed his recent agitations and forebodings with laughter. "Her family," he told his relations, "are a bit old-fashioned. They've got their prejudices, and I don't think they liked the idea, at first, of her being engaged—she's so valuable. But they're getting used to it." He arrived in London in the highest spirits, greeted Rocket as though he had been his life-long friend, and going straight up to his room to dress for dinner, thought to himself that he really did feel at home in the old house. He looked at his fire, at the cosy shape of the room, heard a purring, contented clock ticking away, thought for a moment of Moscow, with its puddles, its mud, its dark, uneven streets, its country roads, its weeks of rain.

"No, I've found my place," he thought, *"this* is home."

And yet, during dinner, his uneasiness, like a forgotten

ghost, crept back to him. Henry had a headache, and had gone to bed.

"He's not been very well lately," said Aunt Aggie to Philip, "that evening with you upset him, I believe—over-excited him, perhaps. I'm glad you liked Manchester." He could not deny that dinner was a little stiff. He was suddenly aware over his pudding that he was afraid of Mrs. Trenchard, and that his fear of her that had been vague and nebulous before his absence was now sharp and defined.

He looked at her, and saw that her eyes were anything but placid and contented, like the rest of her.

"More pudding, Philip?" she asked him, and his heart beat as though he had received a challenge.

Afterwards in the drawing-room he thought to himself: " 'Tis this beastly old house. It's so stuffy"—forgetting that two hours earlier it had seemed to welcome him home. "We'll be all right when we get down to the country," he thought.

Finally he said good-night to Katherine in the dark little passage. As though he were giving himself some desperate reassurance, he caught her to him and held her tightly in his arms:

"Katie—darling, have you missed me?"

"Missed you? I thought the days were never going to pass."

"Katie, I want to be married, here, now, to-night, at once. I hate this waiting. I *hate* it. It's impossible—"

Katherine laughed, looking up into his eyes.

"I like you to be impatient. I'm so happy. I don't think anything can ever be happier. Besides, you know," and her eyes sparkled—"you may change—you may want to break it off—and then think how glad you'll be that we waited."

He held her then so fiercely that she cried out.

"Don't say that—even as a joke. How dare you—even as a joke? I love you—I love you—I love you." He kissed her mouth again and again, then suddenly, with a little movement of tenderness, stroked her hair very softly, whispering to her, "I love you—I love you—I love you—Oh! how I love you!"

That night she was so happy that she lay for many hours staring at the black ceiling, a smile on her lips. He, also, was awake until the early morning. . . .

The departure to the station was a terrific affair. There were Mr. Trenchard, senior, Great Aunt Sarah (risen from a bed of sickness, yellow and pinched in the face, very yellow and pinched in the temper, and deafer than deaf), Aunt Aggie, Aunt Betty, George Trenchard, Mrs. Trenchard, Millie (very pretty), Henry (very sulky), Katherine, Philip, Rocket and Aunt Sarah's maid (the other maids had left by an earlier train)—twelve persons. The train to be caught was the eleven o'clock from Paddington, and two carriages had been reserved. The first business was to settle old Mr. Trenchard and Aunt Sarah. They were placed, like images, in the best corners, Mr. Trenchard saying sometimes in his silvery voice: "It's very kind of you, Harriet," or "Thank ye, Betty, my dear," and once to Millie, "I like to see ye laughing, my dear—very pretty, very pretty". Aunt Sarah frowned and wrinkled her nose, but was, in her high black bonnet, a very fine figure. Her maid, Clarence, was plain, elderly and masculine in appearance, having a moustache and a stiff linen collar and very little hair visible under her black straw hat. She, however, knew just how Great-Aunt Sarah liked to be. . . .

The others in that compartment were Aunt Aggie, George Trenchard (he sat next to his father and told him jokes out of the papers) and Mrs. Trenchard. In the other carriage Katherine and Philip had the corners by the window. Aunt Betty sat next to Philip, Millie and Henry had the farther corners. When the train started, Katherine's heart gave a jump, as it always did when she set off for Garth. "We're really off. We'll really be in Garth by the evening. We'll really wake up there to-morrow morning."

Philip had not seen Henry since his return from Manchester, so he tried to talk to him. Henry, however, was engaged upon a very large edition of "War and Peace," and, although he answered Philip's enquiries very politely, he was obviously determined to speak to no one. Millie had Henry Galleon's "Roads" to read, but she did not study it very deeply—Aunt Betty had a novel called "The Rosary" and her knitting; now and then she would break into little scraps of talk as: "But if I moved the bed across lengthways that would leave room for the bookcase," or "I do think people must be clever to make up conversations in books," or "There's Reading". The lovers, therefore, were left to one another. . . .

Katherine had upon her lap the novel that had so greatly excited Henry; he had insisted upon her reading it, but now it lay idly there, unopened. That little smile that had hovered about her lips last night was still there to-day. Often her eyes were closed, and she might have seemed to be asleep were it not that the little smile was alive—her eyes would open, they would meet Philip's eyes, they would be drawn, the two of them, closer and closer and closer.

They talked together, their voices scarcely above a whisper. The day was one of those that are given sometimes, in a fit of forgetfulness, by the gods, at the beginning of March. It was a very soft, misty day, with the sun warm and golden but veiled. Trees on the dim blue horizon were faintly pink, and streams that flashed for an instant before the windows were pigeon-colour. Everywhere the earth seemed to be breaking, flowers pushing through the soil, rivers released from their winter bondage laughing in their new freedom, the earth chuckling, whispering, humming with the glorious excitement of its preparation, as though it had never had a spring in all its life before, as though it did not know that there would yet be savage winds, wild storms of rain, many cold and bitter days. Blue mist—running water—trees with their bursting buds—a haze of sun and rain in the air—a great and happy peace.

Katherine and Philip, although they saw no one but one another, were aware of the day—it was as though it had been arranged especially for them. The rise and fall of their voices had a sleepy rhythm, as though they were keeping time with the hum of the train:

"I'm so glad," said Katherine, "that your first view of Glebeshire will be on a day like this."

"I'm a little afraid," he answered. "What will you say if I don't like it?"

She seemed really for an instant to be afraid. "But, of course, of course, you will."

"Everyone doesn't. Someone told me the other day that either it was desolate enough to depress you for a lifetime or stuffy like a hot-house, and that the towns were the ugliest in the United Kingdom."

Katherine sighed and then smiled.

"I expect they'd think Manchester the loveliest place on earth," she said. Then, looking at him very intently, she asked him: "Do you regret Russia—the size and the space and the strangeness? I daresay you do. Do you know, Phil, I'm rather jealous of Russia, of all the things you did before I knew you, I wonder whether I'd have liked you if I'd met you then, whether you'd have liked me. I expect you were very different. Tell me about it. I'm always asking you about Moscow, and you're so mysterious—yes, I believe I'm jealous."

Philip looked away from her, out of the window, at the fields with their neat hedges, the gentle hills faintly purple, villages tucked into nests of trees, cows grazing, horses mildly alert at the passing train. For a moment he was conscious of irritation at the tidy cosiness of it all. Then he spoke, dreamily, as though he were talking in his sleep:

"No. That's all behind me. I shall never go back there again. I don't think of it often, but sometimes I fancy I'm there. Sounds will bring it back, and I dream sometimes. . . . One gets so used to it that it's hard now to say what one did feel about it. I had a little flat in a part of the town called the Arbat. Out of my window I could see a church with sky-blue domes covered with silver stars, there was a shop with food, sausages and all kinds of dried fish, and great barrels of red caviare and mountains of cheese. The church had a cherry-coloured wall, with a glittering Ikon at the gate and a little lamp burning in front of it. There were always some cabs at the end of my street, with the cabmen in their fat, bunched-up clothes sleeping very often, their heads hanging from the shafts. Lines of carts from the country would pass down the street with great hoops of coloured wood over the horses' necks and wild-looking peasants in charge of them. They didn't seem wild to me then—they were quite ordinary. Always just before six the bells at the church would ring, one slow, deep note and a little funny noisy jangle as well— one beautiful and unearthly; the other like a talkative woman, all human. . . . In the autumn there'd be weeks of rain and the mud would rise and rise, and the carts and cabs go splashing through great streams of water. When the snow came there'd be fine days and the town on fire, all sparkling and quivering, and every ugly thing in the place would be beautiful. There'd be many days too when the sky would fall lower and lower and the town be like grey blotting-paper and the most beautiful things hideous. Opposite my window there was a half-built house that had been there for three years, and no one had troubled to finish it. There was a beggar at the corner—a fine old man with no legs. He must have made a fortune, because everyone who passed gave him something. It would be fine on a snowy night when the night-watchmen built great fires of logs to keep them warm.

"On a starry night I could see the domes of St. Saviour's Cathedral like little golden clouds—very beautiful."

"And what was the inside of your flat like?" asked Katherine. She had been leaning a little forward, her hands clasped together, deeply interested.

"Oh! very small! I made it as English as I could. It

had central heating and, in the winter, with the double windows, it got very stuffy. I had English pictures and English books, but it was never very comfortable. I don't know why. Nothing in Russia's comfortable. I had a funny old servant called Sonia. She was fond of me, but she drank; she was always having relations to stay with her. I would find funny-looking men in the kitchen in the morning. She had no idea of time, and would cook well or badly as she pleased. She liked to tell fairy stories; she stole and she drank and she lied, but I kept her because I couldn't bother to change her."

He stopped—then began again, but now more dreamily than before, as though he'd been carried far away from the train, from England, from Katherine. "Yes—that was it—one couldn't be bothered. One couldn't be bothered about anything, and one didn't need to bother, because no one else bothered either. Perhaps that's just why I loved it, as I see now that I did love it. No one cared for anything but what was in the air—dreams, superstitions, stories. The country itself was like that too—so vague, so vast and boundless, so careless and heedless, so unpractical, so good for dreams, so bad for work, so unfinished, letting so many things go to pieces, so beautiful and so ugly, so depressing and so cheerful, so full of music and of ugly sounds . . . so bad to live in, so good to dream in. I was happy there and I didn't know it—I was happy and didn't know it." His voice had sunk to a whisper, so that Katherine could not catch his words. She touched the sleeve of his coat.

"Come back, Phil, come back," she said, laughing. "You're lost."

He started, then smiled at her.

"It's all right . . . but it's odd. There are so many things that didn't seem to me to be curious and beautiful then that are so now." Then, looking at Katherine very intently, as though he were calling her back to him, he said:

"But don't talk to me about Russia. It's bad for me. I don't want to think of it. I've left it for ever. And when you ask me questions it revives me, as though it still had some power. . . . You say that you're afraid of it—why," he ended, laughing, "I believe I'm afraid of it too—I don't *want* to think of it. It's England now and Glebeshire and you—and you," he whispered. They were interrupted then by an attendant, who told them that it was time for the first luncheon.

Afterwards, when the shadows were lengthening across the fields and the misty sun rode low above the far hills, they sat silently dreaming of their great happiness. It was an afternoon that was to remain, for both of them, throughout their lives, in spite of all after events, a most perfect memory. There are moments in the histories of all of us when we are carried into heights that by the splendour of their view, the fine vigour of their air, the rapture of their achievement offer to us a sufficient reassurance against the ironic powers. We find in them a justification of our hopes, our confidences, our inspirations, our faith. . . .

So, for these few hours at least, Katherine and Philip found their justification.

This was a moment that two others, also, in that carriage were never afterwards to forget. Millie, under the warm afternoon sun, had fallen asleep. She woke to a sudden, half-real, half-fantastic realisation of Philip. She was awake, of course, and yet Philip was not quite human to her—or was it that he was more human than he had ever been before? She watched him, with her young, eager, inquisitive gaze, over the cover of her book. She watched him steadily for a long time.

She had always liked the clean, bullet-shaped head, his black eyes, his sturdiness and set, square shoulders, his colour and his strength. She had always liked him, but to-day, in this sudden glimpse, he seemed to be revealed to her as someone whom she was seeing for the first time. Millie, in all the freshness of her anticipated attack upon the world, had at this period very little patience for bunglers, for sentimentalists, for nervous and hesitating souls. Now, strangely, she saw in Philip's eyes some hinted weakness, and yet she did not despise him. "I believe," she thought, "he's afraid of us." That discovery came as though it had been whispered to her by someone who knew. Her old conviction that she knew him better than did the others showed now no signs of faltering. "I believe I could help him as they none of them can," she thought. "No, not even Katherine." She had, in spite of her determined, practical common-sense, the most romantic idea of love, and now, as she thought of the two of them wrapped up there before her eyes in one another, she felt irritated by her own isolation. "I wonder whether Katherine understands him really," she thought. "Katherine's so simple, and takes everything for granted. It's enough for her that she's in love. I don't believe it's enough for him." She had always in very early days felt some protecting, motherly element in her love for Katherine. That protection seemed now to spread to Philip as well. "Oh! I do hope they're going to be happy," she thought, and so, taking them both with her under her wing, dozed off to sleep again. . . .

The other was, of course, Henry.

No one could ever call Henry a gay youth. I don't think that anyone ever did, and although with every year that he grows he is stronger, more cheerful and less clumsy and misanthropic, he will never be really gay. He will always be far too conscious of the troubles that may tumble on to his head, of the tragedies of his friends and the evils of his country.

And yet, in spite of his temperament, he had, deep down in his soul, a sense of humour, an appreciation of his own comic appearance, a ready applause for the optimists (although to this he would never, never confess). "He's a surly brute," I heard someone say of him once—but it is possible (I do not say probable) that he will be a great man one of these days, and then everyone will admire his fine reserve, "the taciturnity of a great man"; in one of his sudden moments of confidence he confessed to me that this particular journey down to Glebeshire was the beginning of the worst time in his life—not, of course, quite the beginning. Philip's appearance on that foggy night of his grandfather's birthday was that—and he is even now not so old but that there may be plenty of bad times in store for him. But he will know now how to meet them; this was his first test of responsibility.

He had always told himself that what he really wanted was to show, in some heroic fashion, his love for Katherine. Let him be tested, he cried, by fire, stake, torture and the block, and he would "show them." Well, the test had come. As he sat opposite her in the railway carriage he faced it. He might go up to Philip and say to him: "Look here, is it true? Did you have a mistress in Moscow for three years and have a son by her?" But what then? If Philip laughed, and said: "Why, of course . . . everyone knows it. That's all over now. What is it to you?" He would answer: "It's this to me. I'm not going to have a rotten swelp of a fellow marrying my sister and making her miserable."

Then Philip might say: "My dear child—how young you are! all men do these things. I've finished with that part of my life. But, anyway, don't interfere between me and Katherine, you'll only make her miserable and you'll do no good."

Ah! that was just it. He would make her miserable; he could not look at her happiness and contemplate his own destruction of it. And yet if Philip were to marry her and afterwards neglect her, and leave her as he had left this other woman, would not Henry then reproach himself most bitterly for ever and ever? But perhaps, after all, the story of that wretched man at the Club was untrue, it had been, perhaps, grossly exaggerated. Henry had a crude but finely-coloured fancy concerning the morals of the Man of the World. Had not Seymour dismissed such things with a jolly laugh and "my dear fellow, it's no business of ours. We're all very much alike if we only knew." Had he not a secret envy of

this same Man of the World who carried off his sins so lightly
with so graceful an air? But now it was no case of an
abstract sinner—it was a case of the happiness or unhappiness
of the person whom Henry loved best in life.

A subtler temptation attacked him. He knew (he could not
possibly doubt) that if his parents were told, Philip would
have to go. One word from him to his mother, and the family were rid of this fellow who had come out of nowhere to
disturb their peace. The thing was so infernally easy. As
he sat there, reading, apparently, his novel, his eyes were on
Katherine's face. She was leaning back, her eyes closed,
smiling at her thoughts. What would Katherine do? Would
she leave them all and go with him? Would she hate him,
Henry, for ever afterwards? Yes, that she would probably
do. . . . Ah, he was a weak, feeble, indeterminate creature.
He could make up his mind about nothing. . . . That evening he had had with Philip, it had been glorious and disgusting, thrilling and sordid. He was rather glad that he
had been drunk—he was also ashamed. He was intensely
relieved that none of the family had seen him, and yet he saw
himself shouting to them: "I was drunk the other night, and
I talked to rotten women and I didn't care what happened
to me. . . . I'm a boy no longer."

He hated Philip, and yet, perhaps, Philip was leading
him to freedom. That fellow in the novel about the sea and
the forests (Henry could see him challenging his foes, walking quietly across the square towards his friend, who was
waiting to slay him). He would have admired Philip.
Henry saw himself as that fine solitary figure waiting for his
opportunity. How grand he could be had he a chance, but life
was so lofty, so unromantic, so conventional. Instead of
meeting death like a hero, he must protect Katherine . . .
and he did not know how to do it. . . .

As the sun was sinking in a thick golden web that glittered
behind the dark purple woods—woods that seemed now to
stand like watchers with their fingers upon their lips—the

train crossed the boundary river. That crossing had been, ever since he could remember, a very great moment to Henry. To-day the recognition of it dragged him away from Philip and Katherine, from everything but Glebeshire.

He looked across at Katherine instinctively—she, sitting now upright, gazing out of the window, turned as though she had known and smiled at him. They were in Glebeshire, there was the first valley, mysterious, now like a dark purple cup, there the white winding road that went over the hill on to Rasselas, Liskane, Clinton and Truxe, there was the first break in the hills, where you always peered forward expecting to catch a shimmer of the sea, here that cluster of white cottages that, when he had been small, had seemed to be tumbling down the hill, very dangerous to live in . . . at last the pause at Carlyon, the last stop before Rasselas.

It was quite dark now. The light had suddenly been drawn from the sky, and the earth was filled with new sounds, new scents, new mysteries. The train stopped for a minute before Rasselas, and, suddenly all about it, through the open window there crowded whispers, stealthy movements, the secret confidences of some hidden stream, the murmured greetings of the trees. The train lay there as though it had wanted them all to know how lovely the evening was. On the road that skirted the train a man with a lantern greeted a cart. "Well, good-night to 'ee," a voice said clear and sharp like an invitation; Henry's heart began to beat furiously. Glebeshire had welcomed them.

With a jerk the train stumbled forward again, and they were in Rasselas. The little station, which was of some importance because it was a junction for Pelynt and therefore also for Rafiel, lay very quietly at the bottom of the wooded hill. A porter went down the train swinging a lantern and crying: "Change for P'lynt. Change for P'lynt."

A stream flowed near by, and the scent of a garden flooded the station: there would be already snowdrops and primroses and crocuses. The whole party of them were bundled out on

to the platform—a great pile of luggage loomed in the distance. Heads from the carriage windows watched them, then
a pause, a cry, and the train was off, leaving them all high
and dry, with the wind blowing round their hair and clothes
and ankles like a friendly and inquisitive dog. There was
sea in the wind.

"Smell the sea!" cried Millie. "I must have left it in the
restaurant car," said Aunt Aggie. "Too provoking. I par-
ticularly wanted you to read that article, Harriet. I think
you might have noticed, Millie . . . you were sitting next
to me."

"There's Jacob!" Henry, suddenly happy and excited and
free from all burdens, cried:

"Hallo! Jacob! How are you? How's everyone? How's
Rebekah?"

Jacob, with a face like a red moon, smiled, touched his hat,
stormed at a young man in buttons. "Do 'ee bustle a bit,
John. Didn't I tell 'ee the box with the black 'andles? . . .
very comfortable, Mr. 'Enry, sir, thank 'ee, as I 'opes you
finds yourself. Been a bit o' sickness around down along in
the village . . . but not to 'urt. . . ."

Could they all get in? Of course they could. The luggage
was all on the luggage-cart, and Rock and Clarence with it; a
silver moon, just rising now above the station roofs, peeping
at her, laughed at her serious dignity.

"No, we'll go on the box, Philip and I," said Katherine.
"Of course I shan't be cold. No, really, we'd rather, wouldn't
we, Philip? Plenty of room, Jacob."

They were off, up the little hill, down over the little bridge
and through the little village. Katherine, sitting between
Philip and Jacob, pressing her cheek against Philip's rough
tweed coat, her hand lying in his under the rug, seemed to
slip, dreaming, fulfilling some earlier vision, through space.
She had wondered sometimes, in the earlier days, whether
there could be any greater happiness in life than that ever-

thrilling, ever-satisfying return to Garth. She knew now that there was a greater happiness. . . .

A white world of crackling, burning stars roofed them in; an owl flew by them through the grey dusk; the air smelt of spring flowers and fresh damp soil. The stream that had been with them since their entrance into Glebeshire still accompanied them, running with its friendly welcome at their side. Beyond the deep black hedges cows and horses and sheep moved stealthily: it seemed that they might not disturb the wonderful silence of the night.

"Are you warm enough?" he asked her; he caught her hand more tightly and kissed her cheek, very softly and gently. She trembled with happiness, and pressed more closely against his coat.

"Can you smell the sea yet? You will when you get to the top of Rasselas Hill. This is the high road to Pelynt. It runs parallel with the railway until we get to the cross roads, Pelynt Cross, you know. . . . You'll smell the sea there. You can see it on a clear day. To the left of you there is just Pelynt Moor. It runs for miles and miles, right along by the Drymouth Road. . . . Look through the break in the hedge. Do you see that light across the field? That's John Pollen's cottage. John was murdered just about a hundred years ago. He was an old miser, and some men robbed him, but they never found his head. They say he wanders about still looking for it. . . . Oh, if this could go on for ever. Philip, are you happy?"

"Happy?" . . . Ah! she could feel his body quiver.

"Yes, and now we're coming down to the Well. There's a little wood just at the body of the hill. We always call it the Well because it's so dark and green. It's the most famous wood for primroses in all Glebeshire. They'll be coming now. . . . We'll walk here. . . . I cried once because I thought I was lost here. They forgot me and went home. Then I was comforted by the postman, who found me and carried me home. . . . Jacob, do you remember?"

"Ah, Miss Kathie, doan't 'ee think that I'd forget ought about 'ee. Not likely. And your mother in a fine takin', poor soul, too. We're a-coming to P'lynt Cross now, sir—as famous as any spot o' ground in the 'ole of Glebeshire, sir— Hup, then! Hup, then—Whey—Oh! oh! Hup, then!"

They pulled to the top, leaving the wood in the dip behind them. The wind met them, flinging its salt and freshness in their faces with a rough, wild greeting. Philip could hear suddenly the humming of the telegraph wires, as though they had sprung from their imprisonment in the valley and were chanting their victory. To his left, vague and formless under the starlight, stretched Pelynt Moor, waiting there, scornfully confident in its age and strength and power, for daylight. The salt wind flung its arms around them and dragged them forward; Philip, listening, could hear, very stealthily, with the rhythm of armed men marching, the beating of the sea. . . .

"Now we're near—now we're very near. It'll be Garth Cross in a minute. There it is. Now we turn off down to the Almshouses. We don't really come into the village. . . . There are the Almshouses and the Common. . . . Now round the corner. . . . There it is—there's the Gate—the Gate! . . . Oh! Philip, are you *happy?*"

She was crying a very little: her eyes were blurred as they turned up the long drive, past all the rhododendron bushes, past the lawn with the giant oak at the farther end of it, round the curve to the hall door, with Rebekah standing under the porch to welcome them. Philip was down, and had helped her to the ground. She stood a little away from them all as they laughed and chattered about the door. She wiped her eyes with her gloved hand to stop the tears.

Philip was conscious of standing in a long dark hall with stairs at the end of it and a large oak chest with a glass case that contained a stuffed bird taking up much of the space; that, he always afterwards remembered, was his first impression of the house, that it was absurd to put so large a chest just there where everyone would knock against it. A misty babel of talk surrounded him: he was conscious of a tall old woman wearing a high, stiffly-starched white cap: she had a fine colour, very dark red cheeks, hair a deep black and flashing eyes. She must be between sixty and seventy, but her body was straight and vigorous. This was, he supposed, Rebekah. He saw, in the background, old Mr. Trenchard being helped up the stairs by Rocket; he heard Aunt Betty in a happy twitter, "Ah, now, this is nice . . . this *is* nice . . . how nice this is." He heard Mrs. Trenchard's slow, sleepy voice: "No—the train was punctual, Rebekah, quite punctual. We had luncheon on the train . . . yes, we were quite punctual."

Someone said: "I'll show Philip his room," and George Trenchard, laughing, cried to him: "Come on, Philip, this way—this way." Trenchard, like a boy, bounded up the stairs in front of him. They were old, black, winding and creaking stairs that sighed as you mounted them. Trenchard cried: "To the right now—mind your head!" They turned through a little passage, so low that Philip must bend double and so dark that he could see nothing before him. He put out his hand, touched Trenchard's broad back, and was surprised at his sense of relief. Now they walked along another passage, very narrow, white walls with coloured sporting prints hanging on them. "Ah! here's the Blue Room. Here you are. Hope you'll like it—got a decent view. Brought you hot water? Ah, yes, there it is. When you've washed come down just as you are. Don't bother to change. . . . It's only supper to-night, you know. . . . Right you are."

His room was charming, with cherry-coloured wall-paper on walls that seemed a thousand years old. He flung his windows open, and there was the moon, thin, sharp, quivering with light in the sky, and he could hear the stream that had accompanied him ever since his entry into Glebeshire still singing to him. The night air was so sweet, the trees, that sighed and trembled and sighed again, so intimate. There was an intimacy here that he had never felt in any country before.

There was an intimacy and also, for him, at any rate, some strange loneliness. . . . He closed the window. He found his way down into the hall, and there saw Katherine. "Quick!" she cried. "Quick! I hoped that you'd come down before the others. We've got ten minutes." She was almost dancing with excitement (she his staid, reserved Katherine). She was pulling him by the arm, out through the door, under the porch, into the garden. She ran across the lawn, and he, more slowly, followed her. He caught her and held her close to him.

"You love it, Philip—don't you? You must. Of course you've hardly seen anything to-night. To-morrow we must both get up early, before anyone else, and come down. But look back now. Isn't the house simply—? Isn't it? Don't you feel the happiness and cosiness and friendliness? Oh, you must! You must!"

"When I've got you I don't want anything. Everything is lovely."

"But you're happy now to be here, aren't you?"

"Very happy."

"And you won't be disappointed, will you? You must promise me that you won't be disappointed."

"I promise you."

"And there's so much to show you! Oh! it's so wonderful to have all the old places that I've loved so long, to have them all to show you—to share them all with you. . . . Oh, wonderful, wonderful!"

"Yes, I'll share them all with you. But—but . . . Katherine, darling. No, turn round—come closer. There, like that: I don't want to share *you* with *them*. I don't want to share you with anyone or anything."

"You don't—you can't. Of course you can't. I'm all yours—but then this is part of me, so *it's* all yours too."

"And you couldn't live away from it? You couldn't imagine having to be right away from it—if I *had* to live somewhere else?"

"But why should you? You won't have to live somewhere else. And let's not imagine anything. Things are so lovely, so perfect, as they are. I don't like imagining things. I can't when *this* is all so real."

"Katie . . . Katie . . . No, come closer. Much closer. I don't care if I do hurt you. I want to. I want *you, you, you*. It's what I said last night. Let's marry soon—not this awful year. I feel—I don't know—I imagine too much. I suppose—But I feel as though you'd escape me, as though they'd all come between and take you away. If once you were *mine* I'd never care again. We'd stay anywhere, do anything you like. But this is so hard—to wait like this. To see you caring so much for other people, who don't, perhaps, care for me. I *want* you. I *want* you—*all* of you. And I've only got half."

"Half!" She laughed triumphantly. "You *have* all of me—*all* of me—for *ever!* Philip, how funny you are! Why, you don't trust me! I'd wait for ever if necessary, and never doubt for an instant that anything could come between. I trust you as I trust this place."

A voice broke in upon them. Someone called.

"Katherine! Katherine!"

Slowly she drew away from him. "That's mother. I must go."

He caught her hand. "Stay a little longer. They can wait."

"No, it's mother. She wants me. Come on, Phil darling. Supper time. We'll creep out again afterwards."

She crossed the lawn, expecting Philip to follow her. But he stayed there under the oak tree. He heard the voices laughing and calling in the lighted house. He was suddenly desperately lonely. He was frightened. . . . He crossed hurriedly the lawn, and as he walked he knew that what he wanted was that someone, someone who really knew him, should come and comfort him.

Before he entered the hall he stopped and looked back into the dark garden. Was there someone beneath the oak, some-one who watched him with an ironical, indulgent smile? . . . No, there was no one there. But he knew who it was that could comfort him. With a swift, sharp accusation of dis-loyalty he confessed to himself that it was Anna for whom, during that instant, he had looked.

CHAPTER V

THE FEAST

SOME entries in Millie's diary:

March 12th. Wind and rain like anything. Been in most of the day patching up the screen in my bedroom with new pictures—got them as much like the old ones as possible. Went for an hour's tussle with the wind out to the Cross, and it was fine. Wish I could have got over to Rafiel. The sea must have been fine to-day coming in over the Peak. Father drove Philip over to Polchester in the morning. Felt bored and out of temper in the evening.

March 13th. Katie and Philip had their first tiff this morning—at least first I've seen. He wanted her to go off with him for the day. She'd got to stop and help mother with the Merrimans from Polneaton, coming to tea. Mother said it didn't matter, but I could see that she was awfully pleased when K. stayed. But if I'd been K. I'd have gone. What *does* a family matter when one's in love? and she *is* in love, more than anyone I've ever seen. But I think she's disappointed with Phil for not caring more about Garth, although she never owns it. I'm sorry for him. He wanders about not knowing what to do with himself, and everyone's too busy to think of him. I try, but he doesn't want me, he wants Katherine, and thinks he ought to have her all the time. Aunt Aggie makes things worse in every way she can. . . .

March 15th. Cross all day. Garth isn't quite so nice this time somehow. Is it because of Paris? I don't think so— it used to make one care all the more. I think Philip upsets one. When you see someone criticising something you've always loved, it makes you hot defending it, but also, although you'd never own it, it makes you see weak spots. Then he stirs my imagination as no one ever has done before. I believe he always sees the place he's not in much more vividly than the place he is. If I were Katie I'd marry him to-morrow and make sure of him. Not that he isn't in love with her —he *is*—more every day—but he doesn't want to divide her with us, and she doesn't understand it and we won't have it— so there you are!

March 16th. Henry very queer to-day. I wish they'd send him to Oxford or do something with him. It's so hard on him to let him hang around doing nothing—it's so bad for him, too. I think he hates Philip, but is fascinated by him. He took me into the garden after lunch to-day as though he were going to tell me something very important. He was so very mysterious, and said I could advise him, and he was dreadfully worried. Then he suddenly stopped, said it was nothing, and wasn't it a fine day? I know I shall kill Henry one day. He thinks he's so important and has got a great destiny, whereas he can't even keep his face clean. So I told him, and then I wanted to hug him and comfort him. I'm really awfully fond of him, but I do wish he was nice and smart like other men.

March 17th. Had a long walk with Philip this afternoon. Really I do like him most tremendously, partly, I think, because he always treats me as though I'd come out years ago and knew all about everything. He talked all the time about Katherine, which was natural enough, I suppose. He said (what he'd told me in London) that he was frightened by her idea of him, and wished she thought him more as he was. He said he hated a long engagement, that he wished it were over—then he said that he was a poor sort of fellow for anyone so fine as Katherine, and I said that I didn't think it did to be too humble about oneself and that I always made myself out as grand as I could in my mind.

He said that it was Russia made one like that, that after

you'd been in Russia a little you doubted everyone and everything, most of all yourself. I said that I thought that rather
flabby . . . but I do like him. I don't think Katie ought
to insist so much on his liking Garth. She'll frighten him off
it altogether if she does that.

March 19*th*. Rachel Seddon arrived. Mother asked her
down. She doesn't generally come at this time, and she's
only just back from abroad, but I think she wants to see how
the engagement's getting on. Of course she doesn't like
Philip—you can see that in a moment—and of course he
knows it. But he wants to make her like him. I wish he
didn't care so much whether people like him or no. Henry
quite his old self to-night, and we danced (I tried to teach
him a cake-walk) in my room, and smashed a lamp of Aunt
Aggie's—I'd quite forgotten her ceiling was my floor. The
house is awfully old and shaky—letter from Rose La Touche
—Paris does seem funny to think of here. . . .

Part of a letter that was never posted—
"I haven't written to you all these weeks because I was
determined not to write to Russia until I was settled and
happy and married for life. Then, also, you yourself have
not written. Have you all, over there, forgotten me? Russians never do write letters, do they? I don't suppose I
ought to be disappointed—you warned me. If I'd forgotten
all of you there—but I haven't. I thought for a time that I
had, but I haven't . . . then a bell rings, and all the servants
troop in and kneel down in a row with their heels up, and
George Trenchard reads a bit out of the New Testament and,
very fast, a prayer about 'Thy humble servants', and he has
his eye on the weather out of the window all the time. Afterwards there is the Post—also eggs, bacon, marmalade, brown
bread and white and the family arriving one by one with
'sorry I'm late!' Fancy a Russian saying: 'Sorry I'm late'!
. . . so the day's begun. Afterwards, everyone has their own
especial job. I don't know what my especial job is supposed

to be. George has his writing and the whole place—fences, weeds, horses, dogs—anything you like. He fancies himself Walter Scott at Abbotsford, and is as happy as the day is long; Mrs. Trenchard has the village and the inside of the house (with Katherine her lieutenant). There is no living soul from the infant of a week to the old man of ninety-seven (John Wesley Moyle—he sees visions) who does not have his or her life exactly and precisely arranged. Mrs. Trenchard has a quiet hypnotic power that fills me with terror, because I know that I shall soon be ranged with all the others. She is kindness itself I am sure, and no cloud passing across the sun's face makes less sound—and yet she has always her way. Oh, Paul, old man, I'm frightened of her as I have never been of anyone before. When I see her here I want to run. I had a horrible dream last night. The terror of it is with me still. I thought that I said good-night to everyone and went up to my bedroom. To my surprise I found Mrs. Trenchard there, and instead of my usual bed was an enormous feather-bed—an *enormous* one stretching from wall to wall. 'You will sleep on that to-night,' said Mrs. Trenchard, pointing to it. In some way I knew that if I once lay down upon it I should never get up again. I said 'No, I would not lie down.' 'I think you'd better,' she said in her slow way. 'I think you'd better.' 'No!' I cried, 'I defy you!' Instantly the feather-bed like a cloud rose, filled the room, was above me, under me, around me. It pressed in upon me. I tore at it, and the feathers floated in a great stifling fog against my eyes, up my nose, in my mouth. I screamed for mercy, I fought, I fell, I was suffocating, death was driving down upon me . . . I woke. There's nonsense for you! And yet not such nonsense neither. On a stuffy day here, when everything steams and the trees and grass and hedges close up about the house like an army, when Mrs. Trenchard, with Katherine, is arranging meals and lives, birth and death, when, trying to escape down one of the lanes, they rise so high above one's head that it's like being drowned in a green bath, I tell you the feather-bed is not so far away—suffocation seems no idle dream. The fact of the matter is that there's nothing here for me to do. It didn't matter having nothing to do in Russia—although, as a matter of fact, I always had plenty, because no one else had anything to do that couldn't be stopped at any moment for the sake of a friend, or a drink, or a bit of vague thinking. I suppose it's the order, the neatness, the punctuality and, at the same time, the solid, matter-of-fact assumption that things must be exactly what they look (which they never are) that fusses me. But really of course I came down here to make love to Katherine—and I only get a bit of her. She cherishes the faith that I want the family as badly as I want her, and that the family want me as badly as she does. She has got a thousand little duties here that I had never reckoned on, and they are like midges on a summer's evening. I would throw myself into their life if they would let me, but there doesn't seem any real place for me. It's fighting with shadows. George Trenchard takes me for drives, Millie, Katherine's sister, takes me for walks—Katie herself is, I do believe, with me whenever she can be. . . . I ought to be satisfied. But only last night Great Aunt Sarah, who is in her dotage (or pretends to be), said, in the drawing-room to Millie, in a loud whisper, 'Who is that young man, my dear, sitting over there? I seem to know his face.' That sort of thing doesn't exactly make you feel at home. With all this, I feel the whole time that they are criticising me and waiting for me to make some big blunder. Then they'll say to Katherine, 'You see, my dear!' Oh, of course, I'm an ass to make a fuss. Any sensible fellow would just wait his year, marry Katherine and say good-bye to the lot. But I shan't be able to say good-bye to the lot. That's the whole business . . . partly because I'm weak, partly because Katherine adores them, partly because that is, I believe, Mrs. T.'s plan. To absorb me, to swallow me, to have me ever afterwards, somewhere about the place, a colourless imitation of the rest of them. So they'll keep Katie, and I'm not important

enough to matter. That's her plan. Is she stronger than I?
Perhaps after all I shall snatch Katherine from them and
escape with her—and then have her homesick for ever after.
. . Why am I always imagining something that isn't here?
Russia poisoned my blood—sweet poison, but poison all the
same. You'll understand this letter, but if George Trenchard,
or indeed any ordinary sensible Englishman were to read it,
what an ass he'd think me! 'If he thought more about the
girl he was going to marry than about himself he wouldn't
have all this worry.' But isn't it just that. If, in nine
months from now, I, swallowed whole by Mrs. T., marry
Katie, will that be much fun for her? I shall be a sort of
shadow or ghost. I can see myself running Mrs. Trenchard's
errands, hurrying down to be in time for breakfast (although
she never scolds anyone), sometimes waking, seeing myself,
loathing, despising myself. Ah! Anna would understand . . .
Anna, even when she laughed, understood . . . Anna . . .
I don't think I shall send this. I'm determined to drive you
all from me until, in a year's time, I can think of you safely
again. I described Moscow to Katherine in the train, and
speaking of it, has reminded me . . ."

Katherine could not remember that there had ever been a
year since her eighth birthday when she had missed "The
Feast" at Rafiel. "The Feast" was held always on the 24th
of March, unless that day were a Sunday: it had been held,
old Dr. Pybus, the antiquarian of Pelynt, said, ever since
Phoenician days. To Katherine the event was the crowning
day of the spring. After the 24th there would be, of course,
many cold, blustering days: nevertheless the spring, with
primroses, violets, anemones thick in the four valleys that ran
down to Rafiel, the sky blue with white clouds like bubbles,
the stream running crystal-clear over the red soil, the spring
was here, and "The Feast" was its crowning.

For the fishermen and their families "The Feast" meant a
huge tea in the Schools, great bonfires on the Peak, and a

dance on the fish-market, a drink at 'The Pilchards,' and, above all, for the younger men and women, love and engagements. It was on "The Feast" day that the young men of Rafiel asked the young women whether 'they would walk out', and the young women said 'yes' or 'no' according to their pleasure. On a fine night, with the bonfires blazing to the sky and showers of golden sparks like fire-flies over the quiet sea, there was no happier village in the world than Rafiel. In its little square harbour the stars, and the fires and the amphitheatre-shaped village looked down and the ghosts of the Phoenicians peered over the brow of the hill, sighed for the old times that they once knew, and crept at last, shivering, back into their graves.

This was to be the greatest "Feast" that Katherine had ever known, because Philip was, of course, to be with her. It was to be, for them both, the crowning of their love by the place, the soil, the good Glebeshire earth. To Katherine it seemed that if anything untoward happened on this day, it would be as though Glebeshire itself rejected them. She would confess to no one how solemn it seemed to her. . . .

Uncle Tim was in charge of the party. Timothy Faunder had not, for many, many years missed a "Feast"; thither he went, his outward appearance cynical and careless as ever, but obeying, inwardly, more sacred instincts than he would acknowledge. He would be in charge of Katherine, Millie, Philip, Rachel—Henry did not care to go.

The 24th of March was wonderful weather. Uncle Tim, coming over from his house up the road, to luncheon, said that he had never seen a finer day. He said this to his sister Harriet, standing before the window of her little room, looking down upon the lawn that reflected the sunny shadows like a glass, looking down upon the clumps of daffodils that nodded their heads to him from the thick grass by the garden wall. Harriet was very fond of her brother; she had an intimate relationship with him that had never been expressed in words by either of them. She was a little afraid of him. She was sitting now writing notes. She did not pause as she talked to him, and sometimes she rubbed the side of her nose with her fingers in a puzzled way. She wrote a large sprawling hand, and often spelt her words wrongly.

This conversation was before luncheon.

"Well, Harriet," Tim said. "How are you?"

She looked up for a moment at his big, loose, untidy body, his shaggy beard, his ruffled hair.

"Why do you never brush your hair, Tim? It's such a bad example for Henry. And you're standing in the light. . . . Thank you. . . . Oh—I'm very well. Why didn't you come in last night, as you said you would? . . . Yes, I'm quite well, thank you."

"I went walking," said Timothy. "I do brush my hair, only I am not going to put grease on it for anybody . . . How do you like the young man?"

Mrs. Trenchard nodded her head several times as though she were adding up a sum.

"He likes it here, I think, although of course it must be quiet for him—'And if Tuesday—isn't convenient—suggest —another day—next week!' "

"So you don't like him even so much as you expected to?"

"No." She answered quite abruptly, spreading her large hand flat out upon the table as though, by her sudden pounce, she had caught a fly. "He's weaker than I had fancied, and vainer. . . . More insignificant altogether. . . . Miss Propert, The Close, Polchester. . . ."

"He's weak, yes," said Tim, staring down upon his sister. "But he isn't insignificant. He's weak because his imagination paints for him so clearly the dreadful state of things it would be if affairs went wrong. He wants then terribly to make them right. But he hasn't the character to do much himself, and he knows it. A man who knows he's weak isn't insignificant."

Mrs. Trenchard made no reply.

"Well, what are you going to do about it?" at last said Tim.

"Oh, he'll marry Katherine of course."

"And then?"

"And then they'll live here. . . . 'Dear Canon, I wonder whether . . .'—"

"And then?"

"And then—why then it will be just as it is now."

"Oh! I see!"

Timothy turned his back upon her, staring down upon all the green that came up like a river to the walls of the house. His eyes were grave, his back square, his hands locked tight. He heard the scratching of his sister's pen—otherwise there was deep silence about them. He wheeled round.

"Harriet, look here! I've never—no, I think, never—asked you a favour."

She turned in her chair and faced him, looking up to him with her wide, rather sleepy, kindly eyes—now a little humorous, even a little cynical.

"No, Tim—never," she said.

"Well, I'm going to ask you one now."

"Yes?" Her eyes never flickered nor stirred from his.

"It's this. I like the young man—like him, for God knows what reason. I think I must myself once have seen the world as he does. I know I believed that it could be such a splendid world with such a little effort—if only everyone were nice to everyone. I understand young Philip—I believe that this is a crisis in his life and in Katherine's. There are three possible endings to the engagement. He can marry her, carry her off and live his own life. He can marry her, not carry her off and live your life. The engagement can break down, and he disappear back to where he came from. You love Katherine, you are determined not to lose her, therefore you intend to make the first impossible. You see that Katherine is so deeply attached to him that it will break her heart if he goes—therefore the last is not to be. There remains only the second. To that you devote all your energies. You are quite selfish about it. You see only yourself and Katherine in the matter. You see that he is weak and afraid of you. . . . You will break him in, then turn him into the paddock here to graze for the rest of his life. It would serve you right if Katherine were to run away with him."

"She won't do that," said Mrs. Trenchard quietly.

"Who knows? I wish she would, but she's faithful, faithful, faithful down to the soles of her shoes. . . . Bless her!"

Mrs. Trenchard smiled. "Dear Tim. You are fond of her, I know. . . . There's the luncheon-bell."

"Wait a minute." He stood over her now. "Just listen. I believe you're wrong about Katherine, Harriet. She's old-fashioned and slow compared with the modern girl—we're an old-fashioned family altogether, I suppose. It's the first time she's been in love in her life, and, as I said just now, she's faithful as death—but she'll be faithful to him as well as to you. Let him have his fling, let him marry her and carry her off, go where he likes, develop himself, be a man she can be proud of! It's the crisis of his life and of hers too—perhaps of yours. You won't lose her by letting her go off with him. She'll stick to you all the more firmly if she knows that you've trusted him. But to keep him here, to break his spirit, to govern him through his fear of losing her—I tell you, Harriet, you'll regret it all your life. He'll either run away and break Katie's heart or he'll stay and turn into a characterless, spiritless young country bumpkin, like thousands of other young fellows in this county. It isn't even as though he had the money to be a first-class squire—just enough to grow fat (he's rather fat now) and rotten on. Worse than dear George, who at least has his books.

"And he isn't a stupid fool neither . . . he'll always know he might have been something decent. If I thought I had any influence over him I'd tell him to kidnap Katie to-morrow, carry her up north, and keep her there."

Mrs. Trenchard had listened to him with great attention; her eyes had never left his face, nor had her body moved.

She rose, now, very slowly from her chair, gathered her notes together carefully, walked to the door, turned to him, saying: "How you do despise us all, Tim!" then left the room.

After luncheon they started off. Philip, sitting next to Katherine in the waggonette, was very silent during the drive; he was silent because he was determined that it was on this afternoon that he would tell Katherine about Anna.

Without turning directly round to her he could see her profile, her dark hair a little loose and untidy, her cheek flushed with pleasure, her eyes smiling. "No, she's not pretty," he thought. "But she's better than that. I can't see what she's like—it's as though she were something so close to me and so precious that I could never see it, only feel that it was there. And yet, although I feel that she's un-attainable too—she's something I can never hold completely, because I shall always be a little frightened of her."

He made this discovery, that he was frightened, quite sud-denly, sitting there on that lovely afternoon; he saw the shad-ows from the clouds, swooping, like black birds, down over the valley beneath him: far beyond him he saw a thread of yellow running beside the water of the stream that was now blue in the sunshine and now dark under the hill; there were hosts of primroses down there, and the hedges that now closed the carriage were sheeted with gold: when the hedges broke the meadows beyond them flowed, through the mist, like green clouds, to the hazy sea; the world throbbed with a rhythm that he could hear quite clearly behind the clap-clap of the horses' hoofs—'hum—hum—hum—hum'— The air was warm, with a little breath of cold in it; the dark soil in the ditches glistened as though, very lately, it had been frozen.

Riding there through this beautiful day he was frightened. He was aware that he did not know what Katherine would do when he told her. During his years in Russia he had grown accustomed to a world, inevitably, recklessly, voluble. Rus-sians spoke, on any and every occasion, exactly what was in their mind; they thought nothing of consequences whether to themselves or any other; their interest in the ideas that they were pursuing, the character that they were discussing, the situation that they were unravelling, was always so intense, so eager, so vital that they would talk for days or weeks, if necessary, and lose all sense of time, private feelings, restraint and even veracity. Philip had become used to this. Had Katherine been a member of a Russian family he would, two days after his engagement, have had everything out with them all—he would have known exactly where he stood. With the Trenchards he did not know anything at all; from the moment of his engagement he had been blindfolded, and now he felt as though in a monstrous game of "Blind Man's Buff" he were pushed against, knocked on the elbows, laughed at, bumped against furniture, always in black, grim darkness. Since he had come down to Garth he had lost even Katherine. He felt that she was disappointed in some way, that she had never been quite happy since their journey together in the train. Well, he would put everything straight this afternoon. He would tell her about Moscow, Anna, all his life—tell her that he could not, after their marriage, live at Garth, that it would stifle him, make him worthless and useless, that she must show him that she definitely cared for him more than for her family. . . .

He felt as though, with a great sweeping stroke of his arm, all the cobwebs would be brushed away and he would be free. He rehearsed to himself some of the things that he would say: "You must see, dear, that the family don't like me. They're jealous of me. Much better that we go away for a year or two—right away—and allow them to get used to the idea. Then we can come back."

But what would she say about Anna? Did she know anything about men, their lives and affairs? Would her fine picture of him be dimmed? He hoped a little that it would. He wanted simply to love her, that she should understand him and that he should understand her, and then they two together (the world, Garth, the Trenchards blown to the wind) should—

"That's Tredden Cove, that dip beyond the wood," said Katherine. "We used to go there—"

Yes, he was frightened. He felt as though this afternoon would be the crisis of his life. (There had been already a great many crises in his life.) He was impatient; he wanted to begin, now, in the waggonette. He could imagine turning to her, saying: "Katie, darling, I want to tell you—"

He was conscious that Lady Seddon was watching him. "Jolly day, isn't it?" he said. He thought to himself. "She hates me as the others do."

They had come to the Cross-Roads. Jacob put on the drag, and they began, very slowly, to creak down a precipitous hill. The fantastic element in the affair that Philip had been expecting as a kind of reply to his own sense of his personal adventure seemed to begin with this hill. It resembled no ordinary hill; it plunged down with a sudden curve that seemed to defy the wheels of any carriage; on their right the bank broke sheer away far down to one of the Rafiel four valleys, vivid green now with tufted trees. There was no fence nor wall, and one slip of the wheels would have hurled the carriage over. At a turn of the road a cluster of white cottages, forming one figure together as though they had been a great stone flung from the hill-top by some giant, showed in the valley's cup. At his sense of that remoteness, of that lifting wildness of the rising hills, at the beauty of the green and grey and silver and white, he could not restrain a cry.

Katherine laughed. "That's Blotch End," she said. "One turn and we're at the bottom." The carriage wheeled round, crossed a brown bridge and had started down the road to Rafiel. . . . On one side of the road was a stream that, hurrying down from the valley, hastened past them to the sea; on the other side of them a wooded hill, with trees like sentinels against the sky—then the village street began, ugly at first, as are the streets of so many Glebeshire villages, the straight, uniform houses, with their grey slate roofs, now and then hideous-coloured glass over the doorways, and, ugliest of all, the Methodist chapel with '1870' in white stone over the door. But even with such a street as this Rafiel could do something: the valley stream, hidden sometimes by houses, revealed itself suddenly in chuckling, leaping vistas. Before the houses there were little gardens, thick now with daffodils and prim-roses and hyacinths: through the deep mouth of the forge fires flamed, and a sudden curve of the street brought a bridge, a view of the harbour and a vision of little houses rising, tier on tier, against the rock, as though desperately they were climbing to avoid some flood. This contrast of the wild place itself, with the ugly patches of civilisation that had presented themselves first, was like the voice of the place chuckling at its visitors' surprise.

First the row of villas, the tailor's shop with a pattern pic-ture in the window, the sweet shop, the ironmonger's—now this sudden huddle of twisted buildings, wildly climbing to the very sky, a high, rugged peak guarding the little bay, two streams tossing themselves madly over the harbour ridges, the boats of the fleet rocking as though dancing to some mys-terious measure, a flurry of gulls, grey and white, flashing, wheeling, like waves and foam against the sky, the screaming of the birds, the distant thud of the sea . . . this was Rafiel.

They left the carriage and turned to go back to the schools, where the tea had already begun. Katherine slipped her arm into Philip's: he knew that she was waiting for him to speak about the place, and he knew, too, that she was not expecting his praise as confidently as she would have expected it three weeks ago. A little of her great trust in him was shadowed by her surprise that he had not surrendered to Glebeshire more completely. Now he could tell her that it was to the Trenchards and not to Glebeshire that he had refused to surrender.

She could not tell, of course, that all his attention now was fixed on his determination to tell her everything as soon as he was alone. Walking with him up the road was that secret figure who attends us all—the fine, cherished personality whom we know ourselves to be.

To Philip, more than many others, was the preservation of that secret personality essential. He was, this afternoon, determined to live up to the full height of it.

In the schools, at two long tables, the whole village was feeding: the room was steaming with heat: huge urns at the ends of the tables were pouring out tea with a fierce, scornful indifference, as though they would show what they could do but despised their company. The fishermen, farmers, their wives and families, shining with soap, perspiration and excitement, sat, packed so tightly together that eating seemed an impossibility: there were plates of bread and butter, saffron buns, seed-cake piled up and running over: there were the ladies of the village, who said: "Now, Mr. Trefusis, do try another," or "Mary's rather tired, I think, Mrs. Maxwell. Shall I lift her down?" or "Well, Mrs. Pascoe, out and about again, I see," or "How's the new cottage, Henry? Better than the old one, I expect."

From the other side of the world came: "Aw, thank 'ee, Ma'am—not so bad, thank 'ee. Up to Glossen's Farm they 'ad it praper wild, so they tell me"—"Yes . . . true enough. All over spots 'er arms was, poor worm"—"Didn't worry we, thank 'ee, Miss. Marnin' or evenin' all the same to we . . . Ah, yes, poor Mr. Izards—'e did suffer terrible, poor dear. . . ."

Philip perceived with a sense of irritated isolation how instantly and how easily the other members of his party were swallowed up by the Ceremony. He himself was introduced to a prim young woman in a blue hat, who flung remarks to him over a tea-tray and seemed to regard his well-cut clothes with contempt. The fishermen did not look happy in their stiff Sunday clothes, but he liked their faces. They reminded him more of Russian peasants than any people whom he had seen since his landing in England. No, he must not think about that . . . Russia was banished for ever.

Uncle Timothy, Millie, even Lady Seddon were warmly welcomed, but Katherine was adored. He understood, perhaps for the first time, what that place must mean to her. They called her 'Miss Kathie', they shouted to her across the room, they cracked jokes with her; an old man, with a long white beard like a prophet, stood up and put his hand on her shoulder as he talked to her. Once she broke away from them and came to him.

"Phil, I want you to come and be introduced to a great friend of mine," she said.

He followed her, feeling that all eyes watched him, with criticism and even with hostility. A large, immensely broad man, in a navy blue suit, with a red, laughing face, hair cut very close to his head, and eyes of the honestest, stood up as they came across. He looked at Katherine with the devotion and confidence of a faithful dog.

"This is Mr. Richard Curtis," Katherine said. "He used to pick up shells for me when I was three. He has a boat here with his brother. He's always in good spirits, aren't you, Dick, even when you scald your arm with boiling water?"

This was an allusion to some confidence between them, and as their eyes met, Philip felt a pang of ridiculous jealousy. The man's face was flaming, and his eyes were more devoted than ever. He held out a large, horny hand to Philip. "Excuse me, sir," he said. "I'm proud to shake 'ands with the man wot Miss Katherine is goin' to marry. We thought, once on a time, p'raps as she'd always be 'ere, along with we, but wot we want most is fer 'er to be 'appy—and that we knows now she will be. I 'ope you'll be often down—along, sir, in time to come—that is, sir, if you're not goin' to take 'er right away from us."

"Why, of course not, Dick," said Katherine. "When we're married we're going to live quite close. You've only got to find us a house."

Philip knew that he should say something pleasant; he could think of nothing; he muttered a few words and then turned away, confused, irritated, embarrassed. What had happened to him? He was always so pleasant with everyone, especially with strangers; now, at every turn, he seemed compelled by someone stronger than he to show his worst side. "Oh, if I can only get Katherine out of all this," he thought passionately, "even for a little time. Then I'll come back another man. To have her to myself. Everything's coming between us. Everything's coming between us. . . ."

At last he had his desire. They had left the others. She had led him, out past the row of white cottages, to a rock on the side of the hill, high over the sea, with the harbour below them, the village, curved like a moon in the hills' hollow, behind the harbour, and a little cluster of trees at the hill top striking the blue night sky: opposite them was the Peak rock, black and jagged, lying out into the water like a dragon couchant. They could see the plateau above the Peak where the bonfire was to be, they could see the fish-market silver grey in the evening light, and the harbour like a green square handkerchief with the boats painted upon it. The houses, like an amphitheatre of spectators, watched and waited, their lights turning from pale yellow to flame as the evening colours faded; crying, singing, laughing voices came up to their rock, but they were utterly, finally remote. She leaned her head against his shoulder, and they sat there in silence.

At last, half-dreamily, gazing forward into the sea that, stirred by no wind, heaved ever and again, with some sigh, some tremor born of its own happiness, she talked. "You can see the bonfire and the figures moving around it. Soon the moon will be right above the Peak. . . . Isn't everything quiet? I never knew last year how different this one would be from any that I had ever known before." She turned half towards him, caught his hand and held it. "Phil, you must be very patient with me. I've felt so much that you were part of me that I've expected you to see things always as I

do. Of course that was ridiculous of me. You *can't* love
this place quite as I do—it must take time. . . . You aren't
angry with me, are you?"

"Angry?" he laughed.

"Because the closer I get to you—the longer we're engaged,
the less, in some ways, I seem to know you. I never realised
until you came how shut up as a family we've been, how
wrapt up in ourselves. That must be hard for you to understand. . . ."

"There it goes!" he broke in suddenly.

The bonfire leapt into fire: instantly the village glowed
with flame, a golden pool burnt beneath the Peak, the houses
that had been blue-grey in the dusk now reflected a rosy glow,
and whirling, dancing sparks flew up to join the stars. Little
black figures were dancing round the blaze; down on the fish-
market other figures were moving, and the faint echo of a
fiddle and a horn was carried across the water.

Something said to Philip, 'Tell her—now.'

He plunged with the same tightening of the heart that he
would have known had he sprung from their rock into the
pools of the sea below them. He put his arm more tightly
around her, and there was a desperate clutch in the pressure
of his fingers, as though he were afraid lest she should vanish
and he be left with sky, land and sea flaming and leaping beneath the fire's blaze.

"Katie, I've something I must tell you," he said. He felt
her body move under his arm, but she only said, very quietly:
"Yes, Phil?" Then in the little fragment of silence that followed she said, very cosily and securely: "So long as it isn't
to tell me that you don't love me any more, I don't mind what
it is?"

"No—it isn't that. It's something I should have told you,
I suppose, long ago. I would have told you, only it was all
so over and done with for me that I couldn't imagine its mat-
tering to anyone. I told your father that there was no com-

plication in my life, and that's true—there is none. There's nothing I have nor think nor do that isn't yours."

She said very quietly: "You were in love with someone before you knew me?"

He was surprised and immensely reassured by the quietness and tranquillity of her voice.

"That's it—That's it," he said, eagerly, his heart bounding with relief and happiness. "Look here, Katie. I must tell you everything—*everything,* so that there can't be anything between us any more that you don't know. You see, when I went to Russia first I was very young—very young for my age too. Russia isn't much of a place when you don't know the language and the weather's bad—and I'd gone expecting too much. I'd heard so much about Russia's hospitality and kindness, but I was with English people at first, and most of them were tired to death of Russia, and only saw its worst side and didn't paint it very cheerfully. Then the Russians I did meet had to struggle along in bad French or English (it's all rot about Russians being great linguists), and if a Russian isn't spontaneous he isn't anything at all. Then when I did go to their houses their meals simply killed me. They make one eat such a lot and drink such a lot and sit up all night—I simply couldn't stand it. So at first I was awfully lonely and unhappy—awfully unhappy."

She sighed in sympathy and pressed closer to him.

"I'm not the sort of man," Philip went on, "to stand being lonely. It's bad for me. Some men like it. It simply *kills* me. But after about six months or more I knew a little Russian, and I got to know one or two Russians individually. There's one thing I can tell you—that until you know a Russian personally, so that he feels that he's got some kind of personal part in you, you simply don't know him at all. It's so easy to generalise about Russians. Wait until you've made a friend. . . . I made a friend, several friends. I began to be happier."

Katherine pressed his hand. The bonfire was towering steadily now in a great golden pillar of smoke and flame to heaven. The music of the fiddle and the horn, as though they were its voice, trembled dimly in the air: all the stars were shining, and a full moon, brittle like glass, flung a broad silver road of light across the black Peak and the sea. There was no breeze, but the scent of the flowers from the gardens on the rocks mingled with the strong briny odour of the sea-pinks that covered the ground at their feet.

"The spring came all in a moment, like a new scene at the play. I was introduced to some theatre people, who had a house in the country near Moscow. You've no idea of the slackness and ease of a Russian country house. People just come and go—the doors are all open, meals are always going on—there's always a samovar, and sweets in little glass dishes, and cold fish and meat and little hot pies. In the evening there was dancing, and afterwards the men would just sleep about anywhere. I met a girl there, the first Russian woman who had attracted me. Her name was Anna Mihailovna, and she was a dancer in the Moscow Ballet."

He paused, but Katherine said nothing nor did she move.

"She attracted me because she had never known an Englishman before, and I was exactly what she had always thought an Englishman would be. That pleased me then—I wanted, I even felt it my duty, to be the typical Englishman. It wasn't that she admired the typical Englishman altogether: she laughed at me a great deal, she laughed at my having everything so cut and dried, at my dogmatising so easily, at my disliking Russian unpunctuality and lack of method.

"She thought me rather ridiculous, I fancy, but she felt motherly to me, and that's what most Russian women feel to most men. I was just beginning to love Russia then. I was beginning to dream of its wonderful secrets, secrets that no one ever discovers, secrets the pursuit of which make life one long, restless search. Anna fascinated me—she let me do always as I pleased. She seemed to me freedom itself: I fell madly in love with her."

Katherine's hand gave then a sudden leap in his; he felt the ends of her fingers pressing against his palm. Some of his confidence had left him: some of his confidence not only in himself but in his assurance of the remoteness of his story and the actors in it. He felt as though some hand were dragging him back into scenes that he had abandoned, situations that had been dead. The fire and the sea were veiled, and his eyes, against their will, were fastened upon other visions.

"That year was a very wonderful one for me. We took a flat together, and life seemed to be realised quite completely for me. This, I thought, was what I had always desired . . . and I grew slack and fat and lazy—outside my business—I always worked at that decently. Early in the next year we had a boy. Anna took him with the same happy indifference that she had taken me: she loved him, I know, but she was outside us all, speculating about impossibilities, then suddenly coming to earth and startling one with her reality. I loved her and I loved Moscow—although sometimes too I hated it—but we used also to have the most awful quarrels; I was angry with her, I remember, because I thought that she would never take me seriously, and she would laugh at me for wanting her to. I felt that Russia was doing me no good. Our boy died, quite suddenly, of pneumonia, and then I begged her to marry me and come and live in England. How she laughed at the idea! She didn't want to be married to anyone. But she thought that perhaps England would be better for me. She did not seem to mind at all if I went. That piqued me, and I stayed on, trying to make myself essential to her. I did not care for her then so much as for my idea of myself, that she would break her heart if I went. But she knew that—how she would laugh as she looked at me. . . . She refused to take me seriously. Russia was doing me harm —I got slack, sleepy, indifferent. I longed for England. The chance came. Anna said that she was glad for me to go, and laughed as she said it. I took my chance. . . . I've told you everything," he suddenly ended.

He waited. The tune across the water went: 'La-la-la, la, la-la-la-la, la, la.' Many, many little black figures were turning on the fish-market. The blaze of the bonfire was low and its reflection in the sea smoking red.

When he had finished Katherine had very gently drawn her hand away from his, then suddenly, with a little fierce gesture, pushed it back again.

"What was your boy's name?" she asked, very quietly.

"Paul."

"Poor little boy. Did you care for him very much?"

"Yes, terribly."

"It must have been dreadful his dying."

He felt then a sudden dismay and fear. Perhaps, after all, she was going to dismiss him; he fancied that she was retreating from him—he felt already that she was farther away from him than she had ever been, and, with a desperate urgency, his voice trembling, his hand pressing her arm, he said:

"Katie—Katie—You're disgusted with me. I can feel it. But you must go on loving me—you *must*, you *must*. I don't care for anything but that. All men have had affairs with women. It's all dead with me, as though it had been another man. There's no one in the world but you. I—I—"

His hand shook; his eyes, if she could have seen them, were strained with terror.

She turned to him, put her arms round his neck, drew his head towards her, kissed him on his eyes, his mouth, his cheeks.

"Phil—Phil," she whispered. "How little you understand. My dear—my dear."

Then raising her eyes away from him and staring again in front of her, she said:

"But I want to know, Phil. I *must* know. What was she like?"

"Like?" he repeated, puzzled.

"Yes. Her appearance, her clothes, her hair, *everything*. I want to be able to see her—with my own eyes—as though she were here. . . ."

He stared at her for a moment—then, very slowly, almost reluctantly, he began his description. . . .

CHAPTER VI

O N no day of the year—spring, summer, autumn, or winter, did any inhabitant of Garth House rise before Rebekah. Grimly complete, starch and stiff and taciturn, she would be about the dim house, feeling nothing of the cold blackness of a winter morning, finding apparently no pleasure in the beauty of a summer dawn. Her business was with the House—human beings (yes, Trenchards as well as the rest) she despised—for Houses she could feel reverence . . . they were stronger than she.

Upon the Sunday morning that followed the "Feast" at Rafiel, very early indeed, she was moving about the passages. Looking out on to the lawn and bushes, wet with mist, she knew that it would be a bad day. . . . Weather mattered to her nothing: people (although the Trenchards might think otherwise) mattered to her nothing. Her business was with the House. . . .

That Sunday began badly for Aunt Aggie—and, therefore, for everyone else. Before she woke—in the dusty labyrinth of her half-waking dreams—she knew that her tooth was aching. In her dreams this tooth was of an enormous size, holding, although it was in form and figure a veritable tooth, a huge hammer that it brought down, with a regular beat, upon Aunt Aggie's jaw. She screamed, struggled, fought, awoke—to find that the tooth had receded to its proper place and size, was still faintly beating, but not aching—only threatening. This threat was, in its way, more terrible than

a savage ache. When would the ache begin? Ah, here it
was! . . . no, only the throb. . . . Would hot or cold food
irritate it? Would the wind? . . . She got out of bed and
drew her blind. Her clock told her that the hour was seven.
Why had Annie not called her? Annie had overslept herself
—what was it to Annie if Aunt Aggie were late for Early
Service? But it must be something to Annie. Annie *must*
be warned. Annie . . . Aunt Aggie was conscious that she
had a headache, that the weather was abominable, and that
crossing through the wood to the church would certainly start
the tooth. But she was resolved. Very grimly, her mouth
tightly closed, her heart beating because she was expecting
that, at every moment, that tooth. . . . Aunt Aggie had her
bath, dressed, informed Annie, who came, very greatly agitated, at half-past seven, that this would not be the last she
heard of it, walked off to church. During the singing of the
collection hymn her tooth leapt upon her. . . . It came to her
like some malign and secret enemy, who would influence her
not so deeply through actual pain as through his insistence on
what, please God, he would do afterwards. She hurried
home to breakfast through the wet, grey morning, saying to
herself: "It shall not ache! I forbid it to ache! You hear
me! You shall not!" and always that sinister whisper replied
in her ear: "Wait. Just see what I'll do to you in a moment."

In her bedroom some iodine, which she applied to her gum,
reduced the inside of her mouth to sawdust; through the
dried discomfort of it all her enemy still beat at her heart
ironically.

She was determined that the tooth should not alter her day.
She knew how easily ordinary human beings succumbed—
such weakness should not be hers. Nevertheless her love of
honesty compelled her to admit that, this morning, the house
looked horrible. It had, as she had often told Harriet, been
always overcrowded with 'things'—with mats and jars and
pots and photographs, old books, magazines, ink-bottles, china

ornaments, stones and shells, religious emblems, old calendars, and again photographs, photographs, photographs. . . . It was not that the house was definitely untidy, but that once a thing was there, *there* it remained. The place looked like home, because it was filled with properties that any new-comer would instantly discard. Everything was dim and faded—carpets, curtains, books, pictures; Katherine, Millie, Henry could remember how the water-colour of "Rafiel Beach," the photograph of Trezent Head, the dining-room marble clock, surmounted by the Goddess Diana minus her right leg, the book-case in the drawing-room, with rows and rows of the novels of Anthony Trollope (each in three volumes), the cuckoo clock in the dark corner on the first landing, the glass case with sea shells in the hall near the hatrack, the long row of faded Trenchard and Faunder photographs in the drawing-room, the little corner cupboard with the Sunday games in it—Bible Lotto, puzzle map of Palestine, Bible Questions and Bible Answers—all these things had been "first there" since the beginning of time, even as the oak on the lawn, the rough grass meadows that ran to the very posts of the house, the little wood and the tennis lawn with the brown hole in the middle of it had always been 'there.' Aunt Aggie herself had grown profoundly accustomed to it all—in her heart she would not have had a shell nor a photograph removed from its place. Nevertheless, upon this grey Sunday morning she was oppressed, almost triumphantly, about her sense of the dinginess and confusion of the house. It was as though she said to herself: "There! it's not my tooth at all that makes me feel out of sorts with things. It's simply Harriet's inability to put things straight." She found then that everyone was very quiet at breakfast—'sulky' one could be justified in calling it. Moreover, there were 'sausages again!' Harriet knew perfectly well that Aggie hated sausages—nevertheless she persisted, with the devotion of a blind slave to an august ritual, in having, always, sausages for Sunday breakfast. Aggie was, in spite of her tooth, hungry

this morning, but when, with an unconscious self-conscious-
ness, during a silence, she said: "No sausage for me, thanks.
You know, Betty, that I never care for them." No one said:
"Have an egg, Aggie: it can be boiled in a moment."

Only Harriet, with her attention obviously elsewhere, remarked carelessly: "We can have the ham in, Aggie, if you
like"—to which Aggie could only reply: "You know I dislike cold ham, Harriet."

But, indeed, Sunday breakfast was never a very jolly meal
—how could it be? The hour was throbbing with a consciousness of the impending difficulties and problems of the day.
There was Church, there was Sunday School, there were
callers in the afternoon: there were meals, the very heavy
midday meal with roast beef and Yorkshire pudding, tea with
a great deal of stiff conversation, something in the manner of
Ollendorff, supper, when the chill on the food typified the
exhausted spirits of the tired company. During too many
years had Henry, Millie, Katherine, and still more Aggie,
Betty and Mrs. Trenchard worn Sunday clothes, eaten Sunday meals, suffered Sunday restraint, known Sunday exhaustion for it to be possible for any of them to regard Sunday
in a normal, easy fashion. Very right and proper that they
should so regard it. I would only observe that if there *is* to
be a thorough explosion of Trenchard, of Faunder tempers—
if there is to be, in any kind of way, a "family scene" Sunday
will be, almost certainly, the background selected for it. Aunt
Aggie, looking around her, on this morning, at her assembled
friends and relations, 'thought them all very sulky indeed.
Wrapped up entirely in their own selfish thoughts'. . . . The
day began badly.

Half an hour before church Rachel Seddon and Uncle Tim
were alone together in the drawing-room. She was standing,
prepared and waiting, staring through the windows at the
wild meadow that seemed now soaked with moisture, bent
before the dripping wind. She was thinking very deeply.
She did not at first hear Uncle Tim, and when, turning sud-

denly, she saw him, she thought how exactly he suited the day. By his appearance he instantly justified the atrocious weather: he was wearing a rough grey suit and a low flannel collar: his beard and hair glistened, as though the damp had soaked through them, he carried a muddy trowel in his hand. He came hurriedly into the room, as though he were searching for something. Then when he saw Rachel he stopped, put the trowel down on one of the drawing-room chairs, smiled at her, and came across to her. She had never known him very well, but she had always liked him—his genial aloofness, the sense that he always gave of absolute independence, cheerful but never dogmatic, pleased her. Now she was troubled, and felt that he could help her.

"What's the matter with Katie?" she said, abruptly, looking at him with sharp but deeply honest eyes.

He felt in his tumbled pockets for his pipe and tobacco, then slowly said:

"I was just off for worms—I wanted Henry, but I suppose he's going to church. . . . Katie? . . . Why?"

"I don't know why. I want to know. It's been these last few days—ever since—ever since—Saturday, Friday, Thursday—the day at Rafiel. She's unhappy."

"The lovers have had a quarrel."

"If it were only that! . . . no, that's not Katie, and you know it isn't. Philip's done something—told her something—"

"Ah, you think that because you dislike him."

"I don't know that I do—now. I certainly did at first, but now—here . . . I don't know. He's so much younger than I'd expected, and he is really trying his best to suit himself to the family and the place. I'm sorry for him. I rather like him after all. But *what* is the matter with everyone? Why is the house so uncomfortable? Why can't it all be just smooth and easy? Of course we all hated Katie being engaged at first—I suppose we thought that she might have done better. But now everyone ought to be used to it:

instead of being used to it, it's positively 'nervy' the atmosphere."

"It's simply," said Uncle Tim, pressing down his tobacco into his pipe, "the attack by a Young Man with Imagination upon a family without any. The Young Man's weak of course—people with imagination always are—he's weak and impatient, and insists upon everything being perfect. All the family wants is to be let alone—but it will never be let alone again. The break-up is beginning."

"The break-up?" said Rachel.

"It's like this. If Harriet catches me smoking here in the morning there'll be a row." He picked up the trowel and waved it. "Nearly the whole of our class in England has, ever since the beginning of last century, been happily asleep. It isn't good for people to have a woman on the throne for sixty years—bless her all the same, *and* her making a success of it. So we've slept and slept and slept. The Old Lady died. There was the Boer War: there were motor-cars, flying machines, telephones. Suddenly England was an island no longer. She's *got* to pay attention to other people, other ideas, other customs. She's *got* to look out of her window instead of just snoozing on the sofa, surrounded by her mid-Victorian furniture. Everything's cracking: new classes are coming up, old classes are going down. Birth is nothing: autocracies are anachronisms. . . . A volcano's coming. Everything will be blown sky-high. Then the folk who are left will build a new city—as bad, as stupid, as selfish as the old one, perhaps—but different . . . as different as Garth from China and China from Paradise."

"And Katherine and Philip?" said Rachel.

"Oh, young Mark's just one of the advance-guard. He's smashing up the Trenchards with his hammer—the same way that all the families like us up and down England are being smashed up. If it isn't a young man from abroad, it's a letter or a book or a telephone number or a photograph or a suicide or a Lyceum melodrama. It doesn't matter what it is. The good old backbone of England has got spine disease. When your good grandmother died *your* lot went; now *our* lot is going. . . . When I say going I mean changing."

"There was a funny little man," said Rachel, "whom Uncle John used to know. I forget his name, but he talked in the same way when grandmother died, and prophesied all kinds of things. The world hasn't seemed very different since then, but grandmother was an impossible survival, and *her* lot went, all of them, long before she did. All the same, if you'll forgive me, I don't think that England and possible volcanoes are the point for the moment. It's Katie I'm thinking about. If she's unhappy now what will she be after she's married to him?—If Katie were to make an unhappy marriage, I think it would be the greatest sorrow of my life. I know . . . I've known . . . how easily things can go wrong."

"Ah, things won't go wrong." Uncle Tim smiled confidently. "Young Mark's a good fellow. He'll make Katherine happy all right. But she'll have to change, and changing hurts. She's been asleep like the others. . . . Oh, yes! she has! There's no one loves her better than I, but she's had, in the past, as much imagination as that trowel there. Perhaps now Philip will give her some. She'll lose him if she doesn't wake up. He's restive now under the heavy hands of my dear relations—He'll be gone one fine morning if they don't take care. Katie must look out. . . ." He waved his trowel in the direction of the garden. "All this is like a narcotic. It's so safe and easy and ordered. Philip knows he oughtn't to be comfortable here. Katie, Millie and Henry are beginning to know it. Even Harriet, Aggie, Betty, George will get a tiny glimmering of it one day. But they're too old to change. That's their tragedy. All the same, you see, before this time next year George will be proposing to take Harriet for a trip abroad—Italy probably—a thing he's never done since the day of his marriage."

And at that very moment George entered, very smart and

big and red, with yellow gloves and a flower in his button-hole.

"What's that?" he cried, with his usual roar of laughter. "Who says I'll do what?"

"Take Harriet abroad before this time next year," said Tim.

"I? . . . Not much! . . . We know better than that. England's good enough for us. There isn't a spot in the world to touch this place in the summer—so why should we stir? You'll be saying we ought to go to Russia next, . . . smoking your beastly pipe in here too. Why don't you dress decently and go to church?"

A Church Invasion followed. The Invasion rustled and listened to the bell that called across the garden. 'Com-ing? . . . Com-ing? . . . Com-ing?' . . . Then 'Come! Come! Come!' and said: "Where's Katie? . . . It isn't Litany to-day, so there'll be time before lunch. Where's Henry? . . . We'd better start, the bell's stopping. Just hold my prayer-book a minute, Millie dear, whilst I do this. . . ."

Finally the Invasion called: "Katie! Katie! Katherine! . . . We're going!" and a voice, very far away answered:

"Yes. . . . I'll catch you up! Go on!"

The Invasion left, followed by Uncle Tim, smiling to himself, the trowel in his hand. The house was very still then, relapsing with a little sigh of content into its Sunday quiet: a bird was chattering gently to itself in the wet garden.

Katherine hurried into the drawing-room, her cheeks flushed, buttoning her gloves, her prayer-book under her arm. Her black dress, a little open at the front, had a stiff black lace collar at the back, Elizabethan fashion; now, for the first time in her life, she was wearing something that she had herself thought about and planned. It was for Philip. . . .

She looked about the empty drawing-room, then hurried away through the little wood. How unlike her to be late! She was always the first of the party. But to-day she had been dreaming in her bedroom, sitting, with her hands in her lap, looking out of the window, wondering, longing to know . . . No, she was not jealous. Her curiosity had no tinge of jealousy in it. Why should she be jealous? Was not the thing over, closed? Had not the woman herself dismissed him? That strange figure in that strange country! The wild town, as he had described it, like a village with towers and towers, gold and green and blue, and the carts with painted roofs and the strange writing on the shop-walls . . . and the woman standing there, in the middle of it. This woman, who had known Philip better than Katherine knew him, whom Philip had madly loved, who had borne Philip a son. She was still living there, loving, now, perhaps some-one else, looking back perhaps with some scorn and some pity and some affection to the days when Philip had kissed her, to the hour when their son had died, to that first meeting in the strange country house, where everyone might come and go as they pleased. No, there was no jealousy; but Katherine wanted to have her there, standing in front of her, so that she might study her clothes, her hair, her eyes. Here was a woman whom Philip had madly loved—and he had ceased to love her. Well, he might also cease to love Katherine. But that other woman had dismissed him. Fancy dismissing him! When one had shared with him such experiences how could one ever let him go? . . . Ah, what, *what* was she like? Was her voice soft or harsh? How did she look when Philip made love to her? When Philip made love to her. . . . Yes, there was pain in that.

Katherine hurried under the low porch of the church. She could hear the voice: 'Wherefore I pray and beseech you, as many as are here present, to accompany me with a pure heart. . . .'

As the congregation knelt she slipped into a seat at the back of the church. She had always loved the shabby, ugly little place. It had, for one thing, nothing to boast about—had no fine carvings like the Rafiel Church, no splendid tombs like the two Dunstan St. Firths at Poloynt, no wonderful glass like the Porthcullin memorial window at Borhaze; frankly ugly, whitewashed, with thin narrow grey glass in the side-walls and a hideous purple Transfiguration above the altar, with plain, ugly seats, a terrible modern lectern, a shabby nondescript pulpit, a font like an expensive white sweet, and the most shining and vulgar brass tablet commemorating the Garth heroes of the Boer War.

No other church could ever mean so much to Katherine as this, her shabby friend. She was glad that it was no show place for inquisitive tourists to come tramping over with haughty eyes and scornful boasts. It was her own . . . she loved it because strangers would always say: "How hideous!" because she could remember it on wonderful summer evenings when through the open doors the congregation could hear the tinkling sheep-bells and smell the pinks from the Rectory garden, on wild nights when the sea gales howled round its warm, happy security, on Christmases, on Easters, on Harvest Festivals: she loved it on the evenings when, with its lights covering its plainness, the Garth villagers would shout their souls away over "Onward, Christian soldiers" or "For all the Saints" or would sink into sentimental tenderness over "Abide with me" and "Saviour, again to Thy dear name"; she loved it because here she had been sad and happy, frightened and secure, proud and humble, victorious and defeated . . . as this morning she sank on her knees, burying her face in her hands, she felt at first as though her Friend had found her, had encircled her with His arm, had drawn her into safety. . . .

And yet, after a little while, her unrest returned. As Mr. Smart and the congregation hurried through the psalms for the day, trying, as it were, to beat one another in the friendly race, Katherine felt again that insistent pressure and pursuit. Her mind left the church: she was back again with Philip at Rafiel . . . and now she was searching that mysterious town for that elusive, laughing figure. Katherine

had in her mind a clear picture; she saw a woman, tall and
thin, a dark face with black, ironical eyes, hair jet black, a
figure alert, independent, sometimes scornful, never tragic
or despairing. "If she knew me she would despise me" . . .
this thought came flashing like a sudden stream of light across
the church. "If she knew me she'd despise me . . . despise
me for everything, even perhaps for loving Philip"—and yet
she felt no hostility; of a certainty no jealousy, only a little
pain at her heart and a strange conviction that the world
was altered now simply because there was a new figure in it.
And there were so many things that she wanted to know.
Why had Anna dismissed Philip? Was it simply because
she was tired of him? Was it perhaps for his own sake,
because she thought that he was wasting his life and character
there. No, Anna probably did not think about his character.
. . . Did she still care for him and, now that he was gone,
long for him? Well, Katherine had him now, and no one
should take him. . . . Would she, perhaps, write to Philip
and try to compel him to return? Did she think of the son
who had died? Had she much heart or was she proud and
indifferent?

". . . grant that this day we fall into no sin, neither run
into any kind of danger: but that all our doings may be
ordered by Thy governance to do that which is right. . . ."
Mr. Smart's voice brought back the church, the choir with
two girls in large flowered hats, the little boys, Mr. Hart, the
butcher, and Mr. Swithan, the grocer, the broad backs in the
family pew. Aunt Aggie, Aunt Betty, Henry, Mrs. Trenchard, Millie, Philip, George Trenchard, Rachel Seddon (the
family pew was a hideous box with a door to it, and you
could see only the top half of the Trenchards. . . . They,
however, could see everything: Mrs. Trenchard could see
the choir, and the choir knew it). Because Katherine was
never late, therefore was she denied the opportunity of study-
ing the Collective Trenchard Back. To-day she had it in
front of her, and it seemed, suddenly, to be something with

which she herself had no concern at all. For an amazing, blinding, and most desolating moment she viewed the Trenchards as a stranger might view them. Her loneliness was appalling. She belonged to no one. She had no place nor country: her mother and Philip had left her . . . only a strange woman, watching her to see what she would do, laughed at her. As she stood up and Mr. Smart gave out the hymn, she saw that there was a hole in her glove. She felt shabby and hot, and covered the hole with her other hand, because during that moment she was positively, actively conscious of the other woman's curious, hostile gaze; then, as the hymn began, security came back to her—her heart beat quietly again.

"Why were you late, dear?" said Aunt Aggie, walking back through the wood.

"I dawdled."

"Dawdled! How unlike you, dear! I remember years ago when I dawdled one Sunday mother saying . . . Oh, dear, there it begins again!"

"Is your tooth bad?"

"Never mind, dear, say nothing about it. The last thing I should wish for would be a fuss. I thought poor Mr. Smart at his very worst this morning. Since his last child was born he's never preached a good sermon. Really, it's difficult to be patient with him."

"Have you done anything for it, Aunt Aggie?"

"Iodine. It comes and goes. If it were only steady. . . ."

Katherine knew that it was of the utmost importance to be sympathetic, but all that she could think of in her head was, "How silly to worry about a tooth! How silly to worry about a tooth! . . ." She knew at once that Aunt Aggie saw that she was unsympathetic, and that she resented it deeply

"Mind you say nothing, dear," she said, as they crossed the lawn. "You know that I hate a fuss." And Katherine, who had stopped on the grass and was staring at the horizon, did not even answer. Then Aunt Betty came up and said: "What a delightful sermon! Mr. Smart gets better and better."

Aunt Aggie did not trust herself to speak.

Meanwhile Philip also had been unhappy. He did frankly hate an English Sunday, and to-day the damp-grey heaviness overwhelmed him, so that he was almost melodramatic in his resentment.

Four days now had passed since the "Feast", and he thought that they had been the worst four days of his life. He, positively, had not slept: he had been driven by a wild, uncertain spirit, inspiring him now to this action and now to that, making him cry out in the middle of the night. "What is she thinking about it? Is it changing her love for me? . . . Perhaps she doesn't love me any more, and is afraid to tell me. She didn't seem angry then when I told her, but she may not have realised—now—" He wanted her to tell him everything, and he wanted her also never to allude to the affair again. He had confessed to her, and there was no more to be said—and yet she must say what now, after four days, she felt about it. Meanwhile she said nothing and he said nothing. There was constraint between them for the only time since their first meeting. He had thought that his confession would have smashed the cobwebs—it had only made them the more blinding.

Meanwhile it was all so desperately serious to him that he simply could not endure the watching and waiting family. His insistent desire that 'things should be perfect' had from the beginning been balked by the family's presence, now his sense that they all wanted to take Katherine away from him awoke in him a real hysterical nightmare of baffled impotence. He would willingly have strangled Aunt Aggie, Henry and Mrs. Trenchard, and then set fire to the house and garden. Then, into the middle of it all, came this impossible Sunday.

He set his teeth over the roast beef, Aunt Aggie's complaints and George Trenchard's hearty commonplace; directly luncheon was over he seized Katherine.

"Look here! we must go for a walk—now—at once!"

"My dear Phil! I can't—there's my Sunday School at three. I haven't looked at anything."

"Sunday School! Oh, my God! . . . Sunday School! Look here, Katie, if you don't walk with me first I shall go straight down to the village pond and drown myself."

"No, you mustn't do that". She seemed quite grave about it. "All right—wait for me. I'll be down in two minutes."

They set off along the road to Pelynt Cross, the thin sea mist driving in their faces.

He broke out: "I must go away from here. To-morrow, at once—I simply can't stand it any longer."

"Can't stand what?"

"Seeing you swallowed up by the family, who all hate me and want to get rid of me. You yourself are changing —you aren't frank with me any longer. You don't say what you think. What use am I here anyway? What good is it my hanging round doing nothing? I'm sick of it. I'm losing you—I'm miserable. A Sunday like this is enough to make one commit murder."

She put her hand inside his arm and drew him closer to her.

"I know what it is," she said. "You've been wondering why I haven't spoken to you about what you told me the other day. You've been thinking that I ought to, haven't you?"

"No, it's only that I've wondered whether perhaps you've changed your mind since then. Then you didn't seem to be angry, but, thinking about it afterwards—"

"Why, Phil," she said, "how could there be anything different? It's all gone, finished. You don't suppose that I ever imagined that you'd never loved another woman before

ou met me. I'm interested, that's all. You've told me so
ittle about her. I'd like to know all sorts of things—even
quite little unimportant things—"

"It would be much better," he said slowly, "if we just
eft it and didn't talk about it."

"But I thought you wanted me to talk about it?" she
ried. "How funny you are!"

"No, I didn't *want* you to talk about it. It's only that I
idn't like there being constraint—I don't see why you should
are. It's like talking about someone who's dead."

"But she isn't dead. Do you suppose, Phil—would she,
o you think, like you to go back?"

"No, I'm sure she wouldn't—at least I don't think so."

"Was she the kind of woman who forgets easily, who can
ut people out of her life just as she wants to?"

"Anna . . ." His voice lingered over the name. "No, I
on't think she ever forgot. She was simply independent."

"Would she think of your boy and want him back?"

"She might." He suddenly stopped. "She might. That
vening he was so ill she—"

Katherine looked across the fields to Pelynt Cross, dim and
rey beneath the rain.

"She had a heart, then," she said slowly.

He suddenly wheeled about with his face to Garth. He
poke sharply and roughly in a voice that she had never heard
im use before.

"Don't, Katie—leave her alone. What do you go on about
er for?"

"But if it's all dead?"

"Oh, drop it, I say! That's enough."

She knew that she was a fool, but something—or was it
omebody?—drove her on.

"But you said just now that you wanted me to be frank."
His voice was a cry.

"You'll drive me mad, Katie. You don't seem to have any
onception—"

"Very well. I won't say anything."

They were quite silent after that: the silence swelled, like a rising cloud, between them: it became impossible to break it . . . they were at Garth gates, and they had not spoken. She would have said something, but he turned abruptly off into the garden. She walked, with her head up, into the house.

She went up to her room, arranged her Sunday School books, felt suddenly a grinding, hammering fatigue, as though she had been walking all day; her knees were trembling and her throat was dry. She sat by her window, looking down on to the garden, where the sea mist drove in walls of thin rain against the horizon. Behind the mist the trees seemed to peer at her as though they were wondering who she was. "I don't care," she thought, "he shouldn't have spoken to me like that." But how had it happened? At one moment they had been so close together that no force, no power, would separate them—a word and they had been so far apart that they could not see one another's eyes.

"I don't care. He shouldn't—"

She got up, rubbed her cheeks with her hand because they were burning, and, with a glance at Philip's photograph (someone she had known years ago and would never know again), went out. The house was silent, and she met no one. As she crossed the lawn she thought: "How absurd! We've quarrelled—a real quarrel"—then—"It wasn't my fault. He shouldn't—" She held her head very high indeed as she walked down the road to the Bridge, but she saw no one, felt no rain upon her cheek, was not conscious that she was moving. At the door of the Schools she saw Mrs. Smart, and heard someone say quite sensibly and happily:

"We're early. There won't be many this afternoon, I expect."

"Mrs. Douglas has told me that she won't be able to come— I wonder, Katie, whether you'd mind taking—"

"Why, of course."

Mrs. Smart was little and round and brown like a pippin. She was always breathless from having more to wrestle with than she could grasp. She was nervous, too, and short-sighted, and the one governing motive of her life was to bear her husband a son. She had now four daughters; she knew that her husband felt it very deeply. She had once unburdened herself to Katherine, but, after that, had been shyer with her than before. Katherine, against her will, had been often irritated by Mrs. Smart—she had wondered at her restlessness and incapacity to keep up with the business in hand, but to-day, out of the sinister gloom of that horrible afternoon, the little woman seemed to Katie suddenly sympathetic, eloquent, moving. Katie could hear her voice, rather husky, rather uncertain, on that afternoon of her confession: ". . . and we did really hope that Lucy would be a boy, we really did. He would have been called Edward. Harold has such plans for a son—we have often thought together what we would do . . . and now, I'm afraid. . . ."

Inside the schoolroom door Katie paused, looked at the room with the bare benches arranged in squares, the shining maps of the world and Europe, the case with beetles and butterflies, the hideous harmonium.

She suddenly caught Mrs. Smart's hand and pressed it through the damp little glove. She knew that Mrs. Smart would be surprised—she had never been demonstrative to her before. . . . She moved to her part of the room, three only of her class were present, and to these were added two small boys from another division.

"Now, children," said Mr. Smart's cheerful voice (he always spoke to boys as though he were luring animals into a cage), "let us start with hymn No. 436, shall we?" After the hymn, a prayer, and then, for an hour that subdued, restrained hum which belongs to the Sunday School only; being religious as well as disciplined, persuasive as well as obedient. Katherine now was very proud—as she said: "Well, Robin, and what did Moses do then?" she was thinking—"But he must come to me—that's fair. It was not my fault. He blamed me first for not speaking, and afterwards when I did speak. . . . Besides, if it's all over and finished, why should he mind?" She looked very young as she sat there, her mouth hard and set and her eyes full of trouble. Her sensation was as though she had been suddenly marooned; the desolation, the terror, the awful loneliness came, as the evening fell, creeping up towards her. "Suppose he never makes it up—Suppose he goes away and leaves me." She caught her hands tightly together on her lap and her breath suddenly left her.

"Yes, Johnny. His name was Aaron. That's right."

The ordeal was over; she was hurrying back through the dusk to the lighted house. She went up again to her room, and sat down again by the window. She listened. The house was very still, but she thought that, perhaps, he would guess that she was here, in her bedroom, and would come up. She wished that her heart would stop beating so that she might hear the better.

She listened to every sound, to distant voices, to the whimper of rain upon the window, to the sharp crack of some shutting door. Her whole mind now was concentrated upon his coming: her eyes left the window and turned to the door. She waited. . . .

Quite suddenly, as though someone else had commanded her, she began to cry. She did not move her hands to her face, but little dry sobs shook her body. She hated herself for her weakness, and then that very contempt broke her down completely, so that with her hands pressed against her face desolately and almost, it might seem, ironically, she wept. Through her crying she heard the door open, and, looking up, saw her mother there. Mrs. Trenchard closed the door very carefully. "Why, Katherine!" she said in a whisper as though this were a matter simply between the two of them. "I came to see," said Mrs. Trenchard, "whether you weren't coming in to tea. The Drakes are here."

It was no use to pretend that she had not been crying. She rubbed her eyes with her handkerchief, turning her back for a moment on her mother and gazing down on to the dark lawn that had all melted now into the rain. Then, when she had gained her control, she faced the room again.

"It's nothing, mother. I've had a headache. It's better. I'll lie down a little and then come in. Is Agnes Drake here?"

"Yes. She wants to see you."

"Well. I'll come."

But Mrs. Trenchard did not go away. Her large soft eyes never left her daughter's face.

"What's really the matter, dear?"

"Really—a headache. This weather and then Sunday School. I felt bad in church this morning."

"You've been unlike yourself, dear, for some days."

"No, mother—I've been just the same."

"You've been unhappy."

Katherine raised her head proudly and gave back her mother's gaze.

"There's been nothing—nothing at all—"

But Mrs. Trenchard's eyes never faltered. She suddenly, with an action that was full of maternal love, but love restrained by fear of its rejection, love that had tenderness in its request to be accepted, raised her hands as though she would take her daughter, and hold her safe and never let her depart into danger again.

"Katie—" her voice was soft, and she let her hands fall again. "Give it up, dear. Break the engagement. Let him go."

Katherine did not answer, but she raised her head higher than it had been before, and then, suddenly, as though the irony of her whole relationship with her mother, with Philip, with the very world itself, had driven in upon her, she smiled.

Mrs. Trenchard went on: "You aren't happy, Katie,

darling. We all notice it. It was so sudden, the engagement. You couldn't tell at the time. But now—I've never said anything, have I? You've seen that I've been perfectly fair, but you know that I've never liked him—I said give it its chance. But now that he's been down here, you can judge how different we all are—it's plain that it won't do. Of course you couldn't tell at the time. But now—"

"Ah," Katherine said quietly, "that's why you asked him here. I wondered."

At the sudden hostility in Katherine's voice Mrs. Trenchard started. Then, quite timidly, as though she were asking some great favour, she said:

"You mustn't be angry with me for that. I only care about your happiness. I'm older—If I think that you are not going to be happy I'm worried and distressed of course. What can he be to me compared with you? And lately you yourself have been different—different to all of us . . . Yes . . . You know that if I thought that he would make you happy. . . ." Her voice was quickly sharp sounding on a trembling, quivering note. "Katie—give him up. Give him up. There'll be somebody much better. There are all of us. Give him up, darling. Tell him that you don't love him as you thought you did."

"No, I don't," said Katherine, her voice low. "I love him more than ever I thought I could love anything or anyone. I love him more every day of my life. Why you—all of you—" She broke away from her fierceness. She was gentle, putting her hand against her mother's cheek, then bending forward and kissing her.

"You don't understand, mother. I don't understand myself, I think. But it will be all right. I know that it will. . . . You must be patient with me. It's hard for him as well as for you. But nothing—*nothing*—can change me. If I loved him before, I have twice as much reason to love him now."

Mrs. Trenchard looked once more at Katherine, as though

she were seeing her for the last time, then, with a little sigh, she went out, very carefully closing the door behind her.

Meanwhile, another member of the Trenchard family, namely Henry, had found this especial Sunday very difficult. He always hated Sunday because, having very little to do on ordinary days of the week, he had nothing at all to do on Sunday. Never, moreover, in all his life before had the passing of time been so intolerably slow as it had during these last weeks. The matter with him, quite simply, was that his imagination, which had been first stirred on that afternoon of Philip's appearance, was now as lively and hungry as a starved beast in a jungle. Henry simply didn't know what to do with himself. Miserably uncertain as to his right conduct in the matter of Philip and Katherine, speculating now continually about adventures and experiences in that wider world of which he had had a tiny glimpse, needing desperately some definite business of preparation for business that would fill his hours, and having nothing of the sort, he was left to read old novels, moon about the fields and roads, quarrel with Millie, gaze forebodingly at Katherine, scowl at Philip, have some moments of clumsy sentiment towards his mother, bite his nails and neglect his appearance. He began to write a novel, a romantic novel with three men asleep in a dark inn and a woman stealing up the ricketty stairs with a knife in her hand. That was all that he saw of the novel. He knew nothing at all about its time nor place, its continuation nor conclusion. But he heard the men breathing in their sleep, saw the moonshine on the stairs, smelt the close, nasty, beery smell of the tap-room below, saw the high cheek-bones and large nose of the woman and the gleaming shine of the knife in her hand.

He walked for many miles, to Rafiel, to St. Lowe, to Dumin Head, inland beyond Rasselas, to Pendennis Woods, to Polchester, to the further side of Pelynt—and always, as he walked with his head in the air, his Imagination ran before him like a leaping, towering flame. The visions before his soul were great visions, but he could do nothing with them. He thought that he would go forth and deliver the world, would love all men, prostitutes, lepers, debauchers (like Philip); he flung his arms about, tumbled over his untidy boot laces, saw life as a gorgeous-tinted plain, with fame and glory awaiting him—then returned to Garth, quarrelled with Millie, sulked and bit his nails.

This was a hard time for Henry.

He had determined that he would not present himself in the drawing-room at tea-time, but when half-past four arrived, the afternoon had already stretched to such ghastly lengths that something had to be done. He came slipping, stumbling downstairs, and found Philip, with a waterproof turned up over his ears and every sign of the challenger of wild weather, standing in the hall. Henry would have passed him in silence, but Philip stopped him.

"Look here," he said, in a low mysterious voice, "will you do something for me?"

"What?" said Henry, suspiciously.

"I'm going out for a long walk. Shan't be back until supper. Give this letter to Katherine, and tell her I want her to read it before I get back."

"Why don't you give it to her yourself? She's up in her room."

"Because I want you to."

Henry took the letter, and Philip was gone, sending into the house a little gust of cold wind and rain as he plunged through the door. Henry looked after him, shook his head as though the destinies of the world were on his shoulders, put the letter into his pocket and went into the drawing-room. The Drake family was calling. There were Mrs. Drake, old and sharp and weather-beaten, like a sign post on the top of a hill; her son, Francis Drake, who, unlike his famous namesake, seemed unable to make up his mind about anything, was thin and weedy, with staring eyes, and continually trying to swallow his fist; and little Lettice Drake, aged seven, fifteen years younger than any other in the family; her parents had never entirely got over their surprise at her appearance: she was sharp and bony, like her mother. Mrs. Trenchard, Aunt Aggie and Millie were entertaining; Great-Aunt Sarah was seated in state, in black silk and white cap, and her stern eye was fixed upon Mr. Drake, whose appearance she did not like. This made Mr. Drake very nervous.

Afternoon-tea on Sunday comes at the very moment when the day seems most unbearable—Later, at about six o'clock, Sunday fatigue will happily begin to descend and envelop its victims, but at half-past four one is only able to remember that it is a mistake to have so large a meal in the middle of the day, that Sunday clothes are chill and uncomfortable, and that all the people in whom one has the least interest in life will shortly make their appearance.

There is also the prospect of evening service, followed by cold supper: the earlier hours of the day stretch now behind one at so vast and unwieldy a length that it seems impossible that one will ever reach the end of the day alive. Aunt Aggie felt all this—she also hated the Drakes. She saw that Henry, moody in a corner by himself, regarded her with a cynical eye: her tooth, which had been quiet since luncheon, was throbbing again. She endeavoured to be pleasant to little Lettice, although she hated children, and she knew that children knew it.

"Wonderfully she's grown!" she said, bending down towards the child, who watched her with cold curiosity. "And what's your favourite game now, Lettice? Too old for dolls, I expect."

There was no reply.

"Tell Miss Trenchard about your games, dear," said Mrs. Drake.

There was no reply.

"You must come and play here one day, dear," said Aunt

Aggie. "Such a big room as we've got upstairs—and lots of toys. You'd like that, wouldn't you?"

There was no reply.

"She's shy, I expect," said Mrs. Drake. "So many children are."

Aunt Aggie drew nearer to Lettice.

"You mustn't be shy with me, dear. I'm so proud of children. You shall have *such* a piece of cake in a minute!"

But with a little movement of her bony fingers Lettice Drake, in a voice of chill detachment, said:

"You've got a thpot on your faith," referring to a little black mole on Aunt Aggie's right cheek. The voice was so chill, the indifference so complete that the failure of Aunt Aggie's tactics was obvious to the dullest onlooker. Unfortunately Henry laughed; he had not intended to laugh: he did not feel at all in a humorous mood—but he laughed from nervousness, discomfort and disgust. He knew that Aunt Aggie would not forgive this . . . he hated quarrels with Aunt Aggie. She did not look at him, but her back told him what she was thinking. He wished, bitterly, that he had more self-control; he knew that, of all possible insults, Aunt Aggie would regard most bitterly a mock at her appearance in a public place. The Drakes might be considered a public place.

Mrs. Trenchard said: "Where's Katie? You'd like to see her, Agnes, I'm sure. Perhaps she doesn't know you're here. I'll see. I know you'd like to see her." Mrs. Trenchard went away. Then Aunt Sarah, who had been hitherto absolutely silent, began, her eye never leaving Mrs. Drake's face.

"You're the daughter of Aggie Mummings, whom I used to know. You must be. Poor Aggie . . . I remember your mother quite well—a feeble thing always, never knowing her mind and always wanted people's advice. I used to say to her: 'Aggie, if you let men see how feeble you are you'll never get married'—but she did after all—which shows you never can tell—I think, Millie, I'll have some more hot in this . . . yes, I remember your mother very well, poor thing."

"I've heard her speak of you, Miss Trenchard," said Mrs. Drake.

Mr. Drake suddenly attacked Millie.

"Well now—about Paris—you know—very different from this hole, ain't it?"

"Very different," said Millie. "But I don't consider this 'a hole'."

"Don't you now? Well—that's very interesting. Don't you? . . . I do."

Millie had nothing to say.

"It's slow, you know—horrid slow—just weather, I call it. Whether it's raining or not, you know—. Yes . . . I wonder you don't find it slow after Paris."

"I was at school there, you see," said Millie. "It's different when you're at school."

"I suppose it is. Yes, I s'pose so." He began to cram his fist into his mouth, was surprised at its boniness, regarded it gravely, said: "Well, yes . . . I s'pose so . . . Yes . . . Well . . ." and was silent.

Then Mrs. Trenchard at last returned: Katherine was with her. Henry at once saw that Katherine had been crying. The effect of this discovery upon Henry was elemental in its force. He had, during all his life, regarded Katherine as almost omnipotent in her strength and wisdom. He had, moreover, always thought to himself: "One day she will have her reward," and his vision of Katherine's future happiness and glory had been one of his favourite dreams. Now that cad had been making her cry. . . . He was, at that moment, on the very edge of making a scene . . . he would fling Philip's letter down there, in front of them, Drakes and all. He would cry: "There! that's from the beast who's been making her cry—and I tell you he's a cad. He had a woman for years in Russia and had a son too— that's the kind of fellow he is." But Katherine was smiling and laughing. The Drakes certainly would not see that she had been crying: even Millie did not, apparently, notice it; Millie, having done her duty by the Drakes, was going upstairs to write letters. She said good-bye and left the room . . . two minutes later Henry slipped out after her.

He caught her at the top of the stairs.

"I say," he said. "Come into my room for a minute. I've got something to tell you."

"Oh, bother," answered Millie. "I want to write letters."

"Never mind. You must. It's important."

"Aren't the Drakes awful?" she said, standing inside his door and observing the disorder of his room with a scornful lip.

"Yes, they are," said Henry. "Wasn't Aunt Aggie angry when I laughed?"

"A silly sort of thing to do anyway. *What* a room! You might put those clothes away, and why can't you have another shelf for the books? That table—"

"Oh, rot! Dry up!" Henry moved about uneasily, kicking a book along the floor. "I've got something I want to—I can't keep it to myself any longer."

"What is it? About Philip and Katie?"

"No, not about Katie. At least—not unless he's told her. It's about Philip."

"What is it?" Millie said again.

"He's the most awful cad—an absolute outsider. I've known it for weeks, only I haven't decided what to do."

"I don't believe it," Millie said, slowly. "You don't know enough about men to tell whether a man's an outsider or not. . . . What's he done?"

"In Russia—in Moscow—he had a mistress for years—and they had a son. He's never said anything about it, but it's true. They say he had an awful reputation in Moscow."

"Who's 'they'?" said Millie, slowly. The colour mounted into her cheeks.

"A man I know—a friend of Seymour's. Oh! I know it's true. There isn't any sort of doubt about it."

"I daresay it is. Men are like that," Millie said, with profundity.

"Decent men aren't. Not the sort of man who will marry Katie."

Millie said nothing, and there was a long silence in the room. Then, with a deep sigh, Millie said:

"If it *is* true what does it matter if it's all over?"

"Perhaps it isn't. Besides, if he's that kind of man he'll do it again. And anyway, if Katie were to know—"

"Ah! if Katie were to know—"

They stood there, young (very young) defenders of Katherine. They would both of them, always, afterwards remember that moment, that hour, that Sunday. There came for both of them, suddenly, an active, urgent demand on their participation in a sudden adventure, a real, serious adventure, and they simply did not know what to do with it. With neither of them was their apprehension, disgust, dismay so great as their curiosity. The first thing, after the pause, that Millie said was:

"I wonder what she's like, that other woman I mean."

Henry had been wondering for weeks. He now produced his conclusions.

"It's my idea," he said, "that she was simply bored with him, couldn't endure him any longer. I expect they had awful rows—Russians do, you know, and Philip's got a temper I should think. Then he came home, and—sort of to save his pride because the other woman had kicked him out—made love to the first woman he saw. Katherine *was* the first, you know."

Millie felt a momentary surprise at her brother's unexpected cleverness. Then she shook her head: "No, I'm sure it's not that. He loves Katherine, I know, anyone can see it."

"Well, then," said Henry, with sudden volcanic happiness,

"he's making her awfully miserable. She was crying this afternoon, and I've got a letter in my pocket now that he told me to give to her for her to read while he was out. . . . They've had a quarrel."

"Perhaps he's told her."

"If he's making her unhappy—"

"I wonder what she thinks about it—"

Henry's thought, with all the simplicity that was in his real nature, was only of Katherine. Millie, although she loved her sister, was absorbed by the vision of life—dramatic, tragic, gay, sinister, rapturous—that was slowly being unfolded before her. What she would have liked would have been for both Philip and Katherine to have told her, minutely and precisely, how the affair appeared to them. How she could listen to them if they made her their confidante! Meanwhile she must content herself with Henry.

"What are you going to do?" she asked.

"Do! . . . There are things I can do," he hinted darkly. "Meanwhile, you just keep your eyes open and see whether he's bad to Katherine. If he is we must stop it. That's all that matters."

"I wonder what she was like—that other woman," Millie said, not looking at Henry, but at her own reflection in his looking-glass, then, without another word to him, she turned and left the room.

After she had gone he wondered whether he'd been wise to tell her. She had offered no advice, she had not even, he thought, been immensely interested, she had certainly been, in no way, shocked.

"Girls *are* queer" was his final reflection. When the bell began to ring, with its strange little questioning invitation, he suddenly thought that he would go to church. He sometimes found evening service, with its candles and old familiar tunes and star-lit sky, romantic and moving: to-night he felt that his restlessness and indecision must be influenced. He came downstairs, and found Katherine standing and staring through the little window to the left of the hall door. She started when she heard his voice, as though she had been lost in her own company.

"I've got a letter for you," he said, roughly. "From Philip. He's gone out for a long walk until supper, and he said you were to read it before he came back."

He gave it her. She said nothing. He turned abruptly away, and faced his mother.

She had on her black Sunday hat and was buttoning her gloves.

"I'm going to church."

"Well," said Mrs. Trenchard, "I think we shall be the only ones. Unless Katherine's coming."

"No, I'm not coming," said Katherine.

He walked away with his mother, feeling self-conscious with her, as he always did, but to-night, whether from some especial sense of gloom, of dripping, wet trees, of wind and rain, or from some real perception of agitation in his mother, he felt a strong impulse of protection towards her. He would have liked to have put his arm through hers, to have defied the world to harm her, to run and fetch and carry for her, to help her in any possible way. He had felt this before, but he had never known how to begin, and he knew that any demonstration of any kind would embarrass them both terribly.

Mrs. Trenchard said things like:

"Those two shirts of yours, Henry—those last two blue ones—have shrunk terribly. I'll never go to that place in Oxford Street again. They've shrunk so dreadfully," or "If you think you'd rather have those thicker socks next time you must tell me. . . . Do you like them better?"

Henry was always vexed by such questions. He thought that he should have been managing his own clothes at his age, and he also could not be bothered to give his mind seriously to socks.

"I don't know, mother."

"But you must care for one or the other."

"No, I don't."

"I think the thick ones are better. They don't feel quite so comfortable perhaps. . . . Ah! there's the bell stopping. We shall be late."

In church, influenced by the fickering candles, the familiar chants, the sense of a cosy and intimate trust in a Power who would see one safely through the night, just as one's burning night-light had guarded one when one had been very small, Henry became sentimental and happy. He looked out of the corner of his eye at his mother, at the so familiar wave of her hair, the colour and shape of her cheek, the solid comfort of her figure, and suddenly thought how old she was looking. This came as a revelation to him: he fancied that even in the last week there had been a little change. He moved closer to her: then he saw that her eye was fixed upon a small choirboy who had been eating sweets. The eye was stern and so full of command and assurance that Henry's sentiment suddenly shrivelled into nothing. His mother wanted nobody's help—he sighed and thought about other things. Soon he was singing "Abide with me" in his ugly, untuneful voice, pleased that the choir lingered over it in an abominable fashion, trying now and then to sing 'second', and miserably failing.

But, although he did not know it, Mrs. Trenchard had realised her son's mood. . . .

So, at last, tired, a little hysterical, feeling as though heavy steam rollers had, during the day, passed over their bodies, they were all assembled for supper. Sunday supper should be surely a meal very hot and very quickly over: instead it is, in all really proper English families, very cold and quite interminable. There were, to-night, seated round the enormous table Mrs. Trenchard, Aunt Betty, Aunt Aggie, Katherine, Millie and Henry. George Trenchard and Rachel Seddon were spending the evening with Timothy Faunder:

Philip had not yet returned from his walk. A tremendous piece of cold roast beef was in front of Mrs. Trenchard; in front of Henry were two cold chickens. There was a salad in a huge glass dish, it looked very cold indeed. There was a smaller glass dish with beetroot. There was a large apple-tart, a white blancmange, with little "dobs" of raspberry jam round the side of the dish. There was a plate of stiff and unfriendly celery—item a gorgonzola cheese, item a family of little woolly biscuits, clustered together for warmth, item a large "bought" cake that had not been cut yet and was grimly determined that it never should be, item what was known as "Toasted Water" (a grim family mixture of no colour and a faded, melancholy taste) in a vast jug, item, silver, white table-cloth, napkin-rings quite without end. Everything seemed to shiver as they sat down.

Aunt Aggie, as she saw the blancmange shaking its sides at her, thought that she would have been wiser to have gone straight upstairs instead of coming in to supper. She knew that her tooth would begin again as soon as she saw this food. She had had a wretched day. Katherine, before luncheon, had been utterly unsympathetic, Henry at tea-time had laughed at her. . . . At any rate, in a minute, there would b₃ soup. On Sunday evening, in order to give the servants freedom, they waited upon themselves, but soup was the one concession to comfort. Aunt Aggie thought she would have her soup and then go up quietly to bed. One eye was upon the door, looking for Rocket. Her tooth seemed to promise her: "If you give me soup I won't ache."

"Beef, Aggie—or chicken," said Mrs. Trenchard. "No soup to-night, I'm afraid. They've all got leave to-night, even Rocket and Rebekah. There's a meeting at the Chapel that seemed important . . . yes . . . beef or chicken, Aggie?"

Aunt Aggie, pulling all her self-control together, said: "Beef, please." Her tooth, savage at so direct an insult, leapt upon her.

Aunt Betty, in her pleasant voice, began a story. "I must say I call it strange. In the 'Church Times' for this week there's a letter about 'Church-Kneelers' by 'A Vicar'—complaining, you know . . . Well—"

"Beef or chicken, Millie?" said Mrs. Trenchard.

"Chicken, please," said Millie. "Shall I cut the bread?"

"White, please," said Henry.

"Well—" went on Aunt Betty. "As I was saying, on 'Church-Kneelers' signed by 'A Vicar'. Well, it's a very curious thing, but you remember, Harriet, that nice Mr. Redpath—"

"One moment, Betty, please," said Mrs. Trenchard.

"Not so much as that, Harry. Simply the leg. Thank you, dear. *Simply* the leg. That nice Mr. Redpath—with the nice wife and so many dear little children—he was curate to Mr. Williams of St. Clemens for years. Harriet, *you'll* remember—one year all the children had scarlet fever together, and two of the poor little things died, although I couldn't help thinking that really it was rather a mercy—"

"Mustard, please," said Henry.

"More beef, Aggie?" said Mrs. Trenchard.

"No, *thank* you," said Aggie, snapping her teeth upon a piece of bread. She was thinking: "How selfish they all are! They can't see how I'm suffering!"

"Well, *that* Mr. Redpath—You *must* remember him, Harriet, because he had a red moustache and a rather fine white forehead—when he left Mr. Williams got a living somewhere in Yorkshire, near York, I think, or was it Scarborough? Scarborough, because I remember when I wrote to congratulate him he answered me in such a nice letter, and said that it would be just the place for the children. *You* remember, Katherine, I showed it you."

"Yes," said Katherine.

Henry, hearing her voice, looked across at her and then dropped his eyes upon his plate.

She seemed herself again. Had her letter made her

happy? With a sudden start he realised that Millie also was watching her. . .

"Well, it must have been about 1900 that Mr. Redpath went to Scarborough. I remember it was the year before that dreadful wet school treat here, when we didn't know where to put all the children. I know the year after he went there poor Mrs. Redpath died and left him with all those little children—"

Just at that moment Philip came in. He came with the spray of the sea still wet upon his cheeks, his hair shining with it. His colour flaming, his eyes on fire. He had been, in the wind and darkness, down the Rafiel Road to the point above Tredden Cove where the sea broke inland. Here, deafened by the wind, blinded by the night, the sea-mist, now lashing his face, now stroking it softly with gentle fingers, he had stood on the edge of the world and heard the waters that are beyond the world exult in their freedom and scorn for men. He, too, standing there, had had scorn for himself. He had seen Katherine's eyes as she turned from him in the garden, he had seen his own wretched impatience and temper and selfishness. "By heaven," he thought, as he strode back, "I'll never be so contemptible again. I'll make them all trust me and like me. As for Katherine . . ." and so he burst in upon them, without even brushing his hair first. Also, the only vacant chair was next to Aunt Aggie. . . .

Aunt Betty, who thought that Philip's entry had been a little violent and abrupt, felt that she had better cover it with the continuation of her story.

"And so the next year Mr. Redpath married again—quite a young woman. I never saw her, but Nelly Hickling knew her quite well. She always said that she reminded her of Clara Foster. You know, Harriet, the younger one with the dark hair and pretty eyes."

But Philip had looked across at Katherine, her eyes had met his, and very faintly, as it were secretly, she smiled: the whirl of that encounter had hidden Aunt Betty's voice from him. He did not know that he was interrupting her.

"It was a good walk, and it's raining like anything. The sea was coming in over the Cove like thunder."

No one answered him, and he realised suddenly that all the food was cold. No matter: he was used to Sunday supper by this time, and he was of a ferocious hunger. "Lots of beef, please," he said, with a laugh.

Aunt Aggie shuddered. Her tooth was in her eye and her toes at the same moment; Annie had forgotten to call her, there had been no eggs for breakfast, Katherine at luncheon had been unsympathetic, at tea, before strangers (or nearly strangers), Henry had laughed at her, at supper there had been no soup, Betty, who in the morning had been idiotic enough to think Mr. Smart's sermon a good one, in the evening had been idiotic enough to commence one of her interminable stories, the day had as usual been dreary and heavy and slow, and now that terrible young man, whom she had always hated, must come in, late and dripping, without even washing his hands, makes no apologies, demands food as though he were a butcher, smiles upon everyone with perfect complacency, is not apparently in the least aware of other people's feelings—this horrible young man, who had already made everyone about him miserable and cross and restless: no, deeply though Aunt Aggie had always disliked Philip, she had never really hated him until this evening.

Although he was sitting next to her, he could not possibly have been more unconscious of her. . . .

"You are interrupting my sister," she said.

He started and flushed. "Oh! I beg your pardon," he stammered.

"No, please, it's nothing," said Aunt Betty.

"You were saying something about Mr. Williams, Betty dear," said Mrs. Trenchard.

"No, please, its nothing," said Aunt Betty.

There was silence after that. Philip waited, and then,

feeling that something must be done, said: "Well, Henry, I wish you'd been out with me. You'd have loved it. Why didn't you come?"

"I'm sure he was better at church," said Aunt Aggie. Her tooth said to her: "Go for him! Go for him! Go for him!"

Philip realised then her hostility. His face hardened. What a tiresome old woman she was, always cross and restless and wanting attention! He kept silent. That annoyed her: he seemed so big and overbearing when he sat so close to her.

"And I don't know," she went on, "whether you are really the best companion for Henry."

Everyone looked up then at the bitterness in Aunt Aggie's voice; no one heard Mrs. Trenchard say:

"Do have some tart, Henry."

"What do you mean?" said Philip sharply. His proximity to her made in some way the anger between them absurd: they were so close that they could not look at one another.

"Oh, nothing . . . nothing. . . ." She closed her lips.

"Please . . ." Philip insisted. "Why am I a bad companion for Henry?"

"Because you make him drink . . . disgusting!" she brought out furiously: when she had spoken her eyes went to Katherine's face—then, as she saw Katherine's eyes fixed on Philip's, her face hardened. "Yes. You know it's true," she repeated.

Henry broke in. "What do you say, Aunt Aggie? What do you mean? Drink—I—what?"

"You know that it's true, Henry. That night that you dined with Philip in London—You came back—disgraceful. Philip had to carry you. You fell on the top of the stairs. He had to lift you up and carry you into your room. I watched it all. Well—I didn't mean to say anything. I'm sorry, Harriet, if I—perhaps not quite the right time—but I—I—"

Her voice sank to muttering; her hands shook like leaves

on the tablecloth and her tooth was saying: "Go for him! Go for him! Go for him!"

And for Philip it was as though, after all these weeks of waiting, not only the family but the whole place had at last broken into its definite challenge.

Beyond the room he could feel the garden, the lawn, the oak, the sea-road, the moor, even Rafiel itself, with its little square window-pane harbour, crowding up to the window, listening, crying to him: "You've got to be broken! You've got to go or be broken! . . ." The definite moment had come at last.

His eyes never left Katherine's face as he answered:

"It's perfectly true. I don't know how it happened, but we had been having supper quite soberly together, and then Henry was suddenly drunk. I swear he'd had simply nothing to drink. He was quite suddenly drunk, all in a moment. I was never more surprised in my life. I suppose I should have prevented it, but I swear to you it would have surprised anyone—really, you would have been surprised, Mrs. Trenchard."

Henry, whose face was first flaming, then white, said, sulkily: "It wasn't Philip's fault. . . . I wasn't used to it. Anyway, I don't see why there need be such a fuss about it. What Aunt Aggie wants to drag it in now for just when everyone's tired after Sunday. It isn't as though I were *always* drunk—just once—everyone's drunk sometime."

"I've never said anything," Aunt Aggie began.

"No, that's just it," Philip broke in, suddenly flashing round upon her. "That's just it. You've never said anything until now. Why haven't you? Why, all this time, have you kept it, hugging it to yourself? . . . That's what you've all been doing. You never tell me anything. You never treat me really frankly, but if you've got something you think will do damage you keep it carefully until the best moment for letting it go off. You're all as secret with me as though I were a criminal. You ask me down here, and then keep me out of everything. I know you dislike me and think I oughtn't to marry Katherine—but why can't you say so instead of keeping so quiet? You think I shouldn't have Katherine—but you can't stop it, and you know you can't. . . . I'm sorry." He was conscious of the silence and many pairs of eyes and of much quivering cold food and the ticking of a large grandfather's clock saying: 'You are rude. You *are* rude—You *shouldn't*—do it—You *shouldn't*—do it.'

But he was also conscious of a quivering life that ran, like quicksilver, through the world outside, through all the streams, woods, paths, into the very heart of the sea. His eyes were on Mrs. Trenchard's face.

"I apologise if I've been rude, but to-day—a day like this —awful—" He broke off abruptly, and moved as though he would get up. It was then that the Dreadful Thing occurred.

He pushed his chair, and it knocked against Aunt Aggie's, jolting her. She, conscious that she was responsible for an abominable scene, conscious that she had lost all that fine dignity and self-command in which, through her lifetime, she had seen herself arrayed, conscious of her tooth, of a horrible Sunday, of many Sundays in front of her equally horrible (conscious, above all, of some doubt as to whether she *were* a fine figure, whether the world would be very different without her, conscious of the menace of her own cherished personal allusion), driven forward, moreover, by the individual experiences that Mrs. Trenchard, Millie, Henry, Katherine had had that day (because all their experiences were now in the room, crowding and pressing against their victims), seeing simply Philip, an abominable intrusion into what had formerly been a peaceful and honourable life, Philip, now and always her enemy . . . at the impact of his chair against hers, her tooth said "Go!"

She raised her thin hand and slapped him. Her two rings cut his cheek.

When the House was finally quiet and dark again, Rebekah alone was left. Stiff, solemn, slow, she searched the rooms, tried the doors, fastened the windows, marched with her candle up the back stairs into the heart of the house.

It had been a dull, uneventful Sunday. Nothing had occurred.

CHAPTER VII

TERROR is a tall word; it should not, perhaps, be used, in this trivial history, in connection with the feelings and motives of so youthfully comfortable a character as Philip—nevertheless very nearly akin to terror itself was Philip's emotion on discovering the results of his disgraceful encounter with Aunt Aggie . . . because there were no results.

As he had watched Aunt Aggie trembling, silent, emotional, retreat (after striking Philip she had risen and, without a word, left the room), he had thought that the moment for all his cards to be placed dramatically upon the Trenchard table had at last come. Perhaps they would tell him that he must go; they would openly urge Katherine to abandon him, and then, faced, with force and violence, by the two alternatives, he was assured, absolutely assured, of her loyalty to himself. He saw her, protesting that she would love them all, reminded that (Philip being proved an abomination) she must now choose, finally going out into the world with Philip.

He went to his room that Sunday evening triumphant. No more Trenchard secrets and mysteries—thanks to that horrible old woman, the way was clear. He came down the next morning to breakfast expecting to be treated with chilly politeness, to be asked to interview George Trenchard in his study, to hear Trenchard say: "Well, my dear boy—I'm very sorry of course—but you must see with me that it's better to break off . . ." and then his reply.

"That, sir, must remain with Katherine. I am bound to her. . . ." No, he had no fear of the result. As he came down the stairs on that Monday morning, a fine hot spring day, with the mist of the spring heat hazy above the shining grass, his eyes were lighter, his spirits higher than they had been since his first coming to Garth. He entered the dining-room, and thought that he had dreamt yesterday's incidents.

Millie cried—"Hullo, Phil! Late as usual."

George Trenchard said: "Philip, what do you say to a drive over to Trezent? It's a good day and I've some business there."

Aunt Aggie gave him her withered hand to shake with exactly the proud, peevish air that she always used to him. There was a scratch on his face where her rings had cut him; he looked at her rings . . . yes, he was surely dreaming. Then there crept to him the conviction that the plot—the family plot—seen before vaguely, mysteriously and uncertainly—was now developing before his eyes as something far deeper, far more soundless, far more determined than he had ever conceived. Mrs. Trenchard, smiling there at the head of the table, knew what she was about. That outburst of Aunt Aggie's last night had been a slip—They would make no more.

His little quarrel with Katherine had needed no words to mark its conclusion. He loved her, he felt, just twice as deeply as he had loved her before . . . he was not sure, though, that he was not now a little—a very little—afraid of her. . . .

In the middle of the week, waking, very early on the most wonderful of all spring mornings, his inspiration came to him.

He got up, and about half-past seven was knocking on Katherine's door. She spoke to him from within the room.

"Katie!"

"Yes!"

He whispered to her in the half-lit house, across whose floors the light, carrying the scent of the garden-flowers, shook and trembled; he felt a conspirator.

"Look here! You've got to dress at once and come off with me somewhere."

"Go off!"

"Yes, for the day! I've thought it all out. We can take the pony-cart and just catch the nine o'clock at Rasselas. That'll get us to Clinton by ten. We'll be down in Roche Cove by eleven—spend the day there, catch the eight-thirty back and be in the house again by half-past ten to-night."

There was a pause, filled with the delighted twittering of a company of sparrows beyond the open passage-window.

At last her voice:

"Yes. I'll come."

"Good. . . . Hurry! . . . I'll tell them downstairs."

When the family assembled for breakfast and he told them, his eyes challenged Mrs. Trenchard's.

"Now, look here," his eyes said, "I'm the dreadful young man who is teaching your boy Henry to drink, who's ruining your domestic peace—surely you're not, without protest, going to allow me a whole day with Katherine!"

And her eyes answered him.

"Oh, I'm not afraid. . . . You'll come back. You're a weak young man."

In the train he considered, with a beating heart, his project. The day encouraged adventure, boldness, romance; he was still young enough to believe in the intangible illusion of a Deity Who hangs His signs and colours upon the sky to signify His approval of one bold mortal's projects, and no ironic sense of contrast attacked, as yet, his belief. If the Trenchards refused to make the incident of Sunday night a crisis, he would, himself, force them to recognise it. He had been passive long enough . . . he did not know that, all his life, he had never been anything else.

In the train they talked to one another very little. He

watched her and was bewildered, as are all lovers, by her proximity and her remoteness. The very love that brought her so close to him made her the more remote because it clothed her in strange mystery.

She was further from him than Anna had ever been, because he loved her more deeply . . . and at the thought of Anna—so constant now and so sinister—he had a sudden fear of the success of his project. . . .

Clinton St. Mary is a village, with one ugly street, on the very edge of Roche St. Mary Moor. It has visitors from the outside world because, in a hollow in the moor, lie the remains of St. Arthe Church, one of the earliest Christian buildings in Great Britain, 'buried until lately in the sand, but recently excavated through the kind generosity of Sir John Porthcullis, Bart., of Borhaze, and shown to visitors, 6d. a head—Wednesday and Saturday afternoons free.' Tourists therefore continually patronise 'The Hearty Cow' in Clinton, where there is every day a cold luncheon—ham, chicken, beef, tart, junket, cheese—for half-a-crown a-head. Katherine also had relations here, the Vicar, the Rev. James Trenchard, being a cousin 'and a dear old man'. However, to-day the world should be for themselves alone. In the village they bought ginger-beer, ham-sandwiches, saffron buns, chocolate. They set off across the Moor.

When they had walked a very little way they were suddenly engulfed. Behind them the road, the trees, the village were wrapped in blue haze: to the right, very faintly the yellow sand-hills hovered. In the sandy ground at their feet little pools that caught blue fragments of sky shone like squares of marble: out of the tufts of coarse grass larks rose, circling, like sudden sprays of some flashing into the air as a fountain flashes: no mortal being was visible in this world.

They walked for two hours and exchanged scarcely a word. Philip felt as though he had never had Katherine alone with him before since the day of their engagement—always there had been people between them, and, if not people, then his own silly fancies and imaginations. As he looked his love was now neither reasoning nor hesitating. "I am stronger than you all," he could shout to the ironical heavens, for the first time in all his days. Then she spoke to him, and her voice reminded him of his desperate plans. . . . His confidence left him. It was his great misfortune that he never believed in himself.

Very little, this morning, was Katherine troubled about dreams or fancies. She was happy, as she had always been happy, with absolute simplicity, her trust in the ultimate perfection of the world being so strong in her that a fine day, her closeness to Philip, her own bodily health and fitness were enough to sweep all morbidities far away. She had not been happy lately—some new force had been stirring in her that was strange to her and unreal, like a bad dream.

But now her unhappiness of the last weeks was as faint as the hazy mist, as shadowy as the thin curtain of sea that now spread before them, hung like gauze between two humped and staring sand-hills. They rushed down the deep cup of the sand-valley and up, through the thin wiry grass, to the top, then down again, then up once more to be perched on the very edge of the path that twisted down to their Cove. The sea-breeze, warm and soft, invited them. . . . Down they went.

The Cove was hidden by black rocks, piled together, seeming, through the mist, to be animals herded together to guard its sanctity. Under the rocks the Cove lay, curved like a small golden saucer, the sea forming here a thin glassy lake, protected by a further range of rocks that extended, as though placed there by human agency, across the mouth of the tiny circle. The water within the rocks was utterly clear, the seaweed, red-gold and green, covering the inside of the cup: when the waves broke beyond the barrier they were echoed here by a faint ripple that trembled, in green shadows, like a happy sigh across the surface, and, with this ripple, came the echo of the dull boom that the surging tide was making in the distant caves: this echo was a giant's chuckle, sinister, malevolent, but filtered. When the tide was coming in, the ripples, running in faint lines from side to side, covered the shining surface of the rocks and stones, with layers of water, thin and fine like silk, now purple, now golden, now white and grey.

The silk stretched over the rocks, drew itself taut, then spilt itself suddenly, with a delighted ecstasy, in cascades of shining water, into the breast of the retreating tide. As the tide went out, very reluctantly the colour withdrew from the rocks, leaving them, at last, hard and dry beneath the sun . . . but at the heart of the smooth, glassy cup, on these warm spring days, there was a great peace and content: birds, sea-gulls, sparrows, thrushes, came to the edge of the golden sand, and with trembling, twittering happiness listened to the hollow booming in the distant caves.

Lying there, on the little beach, upon such a spring day as this, man might be assured that the world had been made only for his especial comfort and safety. The intense blue of the sky, the green wall of hill behind him, these things could not change: for an hour of his journey, life, gay rather than solemn, humorous rather than ironic, satisfying and complete, would seem to be revealed to him. He would wonder that he had ever doubted it. . . .

Katherine and Philip lay, for a long time, saying very little, listening to the gentle hiss of the water, watching the line, beyond the rocks, where the sea was suddenly deep blue, feeling the sun upon their faces, and the little breeze that, once and again, with a sudden gesture of merriment ruffled the faces of the golden pools with a flurry of grey splashes and shadows. They ate their sandwiches and saffron buns and drank their ginger-beer, which resembled hot-soap-and-water: Katherine waited. She knew that Philip had something to say to her, that he had brought her here with some purpose, and she seemed to know also that that gentle sunny

hour of the late morning was to be the last moment in some
stage in her life. Her first meeting with him, his proposal
to her, her talk afterwards with her mother, her coming to
Garth with him, his confession at Rafiel, their first quarrel
yesterday—all these had been stages in her growth. She
waited now with a struggle, a maturity that had been far
from her experience a year ago.

He began at last, holding her hand covered by both of his,
searching her eyes with his, very grave; she saw with a
little loving smile to herself that he intended to be of an
immense seriousness, that his sense of humour was very
far away. He began as though he were carrying through
the most tremendous business of his life—and a sparrow,
perched on the water's edge, seemed to watch his gravity with
a twitter of superior amusement.

"Do you mind my talking now a little? There's something
I've got to say."

"It's a beautiful place for talking. There's no Aunt Aggie
. . . only one sparrow to overhear us."

"But it's really important—terribly important. It's simply
this—that last night was a crisis. I'm never going back to
Garth again."

Katherine laughed, but her eyes were suddenly frightened.

"My dear Phil . . . What do you mean?"

"No, I'm not—I mean—at least not until certain things
have happened. You're not going back either—"

"*I'm* not going back?"

"No, not as Miss Katherine Trenchard—one day as Mrs.
Philip Mark, perhaps."

Katherine drew her hand from his, sat up, looked out
to the deep blue line of sea, said, at last, quietly:

"Now please, Philip, explain the joke. The afternoon's
too lovely to be wasted."

"There is no joke. I'm perfectly serious. I can't stand
it any longer. *I cannot stand it*—and when I say 'it' I mean

the family, their treatment of me, their dislike of me, their
determination to swallow me up in their feather-bed and make
an end of me—the whole long engagement; *you're* suffering.
I'm suffering. You were wretched yesterday—so was I.
When you're wretched I could burn the whole family, Garth
and Glebeshire and all included and waste no pity whatever."

But Katherine only laughed:

"Do you know, Phil, you're exaggerating the whole thing
in the most ridiculous manner. It's quite natural—it's because you don't know our habits and manners. Aunt Aggie
lost her temper last night—we were all rather worked up—
Sunday can be awful. She won't lose her temper again. We
had a quarrel. Well, I suppose all lovers have quarrels. You
think they'll all be terribly shocked because you let Henry
drink too much that night in London. That shows that you
simply don't know the family at all, because if you did you'd
know that it's never shocked at anything that it hasn't seen
with its own eyes. Aunt Aggie *saw* Henry, so she *was*
shocked—but for the others . . . If they were to know—
well, what you told me at Rafiel—then—perhaps—"

"Then?" Philip cried eagerly.

"They might be—I don't know what they'd do." She
turned her eyes to his face again. "But you're so impatient,
Phil. You want everything to happen in a minute—You're
discontented because they all have their own lives, which you
can't share. But you're so strange. *I'm* the person whose
life you ought to share, and yet you don't. You've hardly
looked at all this. You've taken no interest at all in the fishermen or the villagers. Garth is nothing to you—"

"I *hate* Garth!" he broke out furiously. "I—" Then he
dropped his voice. "That'll all come later. . . . I'll just say
this about myself. It's only what I've always told you, that
I'm simply not worthy for you to care about me. You may
have had some illusions about me at first. You can't have
any now. I'm weak and backboneless, always wanting things
better than I can have them, ready to be influenced by simply

anyone if they're nice to me, hating it when people aren't nice. I'm no good at all, except for one thing—my love for you."

He bent forward and drew her towards him.

"I have never known anything like it before. I shall never know anything like it again—and just because I do know myself so well I'm going to hold on to it and let nothing take it from me. They, all of them—are doing their best to take it from me. Your mother knows me much better than you do. . . . She despises me completely and she knows the way to influence me."

Katherine would have spoken, but he stopped her.

"Oh, yes, she does. Have you noticed that she and I are never alone together, that we never have talks nor walks nor anything? She is always perfectly kind, but she knows, and I know that she knows, that if I were once to get really intimate with her I might overcome my fright of her, that it's by my imagination of her that she's influencing me. And she is . . . she is . . . she is." His hand trembled against Katherine. "You don't know. You don't see! You love her and think that she's simply your mother. But you don't know. . . . Already she can get me to do anything she likes. If she wants me to waste every day doing nothing, thinking nothing, becoming a stupid bore, with no ambitions, no lips of his own, no energy—and that's what she *does* want—she's making me exactly that. I feel her when she's not there—all over the house, in the garden, in the roads. I can't escape her. In half a year's time, when the wedding day comes, all I shall want is to be allowed to cut the flowers for the dinner-table and to hold your mother's wool when she's winding it."

He paused, stood suddenly upon his feet: "It's like my own mother over again—only Mrs. Trenchard's cleverer . . . but I tell you, Katie, you shan't marry a man like that. If you marry me down there, and we're to spend all our lives there, a year after marriage you'll despise me, hate me for the thing I've become. . . . I've thought it all out. That scene last night decided me. You shan't go back—not until we're married."

He stood proudly facing her, his whole body stirred to his decision. But even then, as she looked at him she saw that his upper lip trembled a little—his upper lip had always been weak. He looked down at her, then sat very close to her, leaning towards her as though he were pleading with her.

"I know that ever since our engagement you've been thinking that I've imagined things. Perhaps I have. Perhaps that's my way, and always has been. And Russia increased my tendency. But if *that's* true then it ought to be taken into account just as much as though I'd got a game leg or was blind of one eye. You can't just dismiss it and say: 'He's a silly ass—he oughtn't to imagine things'. I know that if I were sensible I should just hang on for six months more, marry you and then take you right off. But I know myself —by that time I shall simply do exactly what your mother tells me—and she'll tell me to dig potatoes in the garden."

"You're unjust to yourself, Phil," looking up at him. "You're not so weak . . . and soon you'll love Garth. You'll understand the family, even perhaps mother. It must come —it *must*. I want it so."

"It will never come," he answered her firmly. "You can make up your mind to that now for ever. The only way we can live altogether like a happy family in the future is for me to become a chair or table or one of your aunt's green cushions. That's what I shall become if I don't do something now."

She waited because she saw that he had more to say.

"And do you suppose that even then any of us would be happy? See already how everyone is changed! Millie, Henry, Aunt Aggie, you, even your father. Isn't he always wondering now what's come over everyone? There's a surprised look in his eyes. And it's I! . . . I! . . . I! It's like a pebble in your shoe that you can't find. I'm the pebble, and they'll never be comfortable so long as I'm here.

They're not only threatened with losing you, they're threatened with losing their confidence, their trust, their superstitions."

"I'm one of them," Katherine said. "You forget that. We may be slow and stupid and unimaginative, as you say, but we *are* fond of one another. You're impatient, Phil. I tell you to wait . . . wait!"

"Wait!" He looked out to sea, where the bar of blue was now sown with white dancing feathers. "I can't wait . . . there's something else. There's Anna."

Katherine nodded her head as though she had known that this would come.

"Ever since that day at Rafiel she's been between us; you've known it as well as I. It hasn't been quite as I'd expected. I thought perhaps that you'd be shocked. You weren't shocked. I thought that I'd be confused myself. I haven't been confused. You've wanted to know about her— anything I could tell you. You've simply been curious, as you might, about anyone I'd known before I met you—but the business has been this, that the more you've asked the more I've thought about her. The more she's come back to me. It hasn't been that I've wanted her, even that I've thought tenderly about her, only that your curiosity has revived all that life as though I were back in it all again. I've remembered so much that I'd forgotten."

Katherine took his hand and came close to him. "Yes. I knew that it was like that," she said. "I knew that it was foolish of me to ask questions, to make you talk about her, and I couldn't help myself—I knew that it was foolish, and I couldn't help myself. And the strange thing is that I don't suppose I've ever wondered about anyone whom I didn't know in my life before. I've never been able to imagine people unless I had pictures or something to help me. But now—I seem to see her as though I'd known her all my days. And I'm not jealous—no, truly, truly, I'm not jealous. And yet I don't like her—I grudge—I grudge—"

She suddenly hid her face in the sleeve of his coat and her hand went up to his cheek.

Philip, holding her with his arm as though he were protecting her, went on: "And you've felt that I didn't want you to ask me questions about her—and you've been silent. I knew that you were silent because you were afraid of my restlessness, and that has made restraint between us. You wouldn't speak and I wouldn't speak, and we've both been thinking of Anna until we've created her between us. It's so like her—*so like* her. Why," he went on, "you'll think this absurd perhaps—but I don't know—it's not so absurd when you've lived with her. I wrote and told her about us—about our engagement. I've never had an answer from her, but I can fancy her saying to herself: 'It would be amusing to bring him back to me—not that I want him. I should be bored to death if I had to live with him again—but just for the humour of it. He was always so weak. He'll come if I ask him.'

"I can imagine her saying that, and then I can imagine her just projecting herself over here into the middle of us—simply for the fun of it. I can see her laughing to herself in the way she used to when she saw people behaving in what she thought was a childish fashion. So now she'll think us all childish, and she'll simply come here, her laughing, mocking spirit—and do her best to break us all up."

"You're afraid of her!" Katherine cried, as though she were challenging him.

"Yes. I'm afraid of her," he acknowledged.

"Well, I'm not," she answered. "She can do her utmost. She can laugh as much as she pleases."

"She shall be given no chance," he answered eagerly. "See, Katherine! Listen! . . . All that matters is that we should be married. She can't touch us then—Garth can't touch us, the family can't touch us. I suddenly saw it as an inspiration—that you've got to come up with me now—to London. We'll get a special licence. We'll be married to-morrow. If we catch the five-thirty from Truxe we'll be up there soon after midnight. We can get a trap in Clinton to drive us over. It's got to be. It's just got to be. There can be no alternative."

She shook her head smiling. "What a baby you are, Phil! Just because Aunt Aggie lost her temper last night we've got to be married in half an hour. And what about our promise to father of a year's engagement?"

"That's all right," he answered eagerly. "If your father had wanted to break off the engagement before the year's up he'd have done so, you can be sure."

She laughed. "But I don't want to be married all in a minute. You don't know how women care about trousseaux and presents and bells and—"

"Ah! Please, Katie! . . . It's most awfully serious! Please—"

She was grave then. They stood up together on the little beach, her arm round his neck.

"Phil. I do understand better than you think. But do you know what it would mean if we were to run away now like this? My mother would never forgive me. It would mean that I was throwing off everything—the place, mother, all my life. . . . Of course I would throw it away for you if that were the only course to take. But it isn't the only course. You see life exaggerated, Phil. Everything that happened yesterday has irritated you. To-morrow—"

"To-morrow may be too late," he answered her. "At least give my idea half an hour, I'll go off now for a walk by my-self. In half an hour's time I'll be back. Do your best for me."

She looked at him, bent forward and kissed him.

"Yes, go—Come back in half an hour."

She watched him climb the rocks, wind up the path, turn at the bend and look back to her, then disappear. She sat down on the beach, rested her elbows on her knees and looked out to sea. She was utterly alone: the pool, now spun gold, beneath a sun that was slowly sinking to bars of saffron, quivered only with the reaction of the retreating tide; the rocks were black and sharp against the evening sky.

Katherine, as she sat there, had, at first, a desperate wish for the help of some older person's advice. It was not that she could, for an instant, seriously contemplate this mad proposal of Philip's—and yet he had imparted to her some of his own fear and distrust of the possible machinations of heaven. What he had said was true—that ever since he had told her about Anna it had been as though they had taken some third person into their lives—taken her unwillingly, almost unconsciously, but nevertheless destructively. Then also, although Katherine had denied it, she knew now that what he had said about the family was true. She not only could not hope now that they and Philip would ever live happily together—it was also the fact that they had changed. Her mother had changed—her Aunts, her father, Millie, Henry—they had all changed—changed to her and changed to themselves.

Katherine, moreover, now for the first time in her life criticised her family—even her mother. She felt as though she and Philip had needed help, and that the family, instead of giving it, had made difficulties and trouble. Her mother had, deliberately, made trouble—had been hard and unkind to Philip, had brought him to Garth that he might seem to Katherine unsuited there, had put him into impossible positions and then laughed at him. Her mother had come to her and asked her to give Philip up; in retrospect that scene of yesterday afternoon seemed a deliberate challenge—but a challenge offered behind Philip's back.

Now her whole impulse was that Philip must at all costs be protected and defended, and, for the first time, this afternoon, sitting there alone with the world all hers, she realised how her feeling for him had changed. When she had first known him she had fallen in love with him because she had thought him the strongest, most adventurous, most fearless of mortal souls. Now—she knew that he was weak, afraid of himself, unbalanced, a prey to moods, impulses, terrors—and with that knowledge of him her love had grown, had flung its wide arm about him, had caught him to her heart with a fierce protection that the attraction for his strength had never given her.

With her new knowledge of him came also her direct antagonism with that other woman. She knew that what Philip had said was true, that her curiosity had increased for them both the live actuality of that figure. Katherine had always been afraid of cynical people, who must, always, she felt, despise her for the simplicity of her beliefs, the confidence of her trust. She remembered a woman who had, at one time, been a close friend of Aunt Aggie's, a sharp, masculine woman with pincenez, who, when Katherine had said anything, had looked at her sharply through her glasses, laughed as though she were ringing a coin to see whether it were good metal, and said: 'Do you think so?'

Katherine had hated her and been always helpless before her, clumsy, awkward and tongue-tied. Now it was a woman of that kind whom she was called out to challenge. Her thought in church yesterday was with her now more strongly than ever. "How she would despise me if she knew me! . . ." and then, "what a power she must have if she can come back like this into Philip's life."

And yet not such a power! Always before him was that world where he was not: his fancy, running before him, cried to him: "Yes. There! There! was happiness," or "In such a fashion happiness will come to you"—as though the only end of life was happiness, the security of the ideal moment. Yes, Katherine knew why Anna had laughed at Philip.

Her thoughts turned back again then to his mad idea of their escape to London, and, suddenly, as though some woman were with her whom she had never seen before, some voice within her cried: "Ah! I wish he'd make me go! simply take me prisoner, force me by brutal strength, leave me no will nor power." Her imagination, excited, almost breathless, began to play round this. She saw his return, heard him ask her whether she would go with him, heard her answer that she would not, heard him say: "But you are in my power now. I have arranged everything. Whether you like it or not we go. . . ."

She would protest, but in her surrender, triumphant at heart, she would see her utter defeat of that other woman, whose baffled ghost might whistle across the dark moor back to its own country to find other humours for its decision.

"Poor Ghost," she might cry after it, "you did not know that he would prove so strong!" Nor would he. . . . Her dream faded like the trembling colours in the evening sea.

And otherwise, unless that were so, she could not go. She had no illusions as to what her escape with him would mean. There would be no return for her to Garth—even Glebeshire itself would cast her out. As she thought of all her days, of her babyhood, when the world had been the green lawn and the old oak, of her girlhood, when Rafiel and Polchester had been the farthest bounds, of all the fair days and the wild days, of the scents and the sounds and the cries and the laughter, it seemed that the little cove itself came close to her, pressing up to her, touching her cheek, whispering to her: "You will not go! . . . You will not go! . . . You will not go!" No, of her own will she could not go. The golden pool was very full, swelling with a lift and fall that caught the light of the sun as though the evening itself were rocking it. Against the far band of rocks the tide was breaking with a white flash of colour, and the distant caves boomed like drums. But the peace was undisturbed; birds slowly, with a dreamy beat of wings, vanished into a sky that was almost radiant white . . . and behind her, the dark rocks, more than ever watching, guarding beasts that loved her, waited for her decision.

Then all things faded before her vision of her mother.

That so familiar figure seemed to come towards ɴer with a freshness, a piquancy, as though mother and daughter had been parted for years. "We've misunderstood one another," the figure seemed to say: "there shall never be misunderstanding again." There seemed, at that moment, to be no one else in Katherine's world: looking back she could see, in all her past life, only her mother's face, could hear only her mother's voice.

She remembered the day when she had told her about the engagement, the day when she had forgotten about the Stores, yesterday in her bedroom. . . .

She buried her face in her hands, feeling a wild, desperate despair—as though life were too strong for her and her will too weak.

She felt a touch on her shoulder, and saw that Philip had returned, his face in the dusk was pale like the white sky.

"Well?" he said.

She shook her head, smiling a dismal little smile. "I can't go. . . . You know that I can't."

(That other woman in her whispered: 'Now he must compel you.')

Philip looked out to sea.

"I can't," she repeated. "I can't leave it all."

('Ah! make me go!' that other whispered.)

He turned away from her and looked back at the rocks.

"You care for all this more than for me."

"You know that that is not true. I care for you more than anyone or anything in the world. But these have all been fancies of yours, Phil. In six months time—" she broke off.

('Force me, compel me to go with you,' the other woman whispered to him. But he did not hear.)

"Yes. We'll go back," he said.

They were silent. Suddenly he gripped her shoulder, and they both turned and looked behind them.

"I thought I heard someone laugh," he whispered.

She rose, then before they moved away, put her arm round him with a close, maternal gesture that she had never used to him before.

BOOK III

KATHERINE AND ANNA

CHAPTER I

KATHERINE ALONE

IT happened that in the middle of July there was to be a Trenchard-Faunder wedding in London. It was to be a quite especial Trenchard-Faunder wedding that no Trenchard or Faunder must miss. A Miss Dorothy Faunder, daughter of Colonel Faunder of Foxley Park, Wilts, was to marry her cousin Humphrey Trenchard, second son of Sir Geoffrey Trenchard of Tredent Hall, Truxe, in Glebeshire, and 22 Bryanston Square, W. . . .

The wedding was to be towards the end of the season, before Goodwood and Cowes; and St. Margaret's, Westminster, was to be the scene of the Ceremony. Of course the George Trenchards of Garth would be present—there was never any question of that—but at the same time it was an inconvenient interference with normal life. Trenchards and Faunders saw, as a rule, little of London in the season unless there was a daughter coming out or a wedding or a Presentation at Court. George Trenchard greatly disliked being torn from Garth during July and August, and it was only an exceptional demand that could uproot him.

This demand *was* exceptional. Of course they must all be there.

On the evening before the departure for London Katherine sat alone in her bedroom looking through her bright window on to the garden beneath her. The July evening was close and oppressive—the garden was almost black, with a strange quivering bar of pale yellow light behind the trees. The scents came up to the open window heavily—there was no breeze. Now and then a dog barked as though it were challenging someone. Although there was no breeze, the trees sometimes shivered very faintly.

One star glittered between the black clouds.

Katherine sat at the open window smelling the pinks and the roses, her room dim behind her with a pale metallic glow. She felt oppressed by the evening, and at the same time strangely excited, as though something was about to happen. But beyond this she was conscious of a curious combative loneliness that should have been a miserable thing, but was in reality something challenging and almost defiant. Defiant of what? Defiant of whom? She thought of it as she sat there.

Her thoughts went back to that day that she had spent with Philip at Roche St. Mary Moor. Her loneliness had begun quite definitely from that day. Only a fortnight later Philip had departed. She had not seen him since then. But even had he been with her she thought that he would not, very greatly, have affected her loneliness. He might even have accentuated it. For Philip had behaved very strangely since that afternoon at Roche St. Mary. It was, Katherine thought, as though, having made his bolt for freedom and failed, he simply resigned himself. He only once afterwards alluded to the affair. One day he said to her quite suddenly: "After all, it's worth it—so long as you're there."

"What's worth it?" she had asked him.

"But if you were to leave me," he went on, and stopped and looked at her.

"What's worth it?" she had repeated.

"Being swallowed up," he had answered her. "Your mother and I are going to pay calls together this afternoon."

He had during these last weeks been wonderful about her mother; he had agreed to everything that she proposed, had run errands for her, supported her opinions, "been quite a son to her," Aunt Betty, happy at this transformation, had declared—and he had been perfectly miserable. Katherine knew that.

And his misery had kept them apart. Katherine had never loved him so intensely as she did during those last days, and he had loved her with a kind of passionate, almost desperate, intensity. But their love had never brought them together. There had always been someone between.

It was as good as though he had said to her: "We have still another six months before our marriage. You have told me definitely that you will not give up the family. Your mother is determined not to surrender a bit of you to me, therefore I am to be surrendered to your mother. I am willing that this should be so because I love you, but if I change, if I am dull and lifeless you mustn't be surprised.

"There's the earlier life, which one can't forget all at once, however deeply one wants to. Meanwhile, I hate your mother and your mother hates me. But she'll never let me go unless you force her to. She knows that I can't break away so long as you're here. And she means you to be here always. What would a strong man do? Forget the earlier life, I suppose. So would I if I had you all to myself. But I have to share you—and that gives the earlier life a chance."

Although he had never opened his lips, Katherine heard him saying all this as though he were there in front of her, there with his charm and his hopeless humours about himself, his weakness that she had once thought was strength, and for which now she only loved him all the more.

But the terrible thing about those last weeks had been that, although she knew exactly what he was thinking, they had simply avoided all open and direct discussion. She had wished for it, but what could she say? Only the same things again—that it would be all right when they were married, that he would love the family then, that she would be *his* then and not the *family's*. . . . Always at this point in her argument she was pulled up sharply, because that was a lie. She would not be *his* when they were married. She knew now, quite definitely, that her mother was utterly, absolutely resolved never to let her go.

And meanwhile there was Anna. . . .

Katherine, putting Philip aside for a moment, thought of the members of the family one by one. They were all separated from her. She summoned this ghostly truth before her, there in her dim room with the hot scented air surrounding her, quite calmly without a shudder or a qualm. Her mother was separated from her because, during the last six months, they had never, with one exception, spoken the truth to one another. Aunt Aggie was separated from her because, quite definitely, ever since that horrible Sunday night, she hated Aunt Aggie. Henry was separated from her because during these last months he had been so strange with his alternate moods of affection and abrupt rudeness that she now deliberately avoided him. Aunt Betty was separated from her because she simply didn't see things in the least as they were. Her father was separated from her because he laughed at the situation and refused to consider it at all. Millie— ah! Millie, the friend of all her life!—was separated from her because they were concealing things the one from the other as they had never done in all their days before.

Katherine faced these facts. She had an illusion about her life that she had always been right in the very heart of her family. She did not know that it had been their need of her that had put her there, and that now that she was turning away from them to someone else, they were all rejecting her. They also were unaware of this. They thought and she thought that it had been always a matter of Love between them all—but of course Love in most cases is only a handsome name for selfishness.

So Katherine sat alone in her room and waited for the thunder to come. Meanwhile she was immensely surprised that this discovery of her loneliness did not immediately depress her, but rather aroused in her a pugnacity and an independence that seemed to her to be quite new qualities. And then, following immediately upon her pugnacity, came an overwhelming desire to kiss them all, to do anything in the world that they wished, to love them all more than she had ever done before. And following upon that came an aching, aching desire for Philip, for his presence, his eyes, his hair, his neck, his hands, his voice. . . .

And following upon that came Anna. Anna had become an obsession to Katherine. If, in her earlier life, she had thought very intently of persons or countries remote from her, she would, perhaps, have known how to deal with the woman, but never before, in any crisis or impulse, had her imagination been stirred. If she had ever thought about imagination, she had decided that Rachel Seddon's "Imagination! . . . you haven't got a scrap, my dear!" hurled at her once in the middle of some dispute, was absolutely true. But her love for Philip had proved its preserver, had proved it, roused it, stirred it into a fierce, tramping monster, with whom she was simply unable to deal.

If only, she felt, she had been able to speak of her to Philip! Surely then the questions and the answers would have stripped Anna of her romance, would have shown her to be the most ordinary of ordinary women, someone unworthy of Philip, unworthy of anyone's dreams. But bringing Anna into the air had been forbidden—anything better than to start Philip thinking of her—so that there she had lingered, somewhere in the shadow, romantic, provoking, mocking, dangerous, coloured with all the show of her foreign land, with the towers and plains and rivers of romance.

Nevertheless it had not been all Katherine's imagination. There had been in the affair some other agency. Again and again Katherine had been conscious that, in opposition to her will, she was being driven to hunt for that figure. In the middle of some work or pleasure she would start, half frightened, half excited, conscious that someone was behind her, watching her. She would turn, and in the first flash of her glance it would seem to her that she caught some vanishing figure, the black hair, the thin, tall body, the laughing, mocking eyes.

It was simply, she would tell herself, that her curiosity refused to be quiet. If only she might have known whether Philip thought of Anna, whether Anna thought of Philip, whether Anna wanted Philip to return to her, whether Anna really despised him, whether . . . and then with a little shudder of dismissal, she would banish the Phantom, summoning all her admirable Trenchard common-sense to her aid. . . . "That was past, that was gone, that was dead."

She was, upon this afternoon, at the point of summoning this resolution when the door opened and Millie came in. For a moment so dark was the room that she could not see, and cried: "Katie, are you there?"

"Yes. Here by the window."

Millie came across the room and stood by Katherine's chair. In her voice there was the shadow of that restraint that there had been now between them ever since the Sunday with the Awful Supper.

"It's only the Post. It's just come. Two letters for you—one from Philip that I thought that you'd like to have."

Katherine took the letters, laid them on her lap, looking up at her sister with a little smile.

"Well . . ." said Millie, hesitating, then, half turning, "I must go back to Aunt Betty—I'm helping her with the things."

"No. Don't go." Katherine, who was staring in front of her now into the black well of a garden, lit by the quivering, shaking light, put out her hand and touched Millie's sleeve. Millie stood there, awkwardly, her white cotton dress shining against the darkness, her eyes uncertain and a little timid.

"I ought to go, Katie dear. . . . Aunt Betty—"

"Aunt Betty can wait. Millie, what's the matter?"

"What's the matter?"

"Yes, between us. For a long time it's been—and worse since Philip went away."

"Nothing," said Millie, slowly, then, quite suddenly, with one of those movements so characteristic of her, she flung herself on to her knees, caught Katherine's hands, then stretched forward and pulled Katherine's head down to hers—then kissed her again and again. The two sisters held one another in a close embrace, cheek against cheek, breast to breast. So they stayed for some time.

At last Millie slid down on to the floor and rested there, her head, with all its fair hair ruffled and disordered, on Katherine's lap.

"Well . . ." said Katherine at last, her head against her sister's cheek. "Why, all this time, have you been so queer? Is it because you hate Philip?"

"No, I like him."

"Is it because you hate me?"

"No, I love *you.*"

"Is it because you hate my marrying Philip?"

"No—if you'd do it at once."

"Do it at once?"

"Yes—now—go up to London—Marry him to-morrow—"

"My *dear* Millie! . . . our year isn't up—nearly."

"What does it matter about your year? Better to break your year than to have us all at one another's throats—miserable. And then perhaps after all to lose Philip."

"Lose Philip?"

"Yes. He'll go back to Russia."

The words flashed before Katherine's eyes like lightning through the garden. Her heart gave a furious jump and then stopped.

"Why do you think he'd do that?" she asked at last. "Do you think he doesn't love me?"

"No, it's because he loves you so much that he'd do it. Because he'd rather have none of you than only a bit of you, rather have none of you than share you with us." She turned round, staring into Katherine's eyes. "Oh, I understand him so well! I believe I'm the only one in all the family who does! You think that I'm not grown up yet, that I know nothing about life, that I don't know what people do or think, but I believe that I do know better than anyone! And, after all, it's Philip himself that's made me see! He understands now what he's got to give up if he marries you—all his dreams, all his fun, all his travels, all his imagination. *You* don't want to give up anything, Katie. You want to keep all this, Garth and the sea, even the oldest old man and woman in the place, above all, you want to keep all of us, mother most of all. You know that mother hates Philip and will always make him unhappy, but still you think that it's fair that you should give up nothing and he everything. But you're up against more than Philip, Katie—you're up against all his imagination that won't let him alone however much he wants it to—and then," Millie finally added, turning her eyes back to the other garden—"There's the other woman."

"Why!" Katherine cried—"You know? . . . Who told you?"

"And *you* know?" cried Millie. "He told you after all?"

"But who told you?" Katherine insisted, her hand on Millie's shoulder.

"Henry."

"Then *he* knows. Who else?"

"None of the family, I think, unless Henry's told the others. I've never said a word."

"Who told *him?*"

"A man at his Club."

There was silence. Then Katherine said:

"So *that's* why you've been so queer?"

"Yes. I didn't know whether he'd told you or no. I was afraid to say anything. I thought perhaps he'd told you and it was making you miserable. Then I thought that you ought to know. I thought sometimes that I'd speak to Philip, and then I was afraid of Henry doing something awful, blurting it all out to everybody. I haven't known what to do. But, Katie darling, you aren't unhappy about it, are you?"

"No—not unhappy," said Katherine.

"Because you mustn't be. What does it matter what Phil did before he loved you, whom he knew? What *does* it matter so long as you take her place? If ever anybody loved anybody, Philip loves you. . . ." Then she said quickly, eagerly: "What was she like, Katie? Did he tell you? Did he describe her? Was she lovely, clever? What was her name?"

"Anna," Katie said.

"Does he think of her still? Does he want to see her again?"

"I don't know," Katherine said slowly. "That's what's been so hard all these months. We simply don't talk of her. He doesn't want to think of her, nor of Russia, nor of any of that past life. He says it's all dead—"

"Well," said Millie, eagerly.

"But it isn't to me. I don't hate her, I'm not jealous, it doesn't alter one scrap of my love for Phil, but—I don't know—I feel as though if we talked about it everything would clear away. I'd see then that she was just an ordinary person like anyone else, and I wouldn't bother about her any more, as it is, simply because I don't know anything, I imagine things. I don't know whether Philip thinks of her or not, but I expect that he does, or thinks of my thinking of her, which is the same thing."

"Well, *I've* thought of her!" Millie declared, "again and again. I've wondered a thousand things, why she gave Philip up, whether she loves him still, whether she hates his being in love with someone else, whether she writes to him, what she's like, what she wears. . . . Doesn't it prove, Katie, how shut up we've always been? Why, even in Paris I never really thought about anybody whom I couldn't actually see, and life used to seem too simple if you just did the things in front of your nose—and now it's only the things that aren't anywhere near you that seem to matter." Millie said all this as though she were fifty years old at least. It was indeed a real crisis that she should be admitted into the very heart of all this thrilling affair; she was rewarded at last with her flaming desire, that 'she should share in life.' It was almost as though she herself had a lover.

Katherine waited, then she broke out suddenly: "But it's all so stupid this. Why can't things be perfectly simple? Why can't Philip like them and they like Philip? Why can't Philip and I marry and spend part of the year here and part of the year away?"

"You've got to choose," Millie said, "Mother or Philip— Philip or the family—Philip or Glebeshire. The old life or the new one. You've tried to mix it all up. You can't. Philip can change us. He *is* changing us all, but mix with us never. If he is forced to, he'll simply disappear."

"My dear, what's happened to you?" Katherine cried. "How wise you've become! How you've grown up!"

"I am," said Millie, with a solemnity that proved that 'grown-up' was the last thing that she really was. She sprang to her feet. She spoke as though she were delivering a challenge.

"Katie, if you let things go, if you let Mother have her way, one of two things will happen; either Philip won't be able to stand it and will vanish to Russia, or he'll endure it, will be smothered by us all, and there'll only be the corpse left for your enjoyment.

"Katie!" Her eyes shone with excitement, her voice quivered with the thrill of her intensity. "You must marry him *now*—whilst you're in London. You must chuck us all, show Mother that Philip comes before everything, take it into your own hands, send that Russian woman's ghost back to Russia . . . just as Browning and Mrs. Browning did, slip off one day, buy some smelling-salts at the chemist's and be married!"

She laughed. She clapped her hands.

"Oh! Katie! Katie! . . . It's the only way, the only possible way!"

But Katherine replied: "You're wrong, Millie. I can keep it all. I *will* keep it all. I love Phil, but I love Mother and you and Henry and This—This—all of it. If I were to marry Phil now Mother would never forgive me—you know that she would not. I could never come back. I must lose it all."

"You'd rather lose Philip then?"

"No. *That* never!"

"Well—Anna's after him, Katie. Russia's after him. He's awfully unhappy—and you're unfair. You're giving him nothing, not even himself. You say that you love him, but you want things all your way. I tell you you deserve to lose . . ." then suddenly softening again: "But I'll help you, Katie dear, whatever way it is. Oh! I'm so glad that we've spoken. We're together now, and nothing can part us."

Katherine caught her hand and held her close. "What would Mother do, do you think, if she knew about Anna?" she said, at last.

"I don't know," Millie answered, "Mother's so strange. I believe she'd do nothing. She'd know that if she dismissed him she'd lose you."

Then Katherine suddenly, holding Millie so close to her that their hearts beat as one, said: "I love him so. I love him so. . . . Everything must go if he wants it to."

And then, as though the house, the land, the place that had always been hers, answered her challenge, a lightning flash struck the darkness and the rain broke in a thunder of sound.

All through the wedding-ceremony Katherine felt insanely that she was no longer a Trenchard—insanely because if she was not a Trenchard what was she? Always before in these Trenchard gatherings she had known herself wonderfully at home, sinking down with the kind of cosy security that one greets as one drops into a soft, familiar bed. Every Trenchard was, in one way or another, so like every other Trenchard that a Trenchard gathering was in the most intimate sense of the word a family party. At a Beaminster gathering you were always aware of a spirit of haughty contempt for the people who were still outside, but at a Trenchard or Faunder assembly the people outside did not exist at all. "They were not there." The Beaminsters said: "Those we don't know are not worth knowing." The Trenchards said: "Those we can't see don't exist"—and they could only see one another. All this did not mean that the Trenchards were not very kind to the human beings in the villages and towns under their care. But then these dependents *were* Trenchards, just as old Trenchard chairs and tables in old Trenchard houses were Trenchards.

The Beaminsters had been broken all in a moment because they had tried to do something that their Age no longer permitted them to do. The Trenchards were much more difficult to break, because they were not trying to do anything at all. There was no need for them to be "Positive" about anything. . . .

As old Mrs. Trenchard, mother of Canon Trenchard of Polchester, once said to a rebellious daughter: "My dear, it's no use your trying to do anything. People say that new generations have come and that we shall see great changes. For myself, I don't believe it. England, thank God, is not like one of those foreign countries. England never changes about the Real Things," and by 'England' of course she meant 'Trenchards.'

Katherine knew exactly whom she would see at St. Margaret's, Westminster. From Glebeshire there would be Canon Trenchard, his wife and his two girls, also the Trenchards of Rothin Place, Polchester. There would be Sir Guy Trenchard from Truxe, and Miss Penelope Trenchard from Rasselas. There would be the head of all the Trenchards—Sir Henry Trenchard of Ruston Hall, in Norfolk, and there would be Garth Trenchard, Esq., from Bambury Towers, in Northumberland. There would be the Medlicott Trenchards of South Audley Street, the Robert Trenchards from somewhere in South Kensington (he was a novelist), and the Ruston Trenchards from Portland Place. Of the Faunders there was no end—Hylton Faunder, the famous painter, one of the props of the Royal Academy, the Rev. William Faunder of St. Mary's, Monkston, one of the best of London's preachers, the Misses Faunder of Hampstead, known for their good work, and others, others . . . from Hampshire, Wiltshire, Kent, Suffolk, Durham, Cumberland, every county in England.

Well, there they all were in rows; again and again you beheld the same white high forehead, the same thin and polished nose, the same mild, agreeable, well-fed, uncritical eyes. How well Katherine knew those eyes! She herself had them, of course, but her mother had them so completely, so magnificently, that once you had seen Mrs. Trenchard's eyes you would be able, afterwards, to recognise a Trenchard anywhere. But now, as Katherine looked about the church, it suddenly struck her, with a little shiver of alarm, that all the eyes were blind. She was sitting with her mother and Millie, and she looked at them quickly to see whether they'd noticed anything strange or unusual—but no, very placidly and agreeably, they were enjoying the comfort and 'rightness' of the whole affair. . . .

She was lonely, then, with a sudden shock of acute distress. She felt suddenly, with positive terror, that she did not belong to anyone at all. Philip was miles and miles away; as though it were the voice of prophecy, something seemed to tell her that she would never see him again. The service then seemed endless—she waited desperately for it to close. At last, when they all moved on to 22 Bryanston Square, her impatience simply seemed more than she could control. The presents were there, and many, many beautiful clothes and shining collars and cakes that no one wanted to eat, and over and over again, a voice (it seemed always the same voice) saying: "How nice! How delightful! . . . so glad . . . so fortunate. . . ." At last she was on her way back to Westminster. She had now only this one thought, that unless she were very quick she would never see Philip again. He had said that he would come to her for a moment after the wedding, and, when at the doorway of the drawing-room she caught a reflection of his figure in the mirror, her heart bounded with relief. How silly of her. What had she supposed? Nevertheless, quite breathlessly, she caught his hand.

"Oh, Phil! I'm so glad! . . . Come up to the school-room. We shall be alone there!"

The schoolroom, that had once been the nursery, packed away at the very top of the house, was bathed with the rich evening glow. He caught her in his arms, held her, and she kissed him, passionately, with clinging, eager kisses. Then, with a little happy sigh, she released him.

The old shabby room, with its old shabby books, Charlotte Mary Yonge and Mrs. Ewing and Henty, and the Christmas Supplements on the walls and the old grate that seemed still to be sunk in happy reveries of roasted chestnuts and toffee and toast, reassured her.

"Oh, Phil!" she cried. "I thought I was never going to get to you!"

She looked at him, carefully, luxuriously, with all the happiness of possessing something known and proved and loved. Why, were it the ugliest face in the world, the oldest, shab-biest body, nothing now could change her attachment. That was why, with true love, old age and decay did not, could not matter—and here, after all, was *her* possession, as far from old age as anyone could be, strong and thick-set and with the whole of life before it! But he seemed tired and depressed. He was very quiet, and sat there close to her, holding her hand, loving her, but subdued, saying very little. He *had* changed. He was not now that eager, voluble figure that had burst through the fog on that first wonderful evening so long ago.

"Phil—you're tired!" she said quickly, looking up into his eyes.

"Yes. I am rather," he answered. "It's been awfully hot. Was it very splendid?"

"The wedding? . . . No, horrid. . . . Just like any other, and I can't tell you anything about it, because I didn't notice a thing."

But he didn't ask her. He didn't want to know anything about it. He only wanted to have her there. They sat quietly, very close to one another. Her terror and her loneliness left her. The Abbey clock boomed the hour, and a little clock in the room gave a friendly, intimate echo.

"Your mother's asked me to go back to Garth with you," he suddenly said.

Katherine remembered how triumphant she had been when, upon a certain earlier occasion, he had told her that. Now her alarm returned; her hand trembled on his knee.

"What did you say?"

"Oh! I'm going of course. You'll be there, and I want to do what your mother wishes."

He said this very quietly, and looked at her with a little smile.

"Phil, don't go!" she said suddenly. "You're happier here. We'll be up in October."

"October!" he answered, still very quietly, "that's a long time to wait—and I haven't had very much of you lately. It won't help things very much my staying here—and I want to please your mother," he ended. "I've a kind of idea," he went on, "that she'll get to like me later, when she really gets to know me. I've been thinking all this time in London that I behaved veɪy badly when I was down there before. Wanted everything my own way."

Katherine could say nothing. In between them once more was that shadow. To speak right out would mean the old business all over again, the business that they had both resolutely dismissed. To speak out would mean Anna and the family, and that same demand once more—that Katherine should choose. One word and she knew that he would be pleading with all his force: "Marry me now! Come off with me! Slip out of the house and have it over."

But she could not—she was not ready. Give them all up, cut her life in half, fling them all away? No, still she clung desperately to the belief that she would keep them both, the family and Philip, the old life and the new. She heard Millie urging her, she saw Philip quietly determined to say nothing now until she led the way—but she could not do it, she could not, *could* not do it!

So they sat there, holding hands, his shoulder against hers, until at last it was time for him to go. After he had left her, whilst she was dressing for dinner, she had a moment of panic and almost ran out of the house, just as she was, to find him. But the Trenchard blood reasserted itself; she went down to dinner calm and apparently at ease.

That night, when they had all gone up to their rooms, she stood for a moment waiting outside her bedroom door, then, as though some sudden resolve had come to her, turned and walked to her mother's door. She knocked, entered and found her mother standing in front of her looking-glass. She had slipped off her evening dress, there with her short white sleeves, from which her stout, firm bare arms stood out strong and reliant, with her thick neck, her sturdy legs, she seemed, in spite of her grey hair, in the very plenitude of her strength. Her mild eyes, large and calm, her high white forehead, the whole poise of her broad, resolute back seemed to Katherine to have something defiant and challenging in it. Her mouth was full of hair-pins, but she nodded and smiled to her daughter.

"May I come in, Mother," said Katherine, "I want to speak to you."

Katherine thought of that earlier occasion in that same room when she had first spoken of her engagement. How far apart since then they had grown! It seemed to her to-night,

as she looked at that broad white back, that she was looking
at a stranger. . . . Yes, but an extraordinary stranger, a
really marvellous woman. How curious that Katherine
should have been living during all those years of intimate
affection with her mother and have thought of her never—
no, never at all. She had taken her, her love, her little habits,
her slow voice, her relentless determination, her 'managing'—
all these things and many more—as though they had been inevitably outside argument, statement or gratitude. But now,
simply because of the division that there was between them,
she saw her as a marvellous woman, the strangest mingling
of sweetness and bitterness, of tenderness and hardness, of
unselfishness and relentless egotism. She saw this, suddenly,
standing there in the doorway, and the imminent flash of it
struck her for an instant with great fear. Then she saw
Philip and gained her courage.

"I want to speak to you, Mother," she repeated, moving
into the middle of the room.

"Well, dear . . ." said Mrs. Trenchard, through the hair-
pins. She did not let down her hair, but after another glance
into the mirror, moved away, found a pink woolly dressing-
gown, which she put on. Then sat down on the old sofa, taking up, as she always did, a little piece of work—this time it
was some long red worsted that she was knitting. It curled
away from her, like a scarlet snake, under the flickering light
of the candles on her dressing-table, disappearing into darkness.

Katherine stood in front of her mother, with her hands
behind her, as she had done when she was a very little girl.

"Well, dear, what is it?" said Mrs. Trenchard again.

"Mother—I don't want you to have Philip down at Garth."

"Why not, dear? I thought you would like it."

"He isn't happy there."

"Well, he's only got to say so. . . . He needn't come."

"If he doesn't—he's afraid."

"Afraid of what?"

"Afraid of losing me." Katherine, as she said this, made a little forward movement with her hand as though she were asking for help, but Mrs. Trenchard's eyes were wide and cold.

"Afraid of losing you? . . . My dear, he can't trust you very much!"

"No, no, it isn't that! . . . He knows that you, the others don't like him. He hates Garth—at least he hates it if he's always got to live there. If he's alone here in London he thinks that you'll persuade me never to leave you, that you'll get the tighter hold of me, that—Oh! I can't explain it all!" she broke off quite desperately. "But it isn't good for him to be there, he's unhappy, he's depressed. Mother, *why* do you hate him?" she cried, suddenly challenging the whole room, with its old familiar pictures, its books and furniture to answer her.

"I think," said Mrs. Trenchard, very quietly, counting her stitches and nodding her head at her stocking, "that you're taking all this in a very exaggerated fashion—and you never used to be exaggerated, Katie, my dear—no, you never used to be. I often used to say what a comfort and help I always found you, because you saw things as they were—not like Millie and Henry, who would get excited sometimes over very little. But your engagement's changed you, Katie dear —it really has—more than I should have expected."

Katherine, during this speech, had summoned her control. She spoke now with a voice low and quiet—ridiculously like her mother's an observer might have thought.

"Mother, I don't want to be exaggerated—I don't indeed. But, all these last six months, we've never said to one another what we've thought, have never spoken openly about anything—and now we must. It *can't* go on like this."

"Like what, Katie dear?"

"Never knowing what we're really thinking. We've become a dreadful family—even father's noticed it."

"Certainly," said Mrs. Trenchard slowly. "We were all happier before Philip came."

Katherine's cheeks flushed. "That's unkind, Mother!" she cried. Her voice grew harder. "Please don't say anything about Philip unless you must. It makes everything very difficult. I know that you don't like him. You see him strangely, you put him in the wrong whatever he does. But, Mother," her voice softened again. "It isn't that. We can't alter that. Phil will never be at his best at Garth—not as things are now. But if we were married. Oh! you would see how fine things would be!" Her voice was eager, excited now. "He would be happy and quite, quite different with everyone. I know him. He depends so much—too much— on what people think of him. He knows that you don't like him, and that makes him embarrassed and cross—at his worst. But he's splendid, really, he is, indeed, and you'd see it if we were married and this horrid engagement were over. He's fine in every way, but he's different from us—he's seen so much more, knows life that we can't know, has other standards and judgments. Everyone can't be like us, Mother. There *must* be people who want different things and think different things. Why should he be made into something like us, forced to think as we do? . . . Mother, let us be married soon, at once, perhaps, and then everything will be right—" She stopped, breathless then, in her eagerness, bent down and kissed her mother's cheek.

But Mrs. Trenchard's cheek was very cold.

"Your father said a year," she answered, counting her stitches, "four, five, six—Yes, a year. And you agreed to that, you know."

Katherine turned, with a sharp movement, away, clenching her hands. At that moment she hated her mother, hated with a hot, fiery impulse that urged her to leave the room, the house, the family at that very instant, flinging out, banging the door, and so settle the whole affair for ever.

Mrs. Trenchard made no sound. Her needles clicked. Then she said, as though she had been looking things over:

"Do you think it's good of you, Katherine, considering how much all these years we've all been to one another, to persist in marrying a man whom, after really doing our best, we all of us—yes, all of us—dislike? You're of age, my dear—you can do as you please. It was your father who consented to this engagement, I was not asked. And now, after all these months, it is hardly a success, is it? You are losing us all—and I believe we still mean something to you. And Philip. How can you know about him, my dear? You are in love now, but that—that first illusion goes very quickly after marriage. And then—when it has gone—do you think that he will be a good companion for you, so different from us all, with such strange ideas picked up in foreign countries? You don't know what he may have done before he met you. . . . I don't appeal to your love for us, as once I might have done, but to your common-sense—your common-sense. Is it worth while to lose us, whom you know, in exchange for a man of whom you can know nothing at all? . . . Just give me those scissors off the dressing-table. The little ones, dear."

Katherine turned at the dressing-table. "But," she cried, her voice full of passionate entreaty, "*why* must I give you up because I marry him? Why can't I have you—all of you—and him as well? *Why* must I choose?" Then she added defiantly: "Millie doesn't dislike him—nor Aunt Betty."

"Millie's very young," answered her mother. "Thank you, my dear, and *as* you *are* there, just that thimble. Thank you . . . and your Aunt Betty likes everyone."

"And then," Katherine went on, "why do you see it from everyone's point of view except mine? It's my life, my future. You're settled—all of you, you, father, Aunt Aggie, Aunt Betty—but with Millie and Henry and I everything's to come. And yet you expect us to do all the things, think all the things that you've done and thought. We're different, we're another generation. If we weren't behind everyone else there wouldn't be anything to talk about at all. All parents now," Katherine ended, with an air of profound knowledge, "think of their children. Life isn't what it was fifty years ago."

Mrs. Trenchard smiled a grim little smile. "These are the things, my dear, I suppose, that Philip's been telling you. You must remember that he's been living for years in a country where one can apparently do anything one pleases without being thought wicked, and where you're put in prison a great deal, but only for rather innocent crimes. I don't pretend to understand all that. We may be—perhaps we are—an old-fashioned family, but the fact remains that we were all happy enough a year ago."

She picked up the long trailing serpent, then concluded: "But you're free, Katie dear. Perfectly free."

"If I were to go," said Katie, staring at her mother's face, so like that of an uneloquent baby, "if I were to go off now. If we were to be married at once—would you—would you—turn us out—have no more to do with us?"

She waited as though her whole life hung on her mother's answer.

"I really don't know what's happened to you, Katie," Mrs. Trenchard answered very quietly. "You're like a young woman in a play—and you used to be so sensible. Just give me those scissors again, dear. Certainly if you were to marry Philip to-morrow, without waiting until the end of the year, as you promised, I should feel—we should all feel—that you had given us up. It would be difficult not to feel that."

"And if we wait until the end of the year and then marry and don't live in Glebeshire but somewhere else—will you give us up *then?*"

"My dear, isn't it quite simple? We've given Philip every opportunity of knowing us—we're now just going to give him another. If he loves you he will not want to take you away

from all of us who love you also. He'll do his best to like us
—to settle—"

"To settle!" Katherine cried. "Don't you see that that's
what he's tried to do—and he can't—he can't! It's killing
him—and you want him to be killed! . . . You'd like him
to leave me, and if he won't do that you'll break his will, keep
him under you, ruin his spirit. . . . Mother, let him alone—
If we marry, after six months, let us lead our own lives.
You'll see I shall be as much yours as ever, more than ever.
It will be all right. It must be!"

Mrs. Trenchard said then her final word.

"If you leave us for Philip that is your affair. I do my
best to keep you both. You've talked much, Katie dear, about
our dislike of Philip—what of his dislike of us? Is that
nothing? Doesn't he show it every moment of the day? Unless he hates us less you'll have to choose. You'll have to
choose—let him come down to Garth then—we'll do everything for him."

Katherine would have answered, but a sudden catch in her
mother's voice, a sudden, involuntary closing of the eyes,
made her dart forward.

"Mother, you're tired."

"Yes, my dear, very."

They sat down on the old sofa together. Mrs. Trenchard,
her arms folded, leant back against her daughter's shoulder.

"Just a moment, Katie dear," she murmured, "before I
undress."

Suddenly she was asleep.

Katherine sat stiffly, staring before her into the room. Her
arm was round her mother, and with the pressure of her hand
she felt the soft firmness of the shoulder beneath the dressing-
gown. Often in the old days her mother had thus leant
against her. The brushing of her hair against Katherine's
cheek brought back to the girl thronging memories of happy,
tranquil hours. Those memories flung before her, like reproaching, haunting ghosts, her present unhappiness. Her

love for her mother filled her heart; her body thrilled with the sense of it.   And so, there in the clumsy, familiar room, the loneliest hour of all life came to her.

She was separated from them all.   She seemed to know that she was holding her mother thus for the last time. . . . Then as her hands tightened, in very protest, about the slumbering body, she was conscious of the presence, behind her, just then where she could not see, of the taunting, laughing figure.   She could catch the eyes, the scornful lips, the thin, defiant attitude.

"I'll take him back!   I'll take him back!" the laughing figure cried.

But Katherine had her bravery.   She summoned it all.

"I'll beat you!" she answered, her arms tight around her mother.   "I've made my choice.   He's mine now whatever you try!"

CHAPTER II

THE MIRROR

PHILIP had never had any conceit of himself—that is, he could not remember the time when he had been satisfied with what he had done, or pleased with the figure that he presented. The selfish actions in his life had always arisen from unselfish motives, because he had been afraid of hurting or vexing other people, because he thought other people finer than himself. Even when, as in the case of Seymour, he burst out in indignation at something that he felt to be pretentious and false, he, afterwards, on thinking it over, wondered whether the man hadn't after all been right 'from his point of view.' It was this ability to see the other person's point of view that had been, and would always be, the curse of his life.

Such men as Philip are not among the fine creatures of the world. Very rightly they are despised for their weakness, their lack of resistance, their inability to stand up for themselves. It is possible, nevertheless, that in heaven they will find that they, too, have their fine side. And this possibility of an ultimate divine comprehension irritates, very naturally, their fellow human beings who resent any defence of weakness. Philip himself would have been the first to resent it. He never consoled himself with thought of heaven, but took, now and then, a half-humorous, half-despairing glance at himself, swore, as he had in those long-ago days sworn about his mother, 'how this shall never happen again', and then once more was defeated by his imagination.

In this matter of the Trenchards he saw only too plainly

322

everyone's point of view; even with Aunt Aggie he saw that she was an old disappointed woman who disliked change and loved power so long as she need not struggle for it. Mrs. Trenchard he did not understand, because he was afraid of her. His fear of her had grown and grown and grown, and in that fear was fascination, hatred, and admiration. He felt now quite definitely that he was beaten by her. He had felt that, after she had taken no notice whatever of his public scene with Aunt Aggie. She would now, he believed, take no notice of anything. He knew also, now, of her hold over Katherine. He must stay with Katherine because he loved her. Therefore he must submit to Mrs. Trenchard . . . it was all quite simple.—Meanwhile to submit to Mrs. Trenchard meant, he knew, to such a character as his, extinction. He knew. Oh! . . . better than anyone else in the world— the kind of creature that, under her influence, he would become. He saw the others under her influence, the men and women of the village, the very chickens and pigs in the neighbouring farms. He knew what he had been under his mother, he knew what he had been under Anna, he knew what now he would be under Mrs. Trenchard. Well, extinction was a simple thing enough if you made up your mind to it—why struggle any further?

But day and night, increasingly, as the weeks passed, he was being urged to escape. All this summer, Anna, no longer a suggestion, no longer a memory, but now a vital, bodily presence, was urging him. Her power over him was not in the least because he was still in love with her—he loved only Katherine in all the world—but because of the damnable common-sense of what she said. What she said was this:

"Here you are amongst all these funny people. You are too much in the middle of them to see it plainly for yourself, but I'm a ghost and can see everything quite clearly; I know you—better than you know yourself. This Mrs. Trenchard 's determined never to let her daughter go. You say that you love this young woman, although what you can see in her stupid English solidity I can't imagine. However, you were always a fool. . . . All the same, if you love her it's for *her* sake that you must escape. You know the kind of creature you're going to be if you stay. What does she want with such a man? When she wakes up, about a week after marriage, and finds you under the thumb of her mother, what will happen to her love? She may continue to love you—English women are so stupid—but she'll certainly despise you. Come back to Russia. It isn't that I want you, or will take you back into my life, but she'll find out what you're worth then. If she really loves you she'll have to come after you. *Then* you'll have broken with the family and will be free. Run away, I tell you. It's the only thing to do."

All this he heard during a terribly heavy three weeks with relatives in the North, during a hot and glittering July in London when the world seemed to gyrate with the flashing cabs, the seething crowds, the glass and flowers and scents of a London season. Katherine seemed dreadfully far away from him. He was aware very vividly how bad it was for a healthy young man of his age to have no definite occupation. The men whom he knew in town seemed to him both uninteresting and preoccupied. A day in England seemed of so vast a length. In Russia time had been of no importance at all, and one day had vanished into another without any sound or sign. Here every clock in the town seemed to scream to him that he must take care to make the most of every second. This practical English world, moreover, could offer no friendly solution for the troubles that beset him.

He knew very well that if he asked any man at the club for advice he would be frankly dismissed for a fool. "What! You like the girl but can't bear the Mother-in-law! My dear boy, any music hall will tell you how common that is. Wait till you're married, then you can clear off all right—let the old woman scream as much as you like. What! the girl wants to stay with the mother? Well, again, wait till you're married. The girl will follow you fast enough then!"

How could he expect that any ordinary healthy Englishman would understand the soft, billowy, strangling web that
the Trenchard family had, by this time, wound about him?
Yes, another six months would complete the business. . . .

One hope remained to him—that when they knew of his
immoral life in Moscow they would definitely insist on Katherine's leaving him—and, if it came to that, she would stand
by him. He knew that she would stand by him. He would
himself long ago have told Trenchard had he not been sure
that someone else would do that for him, and that then the
sense of his own subterfuge and concealment would add to
their horror and disgust.

The stronger their disgust the better for him.

The day of that disclosure seemed now his only hope. Let
them fling him off and he knew what Katherine would do! . . .

Upon a torrid afternoon, two days after the Trenchard-
Faunder wedding, an irresistible desire to see Katherine
drove him to the Westminster house. He rang the bell, and
was told by Rocket, who always treated him with an air of
polite distrust, that the ladies were out, but might be in at
any time.

"I will wait," said Philip.

"Very good, sir," said Rocket reluctantly, and showed him
into the drawing-room, cool and damp like a green cave. To
Rocket's own restrained surprise, old Mr. Trenchard was
there sitting quite alone, with a shawl covering his knees, in
a large arm-chair near the empty fireplace.

The old gentleman showed no interest whatever in the
opening of the door, and continued to stare in front of him
through his gold-rimmed eyeglasses, his hands pressed fiercely
into his knees. Rocket hesitated a moment, then withdrew,
closing the door behind him.

Philip advanced slowly into the room. One of his difficulties with old Mr. Trenchard had always been that he was
not sure whether he were truly deaf or no. On certain occasions there had been no question old Mr. Trenchard was not

at all deaf, and then again on others deaf as a crab! He had never shown any marked signs of being aware of Philip's existence. There were many weeks that he spent in his own room, and he could not be said to show a very active consciousness of anyone except Katherine, whom he adored, and Aunt Aggie, whom he hated.

But, altogether, he was to Philip a terrible old man. Like a silver-grey shadow, beautiful perhaps, with the silver buckles on his shoes, his delicate hands and his snow-white hair, but emphatically terrible to Philip, who throve and blossomed under warm human intercourse, and shrivelled into nothing at all under a silent and ghostly disapproval.

But to-day Philip was desperate and defiant. This old man would never die any more than this old drawing-room, reflected in the green mirror, would ever change.

"I'd like to smash that mirror," thought Philip, "smash it into pieces. That would change the room if anything would. Why, I believe the whole family would tumble like a pack of cards if I smashed that mirror. I believe the old man himself would vanish into thin air."

"Good afternoon, sir," Philip said—and then thought to himself: "Why should I be afraid of the old image? He can't eat me!"

He walked over, close to him, and shouted:

"Good afternoon, sir."

The old man never stirred, not an eyelid quivered, but he replied in his clear, silvery voice, "Good afternoon to you."

He might indeed have been an Idol in his old particular temple—the old green room waited around him with the patient austerity that a shrine pays to its deity. The lamp on a distant table flung a mild and decent glow.

"I'm damned if I'm going to be afraid of him," thought Philip, and, taking a chair, he dragged it very close to the other's throne. Sitting there, near to him, it seemed to him that the light, mild though it was, really did go right through the old fellow, his cheeks, like the finest egg-shell china, seemed to catch the glow, store it for an instant in some fine inner receptacle and then pass it out on the other side. It was only the eyes that were not fine. They were true Trenchard eyes, and now, in old age, they were dull and almost dead.

They, ever so faintly, hinted that the beauty, fine as the present glass, was of the surface only, and had, behind it, no soul.

"It's a very hot day," said Philip, in a voice that was intended for a shout if the old man were really deaf and pleasant cheerfulness if he were not, "really very hot indeed. But this room's so very cool. Delightful."

Mr. Trenchard did then very slowly raise his head and look at Philip through his glasses. Then very slowly lowered his eyes again.

"My daughter will be here very shortly to receive you," he said.

"I'd like to talk to *you*," Philip said, still very cheerfully. "We've not had many talks together, have we? and that really isn't right, considering that I'm engaged to your granddaughter."

The old man picked up a magazine that lay on the little table that was in front of him. "Do you ever see Blackwood?" he said, as though he were very politely making conversation for a complete stranger. "It's a magazine for which I have a great liking. It seems to me to keep up its character wonderfully—most agreeable reading—most agreeable reading."

It was then that Philip, looking up, caught a reflection of Mr. Trenchard's face in the Mirror. It may have been imagination or it may have been the effect of shadow, or again it may have been nothing but truth—in any case it seemed to Philip that the old man's expression was an amazing mixture of pathos and wickedness—a quite intolerable expression. Philip made a movement with his hands as though he were brushing away a confusion of cobwebs, then burst out: "Look here, I don't know whether you're deaf or not—if you are it won't matter, and if you aren't we'll have a straight talk at last. You can't move until someone comes in to move you, and that may be a long while yet. You aren't strong enough to knock me down, so that I'm afraid you'll just have to stay here for a while and listen. . . . Of course you know by this time who I am. It's no use your pretending."

Philip paused and looked, but the old man had not stirred at all. His hands were still pressed into his knees, his eyes staring through his glasses, and, as his delicate breathing rose and fell, one black button shone in the lamplight and faded again. This immobility seemed to stir more profoundly Philip's anger.

"I'm going to marry your granddaughter Katherine, and of course you hate it and me too. You're just as selfish as all the others, and more too, I daresay. And you think you can frighten me by just doing nothing except showing you dislike me. But you won't frighten me—no, never—so you needn't expect it. I'm going to marry Katherine and take her right away from you all, so you may as well make up your mind to it."

Philip, flushed in the face and half expecting that the walls of the house would fall in upon him, paused—but there was no change at all in Mr. Trenchard's attitude, unless possibly one shining hand was driven a little more deeply into the knee. There was perhaps some unexpected pathos in the intensity of those pressing fingers, or, perhaps, Philip's desperate challenge was, already, forsaking him. At any rate he went on.

"Why can't you like me? I'm ready enough to like you. I'm not a bad kind of man, and I'll be very good to Katherine, no one could ever be better to anyone than I'll be to her. But why can't we lead our own life? You're an old man— you must have seen a lot in your time—you must know how times alter and one way of thinking gives way to another. You can't keep a family together by just refusing to listen to

anything or anybody. I know that you love Katherine, and
if you love her really, surely you'll want her to lead her own
life. Your life's nearly over—why should you spoil hers
for her?"

He paused again, but now he could not tell whether the
eyes were closed or no. Was the old man sleeping? or was
he fiercely indignant? or was he satirical and smiling? or was
he suddenly going to cry aloud for Rocket?

The uncertainty and the silence of the room worked terribly upon Philip's nerves. He had begun courageously, but
the sound of his voice in all that damp stillness was most unpleasant. Moreover, he was a poor kind of fellow, because he
always, even in the heat of anger, thought a friend better than
an enemy. He was too soft to carry things through.

"He really does look very old," he thought now, looking
at the thin legs, the bones in the neck, the lines on the forehead of the poor gentleman, "and after all it can't be pleasant
to lose Katherine."

"If you'd only," he went on in a milder voice, "give me a
chance. Katherine's much too fond of all of you to give you
up simply because she's married. She isn't that sort at all.
You knew that she'd marry some day. All the trouble has
come because you don't like me. But have you ever tried to?
I'm the sort of man that you've got to like if you're to see the
best of me. I know that's my fault, but everyone has to have
allowances made for them."

Philip paused. There was a most deadly stillness in the
room. Philip felt that even the calf-bound Thackeray and the
calf-bound Waverley novels behind the glass screens in the
large book-case near the door were listening with all their
covers.

Not a movement came from the old man. Philip felt as
though he were addressing the whole house—

He went on. "When you were young you wanted to go
on with your generation just as we do now. You believed
that there was a splendid time coming, and that none of the

times that had ever been would be so fine as the new one. *You* didn't want to think the same as your grandfather and be tied to the same things. Can't you remember? *Can't* you remember? Don't you *see* that it's just the same for us?"

Still no movement, no sound, no quiver of a shadow in the Mirror.

"I'll be good to her, I swear to you, I don't want to do anyone any harm. And after all, what have I done? I was rude one Sunday night, Henry drank too much once, I don't always go to church, I don't like the same books—but what's all that? isn't everyone different, and isn't it a good thing that they are?"

He bent forward—"I know that you can do a lot with them all. Just persuade them to help, and be agreeable about it. That's all that's wanted—just for everyone to be agreeable. It's such a simple thing, really."

He had touched Mr. Trenchard's knee. With that touch the whole room seemed to leap into hostile activity. He had, quite definitely, the impression of having with one step plunged into a country that bristled with foes behind every bush and tree. The warmth of the old man's knees seemed to fling him off and cast him out.

Old Mr. Trenchard raised his head with a fierce, furious gesture like the action of a snake striking.

In a voice that was not silvery nor clear, but shaking and thick with emotion, he said:

"I warn you, young man—if you dare to take my granddaughter away—you'll kill me!"

Before Philip could do more than start back with a gesture of dismay, the door had opened and Mrs. Trenchard and Aunt Aggie had entered.

Meanwhile there was Henry.

Important events had occurred in Henry's life since that Sunday when he had told Millie about Philip's terrible past and had shared in that disastrous supper. He was to go to Cambridge.

This important decision had apparently followed on Aunt Aggie's disclosure of his evil courses, therefore it may be considered that Philip was, in this as in the other recent events in the Trenchard history, responsible. Quite suddenly George Trenchard had lifted up his head and said: "Henry, you're to go to Cambridge next October. I think that Jesus College shall bear the burden of your company. I believe that there are examinations of a kind that you must pass before they will admit you. I have written for papers."

This declaration should, of course, have been enough to fling Henry into a wild ecstasy. Before the arrival of Philip it would undoubtedly have done so. Now, however, he seemed to himself to have progressed already so far beyond Jesus College, Cambridge. To have troubles and experiences so deep and weighty as compared with anything that anyone at Cambridge could possibly have known, and that to propose that he should go there was very little less than an insult. . . . And for this he blamed Philip.

Nevertheless the papers arrived. He was, in reality, no fool, and the Cambridge 'Little Go' is not the most difficult examination under the sun. At the end of May he went up to Cambridge. If one may judge by certain picturesque romances concerned with University life and recently popular amongst us, one is to understand that that first vision of a University thrills with all the passion of one's first pipe, one's first beer and one's first bedmaker or scout, as the case may be. The weather was chill and damp. He was placed in a tiny room, where he knocked his head against the fine old rafters and listened to mice behind the wainscot. His food was horrible, his bedmaker a repulsive old woman, and the streets were filled with young men, who knew not Henry and pushed him into the gutter. He hated everyone whom he saw at the examination, from the large, red-faced gentleman who watched him as he wrote, down to the thin and uncleanly youth who bit his nails at the seat next to his own. He walked down Petty Cury and hated it; he strolled up the King's Parade and hated that too. He went to King's College Chapel and heard a dull anthem, was spoken to by an enormous porter for walking on the grass and fell over the raised step in the gateway. He was conceited and lonely and hungry. He despised all the world, and would have given his eyes for a friend. He looked forward to his three years in this city ("The best time of your life, my boy. What I would give to have those dear old days over again") with inexpressible loathing.

He knew, however, three hours of happiness and exultation. This joy came to him during the English Essay— the last paper of the examination. There were four subjects from which he might choose, and he selected something that had to do with 'The Connection between English History and English Literature.' Of facts he had really the vaguest notion. He seemed to know, through hearsay rather than personal examination, that Oliver Cromwell was something responsible for 'The Pilgrim's Progress', that that dissolute monarch Charles II. had to do with the brillance and audacity of Mr. Congreve and Mr. Wycherley, that Queen Anne in some way produced Pope and Robespierre, Wordsworth, and Queen Victoria, Charlotte Mary Yonge (he had cared very deeply for 'The Daisy Chain'), and our Indian Empire Mr. Rudyard Kipling. He knew it all as vaguely as this, but he wrote—he wrote divinely, gloriously ecstatically, so that the three hours were but as one moment and the grim nudity of the examination-room as the marbled palaces of his own fantastic dreams. Such ecstasy had he known when he began that story about the man who climbed the ricketty stairs. Such ecstasy had been born on that day when he had read the first page of the novel about Forests—such ecstasy had, he knew in spite of itself, received true nourishment from that enemy of their house, Philip.

His spirits fell when he came to himself, saw how many

other gentlemen had also written essays and with what indifference and languor the red-faced gentleman hustled his pages in amongst all the others. Nevertheless, he did come out of that examination-room with some conviction as to the course that his future life would take, and with a kindness, almost a tenderness, towards this grey town that was going to allow him, even to command him, to write essays for the next three years. With Henry one mood succeeded another as rapidly as, in his country, wet weather succeeds fine.

He returned to Garth in an outrageous temper. His main feeling now was that Philip had spoiled Cambridge for him. Philip and his immoral life 'got in' between all that he saw and dropped a misty veil, so that he could think of nothing in the way that tradition had taught him. He had always had a great respect for tradition.

Then as the weeks passed by he was made increasingly unhappy by the strange condition in which he found the family. He was, at heart, the crudest sentimentalist, and his sentimentalism had been fed by nothing so richly as by the cherished conviction that the George Trenchards were the most united family in England. He had always believed this, and had never, until now, considered the possibility of any division. But what now did he find? His mother stern, remote, silent, Millie irritable, uneasy and critical, Aunt Aggie always out of temper, Aunt Betty bewildered and tactless, even his father disturbed and unlike himself. And Katie? . . . He could not have believed that six months would change anyone so utterly.

Instead of the reliable, affectionate and stolid sister who had shared with him all her intimacies, her plans, her regrets, her anticipations, he beheld now a stranger who gave him no intimacies at all, avoided him and hid from him her undoubted unhappiness. It was true of him now as it had ever been that 'he would give his life to make Katherine happy,' but how was he to do anything for her when she would tell him nothing, when she treated him like a stranger, and then blamed him for his hostilities.

If it had been clear that now, after these months of her engagement, she no longer loved Philip, the matter would have been simple. He would have proceeded at once to his father and told him all that he knew about Philip's Moscow life. But she *did* love Philip—more, yes, far more, than ever—nothing could be clearer than that. This love of Katherine's burned, unceasingly, in Henry's brain. With no other human being could he have felt, so urgently, the flame of it but Katherine, whom he had known as he had known himself, so sure, so undramatic, so happily sexless, as she had always seemed to him, that it should be she whom this passion had transformed! From that moment when he had seen her embrace of Philip, his imagination had harried him as a dog harries a rabbit, over the whole scale of the world. . . . Love, too, that he had believed was calm, domestic, friendly, reassuring, was in truth unhappy, rebellious, devastating. In the very heart of her unhappiness seemed to be the fire of her love. This removed her from him as though he had been flung by it into a distant world. And, on every side, he was attacked by this same thing. There were the women whom he had seen that night with Philip, there was the woman who had given Philip a son in Russia, there was here a life, dancing before him, now near him, now far away from him, intriguing him, shaming him, stirring him, revolting him, removing him from all his family, isolating him and yet besetting him with the company of wild, fantastic figures.

He walked the Glebeshire roads, spoke to no one, hated himself, loathed Philip, was lashed by his imagination, aroused at last to stinging vitality, until he did not know whither to turn for safety.

He came up to London for the Faunder-Trenchard wedding. Late in the afternoon that had seen Philip's conver-

sation with old Mr. Trenchard Henry came into the drawing-
room to discover that tea was over and no one was there.
He looked into the tea-pot and saw that there was nothing
there to cheer him. For a moment he thought of Russia, in
which country there were apparently perpetual samovars boiling upon ever-ready tables. This made him think of Philip—
then, turning at some sudden sound, there was Aunt Aggie
in the doorway.

Aunt Aggie looked cold in spite of the warm weather, and
she held her knitting-needles in her hand defiantly, as though
she were carrying them to reassure a world that had unjustly
accused her of riotous living.

"It's simply rotten," said Henry, crossly. "One comes in
expecting tea and it's all over. Why can't they have tea at
the ordinary time?"

"That's it," said Aunt Aggie, settling herself comfortably
into the large arm-chair near the fireplace. "Thinking of
yourself, Henry, of course. Learn to be unselfish or you'll
never be happy in *this* world. I remember when I was a
girl—"

"Look here!" Henry interrupted. "Has Philip been here
this afternoon?"

"Mr. Mark? Yes, he has."

"Did he come to tea?"

"Yes."

She dug her needles viciously into an innocent ball of
wool.

"Yes," said Henry fiercely, "that's why they had it early,
I suppose—and why I don't get any—*of* course."

"All I know is," continued Aunt Aggie, "that he's put your
grandfather into the most dreadful state. He was alone in
here with him it seems, and I'm sure I don't know what he's
said to him, but it upset him dreadfully. I've not been well
myself to-day, and to have your grandfather—"

But Henry again interrupted.

"What did he want coming to-day at all for? He might have waited."

Aunt Aggie, however, did not like to be interrupted when she was discussing her health, so she said now sharply: "Just look at your hands, Henry—Why *can't* you keep them clean. I should have thought going up to Cambridge—"

"Oh! I'm all right," he answered, impatiently. "Anyway, I wonder what he told grandfather."

"Why, what *could* he have told him?" said Aunt Aggie, eagerly, looking up.

"Oh, I don't know—nothing—Only . . . Oh, Rocket, ask them to make some fresh tea. Let me have it in here."

"Certainly, Mr. Henry," said Rocket, removing the tea-pot with an air of strong disapproval.

"Really, Henry!" Aunt Aggie exclaimed. "And simply for yourself! Why, even though I've had the most trying headache all day, I'd never venture to give so much trouble simply for myself."

"Oh, I daresay you'll have some when it comes," Henry answered, carelessly—then, pursuing his thoughts, he continued: "Well, he won't be coming back to Garth with us—that's one comfort."

"Oh, but he is!" cried Aunt Aggie, excitedly. "He is! Your mother's *asked* him to come back with us, and he's accepted. I simply don't understand it. Your mother dislikes him as much as the rest of us do, and why she should *ask* him! It can't be for poor Katie's sake. She's miserable enough when he's at Garth. I'm sure if things go on like this much longer I shall go and take a little house by myself and live alone. I'd really rather than all this unpleasantness."

This threat did not apparently alarm Henry very greatly, for, bursting out suddenly, he cried: "It's beastly! perfectly beastly! There we've all got to sit watching him make Katie miserable. I won't stand it! I *won't* stand it!"

"Why you!" said Aunt Aggie, scornfully. "How can you prevent it? You're only a boy!"

This epithet stung Henry to madness. Ah, if Aunt Aggie only knew all, she'd see that he was very far from being 'only a boy'—if she only knew the burden of secret responsibility that he'd been bearing during all these weeks. He'd keep secret no longer—it was time that everyone should know the kind of man to whom Katherine was being sacrificed. He turned round to his aunt, trembling with anger and excitement.

"You talk like that!" he cried, "but you don't know what I know!"

"What don't I know?" she asked eagerly.

"About Philip—this man Mark—He's wicked, he's awful, he's—abominable!"

"Well," said Aunt Aggie, dropping her needles. "What's he done?"

"Done!" Henry exclaimed, sinking his voice into a horrified and confidential whisper. "He's been a dreadful man. Before, in Russia, there's nothing he didn't do. I know, because there's a friend of mine who knew him very well out there. He lived a terribly immoral life. He was notorious. He lived with a woman for years who wasn't his wife, and they had a baby. There's nothing he didn't do—and he never told father a word." Henry paused for breath.

Aunt Aggie's cheeks flushed crimson, as they always did when anyone spoke, before her, of sexual matters.

At last she said, as though to herself: "I always knew it— I always knew it. You could see it in his face. I warned them, but they wouldn't listen."

Henry meanwhile had recovered himself. He stood there looking into the Mirror. It was a tragic moment. He had done, after all, what, all these months, he had determined to prevent himself from doing. He saw now, in a flash of accusing anger, what would most certainly follow. Aunt Aggie would tell everyone. Philip would be dismissed—Katherine's heart would be broken.

He saw nothing but Katherine. Katherine whom he loved

with all the ardour of his strange undisciplined quixotic soul.
He saw Katherine turning to him, reproaching him, then, hiding her grief, pursuing her old life, unhappy for ever and
ever. (At this stage in his development, he saw everything
in terms of 'for ever and for ever'.) It never occurred to him
that if Philip were expelled out of the Trenchard Eden Katherine might accompany him. No, she would remain, a heart-
broken monument to Henry's lack of character.

He scowled at his aunt, who sat there thrilled and indignant and happy.

"I say!" he burst out. "Of course you mustn't tell anybody!"

Aunt Aggie nodded her head and her needles clicked.

"It must remain with wiser and older heads than yours,
Henry, as to what ought to be done . . ." then to herself
again: "Ah, they'll wish they'd listened to me now."

"But I say," repeated Henry, red in the face, standing in
front of her, "you really mustn't. I told it you as a secret."

"A secret! When everyone in London knows! A nice
thing they'll all think—letting Katherine marry a man with
such a reputation!"

"No, but look here—*you* wouldn't have known anything if
I hadn't told you—and you mustn't do anything—you mustn't
really. Katie loves him—more than ever—and if she were to
lose him—"

"Much better for her to lose him," said Aunt Aggie firmly,
"than for her to be miserable for life—much better. Besides,
think of the abominable way the man's deceived us! Why,
he's no better than a common thief! He—"

"Perhaps he hasn't deceived her," interrupted Henry.
"Perhaps he's told her—"

"Told her!" cried his aunt. "And do you really suppose
that Katherine would stay for one moment with a man whose
life—My dear Henry, how little you know your sister. She
certainly has changed lately under that dreadful man's in-

fluence, but she's not changed so fundamentally as to forget all principles of right and wrong, all delicate feeling."

"I don't know," said Henry slowly, "I don't believe we do know Katie a bit. Girls are so queer. You think they don't know a thing about anything, and really they know more than you do. . . . Anyway," he went on eagerly, "you mustn't say a word. You mustn't really. You must give me your promise."

But before Aunt Aggie could do more than shake her head there was an interruption. The door opened and Philip entered. Aunt Aggie at once rose from her chair, and, with a rustle and a quiver, without looking at the young man, without speaking left the room.

Henry remained, staring at Philip, confused and bewildered, furious with himself, furious with Aunt Aggie, furious with Philip. Yes, now he had ruined Katherine's life—he and Philip between them. That he should not consider it possible that Katherine should have her life in her own hands to make or mar was characteristic of the Trenchard point of view.

Philip, conscious of Aunt Aggie's exit, said: "I was just going—I came back to fetch a book that I left here—one that Katherine lent me."

Henry made his usual lurching movement, as though he would like to move across the room and behave naturally, but was afraid to trust himself.

"That it?" he asked, pointing gloomily to a novel on the table near him.

"That's it," said Philip.

"Hullo!" cried Henry, looking at it more closely. "That's mine!" It was indeed the novel that had to do with forests and the sea and the liberty of the human soul, the novel that had been to Henry the first true gospel of his life and that had bred in him all the troubles, distrusts and fears that a true gospel is sure to breed. Henry, when the original book had been delivered back to Mudie's had with ceremony and worship bought a copy for himself. This was his copy.

"It's my book," Henry repeated, picking it up and holding it defiantly.

"I'm very sorry," said Philip stiffly. "Of course I didn't know. Katherine spoke as though it were hers."

"Oh, you can take it," Henry said, frowning and throwing it back on the table.

Philip looked at him, then suddenly, laughing, walked over to him, "What's the matter, Henry?" he said catching his arm. "I'll have it out with the lot of you, I swear I will. You, none of you, say anything—you all just look as though you didn't know me. You yourself, these last months, have looked as though you'd like to stick a dagger into my back. Now, really, upon my word, I don't know what I've done. I'm engaged to Katherine, but I've behaved as decently about it as I can. I'm not going to take her away from you all if I can help it. I've made up my mind to that, now that I see how much she cares for you all. I've done my best . . . I really have. Now, what is it?"

Henry was, in spite of himself, touched by this appeal. He glanced at Philip's face and thought, again in spite of himself, what a nice one it was. A horrible suspicion came to him that he liked Philip, had always liked him, and this abominable whisper, revealing treachery to all his principles, to all his traditions, to all his moral code, above all to Katherine, infuriated him. He tore his arm away.

"If you want to know," he cried, "it's because I think you're a beast, because you're not fit to touch Katie—because —because—I know all about you!"

Philip stood there; for a moment a smile trembled to his lips, then was dismissed.

"What do you mean?" he said, sternly.

"Mean?" cried Henry, allowing himself to be carried along on a tide of indignation that seemed, in some way, in spite of itself, to be quite genuine. "Mean? I mean that I've known for weeks and weeks the kind of man *you* are! I know what you did in Moscow for years and years, although you may look so quiet. Do you think you're the sort of man to marry Katherine? Why, you aren't fit to touch her hand."

"Would you mind," said Philip quietly, "just telling me exactly to what you are referring?"

"Why," said Henry, dropping his voice and beginning to mumble, "you had—you had a mistress—in Moscow for years, and everyone knew it—and you had a baby—and it died. Everyone knows it."

"Well," said Philip quietly, "and what then?"

"Oh, you're going to deny it, I suppose," said Henry, "but I tell you—"

"No," said Philip, "I'm not going to think of denying it. I don't know where you got your information from, but it's perfectly true. At the same time I can't see that it's your particular business or, indeed, anyone's. The affair's absolutely done with—old history."

"No, I suppose," cried Henry, "it doesn't seem to be anything to you. You don't know what a decent family thinks of such things. It's nothing to you, of course. But we happen to care for Katherine more than—more than—you seem to know. And—and she's everything to us. And we're not going to let her—to let her marry someone who's notoriously a—a bad man. No, we're not. It may seem odd to you, but we're *not*."

Philip was standing now beneath the Mirror, in front of the fireplace, his hands behind his back.

"My dear Henry," he said, "it's extremely pleasant to me to hear that you're so fond of Katherine—but has it ever occurred to any of you that she may possibly have a life of her own, that she isn't going to be dependent on all of you for ever? . . . And as for you, Henry, my boy, you're a nice character, with charming possibilities in it, but I'm afraid that it can't be denied that you're a bit of a prig—and I don't know that Cambridge is exactly the place to improve that defect."

Philip could have said nothing more insulting. Henry's face grew white and his hands trembled.

His voice shaking, he answered: "You can say what you like. All I can tell you is that if you don't give up Katherine I'll tell Father at once the sort of man you are—tell them all. And then you'll have to go."

At Philip's heart there was triumph. At last the crisis was threatened for which he had, all this time, been longing. He did not for an instant doubt what Katherine would do. Ah! if they drove him away she was his, his for ever! and, please God, they would never see Glebeshire again!

He was triumphant, but he did not give Henry his mood.

"You can do what you please, my son," he answered, scornfully. "Tell 'em all. But brush your hair next time you come down to the drawing-room for tea. Even in Russia we do that. You don't know how wild it looks. . . . Now, just hand me that book and I'll clear out. Meanwhile don't be so childish. You're going to Cambridge, and really *must* grow up. Take my advice. Brush your hair, put on a clean collar, and don't be a prig."

Henry, white with passion, saw nothing but Philip's face. Philip the enemy and scorn of the house, Philip the ravisher of Katherine, Philip author of all evil and instigator of all wickedness.

He picked up the book and flung it at Philip's head.

"There's your book!" he screamed. "Take it! . . . You —you cad!"

The book crashed into the centre of the mirror.

There was a tinkle of falling glass, and instantly the whole room seemed to tumble into pieces, the old walls, the old prints and water-colours, the green carpet, the solemn bookcases, the large arm-chairs—and with the room, the house, and with the house Westminster, Garth, Glebeshire, Trenchard and Trenchard tradition—all represented now by splinters and fragments of glass, by broken reflections of squares and stars of green light, old faded colours, deep retreating shadows.

"Oh!" cried Henry! "Oh!"

"Thank Heaven!" laughed Philip triumphantly. "One of you've done something at last!"

CHAPTER III

THAT return to Garth was, for everyone concerned, a miserable affair. It happened that the fine summer weather broke into torrents of rain. As they drove up to the old house they could hear the dripping of water from every nook and corner. As Henry lay awake that first night the hiss and spatter of the rain against his window seemed to have a personal grudge against him. "Ah—you fool—s-s-s—you s-s-s-illy a-s-s-s. *Put* your *pride* in your *pocket*—s-s-s-illy a-s-s."

When he slept he dreamt that a deluge had descended upon the earth, that all were drowned save he, and that he was supported against the flood only by the floor of the house that swayed and swayed. Suddenly with a crash in it fell—he awoke to find that he had tumbled out of bed on to the carpet.

For days a steaming, clammy mist, with a weight and a melancholy peculiar to Glebeshire, hung over the world.

They lived in hot steam, their hair was damp and their hands chill. It was poor days for the beginning of August. Rebekah was in a bad temper; no one knew what it was that had displeased her, but she had a wicked nephew who wrote, at certain times, to plead for money, and always for many days after receiving a letter from him she was displeased with everyone. She walked now like a tragedy queen in her tall white cap and stiff white apron; only Mrs. Trenchard could be expected to deal with her, and Mrs. Trenchard had other things that occupied her mind.

Henry's eye was now forever on his mother. He waited

344

for the moment when Aunt Aggie would speak, that quite inevitable moment.

He thought that he had never truly seen his mother before. In old days, in that strange, dim world before Philip's arrival, she had seemed to him someone to be cherished, to be protected, someone growing a little old, a little cheerless, a little lonely. Now she was full of vigour and dominion. When she said to him: "Did you put on that clean under-clothing this morning, Henry?" instead of sulking and answering her question with an obvious disgust, he assured her earnestly that he had done so. He admired now her strong figure, her pouring of tea at breakfast, her sharp rebukes to the gardener, and her chiding of Uncle Tim when he entered the drawing-room wearing muddy boots. Yes, he admired his mother. So he trembled at the thought of her cold, ironic anger when she heard of Philip's past.

On the day after their arrival at Garth he told Millie what he had done. He had long ago realised that, since her return from Paris, Millie had been a quite unaccountable creature. It was not only her French education. He attributed this change also to the dire influence of Philip. He noticed with disgust that she behaved now as though she were a woman of the world, implying, at the same time, that he was still an uncleanly and ignorant schoolboy. He knew that she would be indignant and scornful at his indiscretion, nevertheless he was driven by loneliness to confide in her.

They walked together to the village that they might fetch the afternoon post, otherwise unrescued until the following morning.

Millie was in a bad temper.

"I never knew anyone walk in the mud as you do, Henry. Your boots are filthy in a minute. You walk into every puddle you can see. You always did."

The trees hung ghostly out of the mist like mocking scarecrows. Every once and again moisture from somewhere trickled down between Henry's neck and collar.

"Look here, Millie," he said gloomily, "I want your advice."

"You've done something silly again, I suppose," she answered loftily.

Glancing shyly at her, he thought that she was looking very pretty. Strange, the number of new things that he was noticing now about the family. But she *was* pretty—a great deal prettier than Katherine; in fact, the only pretty one of the family. He liked her soft hair, so charming under her large flopping garden-hat, her little nose, her eyes black and sparkling, the colour of her cheeks, her tall and slim body that carried her old cotton dress so gracefully. Everything about her was right and beautiful in a way that no other members of the family could achieve. Katherine was always a little clumsy, although since her engagement to Philip she had taken more care. . . . There was something light and lovely about Millie that no care would produce if you had not got it. He was proud of her, and would have liked that she should be nice to him.

"Yes," he said, "I've been an awful fool. . . . I've told Aunt Aggie about Philip."

Millie stopped and stood, staring at him.

"You've told Aunt Aggie?" she cried furiously.

"Yes," he repeated, blushing, as he always did when he was scolded.

"Oh! you *silly* ass!" She was so deeply exasperated that she could scarcely speak.

"You SILLY ass! I might have guessed it—And yet all the time I'd hoped that at least. . . . And Aunt Aggie of all people! . . . and now Katherine and mother!"

"Oh, you chattering, blundering idiot!"

She walked forward at a furious pace; he plunged after her.

"That's all right," he said, "when you've done cursing you'll be cooler. I *know* I'm an ass, but Aunt Aggie irritated me and got it all out of me. Aunt Aggie's the devil!"

"Of course she is, and *of course* you'll choose her out of everyone, when she *hates* Philip and would wring his neck to-morrow if her hands were strong enough."

"Well, I hate him too," said Henry.

"Oh, no you don't," answered Millie, "you think you do. You're proud of thinking you hate him, and you lose your temper because he laughs at you, and then you throw books at his head, but you don't really hate him."

"How do you know I throw books at his head?"

"Oh, you don't suppose we, any of us, believed that story about you and Philip having a kind of game in the drawing-room just for fun. . . . Father was furious about it, and said the mirror was unreplaceable, and the sooner you went to Cambridge and stopped there the better—and I think so too.   Oh! you've just spoilt everything!"

"It's only about Katie I'm thinking," he answered doggedly.   "It may, after all, be true what Aunt Aggie said, that it will be much better for her in the end for the thing to be broken off, even though it hurts her now."

"Better for her!" cried Millie scornfully.   "Don't you know that, however deeply she loved Philip when it all began, it's nothing to the way that she loves him now? . . . Of course now there'll be a scene.   Philip will be turned off for ever and—" She broke off, then said, staring at Henry: "Supposing, after all, Katie were to go with him!"

Henry shook his head.   "She'd never do that, however much Philip is to her.   Why, it would mean giving up Garth and us for ever!   Mother would never forgive her!   After all, she's only known Philip six months, and I heard her say the other day in London she loves Garth more than ever. And even if Mother *did* forgive her, in the end she'd never be able to come back here as one of us again.   You and I will love her whatever she does, but Mother and Father and the aunts . . . I believe it would simply kill them—"

"I'm not so sure," said Millie slowly, "that Mother thinks that.   I believe she's half afraid of Philip running off and then Katie following him. That's why she's been so nice to him lately, although she can't bear him. Of course if she knew all this that we know he'd *have* to go—she wouldn't have him in the house five minutes, and Father would do what Mother told him of course. And now that you've been an idiot enough to tell Aunt Aggie, it's all up. . . . The only hope is that Katie will chuck it all and follow him!"

"What!" cried Henry aghast. "You'd like her to!"

"Why, of course," said Millie, "there isn't anything compared with the sort of thing Katie feels for Philip—Home and the family? Why, they've all *got* to go in these days! That's what people like the aunts and fathers and the rest of the old fogeys round here don't see. But they'll *have* to see soon. . . . But mother's cleverer than they are. At least she is about Katie, because she loves her so much."

"My word!" said Henry, in the husky voice that always came when he admired anybody. "You've changed an awful lot lately, Millie."

"Yes, I suppose I have," she answered, complacently.

They talked very little after that, for the reason that in the village Henry bought Millie some bulls-eyes, because he felt in a confused kind of way that he admired her more than he had ever done.

Millie had also another reason for silence; she was thinking very hard. During those few days in London she had lived in a world of thrilling expectation. She hoped that every moment would announce the elopement of Katherine and Philip. After her conversation with her sister, it had seemed to her that this elopement was inevitable. On every occasion of the opening of a door in the London house her heart had leapt in her breast. She had watched the lovers with eyes that were absorbed. Ah! if only they would take her more thoroughly into their confidence, would put themselves into her hands. She'd manage for them—she'd arrange everything most beautifully. This was the most romantic hour of her life. . . .

But now, after Henry's revelation, Millie's thoughts were turned upon her mother. Of course her mother would expel Philip—then there was a danger that Philip would return to that living, fascinating creature in Russia, the mysterious, smiling Anna. Millie had created that figure for herself now, had thought and wondered and dreamed of her so often that she saw her bright and vivid and desperately dangerous, thin and dark and beautiful against a background of eternal snow.

There they were—her mother and Anna and Katherine, with Philip, poor Philip, in between them all. It was truly a wonderful time for Millie, who regarded all this as a prologue to her own later dazzling history. She did not know that, after all, she blamed Henry very desperately for his foolishness. The thrilling crisis was but brought the nearer.

Meanwhile the first thing that she did was to inform Katherine of Henry's treachery.

Katherine received the news very quietly.

"And now," said Millie eagerly, "what will you do, Katie darling?"

"Wait and see what Mother does," said Katie.

"She'll be simply horrified," said Millie. "If she sends Philip away and forbids you ever to see him again, what will you do?"

But Katherine would not answer that.

"Let's wait, Millie dear," she said gently.

"But you wouldn't let him *go*?" Millie pursued, "not back to Russia and that awful woman."

"I trust Philip," Katherine said.

"You can never trust a man," Millie said gravely. "I know. One of our girls in Paris was let in terribly. She—"

Katherine interrupted her.

"Philip isn't like anyone else," she said.

And Millie was dismissed.

But when Katherine was alone she sat down and wrote a letter. This was it:

"My darling Rachel,

Do you remember that a long time ago, one day when I came to see you in London, you said that if I were ever in trouble I was to tell you and you'd understand *anything?* Well, I'm in trouble now—bad trouble. Things are growing worse and worse, and it seems now that whichever way I act, something's got to be hopelessly spoiled. To any ordinary outsider it would mean such a small business, but really it's the *whole* of my life and of other people's too. You're *not* an outsider, and so I know that you'll understand. I can't tell you more now—I don't know what will happen, how I'll act, or anything. But I shall know soon, and then I shall want your help, dreadfully. I'm sure you'll help me when I ask you to.

You do like Philip better now, don't you? I know that you didn't at first, but that was because you didn't really know him. *I* didn't really know him either then, but I know him now, and I love him twice as much as ever I did.

This will seem a silly letter to you, but I want to feel that I've got someone behind me. Millie's a dear, but she isn't old enough to understand. Don't be frightened by this. If anything happens I'll write at once.

Your loving

K."

Meanwhile the family life proceeded, outwardly, on its normal way. August was always a month of incident—picnics to Rafiel and St. Lowe and Damen Head, sometimes long expeditions to Borhaze or Pelynt, sometimes afternoons in Pendennis or Rothin Woods. There were expeditions in which relations from Polchester or Clinton, or friends from Liskane and Polewint shared, and, in the cover of them, the family supported quite successfully the Trenchard tradition of good manners, unruffled composure, and abundant leisure. As members of a clan so ancient and self-reliant that no enemy, however strong, however confident, could touch them, they sat about their luncheon baskets on the burning sand, whilst the fat pony cropped in the dark hedges above the beach and the gulls wheeled and hovered close at hand.

This was well enough, but the long summer evenings betrayed them. In earlier days, when relationships were so sure and so pleasant that the world swept by in a happy silence, those summer evenings had been lazy, intimate prologues to long nights of undisturbed sleep. They would sit in the drawing-room, the windows open to the garden scents and the salt twang of the sea, moths would flutter round the lamps, Millie would play and sing a little at a piano that was never quite in tune. Aunt Betty would struggle happily with her "Demon Patience," George Trenchard would laugh at them for half-an-hour, and then slip away to his study. Mrs. Trenchard and Aunt Aggie would knit and discuss the village, Henry would lie back in an arm-chair, his nose deep in a book, Katherine would be at anybody's service—the minutes would fly, then would come Rebekah with hot milk for some and toast-and-water for others, there would be prayers, and then "good-night, ma'am". "Good-night, sir", from the three maids, the cook and Rebekah, then candles lighted in the hall, then climbing slowly up the stairs, with clumsy jokes from Henry and last words from Mrs. Trenchard, such as "Don't forget the Williams' coming over to-morrow, Katie dear," or "Some of that quinine for your cold, Aggie, *I* suggest," or "I've put the new collars on your bed, Henry," then the closing of doors, then a happy silence, utterly secure. That had been the old way.

Outwardly the August nights of this year resembled the old ones—but the heart of them beat with panic and dismay. Philip had thought at first that it was perhaps his presence that caused the uneasiness, and one evening he complained of a headache and went up to his room after dinner. But he learnt from Katherine that his absence had merely emphasised everything. They must be all there—it would never do to show that there was anything the matter. Millie played the piano, Aunt Betty attempted her "Patience" with her usual little "Tut-tut's" and "Dear me's." Mrs. Trenchard and Aunt Aggie sewed or knitted, but now the minutes dragged in endless procession across the floor, suddenly someone would raise a head and listen, Henry, pretending to read a book, would stare desperately in front of him, then noticing that Aunt Aggie watched him, would blush and hold his book before his face; with relief, as though they had escaped some threatening danger, they would greet the milk, the 'toast-and-water', the maids and the family prayers.

There was now no lingering on the staircase.

There are many families, of course, to whom the rebellion or disgrace of one of its members would mean but little, so slightly had been felt before the dependence of one soul upon another. But with the Trenchards that dependence had been *everything,* the outside world had been a fantastic show, unreal and unneeded: as the pieces of a pictured puzzle fit one into another, so had the Trenchards been interwoven and dependent . . . only in England, perhaps, had such a blind and superior insularity been possible . . . and it may be that this was to be, in all the records of history, the last of such a kind—*"Nil nisi bonum"*. . . .

To Philip these summer days were darkened by his consciousness of Mrs. Trenchard. When he looked back over the months since he had known her, he could remember no very dramatic conversation that he had had with her, nothing tangible anywhere. She had been always pleasant and agreeable to him, and, at times, he had tried to tell himself that, after all, he might ultimately be happy 'eaten up by her,' as Jonah was by the whale. Then, with a little shiver, he knew the truth—that increasingly, as the days passed, he both hated and feared her. She had caught his will in her strong hands and was crushing it into pulp.

He made one last effort to assert himself, even as he had tried his strength against Katherine, against Henry, against Aunt Aggie, against old Mr. Trenchard. This little conversation that he had in the Garth garden with Mrs. Trenchard upon one of those lovely summer evenings was of the simplest and most undramatic fashion. Nevertheless it marked the end of his struggle; he always afterwards looked back upon those ten minutes as the most frightening experience of his life. Mrs. Trenchard, in a large loose hat and gauntleted gardening gloves, made a fine cheerful, reposeful figure as she walked slowly up and down the long lawn; she asked Philip to walk with her; the sun flung her broad flat shadow like a stain upon the bright grass.

They had talked a little, and then he had suddenly, with a tug of alarm at his heart, determined that he would break his chains. He looked up at her placid eyes.

"I think," he said—his voice was not quite steady—"that Katherine and I will live somewhere in the North after our marriage. Quite frankly I don't think Glebeshire suits me."

"And Katie," said Mrs. Trenchard, smiling.

"Katie . . . she—she'll like the North when she's tried it for a little."

"You'll rob us of her?"

"Not altogether, of course."

"She'll be very miserable away from Glebeshire . . . very miserable. I've seen such a nice little house—Colve Hall—only two miles from here—on the Rafiel road. I don't think you must take Katie from Glebeshire, Philip."

That was a challenge. Their eyes met. His dropped.

"I think it will be better for her to be away after we are married."

"Why? Do you hate us all?"

He coloured. "I'm not myself with you. I don't know what to do with your kind of life. I've tried—I have indeed —I'm not happy here."

"Aren't you selfish? If you rob Katie of everything— will you be happy then?"

Yes, that was it. He could see their future life, Katherine, longing, longing to return, excited, homesick!

Although he did not look up, he knew that she was smiling at him.

"You are very young, Philip," she said. "You want life to be perfect. It can't be that. You must adapt yourself. I think that you will both be happier here in Glebeshire—near us."

He would have broken out, crying that Katherine was his, not theirs, that he wanted her for himself, that they must be free. . . . Of what use? That impassivity took his courage and flattened it all out as though he were a child of ten, still ruled by his mother.

"Shall we go in?" said Mrs. Trenchard. "It's a little cold."

It was after this conversation that he began to place his hope upon the day when his Moscow misdeeds would be declared—that seemed now his only road to freedom.

Upon one lovely summer evening they sat there and had, some of them, the same thought.

Millie, slim and white, standing before the long open window, stared into the purple night, splashed with stars and mysterious with tier-like clouds. She was thinking of Anna, of all that life that Philip had, of what a world it must be where there are no laws, no conventions, no restraints. That woman now had some other lover, she thought no more, perhaps, of Philip—and no one held her the worse. She could do what she would—how full her life must be, how adventurous, packed with colour, excitement, battle and victory. And, after all, it might be, to that woman, that this adventure meant so little that she did not realise it *as* an adventure. Millie's heart rose and fell; her heart hurt her so that she pressed her hand against her frock. She wanted her own life to begin—at once, at once. Other girls had found the beginning of it during those days in Paris, but some English restraint and pride—she was intensely proud—had held her back. But now she was on fire with impatience, with long-

ing, with courage. . . . As she stared into the night she
seemed to see the whole world open, like a shining silver plate,
held by some dark figure for her acceptance. She stretched
out her hands.

"Take care you don't catch cold by that open window,
Millie dear," said her mother.

Henry also was thinking of Anna. From where he sat
he could, behind his book, raising his eyes a little, see Philip.
Philip was sitting, very straight and solid, with his short
thick legs crossed in front of him, reading a book. He never
moved. He made no sound. Henry had, since the day when
he had broken the mirror, avoided Philip entirely. He did
not want to consider the man at all; of course he hated the
man because it was he who had made them all miserable,
and yet, had the fellow never loved Katherine, had he remained outside the family, Henry knew now that he could
have loved him.

This discovery he had made exactly at the moment when
that book had fallen crashing into the mirror—it had been
so silly, so humiliating a discovery that he had banished it
from his mind, had refused to look into it at all.

But that did not mean that he did not contemplate Philip's
amazing life. He contemplated it more intensely every day.
The woman had all the mystery of invisibility, and yet Henry
thought that he would know her if he saw her. He coloured
her according to his fancy, a laughing, tender figure who
would recognize him, did she meet him, as the one man in the
world for whom she had been searching.

He imagined to himself ridiculous conversations that he
should have with her. He would propose to marry her,
would declare, with a splendid nobility, that he knew of her
earlier life, but that "that meant nothing to him." He would
even give up his country for her, would live in Russia,
would . . . Then he caught Philip's eye, blushed, bent to
pull up his sock, said, in a husky, unconcerned voice:

"Do play something, Millie. Something of Mendelssohn."

Philip also was thinking of Anna. Through the pages of his stupid novel, as though they had been of glass, he saw her as she had last appeared to him on the platform of the Moscow station. She had been wearing a little round black fur hat and a long black fur coat, her cheeks were pale, her eyes mocking, but somewhere, as though in spite of herself, there had been tenderness. She had laughed at him, but she had, for only a moment perhaps, wished that he were not going. It was that tenderness that held him now. The evening, through which he was now passing, had been terrible—one of the worst that he had ever spent—and he had wondered whether he really would be able to discipline himself to that course on which he had determined, to marry Katherine under the Trenchard shadow, to deliver himself to Mrs. Trenchard, even as the lobster is delivered to the cook. And so, with this desperation, had come, with increasing force, that memory of Anna's tenderness.

He did not want to live with her again, to renew that old life—his love for Katherine had, most truly, blotted out all the fire and colour of that earlier passion, but he wanted— yes, he wanted most passionately, to save his own soul.

Might it not, after all, be true, as that ghostly figure had urged to him, that it would be better for him to escape and so carry Katherine after him—but what if she did not come?

He heard Mrs. Trenchard's voice as she spoke to Millie, and, at that sound, he resigned himself . . . but the figure still smiled at him behind that glassy barrier.

Katherine also thought of Anna. She was sitting just behind Aunt Betty watching, over the old lady's shoulder, the 'Patience'.

"There," said Aunt Betty, "there's the ten, the nine, the eight. Oh! if I only had the seven!"

"You can get it," said Katherine, "if you move that six and five."

"How stupid I am!" said Aunt Betty, "thank you, my dear, I didn't see."

Katherine saw dancing in and out between the little cards
a tiny figure that was yet tall and strong, moving there a teas-
ing, taunting puppet, standing also, a motionless figure, away
there, by the wall, watching, with a cynical smile, the room.
Beneath the thin hands of the old lady the cards fluttered,
shifted, lay with their painted colours on the shining table,
and, in accompaniment with their movement, Katherine's
thoughts also danced, in and out, round and round, chasing
the same old hopeless riddle.   Sometimes she glanced across
at her mother. Perhaps already Aunt Aggie had told
her. . . . No, she had not.   Her mother's calm showed that
she, as yet, knew nothing.   Katherine, like the others, did
not doubt what her mother would do. She would demand
that the engagement should be broken off; they would all,
ranged behind her broad back, present their ultimatum—And
then what would Katherine do? . . . Simply, sitting there,
with her fingers fiercely interlaced, her hands pressed against
her knee, she did not know. She was exhausted with the
struggle that had continued now for so many weeks, and
behind her exhaustion, waiting there, triumphant in the expectation of her success, was her rival.

Then, suddenly, as they waited there came to them all the
idea that the hall door had been opened and gently closed.
They all, Mrs. Trenchard, Aunt Aggie, Millie, Henry, Katherine, started, looked up.

"Did someone come in?" said Mrs. Trenchard, in her mild
voice. "I thought I heard the hall door—Just go and see,
Henry."

"I'll go," said Katherine quickly.

They all waited, their heads raised.   Katherine crossed
the room, went into the hall that glimmered faintly under a
dim lamp, paused a moment, then turned back the heavy han-
dle of the door.   The door swung back, and the lovely summer night swept into the house.   The stars were a pattern of
quivering light between the branches of the heavy trees that
trembled ever so gently with the thrilling sense of their happi-

ness. The roses, the rich soil soaked with dew, and the distant murmur of the stream that ran below the garden wall entered the house.

Katherine waited, in the open door, looking forward. Then she came in, shutting the door softly behind her.

Had someone entered? Was someone there with her, in the half-light, whispering to her: "I'm in the house now—and I shall stay, so long as I please—unless you can turn me out."

She went back into the drawing-room.

"There was no one," she said. "Perhaps it was Rebekah."

"There's rather a draught, dear," said Aunt Aggie, "my neuralgia . . . thank you, my dear."

"I've done it!" cried Aunt Betty, flushed with pleasure. "It's come out! If you hadn't shown me that seven, Katie, it never would have come!"

Upon the very next afternoon Aunt Aggie made up her mind. After luncheon she went, alone, for a walk; she climbed the fields above the house, threaded little lanes sunk between high hedges, crossed an open common, dropped into another lane, was lost for awhile, finally emerged on the hill above that tiny Cove known as Smuggler's Button. Smuggler's Button is the tiniest cove in Glebeshire, the sand of it is the whitest, and it has in the very middle a high jagged rock known as the Pin. Aunt Aggie, holding an umbrella, a black bonnet on her head and an old shabby rain-coat flapping behind her, sat on the Pin. It was a long way for her to have come—five miles from Garth—and the day was windy, with high white clouds that raced above her head like angry birds ready to devour her. Aunt Aggie sat there and looked at the sea, which approached her in little bowing and beckoning white waves, as though she were a shrivelled and pouting Queen Victoria holding a drawing-room. Once and again her head trembled, as though it were fastened insecurely to her body, and her little fat, swollen cheeks shook like jelly.

Sometimes she raised a finger, encased in a black glove, and waved it in the air, as though she were admonishing the universe.

She clutched vigorously in one hand her umbrella.

She gazed at the sea with passion. This love for the sea had been a dominant power in her ever since she could remember, and had come she knew not whence. It had been, in earlier days, one of the deep, unspoken bonds between herself and Katherine, and it had been one of her most active criticisms of Millie that 'the girl cared nothing about the sea whatever'. But she, Aunt Aggie, could not say why she loved it. She was no poet, and she knew not the meaning of the word 'Enthusiasm'. She was ashamed a little of her passion, and, when she had walked five miles to Smuggler's Button or seven miles to Lingard Sand 'just to look at it', she would walk stiffly home again, would give no answer to those who asked questions, and, if driven into a corner would say she had been 'just for a walk.' But she loved it in all its moods, grave, gay and terrible, loved it even when it was like a grey cotton garment designed for the poor or when it slipped into empty space under a blind and soaking mist. She loved the rhythm of it, the indifference of it, above all, the strength of it. Here at last, thank God, was something that she could admire more than herself.

She had, nevertheless, always at the back of her mind the thought that it would be bad for it if it knew how much she thought of it; she was always ready to be disappointed in it, although she knew that it would never disappoint her—she was grim and unbending in her attitude to it lest, in a moment of ecstasy, she should make cheap of her one devotion. To-day she did not actively consider it. She sat on the rock and made up her mind that she would take steps 'that very day.' Harriet, her sister-in-law, had, during these last months, often surprised her, but there would be no question of her action in this climax of the whole unfortunate business.

"The young man," as she always called Philip, would never

show his face in Trenchard circles again. Harriet might forgive, because of her love for Katherine, his impertinence, his conceit, his irreligion, his leading Henry into profligacy and drunkenness, she *would* not—*could* not—forgive his flagrant and open immorality, an immorality that had extended over many years. As she thought of this vicious life she gave a little shiver—a shiver of indignation, of resolution, of superiority, and of loneliness. The world—the gay, vital, alluring world, had left her high and dry upon that rock on which she was sitting, and, rebuke and disapprove of it as she might, it cared little for her words.

It was, perhaps, for this reason that she felt strangely little pleasure in her approaching triumph. She had hated "the young man" since her first meeting with him, and at last, after many months of patient waiting, the means had been placed in her hands for his destruction. . . . Well, she did not know that she cared to-day very greatly about it. She was old, she was tired, she had neuralgia in one side of her face, there was a coming headache in the air. Why was it that she, who had always held so steadily for right, whose life had been one long struggle after unselfishness, who had served others from early morning until late at night, should now find no reward, but only emptiness and old age and frustration? She had not now even the pleasure of her bitternesses. They were dust and ashes in her mouth.

She resolved that at once, upon that very afternoon, she would tell Harriet about Philip—and then suddenly, for no reason, with a strange surprise to herself, she did a thing that was quite foreign to her; she began to cry, a desolate trickling of tears that tasted salt in her mouth, that were shed, apparently, by some quite other person.

It seemed to her as she turned slowly and went home that that same Woman who had encountered life, had taken it all and tasted every danger, now, watching her, laughed at her for her wasted, barren days. . . .

By the time, however, that she reached Garth she had

recovered her spirits; it was the sea that had made her melancholy. She walked into the house with the firm step of anticipated triumph. She went up to her bedroom, took off her bonnet, washed her face and hands, peeped out on to the drive as though she expected to see someone watching there, then came down into the drawing-room.

She had intended to speak to her sister-in-law in private. It happened, however, that, on going to the tea-table, she discovered that the tea had been standing for a considerable period, and nobody apparently intended to order any more—at the same time a twinge in her left jaw told her that it had been foolish of her to sit on that rock so long.

Then Philip, who had the unfortunate habit of trying to be friendly at the precisely wrong moment, said, cheerfully:

"Been for a walk all alone, Aunt Aggie?"

She always hated that he should call her Aunt Aggie. To-day it seemed a most aggravated insult.

"Yes," she said. "You've had tea very early."

"George wanted it," said Mrs. Trenchard, who was writing at a little table near a window that opened into the sunlit garden. "One never can tell with you, Aggie, what time you'll like it—never can tell, surely."

There! as though that weren't directly charging her with being a trouble to the household. Because *they'd* happened to have it early!

"I call it very unfair—" she began nibbling a piece of bread and butter.

But the unfortunate Philip gaily continued: "When we are married, Aunt Aggie, and you come to stay with us, you shall have tea just when you like."

He was laughing at her, he patronised her! He dared—! She trembled with anger.

"I shall never come and stay with you," she said.

"Aunt Aggie!" cried Katherine, who was sitting near her mother by the window.

"No, never!" Aunt Aggie answered, her little eyes flashing and her cheeks shaking. "And if I had my way you should never be married!"

They all knew then that at last the moment had come. Henry started to his feet as though he would escape, Katherine turned towards her mother, Philip fixed his eyes gravely upon his enemy—only Mrs. Trenchard did not pause in her writing. Aunt Aggie knew then that she was committed. She did not care, she was glad if only she could hurt Philip, that hateful and intolerable young man.

Her hands trembled, her rings making a tiny clatter against the china; she saw only her sister-in-law and Philip.

Philip quietly said:

"Why do you hope that Katherine and I will never marry, Aunt Aggie?"

"Because I love Katherine—because I—we want her to make a happy marriage. Because if she—knew what I know she would not marry you."

"My dear Aggie!" said Mrs. Trenchard, softly, from the writing-table—but she stayed her pen and waited, with her head turned a little, as though she would watch Katherine's face without appearing to do so.

"And what do you know," pursued Philip quietly, "that would prevent Katherine from marrying me?"

"I know," she answered fiercely, the little gold cross that hung round her throat jumping against the agitation of her breast, "that you—that you are not the man to marry my niece. You have concealed things from her father which, if he had known, would have caused him to forbid you the house."

"Oh! I say!" cried Henry, suddenly jumping to his feet.

"Well," pursued Philip, "what are these things?"

She paused for a moment, wondering whether Henry had had sufficient authority for his statements. Philip of course would deny everything—but she had now proceeded too far to withdraw.

"I understand," she said, "that you lived in Russia with a woman to whom you were not married—lived for some years, and had a child. This is, I am ashamed to say, common talk. I need scarcely add that I had not intended to bring this disgraceful matter up in this public fashion. But perhaps after all it is better. You have only yourself to blame, Mr. Mark," she continued, "for your policy of secrecy. To allow us all to remain in ignorance of these things, to allow Katherine—but perhaps," she asked, "you intend to deny everything? In that case—"

"I deny nothing," he answered. "This seems to me a very silly manner of discussing such a business." He addressed his words then to Mrs. Trenchard. "I said nothing about these things," he continued, "because, quite honestly, I could not see that it was anyone's affair but my own and Katherine's. I told Katherine everything directly after we were engaged."

At that Aunt Aggie turned upon her niece.

"You knew, Katherine? You knew—all these disgraceful—these—" Her voice broke. "You knew and you continued your engagement?"

"Certainly," answered Katherine quietly. "Whatever life Philip led before he knew me, was no business of mine. It was good of him to tell me as he did, but it was not my affair. And really, Aunt Aggie," she continued, "that you could think it right to speak like this before us all—to interfere—"

Her voice was cold with anger. They had none of them ever before known this Katherine.

Aunt Aggie appealed to her sister-in-law.

"Harriet, if I've been wrong in mentioning this now, I'm sorry. Katherine seems to have lost her senses. I would not wish to condemn anyone, but to sit still and watch whilst my niece, whom I have loved, is given to a profligate—"

Katherine stood, with the sunlight behind her; she looked at her aunt, then moved across the room to Philip and put her hand on his shoulder.

They all waited then for Mrs. Trenchard; they did not doubt what she would say. Katherine, strangely, at that moment felt that she loved her mother as she had never loved her before. In the very fury of the indignation that would be directed against Philip would be the force of her love for her daughter.

This pause, as they all waited for Mrs. Trenchard to speak, was weighted with the indignation that they expected from her.

But Mrs. Trenchard laughed: "My dear Aggie: what a scene! really too stupid. As you have mentioned this, I may say that I have known—these things—about Philip for a long time. But I said nothing because—well, because it is really not my business what life Philip led before he met us. Perhaps I know more about young men and their lives, Aggie, than you do."

"You knew!" Henry gasped.

"You've known!" Aggie cried.

Katherine had, at the sound of her mother's voice, given her one flash of amazement: then she had turned to Philip, while she felt a cold shudder at her heart as though she were some prisoner suddenly clapt into a cage and the doors bolted.

"Yes," said Mrs. Trenchard, "Mr. Seymour came a long time ago and told me things that he thought I ought to know. I said to Mr. Seymour that he must not do such things, and that if I ever spoke of it to Philip I should give him his name. I disapprove of such things. Yes, it was Mr. Seymour—I think he never liked you, Philip, because you contradicted him about Russia. He's a nice, clever boy, but I daresay he's wrong in his facts. . . ." Then, as they still waited in silence, "I really think that's all, Aggie. You must forgive me, dear, but I don't think it was quite your business. Katherine is over age you know, and in any case it isn't quite nice in the drawing-room—and really only because your tea was cold, Aggie dear."

"You've known . . . you'll do nothing, Harriet?" Aggie gasped.

Mrs. Trenchard looked at them before she turned back to her writing-table.

"You can ring for some fresh tea if you like," she said.

But for a moment her eyes had caught Philip's eyes. They exchanged the strangest look. Hers of triumph, sarcastic, ironic, amazingly triumphant, his of a dull, hopeless abandonment and submission.

Her attack at last, after long months of struggle, had succeeded. He was beaten. She continued her letter.

CHAPTER IV

THE WILD NIGHT

TEN minutes later Katherine and Philip were alone in the garden. There were signs that the gorgeous summer afternoon was to be caught into thunder. Beyond the garden-wall a black cloud crept toward the trees, and the sunlight that flooded the lawn seemed garish now, as though it had been painted in shrill colours on to the green; the air was intensely hot; the walls of the house glittered like metal.

They stood under the great oak bobbing in front of them.

"Well," said Philip at last, "that's the end, Katie dear—your mother's a wonderful woman."

Katherine was silent. He went on:

"That was my last hope. I suppose I'd been counting on it more than I ought. You'd have come with me, I know, if they'd turned me out? Not a bit of it. Your mother's a wonderful woman, I repeat." He paused, looked into her eyes, seemed to be startled by the pain in them. "My dear, don't mind. She only wants to keep you because she can't get on without you—and I shall settle down all right in a bit. What a fuss, after all, we've been making."

Katherine said: "Tell me, Phil, have there been times, lately, in the last week, when you've thought of running away, going back to Russia? Tell me honestly."

"Yes," he answered, "there have—many times. But I always waited to see how things turned out. And then to-day when the moment *did* come at last, I saw quite clearly that I couldn't leave you *ever*—that anything was better than being without you—*anything*—So that's settled."

"And you've thought," Katherine pursued steadily, "of what it will be after we're married. Mother always wanting me. Your having to be in a place that you hate. And even if we went to live somewhere else, of Mother always keeping her hand on us, never letting go, never allowing you to be free, knowing about Anna—their *all* knowing—you've faced it all?"

"I've faced it all," he answered, trying to laugh. "I can't leave you, Katie, and that's the truth. And if I've got to have your mother and the family as well, why, then, I've got to have them. . . . But, oh! my dear, how your mother despises me! Well, I suppose I *am* a weak young man! And I shall forget Russia in time. . . . *I've got to!*" he ended, almost under his breath.

She looked at him queerly.

"All right," she said, "I know now what we've got to do."

"What do you mean?" he asked.

"Wait. I must go and speak to Uncle Tim. I shall be an hour. Be ready for me out here under this tree in an hour's time. It will be seven o'clock."

"What do you mean?" he asked her again, but she had gone.

She had picked up an old garden hat in the hall, and now very swiftly hurried up the village road. She walked, the dust rising about her and the black cloud gaining in size and strength behind her. Uncle Tim's house stood by itself at the farther end of the village. She looked neither to right nor left, did not answer the greeting of the villagers, passed quickly through the little garden, over the public path and rang the rusty, creaking bell. An old woman, who had been Uncle Tim's housekeeper for an infinite number of years, opened the door.

"Ah, Miss Kathie," she said, smiling. "Do ee come in. 'E's gardenin', poor soul. All of a sweat. Terrible 'ot 'tis, tu. Makin' up thunder I'm thinkin'."

Katherine went into the untidy, dusty hall, then into her

uncle's study. This had, ever since her childhood, been the same, a litter of bats, fishing-rods, specimens of plants and flowers drying on blotting paper, books lying in piles on the floor, and a pair of trousers hanging by a nail on to the back of the door.

She waited, seeing none of these familiar things. She did not, at first, see her uncle when he came in from the garden, perspiration dripping down his face, his old cricket shirt open at the neck, his grey flannel trousers grimed with dust.

"Hullo, Katie!" he cried, "what do *you* want? And if it's an invitation to dinner tell 'em I can't come." Then, taking another look at her, he said gravely, "What's up, my dear?"

She sat down in an old arm-chair which boasted a large hole and only three legs; he drew up a chair close to her, then suddenly, as though he saw that she needed comfort, put his arms round her.

"What's the matter, my dear?" he repeated.

"Uncle Tim," she said, speaking rapidly but quietly and firmly, "you've got to help me. You've always said that you would if I wanted you."

"Why, of course," he answered simply. "What's happened?"

"Everything. Things, as you know, have been getting worse and worse at home ever since—well, ever since Phil and I were engaged."

"Yes, I know," he said.

"It hasn't been Phil's fault," she broke out with sudden fierceness. "He's done everything. It's been my fault. I've been blind and stupid from the beginning. I don't want to be long, Uncle Tim, because there's not much time, but I must explain everything so that you shall understand me and not think it wrong. We've got nearly two hours."

"Two hours?" he repeated, bewildered.

"From the beginning Mother hated Phil. I always saw it of course, but I used to think that it would pass when she knew Phil better—that no one could help knowing him with-

out loving him—and that was silly, of course.   But I waited,
and always hoped that things would be better.   Then in the
spring down here there was one awful Sunday, when Aunt
Aggie at supper made a scene and accused Philip of leading
Henry astray or something equally ridiculous.   After that
Philip wanted me to run away with him, and I—I don't
know—but I felt that he ought to insist on it, to make me go.
He didn't insist, and then I saw suddenly that he wasn't
strong enough to insist on anything, and that instead of being
the great character that I'd once thought him, he was really
weak and under anyone's influence.   Well, that made me
love him in a different way, but more—much more—than I
ever had before.   I saw that he wanted looking after and protecting.   I suppose you'll think that foolish of me," she said
fiercely.

"Not at all, my dear," said Uncle Tim, "go on."

"Well, there was something else," Katherine went on.
"One day some time before, when we first came to Garth, he
told me that when he was in Russia he had loved another
woman.   They had a child, a boy, who died.   He was afraid
to tell me, because he thought that I'd think terribly of him.

"But what did it matter, when he'd given her up and left
her?   Only this mattered—that I couldn't forget her.   I
wasn't jealous, but I was curious—terribly.   I asked him
questions, I wanted to see her as she was—it was so strange
to me that there should be that woman, still living somewhere,
who knew more, much more, about Phil than I did.   Then
the more questions I asked him about her the more he thought
of her and of Russia, so that at last he asked me not to speak
of her.   But then she seemed to come between us, because we
both thought of her, and I used to wonder whether he wanted
to go back to her, and *he* wondered whether, after all, I was
jealous about her.   Then things got worse with everyone.   I
felt as though everyone was against us.   After the Faunder
wedding Henry and Phil had a quarrel, and Henry behaved
like a baby.

"I've had a dreadful time lately. I've imagined *anything*. I've been expecting Phil to run away. Millie said he would —Mother's been so strange. She hated Phil, but she asked him to Garth, and seemed to want to have him with her. She's grown so different that I simply haven't *known* her lately. And Phil too—it's had a dreadful effect on him. He seems to have lost all his happiness—he hates Garth and everything in it, but he's wanted to be near me, and so he's come. So there we've all been." She paused for a moment, then went on quickly. "Just now—this afternoon—it all came to a climax. Aunt Aggie had found out from Henry about the Russian woman. She lost her temper at tea, and told Mother before us all. Phil has been expecting this to happen for weeks, and had been almost hoping for it, because then he thought that Mother and Father would say that he must give me up, and that then I would refuse to leave him. In that way he'd escape.

"But it seemed"—here Katherine, dropping her voice, spoke more slowly—"that Mother had known all the time. That horrid Mr. Seymour in London had told her. She'd known for *months,* and had never said anything—Mother, who would have been *horrified* a year ago. But no—She said *nothing*. She only told Aunt Aggie that she oughtn't to make scenes in the drawing-room, and that it wasn't her business.

"Philip saw then that his last chance was gone, that she meant *never* to let me go, and that if she must have him as well she'd *have* him. He's sure now that I'll never give Mother up unless she makes me choose between him and her —and so he's just resigned himself."

Uncle Tim would have spoken, but she stopped him.

"And there's more than that. Perhaps it's foolish of me, but I've felt as though that woman—that Russian woman— had been coming nearer and nearer and nearer. There was an evening the other night when I felt that she'd come right inside the house. I went into the hall and listened. That

must seem ridiculous to anyone outside the family, but it may
be that thinking of anyone continually *does* bring them—
does do something. . . . At least for me now she's here, and
she's going to try and take Phil back again. Mother wants
her, it's Mother, perhaps, who has made her come. Mother
can make Phil miserable in a thousand ways by reminding
him of her, by suggesting, by . . ." With a great cry
Katherine broke off: "Oh, Mother, Mother, I did love you
so!" and bursting into a passion of tears, clung to her uncle
as though she were still a little child.

Then how he soothed her! stroking her hair, telling her that
he loved her, that he would help her, that he would do anything for her. He held her in his arms, murmuring to her
as he had done so many years ago:

"There, Katie, Katie . . . it's all right, it's all right.
Nobody will touch you. It's all right, it's all right."

At last, with a sudden movement, as though she had
realised that there was little time to waste, she broke from
him and stood up, wiping her eyes with her handkerchief;
then, with that strange note of fierceness, so foreign to the
old mild Katherine, she said:

"But now I see—I see everything. What Millie said is
true—I can't have it both ways, I've got to choose. Mother
doesn't care for anything so much as for beating Philip, for
humiliating him, for making him do everything that she says.
That other woman too—she'd like to see him humiliated,
laughed at—I *know* that she's like that, cruel and hard.

"And he's only got me in all the world. I can beat that
other woman only by showing her that I'm stronger than she
is. I thought once that it was Phil who would take me and
look after me, but now it is *I* that must look after him.

"If we stay, if we do as Mother wishes, we shall never escape. I love everything here, I love them all, I can't leave
them unless I do it now, *now*! Even to-morrow I shall be
weak again. Mother's stronger than we are. She's stronger,

I do believe, than anyone. Uncle Tim, we must go to-night!"

"To-night!" he repeated, staring at her.

"Now, at once, in an hour's time. We can drive to Rasselas. There's the London Express at eight o'clock. It's in London by midnight. I can wire to Rachel. She'll have me. We can be married, by special licence, to-morrow!"

He did not seem astonished by her impetuosity. He got up slowly from his chair, knocked over with his elbow the blotting-paper upon which were the dried flowers, swore, bent down and picked them up slowly one by one, rose at last and, very red in the face with his exertions, looked at her. Then he smiled gently, stroking his fingers through his beard.

"My dear, how you've changed!" he said.

"You understand, Uncle Tim," she urged. "I couldn't tell Millie. They'd make it bad for her afterwards, and it would hurt Mother too. I don't want Mother to be left alone. It's the only thing to do. I saw it all in a flash this evening when Mother was speaking. Even to-morrow may be too late, when I see the garden again and the village and when they're all kind to me. And perhaps after all it will be all right. Only I must show them that Phil comes first, that if I must choose, I choose Phil."

She paused, breathlessly. He was grave again when he spoke:

"You know, my dear, what you are doing, don't you? I won't say whether I think you right or wrong. It's for you to decide, and only you. But just think. It's a tremendous thing. It's more than just marrying Philip. It's giving up, perhaps, everything here—giving up Garth and Glebeshire and the house. Giving up your Mother may be for ever. I know your Mother. It is possible that she will never forgive you."

Katherine's under lip quivered. She nodded her head.

"And it's hurting her," he went on, "hurting her more than ever anything has done. It's her own fault in a way. I

warned her long ago. But never mind that. You must realise what you're doing."

"I do realise it," Katherine answered firmly. "It needn't
hurt her really, if her love for me is stronger than her hatred
of Philip. I've thought it all out. If she loves me she'll
see that my love for her isn't changed at all,—that it's there
just as it always was; that it's only that she has *made* me
choose, either Phil's happiness or unhappiness. I can only
choose one way. He's ready to give up everything, surrender
all the splendid things he was going to do, give up half of me,
perhaps more, to the family—perhaps more. He hates the
life here, but he'll live it, under Mother and grandfather and
the rest, for my sake. It isn't fair that he should. Mother,
if she loves me, will see that. But I don't believe," here
Katherine's voice trembled again, "that she cares for *anything*
so much as beating Philip. He's the first person in the world
who ever opposed her. . . . She knows that I'll love her always, always, but Phil's life shan't be spoilt. Nothing matters beside that."

She stopped, her breast heaving, her eyes flashing; he
looked at her and was amazed, as in his queer, isolated life
he had never been before, at what love can do to the soul.

"Life's for the young," he said, "you're right, Katherine.
Your Mother will never forgive me, but I'll help you."

"No," Katherine said, *"you're* not to be involved, Uncle
Tim. Mother mustn't lose *anyone* afterwards. You're to
know nothing about it. I shall leave a note with someone to
be taken up to the house at half-past nine. I've told you because I wanted you to know, but you're not to have anything
to do with it. But you'll love me just the same, won't you?
You won't be any different, will you? I had to know that.
With you and Millie and Aunt Betty and Father caring for
me afterwards, it won't be quite like breaking with the family. Only, Uncle Tim, I want you to do for me what you
can with Mother. I've explained everything to you, so that
you can tell her—show her."

"I'll do my best," he said. Then he caught her and hugged her.

"Good luck," he said—and she was gone.

Although she had been less than her hour with her uncle, she knew that she had no time to spare. She was haunted, as she hurried back again down the village road by alarms, regrets, agonising reproaches that she refused to admit. She fortified her consciousness against everything save the immediate business to which she had bound herself, but every tree upon the road, every hideous cottage, every stone and flower besieged her with memories. "You are leaving us for ever. Why? For Panic? . . . For Panic?" . . . She could hear the voices that would follow the retreat. "But why did she run away like that? It wasn't even as though their engagement had been forbidden. To be married all in a hurry and in secret—I don't like the look of it. . . . She was always such a quiet, sensible girl."

And she knew—it had not needed Uncle Tim's words to show her—that this act of hers was uprooting her for ever from everything that had made life for her. She would never go back. More deeply than that, she would never belong again, she, who only six months ago had been the bond that had held them all together. . . .

And behind these thoughts were two figures so strangely, so impossibly like one another—the first that woman, suddenly old, leaning back on to Katherine's breast, fast asleep, tired out, her mother—the second that woman who, only that afternoon, had turned and given both Katherine and Philip that look of triumph. . . . "I've got you both—You see that I shall never let you go. You cannot, cannot, cannot, escape." That also was her mother.

She stopped at the village inn, 'The Three Pilchards', saw Dick Penhaligan, the landlord, and an old friend of hers.

"Dick, in half-an-hour I want a jingle. I've got to go to Rasselas to meet the eight train. I'll drive myself."

"All right, Miss Katherine," he said, looking at her with

affection. " 'Twill be a wild night, I'm thinkin'. Workin' up wild."

"Twenty minutes, Dick," she nodded to him, and was off again. She crossed the road, opened the little wicket gate that broke into the shrubbery, found her way on to the lawn, and there, under the oak, was Philip, waiting for her. As she came up to him she felt the first spurt of rain upon her cheek. The long lighted windows of the house were watching them; she drew under the shadow of the tree.

"Phil," she whispered, her hand on his arm, "there isn't a moment to lose. I've arranged everything. We must catch the eight o'clock train at Rasselas. We shall be in London by twelve. I shall go to Rachel Seddon's. We can be married by Special Licence to-morrow."

She had thought of it so resolutely that she did not realise that it was new to him. He gasped, stepping back from her.

"My *dear* Katie! What *are* you talking about?"

"Oh, there isn't any *time*," she went on impatiently. "If you don't come I go alone. It will be the same thing in the end. I saw it all this afternoon. Things *can't* go on. I understood Mother. I know what she's determined to do. We must escape or it will be too late. Even to-morrow it may be. I won't trust myself if I stay; I'm afraid even to see Mother again, but I *know* I'm right. We have only a quarter of an hour. That suit will do, and of course you mustn't have a bag or anything. There's that cousin of yours in the Adelphi somewhere. You can go to him. We must be at the 'Three Pilchards' in a quarter of an hour, and go separately, of course, or someone may stop us. . . . "

But he drew back. "No, no, no," he said. "Katie, you're mad! Do you think I'm going to let you do a thing like this? What do you suppose I'm made of? Why. if we were to go off now they'd never forgive you, they'd throw you off—"

"Why, of course," she broke in impatiently, "that's exactly why we've got to do it. You proposed it to me yourself once, and I refused because I didn't understand what our staying here meant. But I do now—it's all *settled,* I tell you, Phil, and there's only ten minutes. It's the last chance. If we miss that train we shall never escape from Mother, from Anna, from anyone. Oh! I know it! I know it!"

She scarcely realised her words; she was tugging at his sleeve, trying to drag him with her.

But he shook her off. "No, Katie, I tell you I'm not such a cad. I know what all this means to you, the place, the people, everything. It's true that I asked you once to go off, but I didn't love you then as I do now. I was thinking more of myself then—but now I'm ready for anything here. You know that I am. I don't care if only they let me stay with you."

"But they won't," Katherine urged. "You know what they'll do. They'll marry us, they'll make you take a house near at hand, and if you refuse they'll persuade you that you're making me miserable. Oh! Phil! don't you see—if I were sure of myself I'd never run off like this, but it's from myself that I'm running. That's the whole point of everything. I can't trust myself with Mother. She has as much influence over me as ever she had. I felt it to-day more than I've ever felt it. There she is over both of us. You know that you're weaker with her than I am. It isn't that she does anything much except sit quiet, but I love her, and it's through that she gets at both of us. No, Phil, we've got to go—and *now.* If not now, then never. I shan't be strong enough to-morrow. Don't you *see* what she can do in the future, now that she knows about Anna. . . . " Then, almost in a whisper, she brought out: "Don't you see what *Anna* can do?"

"No." he said, "I won't go. It's not fair. It's not—"

"Well, she answered him, "it doesn't matter what you do, whether you go or not. I shall go. And what are you to do then?"

She had vanished across the lawn, leaving him standing

there. Behind all his perplexity and a certain shame at his inaction, a fire of exultation inflamed him, making him heedless of the rain oɪ the low muttering thunder far away. She loved him! She was freeing him! His glory in her strength, her courage, flew like a burning arrow to his heart, killing the old man in him, striking him to the ground, that old lumberɪing body giving way before a new creature to whom the whole world was a plain of victory. He stood there trembling with his love for her. . . .

Then he realised that, whatever he did, there was no time to be lost. And after all what was he to do? Did he enteɪ and alarm the family, tell them that Katherine was flying to London, what would he gain but her scorn? How much would he lose to save nothing? Even as he argued with himself some stronger power was dragging him to the house. He was in his room; he had his coat and hat from the hall; he saw no one; he was in the dark garden again, stepping softly through the wicket-gate on to the high road—Then the wind of the approaching storm met him with a scurry of rain that slashed his face. He did not know that now, for the first moment since his leaving Russia, Anna was less to him than nothing. He did not know that he was leaving behind him in that dark rain-swept garden an indignant, a defeated ghost. . . .

Meanwhile Katherine had gone, rapidly, without pause, to her bedroom. She was conscious of nothing until she reached it, and then she stood in the middle of the floor, struck by a sudden, poignant agony of reproach that took, for the moment, all life from her. Her knees were trembling, her heart pounding in her breast, her eyes veiled by some mist that yet allowed her to see with a fiery clarity every detail of the room. They rose and besieged her, the chairs, the photographs, the carpet, the bed, the wash-hand-stand, the pictures, the window with the old, old view of the wall, the church-tower, the crooked apple-tree clustered in a corner, the bed of roses, the flash of the nook beyond the lawn. She covered her eyes with her hand. Everything was still there, crying to her "Don't leave us! Is our old devotion nothing, our faithful service? Are you, whom we have trusted, false like the rest?"

She swayed then; tears that would never fall burnt her eyes. The first rain lashed her window, and from the trees around the church some flurry of rooks rose, protesting against the coming storm. She drove it all down with a strong hand. She *would* not listen. . . .

Then, as she found her coat and hat, a figure rose before her, the one figure that, just then, could most easily defeat her. Her Mother she *would* not see, Millie, Henry, the Aunts could not then touch her. It was her Father.

They were breaking their word to him, they who were standing now upon their honour. His laughing, friendly spirit, that had never touched her very closely, now seemed to cling to her more nearly than them all. He had kept outside all their family trouble, as he had kept outside all trouble since his birth. He had laughed at them, patted them on the shoulder, determined that if he did not look too closely at things they must be well, refused to see the rifts and divisions and unhappiness. Nevertheless he must have seen something; he had sent Henry to Cambridge, had looked at Millie and Katherine sometimes with a gravity that was not his old manner.

Seeing him suddenly now, it was as though he knew what she was about to do, and was appealing to her with a new gravity: "Katie, my dear, I may have seemed not to have cared, to have noticed nothing, but now—don't give us up. Wait. Things will be happier. Wait. Trust us."

She beat him down; stayed for another moment beside the window, her hands pressed close against her eyes.

Then she went to her little writing-table, and scribbled very rapidly this note:

"Darling Mother,

I have gone with Philip by the eight train to London. We shall be married as soon as possible. I shall stay with Rachel until then. You know that things could not go on as they were.

Will you understand, dear Mother, that if I did not love you so deeply I would not have done this? But because you would not let Phil go I have had to choose. If only you will understand that I do not love you less for this, but that it is for Phil's sake that I do it, you will love me as before. And you know that I will love you always.

Your devoted daughter,
Katherine."

She laid this against the looking-glass on her dressing-table, glanced once more at the room, then went.

Upon the stairs she met Henry.

"Hullo!" he cried, "going out? There's a lot of rain coming."

"I know," she answered quietly. "I have to see Penhaligan. It's important."

He looked at her little black hat; her black coat. These were not the things that one put on for a hurried excursion into the village.

"You'll be late for dinner," he said.

"No, I shan't," she answered, "I must hurry." She brushed past him; she had an impulse to put her arms round his neck and kiss him, but she did not look back.

She went through the hall; he turned on the stairs and watched her, then went slowly to his room.

When she came out on to the high road the wind had fallen and the rain was coming in slow heavy drops. The sky was all black, except that at its very heart there burnt a brilliant star; just above the horizon there was a bar of sharp-edged gold. When she came to the 'Three Pilchards' the world was lit with a strange half-light so that, although one could see all things distinctly, there was yet the suggestion that nothing was what it seemed. The 'jingle' was there, and Philip standing in conversation with Dick Penhaligan.

"Nasty night 'twill be, Miss Katherine. Whisht sort o' weather. Shouldn't like for 'ee to get properly wet. Open jingle tu."

"That's all right, Dick," she answered. "We've got to meet the train. I've been wet before now, you know."

She jumped into the trap and took the reins. Philip followed her. If Mr. Penhaligan thought there was anything strange in the proceeding he did not say so. He watched them out of the yard, gave a look at the sky, then went whistling into the house.

They did not speak until they had left the village behind them, then, as they came up to Pelynt Cross, the whole beauty of the sweep of stormy sky burst upon them. The storm seemed to be gathering itself together before it made its spring, bunched up heavy and black on the horizon, whilst the bar of gold seemed to waver and hesitate beneath the weight of it. Above their heads the van of the storm, twisted and furious, leaned forward, as though with avaricious fingers, to take the whole world into its grasp.

At its heart still shone that strange glittering star. Beneath the sky the grey expanse of the moon quivered with anticipation like a quaking bog; some high grass, bright against the sky, gave little windy tugs, as though it would release itself and escape before the fury beat it down. Once and again, very far away, the rumble of the thunder rose and fell, the heavy raindrops were still slow and measured, as though they told the seconds left to the world before it was devastated.

Up there, on the moor, Phiilp put his arm round Katherine. His heart was beating with tumultuous love for her, so that he choked and his face was on fire; his hand trembled against her dress. This was surely the most wonderful thing

that had ever happened to him. He had seemed so utterly
lost, and, although he had known that she loved him, he had
resigned himself to the belief that her love stayed short of sacrifice. He had said to himself that he was not enough of a
fellow for it to be otherwise. And now he did not care for
any of them! No one, he realised, had ever, in all his life,
made any great sacrifice for him—even Anna had let him go
when he made life tiresome for her.

Surging up in him now was the fine vigour of reassurance
that Katherine's love gave to him. It was during that drive
to Rasselas station that he began, for the first time, to believe
in himself. He did not speak, but held Katherine with his
arm close to him, and once, for a moment, he put his cheek
against hers.

But she was not, then, thinking of Philip, she was scarcely
aware that he was with her. Her whole will and purpose
was concentrated on reaching the station in time. She
thought: "If we missed that train we're finished. We'll
have to come back. They'll have found my note. Mother
won't be angry outwardly, but she'll hate Phil twice as much
as ever, and she'll never loose her hold again. She'll show
him how ashamed he should be, and she'll show me how deeply
I've hurt her. We shall neither of us have the courage to
try a 'second time'."

How was it that she saw all this so clearly? Never before
these last months had she thought of anything save what was
straight in front of her. . . . The world was suddenly un-
rolled before her like a map of a strange country.

Meanwhile, although she did not know it, she was wildly
excited. Her imagination, liberated after those long years
of captivity, flamed now before her eyes. She felt the storm
behind her, and she thought that at the head of it, urging it
forward, was that figure who had pursued her, so remorse-
lessly, ever since that day at Rafiel when Philip had confessed to her.

Anna would keep them if she could, she would drag them back, miserable fugitives, to face the family—and then how she would punish Philip!

"Oh, go on! Go on!" Katherine cried, whipping the pony; they began to climb a long hill. Suddenly the thunder broke overhead, crashing amongst the trees of a dark little wood on their right. Then the rain came down in slanting, stinging sheets. With that clap of thunder the storm caught them, whirled up to them, beat them in the face, buffeted in their eyes and ears, shot lightning across their path, and then plunged them on into yet more impenetrable darkness. The world was abysmal, was on fire, was rocking, was springing with a thousand gestures to stop them on their way. Katherine fancied that in front of her path figures rose and fell, the very hedges riding in a circle round about her.

"Oh! go on! Go on!" she whispered, swaying in her seat, then feeling Philip's arm about her. They rose, as though borne on a wave of wild weather, to the top of the hill. They had now only the straight road; they could see the station lights. Then the thunder, as though enraged at their persistence, broke into a shattering clatter—the soil, the hedges, the fields, the sky crumbled into rain; a great lash of storm whipped them in the face, and the pony, frightened by the thunder, broke from Katherine's hand, ran wildly through the dark, crashed with a shuddering jar into the hedge. Their lamps fell; the 'jingle', after a moment's hesitation, slipped over and gently dropped them on to the rain-soaked ground.

Katherine was on her feet in an instant. She saw that by a happy miracle one of the lamps still burned. She went to the pony, and found that, although he was trembling, he was unhurt. Philip was trying to turn the 'jingle' upright again.

"Quick!" she cried. "Hang the lamp on the cart. We must run for it—the shaft's broken or something. There's no time at all if we're to catch that train. Run! Run! Phil! There's sure to be someone coming in by the train who'll see the jingle'."

They ran; they were lifted by the wind, beaten by the rain, deafened by the thunder, and Katherine as she ran knew that by her side was her enemy:

"You shan't go! You shan't go! I've got you still!"

She could hear, through the storm, some voice crying, "Phil! Phil! Come back! Come back!"

Her heart was breaking, her eyes saw flame, her knees trembled, she stumbled, staggered, slipped. They had reached the white gates, had passed the level crossing, were up the station steps.

"It's in! It's in!" gasped Philip. "Only a second!"

She was aware of astonished eyes, of the stout station-master, of someone who shouted, of a last and strangely distant peal of thunder, of an open door, of tumbling forward, of a whistle and a jerk, and then a slow Glebeshire voice:

"Kind o' near shave that was, Miss, I'm thinkin'."

And through it all her voice was crying exultantly: "I've beaten you—you've done your worst, but I've beaten you. He's mine now for ever"—and her eyes were fastened on a baffled, stormy figure left on the dark road, abandoned, and, at last, at last, defeated. . . .

CHAPTER V

THE TRENCHARDS

HENRY waited, for a moment, on the stairs. He heard the door close behind Katherine, heard the approaching storm invade the house, heard the cuckoo-clock in the passage above him proclaim seven o'clock, then went slowly up to his room. Why had Katherine gone out to see Penhaligan in those clothes, in such weather, at such an hour? . . . Very strange. . . . And her face too. She was excited, she had almost kissed him. . . . Her eyes. . . .

He entered his familiar room, looked with disgust at his dinner-jacket and trousers lying upon the bed (he hated dressing for dinner), and then wandered up and down, dragging a book from the bookcase and pushing it impatiently back again, stumbling over his evening slippers, pulling his coat off and allowing it to fall, unregarded, on to the floor.

Katherine! . . . Katherine? . . . What was 'up' with Katherine?

He had, in any case, been greatly upset by the events of the day. The crisis for which he had so long been waiting had at length arrived, and, behold, it had been no crisis at all. Superficially it had been nothing . . . in its reality it had shaken, finally, destructively, the foundations of everything upon which his life had been built. He remembered, very clearly, the family's comments upon the case of a young man known to them all, who, engaged to a girl in Polchester, had confessed, just before the marriage, that he had had a mistress for several years in London, who was however now happily married to a gentleman of means and had no further

claim on him. The engagement had been broken off, with the
approval of all the best families in Glebeshire. Henry remembered that his mother had said that it was not only the
immorality of the young man but also his continued secrecy
concerning the affair that was so abominable, that, of course,
"young men must be young men, but you couldn't expect a
nice girl"—and so on.

He remembered all this very clearly, and he had decided
at the time that if he ever had a mistress he would take very
good care that no one knew about her. That had been a year
ago . . . and now! He was bewildered, almost breathless
with a kind of dismayed terror as to what the world might
possibly be coming to. His mother! of whom at least one
thing had surely been unalterable—that she, herself, would
never change. And now she had taken this thing without
horror, without anger, almost with complacency.

She had known of it for months!

It was as though he had cherished a pet with the happy
conviction that it was a kitten and had suddenly discovered
it to be a cub. And out of this confusion of a wrecked and
devastated world there emerged the conviction "that there was
something more behind all this", that "his mother had some
plan." He did not see at all what her plan could possibly
be, but she appeared before him now as a sinister and menac-
ing figure, someone who had been close to him for so many
years, but whose true immensity he had never even remotely
perceived.

He, Henry, had, from other points of view, risen out of
the affair with considerable good fortune. He had not, as far
as he could perceive, earned Katherine's undying hatred; he
had not even made a fool of himself, as might naturally be
expected. It was plain enough now that Philip was to be
with them for ever and ever, and that therefore Henry must
make the best of him. Now indeed that it had come to this,
Henry was not at all sure that he might not like Philip very
much indeed. That night at the 'Empire' had been the be-

ginning of life for Henry, and the indifference of his mother to Philip's past and the knowledge that Katherine had long been aware of it made him not a little ashamed of his indignation and tempers. Nevertheless Philip *had* that effect upon him, and would have it many times again no doubt. For a clear and steady moment Henry, looking at himself in his looking-glass, wondered whether he were not truly the most terrible of asses.

However, all this was of the past. It was with a sense of advancing to meet a new world that he went down to dinner.

In the drawing-room he found his mother alone. She was wearing an evening dress of black silk, and Henry, whose suspicion of the world made him observant, noticed that she was wearing a brooch of old silver set with pearls. This was a family brooch, and Henry knew that his mother wore it only 'on occasions'; his mother's idea of what made an 'occasion' was not always that of the outside world. He wondered what the occasion might be to-night.

He had, for long, been unconsciously in the habit of dividing his mother into two persons, the figure of domination and power who kept the household in awe and was mysterious in her dignity and aloof reserve, and the figure of maternal homeliness who spoke to one about underclothes, was subject to human agitations and pleasures; of the first he was afraid, and would be afraid until he died. The second he loved. His mother to-night was the first of these. She looked, in his eyes, amazingly young. Her fair grey hair, her broad shoulders, her straight back, these things showed Henry's mother to be younger than ever Henry would be. The pearl brooch gleamed against the black silk that covered her strong bosom; her head was carried high; her eyes feared no man nor woman alive.

Therefore Henry, as was his manner on such an occasion, did his best to slip quietly into a chair and hide his diminished personality in a book. This, however, was not permitted him.

"Henry," his mother said softly, "why did you not tell me earlier the things that you had heard about Philip?"

Henry blushed so intensely that there was a thin white line just below the roots of his hair.

"I didn't want to make Katie unhappy," he muttered.

"I should have thought your duty to your parents came before your duty to Katherine," his mother replied.

"It wasn't you who was going to marry Philip," he answered, not looking at his mother.

"Nevertheless it's possible that older heads—yes, older heads—"

"Oh! well! it's all right," he burst out, "I'm sick of the thing, and you and father don't seem to mind anything about it—"

"I haven't told your father," she interrupted.

"Haven't told Father?" Henry repeated.

"No. Father doesn't think of such things. If everything goes well, as I am sure that everything will, Father will want to know nothing further. I have every confidence in Philip."

"Why!" Henry burst out, "I always thought you hated Philip, Mother. I simply don't understand."

"There are quite a number of things you don't understand, Henry dear," his mother answered. "Yes, quite a number. Philip was perhaps not at home with us at first—but I'm sure that in time he will become quite one of the family—almost as though he had been born a Trenchard. I have great hopes. . . . Your tie is as usual, Henry, dear, above your collar. Let me put it down for you."

Henry waited whilst his mother's cool, solid fingers rubbed against his neck and sent a little shiver down his spine as though they would remind him that he was a Trenchard too and had better not try to forget it. But the great, overwhelming impression that now dominated him was of his mother's happiness. He knew very well when his mother was happy. There was a note in her voice as sure and melodious as the rhythm of a stream that runs, somewhere hidden, between the rocks. He had known, on many days, that deep joy of his mother's—often it had been for no reason that he could discover.

To-night she was triumphant; her triumph sang through every note of her voice.

The others come in. George Trenchard entered, rubbing his hands and laughing. He seemed, every week, redder in the face and stouter all over; in physical reality he added but little to his girth. It was the stoutness of moral self-satisfaction and cheerful complaisance. His doctrine of pleasant aloofness from contact with other human beings had acted so admirably; he would like to have recommended it to everyone had not such recommendation been too great a trouble.

He was never, after this evening, to be aloof again, but he did not know that.

"Well, well," he cried. "Punctual for once, Henry. Very nice, indeed. Dear me, Mother, why this gaudiness? People coming to dinner?"

She looked down at her brooch.

"No, dear. . . . No one. I just thought I'd put it on. I haven't worn it for quite a time. Not for a year at least."

"Very pretty, very pretty," he cried. "Dear me, what a day I've had! So busy, scarcely able to breathe!"

"What have you been doing, Father?" asked Henry.

"One thing and another. One thing and another," said George airily. "Day simply flown."

He stood there in front of the fire, his legs spread, his huge chest flung out, his face flaming like the sun.

"Yes, it's been a very pleasant day," said Mrs. Trenchard, "very pleasant."

"Where's Katie?" asked her father. "She's generally down before anyone."

Henry, who, in the contemplation of his mother, had forgotten, for the moment, his sister's strange behaviour, said: "Oh! she'll be late, I expect. I saw her go out about seven. Had to see Penhaligan about something important, she told me. Went out into all that storm."

As he spoke eight o'clock struck.

Mrs. Trenchard looked up.

"Went out to see Penhaligan?" she asked.

"Yes, Mother. She didn't tell me why."

Aunt Betty came in. Her little body, her cheerful smile, her air as of one who was ready to be pleased with anything, might lead a careless observer into the error of supposing that she was a quite ordinary old maid with a fancy for knitting, the Church of England, and hot water with her meals. He would be wrong in his judgment; her sharp little eyes, the corners of her mouth betrayed a sense of humour that, although it had never been encouraged by the family, provided much wise penetration and knowledge. Any casual acquaintance in half an hour's talk would have discovered in Aunt Betty wisdom and judgment to which her own family would, until the day of its decent and honourable death, be entirely blind.

Just now she had lost her spectacles.

"My spectacles," she said. "Hum-hum—Very odd. I had them just before tea. I was working over in that corner—I never moved from there except once when—when—Oh! there they are! No, they are not. And I played 'Patience' there, too, in the same corner. Very odd."

"Perhaps, dear," said Mrs. Trenchard, "you left them in you bedroom."

"No, Harriet, I looked there. Hum-hum-hum. Very odd it is, because—"

Millie came in and then Aunt Aggie.

"Is Father coming down to-night?" said George.

"Yes," said Mrs. Trenchard. "He said that he felt better. Thought it would be nice to come down. Yes, that it would be rather nice. . . . Aggie, dear, that's your sewing, isn't it? You left it here this morning. Rocket put it between the pages of my novel to mark the place. I knew it was yours—"

"Yes, it's mine," said Aunt Aggie, shortly.

Meanwhile Henry, looking at the door, waited for Katherine. A strange premonition was growing in him that all was not well. Katherine and Philip, they had not appeared —Katherine and Philip. . . . As he thought of it, it occurred to him that he had not heard Philip moving as he dressed. Philip's room was next to Henry's, and the division was thin; you could always hear coughs, steps, the pouring of water, the opening and shutting of drawers.

There had been no sounds to-night. Henry's heart began to beat very fast. He listened to the wind that, now that the storm had swung away, was creeping around the house, trying the doors and windows, rattling something here, tugging at something there, all the pipes gurgled and spluttered with the waters of the storm.

"Ah! there they are!" cried Aunt Betty.

Henry started, thinking that she must herald the entry of Katherine and Philip; but no, it was only the gold-rimmed spectacles lying miraculously beneath the sofa.

"Now, how," cried Aunt Betty, "did they get there? Very odd, because I remember distinctly that I never moved from my corner."

"Well," said George Trenchard, who, now that his back was warmed by the fire, wanted his front warmed too, "how much longer are we to wait for dinner? Katie and Philip. Playing about upstairs, I suppose."

Quarter-past eight struck, and Rocket, opening the door, announced that dinner was ready.

"Suppose you just go up and see what Katie's doing, Millie dear," said Mrs. Trenchard.

Millie left them and ran quickly upstairs. She pushed back Katie's door, then, stepping inside, the darkness and silence and a strange murmurous chill caught her, as though someone had leapt, out of the dusk, at her throat. She knew then instantly what had occurred. She only said once, very softly, "Katie!" then gently closed the door behind her, as though she did not want anyone else to see the room.

She stayed there; there, beside the door, for quite a long time. The room was very dark, but the looking-glass glimmered like a white, flickering shadow blown by the wet wind that came in through the open window. Something flapped monotonously.

Millie, standing quite motionless by the door, thought to herself "Katherine and Philip! They've done it! . . . at last, they've done it!" At first, because she was very young and still believed in freedom and adventure as the things best worth having in life, she felt nothing but a glad, triumphant excitement; an excitement springing not only from her pleasure in any brave movement, but also from her reassurance in her beloved sister, her knowledge that after all Katherine *did* believe in Love beyond every other power, was ready to venture all for it. Her own impulse was to run after them, as fast as she could, and declare her fidelity to them.

At last she moved away from the door to the dressing-table and lit a candle. It's soft white flame for a moment blinded her. She had an instant of hesitation; perhaps after all she had flown too rapidly to her desired conclusions, the two of them were waiting now in the drawing-room for her. . . . Then she saw Katherine's note propped against the looking-glass.

She took it up, saw that it was addressed to her mother, and realised, for the first time, what this would mean to them all. She saw then—THE OLD ONES—Grandfather, Mother, Father, Aunt Sarah, Aunt Aggie, Aunt Betty. She was sorry for them, but she knew, as she stood there, that she did not care, really, whether they were hurt or no. She felt her own freedom descend upon her, there in Katie's room, like a golden, flaming cloud. This was the moment for which, all her life, she had been waiting. The Old Ones had tried to keep them and tie them down, but the day of the Old Ones was past, their power was broken. It was the New Generation that mattered —Katherine and Philip, Millie and Henry, and all their kind; it was *their* world and *their* dominion—

She suddenly, alone there, with the note in her hand, danced a little dance, the candle-flame flickering in the breeze and Katherine's white, neat bed so cold and tidy.

She was not hard, she was not cruel—her own time would come when she would cry for sympathy and would not find it, and must set her teeth because her day was past . . . now was her day—She seized it fiercely.

Very quietly she went downstairs. . . .

She opened the drawing-room door: as she entered all their eyes met her and she knew at once, as she saw Henry's, that he was expecting her announcement.

She looked across at her mother.

"Katherine's room's empty," she said. "There's no one there at all." She hesitated a moment, then added: "There was this note for you, Mother, on her dressing-table."

She went across the room and gave it to her mother. Her mother took it; no one spoke.

Mrs. Trenchard read it; for a dreadful moment she thought that she was going to give way before them all, was going to cry out, to scream, to rush wildly into the road to stop the fugitives, or slap Aunt Aggie's face. For a dreadful moment the battle of her whole life to obtain the mastery of herself was almost defeated—then, blindly, obeying some impulse with which she could not reason, of which she was scarcely conscious, some strong call from a far country, she won a triumphant victory.

"It's from Katherine!" she said. "The child's mad. She's gone up to London."

"London!" George Trenchard cried.

"London!" cried Aunt Aggie.

"Yes. With Philip. They have caught the eight train.

They are to be married to-morrow. 'Because I would not let Philip go,' she says. But she's mad—"

For an instant she gripped the mantelpiece behind her. She could hear them, only from a distance, as though their voices were muffled by the roar of sea or wind, their exclamations.

Her husband was, of course, useless. She despised him. He cried:

"They must be stopped! They must be stopped. This is impossible! That fellow Mark—one might have guessed! They must be stopped. At once! At once!"

"They can't be." She heard her voice far away with the others. "They can't be stopped. The train left at eight o'clock, nearly half an hour ago. There's nothing to be done."

"But, of course," cried George, "there's *something* to be done. They must be stopped at once. I'll go up by the next train."

"There's no train until six to-morrow morning—and what good would you do? They're engaged. You gave your permission. Katherine's of age. It is her own affair."

They all cried out together. Their voices sounded to Mrs. Trenchard like the screams of children.

Through the confusion there came the sound of an opening door. They all turned, and saw that it was old Mr. Trenchard, assisted by Rocket.

"Why don't you come in to dinner?" he said, in his clear, thin voice. "I went straight into the dining-room because I was late, and here you all are, and it's nearly half-past eight."

The same thought instantly struck them all. Grandfather must know nothing about it; a very slight shock, they were all aware, would *kill* Grandfather, and there could not possibly be any shock to him like this amazing revolt of Katherine's. Therefore he must know nothing. Like bathers asserting themselves after the first quiver of an icy plunge, they fought their way to the surface.

Until Grandfather was safely once more alone in his room

the situation must be suspended. After all, there was *nothing* to be done! He, because he was feeling well that evening, was intent upon his dinner.

"What! Waiting for Katherine?" he said.

"Katherine isn't coming down to dinner, Father," Mrs. Trenchard said.

"What, my dear?"

"Katherine isn't coming down to dinner."

"Not ill, I hope."

"No—a little tired."

George Trenchard was the only one who did not support his part. When the old man had passed through the door, George caught his wife's arm.

"But, I say," he whispered, "something—"

She turned for an instant, looking at him with scorn.

"Nothing!" she said. "It's too late."

They went in to dinner.

It was fortunate that Grandfather was hungry; he did not, it seems, notice Philip's absence.

"Very nice to see you down, Father," Mrs. Trenchard said pleasantly. "Very nice for us all."

"Thank ye, my dear. Very agreeable—very agreeable. Quite myself this evening. That rheumatism passed away, so I said to Rocket, 'Well, 'pon my word, Rocket, I think I'll come down to-night.' Livelier for us all to be together. Hope Katie isn't ill, though?"

"No—no—nothing at all."

"I saw her this morning. She seemed quite well."

"A little headache, Father dear. She thought she was better by herself."

"Dear Katie—never do to have her ill. Well, George. What's the matter with 'ee? Looking quite hipped. Dig your father in the ribs, Millie, my dear, and cheer him up a bit."

So seldom was old Mr. Trenchard in his merry mood, and so difficult of him to be in it now. So often he was consumed with his own thoughts, his death, perhaps, the present degradation of the world, the tyranny of aches and pains, impatience with the monotonous unvariety of relations, past Trenchard glories, old scenes and days and hours . . . he, thus caught up into his own life, would be blind to them all. But to-night, pleased with his food because he was hungry, and because his body was not paining him anywhere just now, he was interested in them. His bright little eyes darted all about the table.

There came at last the question that they dreaded:

"Why, where's the young man? Katie's young man?"

A moment's silence, and then Mrs. Trenchard said quietly, and with her eyes upon the new "girl," introduced into the house only last week and fresh to the mysteries of a dinner-table:

"He's dining with Timothy to-night, Father."

Rocket could be heard whispering to Lucy, the 'girl':

"Potatoes first—then the sauce."

Of them all, it was George Trenchard who covered with least success the yawning chasm, even Aunt Betty, although her hands shook as she crumbled her bread, had not surrendered her control.

But for George this was the first blow, in all his life, to reach his heart. Nothing really had ever touched him before. And he could not understand it—he simply could not understand it. It had been as sudden as an earthquake, and then, after all, there had been nothing to be done. That was the awful thing. There had been nothing to be done. . . . It was also so mysterious. Nothing had ever been mysterious to him before. He had been dimly aware that during these last months all had not been well, but he had pursued his old safe plan, namely, that if you didn't mention things and just smiled upon life without inviting it to approach you closely, all would, in the end, be well.

But now he could no longer hold aloof—he was in the middle of something, as surely as though he had been plunged into a deep tub of tossing, foaming water. Katherine . . . Katie . . . dear, devoted Katie . . . who had always loved him and done as he wished; Katie, nearest of all human beings to his heart, and nearest because he had always known that she cared for him more than for any other human being. And now it was obvious that that was not so, it was obvious that she cared more for that young man, that abominable young man. . . . O, damn it! damn it! *damn it!* Katherine was gone, and for no reason, for nothing at all except pride and impatience. Already, as he sat there, he was wondering how soon, by any means whatever, he could establish pleasant relations with her, and so make his life comfortable once more. But, beyond Katherine, there was his wife. What was he to do about Harriet? For so many years now he had decided that the only way to deal comfortably with Harriet was not to deal with her, and this had seemed to work so well . . . but now . . . now . . . he *must* deal with her. He saw that she was in terrible distress; he knew her well enough to be sure of that. He would have liked to have helped and comforted her; it really distressed him to see anyone in pain, but he discovered now, with a sharp surprise, that she was a complete stranger, that he did not know any more about the real Harriet Trenchard than he did about Lucy, the maid-servant. There was approaching him that awful moment when he would be compelled to draw close to her . . . he was truly terrified of this.

It was a terrible dinner for all of them; once Lucy dropped a knife, and they started, all of them, as though a bomb had screamed through the ceiling. And perhaps, to the older ones, there was nothing in it more alarming than the eyes, the startled, absorbed and challenging eyes, of Millie and Henry. . . .

Slowly, as the dinner progressed, old Mr. Trenchard discovered that something was the matter. He discovered it as surely by the nervous laughter and chatter of Aunt Betty as by the disconcerted discomfort of his son George. His merri-

ment fell away from him; he loved 'Angels on Horseback'—
to-night there were 'Angels on Horseback', and he ate
them with a peevish irritation. Whatever was the matter
now? He felt lost without Sarah; *she* knew when and why
things were the matter more quickly than anyone, aware of
her deafness, would consider possible. But before he was
assisted from the table he was sure that the "something" was
connected with his dear Katherine. . . . The men did not
stay behind to-night. In the hall they were grouped together,
on the way to the drawing-room, waiting for the old man's
slow progress.

He paused suddenly beside the staircase.

"George," he said, "George, just run up and see how
Katie is. Give her my love, will 'ee?"

George turned, his face white. Mrs. Trenchard said:

"She's probably asleep, Father. With her headache—it
would be a pity to wake her."

At that moment the hall door pushed slowly open, and
there, the wind eddying behind him, his ulster up over his
neck, his hair and beard wet with the rain, stood Uncle
Timothy.

"Hullo!" he cried, seeing them all grouped together. But
old Mr. Trenchard called to him in a voice that trembled
now with some troubled anticipation:

"Why, your dinner's soon done? Where's the young man?"

Uncle Timothy stared at them; he looked round at them,
then, at a loss for the first time in his life, stammered: "Why,
don't you know . . . ?"

The old man turned, his stick shaking in his hand:
"Where's Katherine? Katie. . . . What's happened to
Katie? What's this mean?"

Mrs. Trenchard looked at him, then said:

"It's all right, Father—really. It's quite all right."

"It's not all right." Fright like the terror of a child alone
in the dark was in his eyes. "What have you done with her?"

Her voice cold, without moving, she answered:

"Katherine went up by the eight o'clock train to London with Philip.   She has gone to Rachel Seddon."

"With Philip? . . . What do you say? I can't hear you."

"Yes.   She is to stay with Rachel Seddon."

"But why? What have you done? Why did you tell me lies?"

"We have done nothing.   We did not know that she was going."

"You didn't know? . . . then she's left us?"

Mrs. Trenchard said nothing.

He cried: "I told him—what it would be—if he took her . . . Katie!"

Then, his stick dropping with a rattle on to the stone floor, he fell back.   Rocket caught him.

There was a movement forward, but Mrs. Trenchard, saying swiftly, "George . . . Rocket," had swept them all outside the figure—the figure of an old, broken, tumbled-to-pieces man, held now by his son and Rocket, huddled, with his white, waxen hand trailing across George Trenchard's strong arm.

Harriet Trenchard said to her brother:

"You knew!" then turned up the stairs.

In the drawing-room Aunt Aggie, Aunt Betty, Millie and Henry faced Uncle Timothy.

"Well!" said Aunt Aggie, "so you know all about it. . . . You've killed Father!" she ended with a grim, malignant triumph.

He answered fiercely: "Yes, I knew.   That's why I came.   She said that she would send up a note from the village.   I thought that you wouldn't have heard it yet.   I came up to explain."

They all burst upon him then with questions:

"What?"   "Did you see her?"   "What did she say?" "Where was she?"

"Of course I saw her.   She came to me before she went off."

"She came and you didn't stop her!"   This from Aunt

Aggie. He turned then and addressed himself solely to her. "No. I didn't stop her. I gave her my blessing."

Aunt Aggie would have spoken, but he went on: "Yes, and it's you—you and Harriet and the others—who are responsible. I warned Harriet months ago, but she wouldn't listen. What did you expect? Do you think the world's always going on made for you and you alone? The more life's behind you the more important you think you are, whereas it doesn't matter a damn to anybody what you've done compared with what others are going to do. You thought you could tie Katherine and Philip down, take away their freedom? Well, you couldn't, that's all."

"Yes," cried Aunt Aggie, who was shaking with anger, "it's such doctrines as yours, Timothy, that lead to Katherine and others doing the dreadful things they do. It's all freedom now and such words, and young men like Mr. Mark, who don't fear God and have no morals and make reprobates of themselves and all around them, can do what they please, I suppose. You talk about common-sense, but what about God? What about the Commandments and duty to your parents? They may think what they like abroad, but, Heaven be praised, there are some of us still in England who know our duty."

He had recovered his control before she ended her speech. He smiled at her.

"The time will come," he answered, "and I daresay it isn't so distant as you think, when you and you fellow-patriots, Aggie, will learn that England isn't all alone, on her fine moral pedestal, any longer. There won't be any pedestal, and you and your friends will have to wake up and realise that the world's pushed a bit closer together now-a-days, that you've got to use your eyes a bit, or you'll get jostled out of existence. The world's going to be for the young and the independent and the unprejudiced, not the old and narrow-minded.

"Philip Mark's woken you all up, and thank God he has!"

"Heaven forgive you," Aunt Aggie answered, "for taking His name. You've got terrible things to answer to Him for, Timothy, when the time comes."

"I'm not afraid, Aggie," he said.

But it was Millie who spoke the final word.

"Oh, *what* are you all talking about!" she broke in. "What does it matter *who's* good or bad or right or wrong. It's Katie's *happiness* that matters, nothing else. Of *course*, she's gone. She ought to have gone months ago. You all wanted to make her and Phil live *your* life just as you wished it, and Phil, because he loved Katie so much, was ready to, but *why* should they? You say you all loved her, but I think it was just selfishness. I've been as bad as the rest of you. I've been thinking of myself more than Katie, but at heart now I'm glad, and I hope they'll be happy, happy for ever."

"And your Mother?" said Aunt Aggie. "Did Katherine owe her nothing?"

"Yes," answered Millie, stoutly, "but she didn't owe her all her life. Mother's still got her if she wants her. Katie will never change—she isn't that kind. It's mother's pride that's hurt, not her love."

Aunt Betty, who had been quite silent, said:

"I do indeed hope that she will be very happy . . . but life will never be the same again. We mustn't be selfish, of course, but we shall miss her—terribly."

At a later hour George Trenchard, in pyjamas and a dressing gown, knocked on his wife's door. She opened it, and he found her fully clothed; she had, it seemed to him, been reading.

He looked at her; he felt very wretched and uncomfortable.

"Father's asleep," he said.

"I'm glad of that," she answered.

"I think he'll be none the worse in the morning."

"I nope not. Dr. Pierson seemed reassured."

There was a pause; in spite of his bedroom slippers, his feet were cold.

"Harriet."

"Yes, George."

"I only wanted to say—well, I don't know—only that—I'm sorry if this—this business of Katherine's—has been a great blow to you."

Her mind returned to that day, now so long ago, when, after her visit to the Stores, she had gone to his study. Their position now was reversed. But she was tired; she did not care. George did not exist for her.

"It has surprised me, of course," she answered, in her even, level voice. "I thought Katherine cared more for us all than she has shown that she does. I certainly thought so. Perhaps my pride is hurt."

By making this statement—not especially to George, but to the world in general—she could say to herself: "You see how honest you are. You are hiding nothing."

He meanwhile hated his position, but was driven on by a vague sense that she needed comfort, and that he ought to give it her.

"See here, Harriet," he said, awkwardly, "perhaps it needn't be so bad. Nothing very terrible's happened, I mean. After all, they were going to marry anyway. They've only done it a bit sooner. They might have told us, it's true—they ought to have told us—but, after all, young people will be young people, won't they? We can't be very angry with them. And young Mark isn't quite an Englishman, you know. Been abroad so long."

As he spoke he dwindled and dwindled before her until his huge, healthy body seemed like a little speck, a fly, crawling upon the distant wall.

"Nothing very terrible's happened" . . . *"Nothing very terrible's happened"* . . . "NOTHING VERY TERRIBLE'S HAPPENED."

George, who, during these many years had been very little

in her life, disappeared, as he made that speech, utterly and entirely out of it. He was never to figure in it again, but he did not know that.

He suddenly sat down beside her on the old sofa and put his arm round her. She did not move.

They sat there in utter silence. At last desperately, as though he were committing the crime of his life, he kissed her. She patted his hand.

"You look tired," he said, feeling an immense relief, now that he had done his duty. "You go to bed."

"Good night, George dear," she said.

He raised his big body from the sofa, smiled at her and padded away. . . .

When he had gone and she was alone, for a terrible time she fought her defeat. She knew now quite clearly that her ruling passion during all these months had not been, as she had supposed, her love of Katherine, but her hatred of Philip.

From the first moment of seeing him she had known him for her enemy. He had been, although at the time she had not realised it, the very figure whose appearance, all her life, she had dreaded; that figure, from outside, of whose coming Timothy had long ago prophesied. How she had hated him! From the very first she had made her plans, influencing the others against him, watching how she might herself most securely influence him against himself, breaking in his will, using Katherine against him; finally, when Seymour had told her the scandal, how she had treasured it up for the moment when he, because of his love for Katherine, should be completely delivered over to her!

And the moment had come. She had had her triumph! She had seen his despair in his eyes! She had got him, she thought, securely for ever and ever.

Then how she had known what she would do in the future, the slave that she would make of him, the ways that she would trouble him with Katherine, with that Russian woman, with Aggie, with all of them!

Ah! it had been so perfect! and—at the very moment of her triumph—he had escaped!

That love for Katherine that had been a true motive in her earlier life, a true motive even until six months ago, was now converted into a cold, implacable resentment, because it was Katherine who had opened the door of Philip's cage. Strange the complexities of the human heart! That very day, as she won her triumph she had loved her daughter. She had thought: "Now that I have beaten him I can take you back to my heart. We can be, my dear, as we used to be"—but now, had Katherine entered the room, she would have been spurned, dismissed for ever.

In the lust of love there is embedded, as the pearl is embedded in its shell, a lust of hate. Very closely they are pressed together. Mrs. Trenchard was beaten—beaten by her daughter, by a new generation, by a new world, by a new age—beaten in the very moment of her victory.

She would never forgive.

What was left to her?

Her heart was suddenly empty of love, of hatred, of triumph, of defeat. She was tired and lonely. Somewhere, dimly, from the passage, the cuckoo-clock proclaimed the hour.

The house! That at least was left to her. These rooms, these roofs, the garden, the village, the fields, the hedges the roads to the sea. The Place had not deceived her, had not shared in the victory over her; it had, rather, shared in her defeat.

It seemed, as she stood there, to come up to her, to welcome her, to console her.

She put a shawl over her shoulders, went softly through the dark passages, down into the drawing-room.

There, feeling her way, she found candles and lit them. She went to her cabinet, opened drawers, produced papers, plans, rows of figures. Here was a plan of a new barn behind the house, here the addition of a conservatory to the drawing-room. Before her was a map of South Glebeshire, with the roads, the fields, the farms. She began to work, adding figures, following the plans, writing. . . .

The light of the summer morning found her working there in the thin candle-light.

CHAPTER VI

THE CEREMONY

AT about half-past four upon the afternoon of November 8th, 1903, the drawing-room of No. 5 Rundle Square Westminster, was empty. November 8th was, of course, Grandfather Trenchard's birthday; a year ago on that day Philip Mark had made his first entrance into the Trenchard fastnesses. This Eighth of November, 1903, did not, in the manner of weather, repeat the Eighth of November, 1902. There had been, a year ago, the thickest of fogs, now there was a clear, mildly blue November evening, with the lamps like faint blurs of light against a sky in which tiny stars sparkled on a background that was almost white. It was cold enough to be jolly, and there was a thin wafer-like frost over the pools and gutters.

A large fire roared in the fireplace; the room seemed strangely altered since that day when Henry had read his novel and thought of his forests. In what lay the alteration? The old green carpet was still there; in front of the fireplace was a deep red Turkey rug—but it was not the rug that changed the room. The deep glass-fronted bookcases were still there, with the chilly and stately classics inside them; on the round table there were two novels with gaudy red and blue covers. One novel was entitled "The Lovely Mrs. Tempest", the other "The Mystery of Dovecote Mill"—but it was not the novels that changed the room. The portraits of deceased Trenchards, weighted with heavy gold, still hung upon the walls; there was also, near the fireplace, a gay water-colour of some place on the Riviera, with a bright parasol in the foreground and the bluest of all blue seas in the background—but it was not the water-colour that changed the room.

No, the change lay here—the Mirror was gone.

After Henry had broken it, there was much discussion as to whether it should be mended. Of course it would be mended—but when?—Well, soon. Meanwhile it had better be out of the way somewhere . . . it had remained out of the way. Until it should be restored, Sir George Trenchard, K.C.B., 1834-1896, a stout gentleman with side whiskers, hung in its place.

Meanwhile it would never be restored. People would forget it; people wanted to forget it . . . the Mirror's day was over.

It was, of course, impossible for Sir George Trenchard to reflect the room in his countenance or in his splendid suit of clothes, and the result of this was that the old room that had gathered itself so comfortably, with its faded and mossy green, into the shining embrace of the Mirror, had now nowhere for its repose; it seemed now an ordinary room, and the spots of colour—the Turkey rug, the novels, the water-colour, broke up the walls and the carpet, flung light here and light there, shattered that earlier composed remoteness, proclaimed the room a comfortable place that had lost its tradition.

The Room was broken up—the Mirror was in the cellar.

Henry came in. He had had permission to abandon—for one night—his labours at Cambridge to assist in the celebration of his grandfather's birthday, the last, perhaps, that there would be, because the old man now was very broken and ill. He had never recovered from the blow of Katherine's desertion.

The first thing that Henry had done on his arrival in London had been to pay a visit to Mrs. Philip Mark. Katherine and Philip lived in a little flat in Knightsbridge—Park Place—and a delightful little flat it was. This was not the first visit that Henry had paid there; George Trenchard, Millie, Aunt Betty had also been there—there had been several merry tea-parties.

The marriage had been a great success; the only thing that marred it for Katherine was her division from her mother. Mrs. Trenchard was relentless. She would not see Katherine, she would not read her letters, she would not allow her name to be mentioned in her presence. Secretly, one by one, the others had crept off to the Knightsbridge flat. . . . They gave no sign of their desertion. Did she know? She also gave no sign.

But Katherine would not abandon hope. The time must come when her mother needed her. She did not ask questions of the others, but she saw her mother lonely, aged, miserable; she saw this from no conceit of herself, but simply because she knew that she had, for so many years, been the centre of her mother's life. Her heart ached; she lay awake, crying, at night, and Philip would strive to console her but could not. Nevertheless, through all her tears, she did not regret what she had done. She would do it again did the problem again arise. Philip was a new man, strong, happy, reliant, wise . . . she had laid the ghosts for him. He was hers, as though he had been her child.

Henry, upon this afternoon, was clearly under the influence of great excitement. He entered the drawing-room as though he were eager to deliver important news, and then, seeing that no one was there, he uttered a little exclamation and flung himself into a chair. Anyone might see that a few weeks of Cambridge life had worked a very happy change in Henry; much of his crudity was gone. One need not now be afraid of what he would do next, and because he was himself aware of this development much of his awkwardness had left him.

His clothes were neat; his hair was brushed. He might still yield at any moment to his old impetuosities, his despairs and his unjustified triumphs, but there would now be some further purpose beyond them; he would know now that there were more mportant things in life than his moods.

He looked at the place where the Mirror had been and blushed; then he frowned. Yes, he had lost his temper badly that day, but Philip had had such an abominable way of showing him how young he was, how little of life he knew. All the same, Philip wasn't a bad sort,—and he *did* love Katie—'like anything!'

Henry himself thrilled with the consciousness of the things that he intended to do in life. He had attended a debate at the Cambridge Union, and himself, driven by what desperate impulse he did not know, had spoken a few words. From that moment he had realised what life held in store for him. He had discovered other eager spirits; they met at night and drank cocoa together. They intended nothing less than the redemption of the world; their Utopian City shone upon no distant hill. They called themselves the Crusaders, and some time before the end of the term the first number of a periodical written by them was to startle the world. Henry was the Editor. His first Editorial was entitled: "Freedom: What it is".

And only a year ago he had sat in this very room reading that novel and wondering whether life would ever open before him. It had opened—it was opening before them all. He did not know that it had been opening thus for many thousands of years. He knew nothing of the past; he knew nothing of the future; but he saw his City rising, so pure and of marvellous promise, before his eyes. . . .

As he looked back over the past year and surveyed the family, it was to him as though an earthquake had blown them all sky-high. A year ago they had been united, as though no power could ever divide them. Well, the division had come. There was now not one member of the family who had not his, or her, secret ambitions and desires. Aunt Aggie intended to live in a little flat by herself. She found "the younger ones impossible." George Trenchard bought land at Garth. Mrs. Trenchard intended to pull down some of the Garth house and build a new wing.

She was immersed all day in plans and maps and figures; even her father-in-law's illness had not interfered with her determination.

Millie had made friends with a number of independent London ladies, who thought Women's Suffrage far beyond either cleanliness or Godliness. She talked to Henry about her companions, who hoped for a new City in no very distant future, very much as Henry's friends at Cambridge did. Only, the two Cities were very different. Even Katherine and Philip were concerned in some Society for teaching poor women how to manage their children, and Philip was also interested in a new Art, in which young painters produced medical charts showing the internal arrangements of the stomach, and called them "Spring on the Heath" or "Rome— Midday."

And through all the middle-class families in England these things were occurring. "Something is coming. . . ." "Something is coming. . . ." "Look out. . . ." "Look out. . . ."

This was in 1903. Henry, Millie, Katherine had still eleven years to wait for their revolution, but in at least one corner of happy England the work of preparation had been begun.

The door opened, and Henry's reveries were interrupted by the entrance of Millie. He started, and then jumped up on seeing her; for a moment, under the power of his thoughts, he had forgotten his news; now he stammered with the importance of it.

"Millie!" he cried.

"Hullo, Henry," she said, smiling. "We expected you hours ago."

He dropped his voice. "I've been round to see Katie. Look here, Millie, it's most important. She's coming here to see Mother."

Millie glanced behind. They carried on then the rest of their conversation in whispers.

"To see Mother?"

"Yes. She can't bear waiting any longer. She felt that she *must* be here on Grandfather's birthday."

"But—but—"

"Yes, I know. But she thinks that if she sees Mother alone and she can show her that nothing's changed—"

"But *everything's* changed. She doesn't *know* how different Mother is."

"No, but she thinks if they both *see* one another—at any rate she's going to try."

"Now?"

"Yes. In a few minutes. I'll go up and just tell Mother that there's a caller in the drawing-room. Then leave them alone together—"

Millie sighed. "It would be too lovely for anything if it really happened. But it won't—it can't. Mother's extraordinary. I don't believe she ever loved Katie at all, at least only as an idea. She'll *never* forgive her—*never*—and she'll always hate Philip."

"How's Grandfather?"

"Very bad. He says he *will* come down to-night, although it'll probably kill him. However, now they've arranged that his presents shall be in the little drawing-room upstairs. Then he won't have so far to go. He's awfully bad, really, and he's as hard about Katie as Mother is. He won't have her name mentioned. It's simply, *I* believe, that it's terrible to him to think that she could love Philip better than him!"

"And how's everyone else?"

"Oh, well, it's all right, I suppose. But it isn't very nice. I'm going off to live with Miss Emberley as soon as they'll let me. Aunt Aggie's been *awful*. And then one day she went suddenly to see Katie, and Mother found out somehow. Mother never said anything, but Aunt Aggie's going to take a flat by herself somewhere. And since that she's been nicer than I've ever known her. Quite soft and good-tempered."

"Does Mother know that we all go to see Katie?"

"Sometimes I think she does—sometimes that she doesn't. She never says a word. She seems to think of nothing but improving the place now. She must be very lonely, but she doesn't show anyone anything. All the same it's impossible without Katie—I—"

At that moment the bell of the hall-door rang. They stood silently there listening.

For a moment they stared at one another, like conspirators caught in the act of their conspiracy. The colour flooded their cheeks; their hearts beat furiously. Here and now was Drama.

They heard Rocket's footstep, the opening door, Katherine's voice. They fled from the room before they could be seen.

Katherine, when she stood alone in the room in whose life and intimacy she had shared for so many years, stared about her as though she had been a stranger. There was a change; in the first place there was now her own room, made for her and for Philip, that absorbed her mind; in comparison with it this room, that had always appeared to her comfortable, consoling, protective, was now old-fashioned and a little shabby. There were too many things scattered about, old things, neither beautiful nor useful. Then the place itself did not seem to care for her as it had once done. She was a visitor now, and the house knew it. Their mutual intimacy had ceased.

But she could not waste many thoughts upon the room. This approaching interview with her mother seemed to her the supreme moment of her life. There had been other supreme moments during the past year, and she did not realise that she was now better able to deal with them than she had once been. Nevertheless her mother *must* forgive her. She would not leave the house until she had been forgiven. She was hopeful. The success of her marriage had given her much self-confidence. The way that the family had, one after another, come to see her (yes, even Aunt Aggie) had immensely reassured her. Her mother was proud; she needed that submission should be made to her.

Katherine was here to make it. Her heart beat thickly with love and the anticipated reconciliation.

She went, as she had done so many, many times, to the Mirror over the fireplace to tidy herself. Why! the Mirror was not there! Of course not—that was why the room seemed so changed. She looked around her, smiled a little. A fine girl, anyone seeing her there would have thought her. Marriage had given her an assurance, a self-reliance. She had shrunk back before because she had been afraid of what life would be. Now, when it seemed to her that she had penetrated into the very darkest fastnesses of its secrets, when she felt that nothing in the future could surprise her ever again, she shrank back no longer.

Her clothes were better than in the old days, but even now they did not fit her very perfectly. She was still, in her heart, exactly the same rather grave, rather slow, very loving Katherine. She would be stout in later years; there were already little dimples in her cheeks. Her eyes were soft and mild, as they had ever been.

The door opened, and Mrs. Trenchard entered.

She had expected some caller, and she came forward a few steps with the smile of the hostess upon her lips. Then she saw her daughter, and stopped.

Katherine had risen, and stood facing her mother. With a swift consternation, as though someone had shouted some terrifying news into her ear, she realised that her mother was a stranger to her. She had imagined many, many times what this interview would be. She had often considered the things that she would say and the very words in which she would arrange her sentences. But always in her thoughts she had had a certain picture of her mother before her. She had seen an old woman, old as she had been on that night when she had slept in Katherine's arms, old as she had been at that moment when Katherine had first told her of her engagement to Philip. And now she thought this old woman would face her, maintaining her pride but nevertheless ready, after the separation of these weeks, to break down before the vision of Katherine's own submission.

Katherine had always thought: "Dear Mother. We *must* have one another. She'll feel that now. She'll see that I'm exactly the same. . . ."

How different from her dreams was this figure. Her mother seemed to-day younger than Katherine had ever known her. She stood there, tall, stern, straight, the solidity of her body impenetrable, inaccessible to all tenderness, scornful of all embraces. She was young, yes, and stronger.

At the first sight of Katherine she had moved back as though she would leave the room. Then she stayed by the door. She was perfectly composed.

"Why have you come?" she said.

At the cold indifference of that voice Katherine felt a little pulse of anger beat, far away, in the very heart of her tenderness.

She moved forward with a little gesture.

"Mother, I had to come. It's Grandfather's birthday. I couldn't believe that after all these weeks you wouldn't be willing to see me."

She stopped. Her mother said nothing.

Katherine came nearer. "I'm sorry—terribly sorry—if I did what hurt you. I felt at the time that it was the only thing to do. Phil was so miserable, and I know that it was all for my sake. It wasn't fair to let him go on like that when I could prevent it. You didn't understand him. He didn't understand you. But never, for a single instant, did my love for you change. It never has. It never will. Mother dear, you believe that—you *must* believe that."

Did Mrs. Trenchard have then for a moment a vision of the things that she might still do with life? With her eyes, during these weeks, she had seen not Katherine but her own determination to vindicate her stability, the stability of all her standards, against every attack. They said that the world was changing. She at least could show them that she would not change. Even though, in her own house, that revolution had occurred about which she had been warned, she would show them that she remained, through it all, stable, unconquered.

Katherine had gone over to the enemy. Well, she would fasten her life to some other anchor then. It should be as though Katherine and Katherine's love had never existed. There was offered her now her last chance. One word and she would be part of the new world. One word . . .

She may for an instant have had her vision. The moment passed. She saw only her own determined invincibility.

"You had your choice, Katherine," she said. "You made it. You broke your word to us. You left us without justification. You have killed your Grandfather. You have shown that our love and care for you during all these years has gone for nothing at all."

Katherine flushed. "I have not shown that—I. . . ." She looked as though she would cry. Her lips trembled. She struggled to compose her voice—then at last went on firmly:

"Mother—perhaps I was wrong. I didn't know what I did. It wasn't for myself—it was for Philip. It isn't true that I didn't think of you all. Mother, let me see Grandfather—only for a moment. He will forgive me. I know —I know."

"He has forbidden us to mention your name to him."

"But if he sees me—"

"He is resolved never to see you again."

"But what did I do? If I speak to him, if I kiss him—I must go to him. It's his birthday. I've got a present—"

"He is too ill to see you." This perhaps had moved her,

ecause she went on swiftly: "Katherine, what is the use of
his? It hurts both of us. It can do no good. You acted
s you thought right. It seemed to show me that you had
o care for me after all these years. It shook all my confi-
ence. That can never be between us again, and I could
ot, I think, in any way follow your new life. I could never
orget, and you have now friends and interests that must
xclude me. If we meet what can we have now in common?
f I had loved you less, perhaps it would be possible, but as it
s—no."

Katherine had dried her tears.

They looked at one another. Katherine bowed her head.
She had still to bite her lips that she might not cry, but she
ooked very proud.

"Perhaps," she said, very softly, "that one day you will
want—you will feel— At least I shall not change. I will
ome whenever you want me. I will always care the same.
One day I will come back, Mother dear."

Her mother said only:

"It is better that we should not meet."

Katherine walked to the door. As she passed her mother
he looked at her. Her eyes made one last prayer—then
hey were veiled.

She left the house.

A quarter of an hour later Henry came into the room, and
ound his Mother seated at her desk, plans and papers in
ront of her. He could hear her saying to herself:

"Fifteen—by fourteen. . . . The rockery *there*—Five
teps, then the door. . . . Fifteen pounds four shillings and
ixpence. . . ."

Katherine was not there. He knew that she had been re-
ected. His mother showed no signs of discomposure.
Their interview must have been very short.

He went to the window and stood there, looking out. In

a moment Rocket would come and draw the blinds. Rund
Square swam in the last golden light.

Tiny flakes of colour spun across the pale blue that wa
almost white. They seemed to whirl before Henry's eyes.

He was sorry, terribly sorry, that Katherine had faile
but he was filled to-day with a triumphant sense of the glor
and promise of life. He had been liberated, and Katherin
had been liberated. Freedom, with its assurances for a
the world, flamed across the darkening skies. Life seeme
endless: its beckoning drama called to him. The anticip
tion of the glory of life caught him by the throat so that I
could scarcely breathe. . . .

At that moment in the upstairs room old Mr. Trenchar
suddenly struggling for breath, tried to call out, failed, fe
back, on to his pillow, dead.

THE END